What They're Saying...

"The Riviera nightclub always fascinated me as a kid. The star power that lit up that stage was almost as bright as the New York skyline it looked out on. Tom Austin brings you in the front door."
— **Bob Gaudio**, *composer; member, Songwriters Hall of Fame; member, Rock and Roll Hall of Fame.*

"When I was a teenager just beginning my singing career, Al Martino — my friend and a wonderful singer — took me to the Riviera for dinner and a show. I'll never forget how this Fort Lee, New Jersey nightclub knocked me out. Perched at the edge of the Palisades over-looking the George Washington Bridge, it was the ultimate in style, class, and excitement. High Society, the Mob, and the greatest entertainers in America all rubbed elbows. Tom Austin's new novel takes me back to that time and place of leggy chorus girls and revolving bandstands and hidden casinos. I wish it had lasted longer, so that I could have performed there."
— **Frankie Avalon**, *star of stage, screen, and television.*

"Next to his family, the Riviera in Fort Lee, New Jersey was my dad's life. I wish he were still here, so he could read Tom Austin's new book, which recreates that one-of-a-kind nightclub and its colorful era."
— **Susan Miller**, *daughter of Riviera owner Bill Miller.*

D0776575

BRIDGE TO THE
RIVIERA

By Tom Austin

Published by Ertel Publishing

For information address inquiries to
Ertel Publishing
506 South High Street
Yellow Springs, Ohio 45387

First edition published September 2015 by Ertel Publishing
506 South High Street
Yellow Springs, Ohio 45387

Designed by Rachel Ertel

ISBN: 978-0-578-16909-5

Dedication

This book is dedicated to *Ben Marden* and *Bill Miller*. Two tireless theatrical visionaries who not only shared the same initials but shared the same grit and fortitude that knew no bounds in order to make their beloved Riviera the undisputed "Showplace of America."

Foreword

"The Riviera Nightclub in Fort Lee, New Jersey was a legendary part of the American scene from 1931 to January 1, 1954. Fort Lee native Tom Austin, a performer of note in his own right, tells the story as only one could who was there and saw this Emerald City of entertainment and night life. The Fort Lee Film Commission and Fort Lee Historical Society are proud to call Tom one of our own. His story is not only Fort Lee's story but America's story of a time when stars weren't just in the skies but in a nightclub atop the Jersey Palisades."

—*Tom Meyer, Fort Lee Film Commission*

Preface

One of New York's favorite nightclubs from the 1930s through the early 1950s wasn't in New York. The world famous Riviera opened on the craggy cliffs of the Palisades high above the Hudson River in Bergen County, New Jersey in 1931, where my Dad would become an integral part of its history.

I was born in 1939 into a family of hard working people who came to the Fort Lee area by horse and wagon in 1904, settling in Coytesville a rural enclave located at the north end of Fort Lee. I was named after my Grandfather Tom who had started a small trucking company on the Lower East side of New York after he arrived from England. Like so many others at the time, Fort Lee was beckoning all young entrepreneurs to take the ferry across the pond to seek their fortune in the burgeoning motion picture business, which originated in Fort Lee.

By 1920, however, the movie business, seeking better weather conditions, began its cross country trek to California and the Prohibition era was underway. Grandpa shifted his efforts from hauling movie scenery to hauling liquor and moving the contents of raided "Speakeasy" operations around New York. In 1929, my dad Alfred, who earned the family nickname of "Mott Street Al," met my mother at a baseball game in Fort Lee. Mom was a small time singer and contest winning Charleston dancer who sang and danced with her brother George's band called the Continentals. The trucking business went bust during the Great Depression and everyone was out of work. The only source of income was from "day work" as Dad called it where men would have to stand in a "shape up" line and hopefully be picked for hard labor to earn a day's pay.

In October of 1931, when the George Washington Bridge was completed, entrepreneur Ben Marden opened a huge, lavish nightclub restaurant on the Jersey side of the Hudson in Fort Lee. Patrons crossed the bridge to enjoy the Riviera's illegal gambling, illegal liquor, and fantastic performances with gorgeous showgirls, all under the watchful eye of the Mob. Fort Lee locals, including my family, once again found work, becoming the service force of the operation. Dad got a job at the Riviera as a stage door security officer. His duty was to see to it that everyone behaved and didn't disrupt the operation or the flow of money pouring in.

Every morning around 6 a.m. when he came home from work, Dad would sit on the edge of my bed and tell me stories of the events, good and bad, that had taken place at the Riviera the night before. I would hear stories about Frank Sinatra or Eddie Fisher or maybe some famous Mob guys who showed up to meet the stars. At family gatherings, I would be fascinated as my uncles and Dad related stories and gossip of the events in our town concerning show business and the Mob. My eight-year-old mind was becoming a storehouse of information regarding the Riviera and its colorful characters. As the years passed, Dad's fascinating stories stayed with me, and eventually I memorized them - for a reason that I was unaware of at the time.

It wasn't until I reached my late 60s that a friend of mine named Ron Kase talked me into co-writing a nonfiction book about the events that took place at the Riviera. I wanted to record the factual events for people so that they could enjoy them as much as I did. I wanted the great memories of the Riviera to live on forever. Together, Ron and I wrote Bill Miller's Riviera: America's Showplace in Fort Lee, New Jersey which was published in 2011. The book includes dozens of the autographed photographs of stars and celebrities that Dad brought home to us.

That first book led the Fort Lee Film Commission, under the direction of Nelson Page and Tom Meyer, to come to me and say, "You're holding back. You must write the real behind-the-scenes story that was handed down to you by your dad. The world needs to know that before Hollywood and Las Vegas, our town of Fort Lee was the Mecca of big-time show business and that most of the grandiose ideas used to bring those places to life originated in our town of Fort Lee, New Jersey."

I accepted the challenge and began to dig deep in historic archives, researching my characters and events surrounding the origins of the Riviera. Through interviews with the owner's family members, court records, FBI files, newspaper articles, books, local folk tales and Dad's stories, I readied myself to render a tale that would both entertain the reader and stay true to the history of the Riviera.

What I realized immediately was that *Bridge to the Riviera* had to be written as a historic novel. It was necessary to communicate the conversations of the characters in a fictional manner, based on the author's imagination, in a way that would lead the story on a credible timeline of events. The story is told through the eyes of the main character, the young half Jewish, half Italian Gio Arrigo. Although Gio is quiet and non-assuming he is a presence recognized by all.

I hope you enjoy this trip back to the time when the Riviera in Fort Lee was the unparalleled trendsetter in entertainment excitement.

Acknowledgements

I first want to thank Patrick Ertel and his wife Vicki for believing in this project and to all those people at Ertel Publishing for their tireless efforts in making it happen. In addition I owe a debt of gratitude to Tom Meyer and Nelson Page of the Fort Lee Film Commission for encouraging me to write this backstage, behind the scenes story of the Riviera and of the men who built it. A million thanks go out to Jim Waltzer for helping me put the polish on my manuscript and keeping me on track to make my book the best that it could be. To the Miller family, Susan, Judy, Denise, Mary, David Vine and Barney Miller, thank you for your support and good wishes. To Barbara, thank you for covering the bases for me at my day gig while I did the research for this book. Finally and most important, to my wife Lorraine and my sons Michael and Tom thank you for always standing in support of me and never complaining when I have my head in the clouds off on another artistic adventure.

Prologue

A hush came over the audience, as the Riviera showroom grew dark. Four spotlights danced around the room, pausing momentarily on the celebrities who came to see Frank Sinatra make his comeback. Waiter captain Lou Gallo was quick-stepping a contingent of New York Yankee late arrivals to their table, young players named Mantle, Berra, Martin, and Ford—World Series victors over the Dodgers the previous fall. They briefly shook outstretched hands, as they moved past the first-tier banquettes to be seated. Columnist Walter Winchell was all smiles, as he patted TV show host Ed Sullivan on the back, broke from conversation, and rushed back to his own table. Beautiful Ava Gardner chatted with composer Harold Arlen, as photogs bombarded her with attention. Chicago gangsters Rocco, Charlie and Joe Fischetti sat ringside, waiting for their favorite singer. Jersey counterparts Willie Moretti, Joe Adonis, Albert Anastsia, Gyp DeCarlo, and Longie Zwillman appeared startled, as the spotlights hit their tables. Politicians, gangsters, clergy, press, sports and show biz celebrities along with just plain people, all came out to welcome back the man who had defied the odds and regained his standing atop the entertainment world.

Through the tall windows, lights on the George Washington Bridge twinkled like a magical sequence of stars. A hush came over the 1200-seat showroom, as four spotlights that had been sparring with the audience focused on the stage and the drummer laid down a sustained single stroke roll on his timpani. A rich baritone voice leapt from the house speakers.

"Ladies and gentleman, Bill Miller's Riviera proudly presents the one and only, Mister Frank Sinatra."

The room exploded as if it were Yankee Stadium and Mantle had just sent one into orbit. The orchestra jumped on an up-tempo arrangement. After what seemed endless, heart-stopping moments, Sinatra—with spotlights converging—emerged from behind the black bandstand curtain, wearing a perfectly tailored, grey sharkskin suit glistening in the lights. Still skinny, still taut and electric. The crowd sent out a second explosion—greater than the first—that, without the sturdy nightclub walls deflecting it, might have reached skyscrapers of Manhattan, rising fortress-like across the bridge. Accepting the adulation, Sinatra shrugged his shoulders, as he turned to the bandleader, then faced the audience again, in full swagger. "Kick it, boys," he said to the band behind him, and off they went into history.

BRIDGE TO THE RIVIERA

Chapter 1

As I drove across the George Washington Bridge on my way back
to New Jersey, I noticed that, off to the right near the edge of those
500-foot-high cliffs, where the most famous nightclub in the world
once stood, the trees were much shorter than all of the other trees
surrounding that spot. It was hard to believe that so many years
had passed since the Riviera closed in 1953; what a shame I thought,
a damn shame.

When I reached Fort Lee on the Jersey side of the river, I hung
a quick right, headed down to Hudson Terrace, and parked my car
on the shoulder of the road below the tollgates for the Palisades
Interstate Parkway. Was I crazy? Was it ridiculous to feel such an
urge to climb those steep stairs next to the bridge, walk the cliff
trail just to see the ruins, and visit the place that I loved so much?
Going there was like visiting a cemetery to pay my respects to an
old friend. I had been planning to come to this place for the past
month after getting out of the hospital, so why turn back now?
This was my sacred place, a place I knew so much about, that special place of such importance in my life. I just had to come back to
revisit and pay tribute.

I opened the trunk of my car and took out a small bag containing a few items I needed for searching the ruins of this grand
old lady. Nothing fancy—just a pair of binoculars, a small garden shovel, a rake and, most importantly, a small box containing a
creased photograph and a beautiful cameo pin framed in gold. This
last item had its own special meaning to me. It needed to be buried
here along with my memories.

Why am I doing this, I thought? I really shouldn't be out here
taking a chance on falling and hurting myself, climbing around
this rubble at my age. The truth of the matter is that, if something happened, no one would ever find me up here on the cliffs
and, anyway, who really gives a damn about me? No one would
miss me if I checked out right now, and that's for sure. "Look at

those beautiful pieces of blue tile over there in the weeds," I heard myself saying out loud.

This must have been the spot where all those chauffeur-driven Cadillacs and Lincolns would pull up to the main entrance and drop off their people. I can still see those flashy cars gleaming in the night.

It was all so wonderful, so glamorous, people coming from all over the world to see the lavish shows right here on this spot. And I was in the middle of it all.

Funny, I guess the beautiful showgirls who danced here are all grandmothers or even great-grandmothers by now, if they are still with us, I thought.

After the Riviera closed, I regularly took out my big photo album to show friends autographed pictures of Frank Sinatra, Peggy Lee, Tony Martin, Dean Martin, Jerry Lewis, and all the others who played the handsome club that overlooked the Hudson. It was always wonderful to reminisce. Everyone was impressed with those pictures of the stars. Friends, who never had been there, could not believe that the Riviera could seat 1,200 for dinner and 200 more in the lounge and bar, or that it had a revolving dance floor and even a revolving bandstand capable of featuring two bands at once. People were amazed that the roof could actually roll off the building and that, otherwise hidden by the roof, a gambling casino run by the most famous mobsters of the time drew high rollers. The Mob guys dubbed it the "Carpet Joint" because it was so luxurious. (They called their low-class, backroom casinos "dice barns.")

The memories are indelible. When Frank Sinatra came here to make his comeback, the place was so packed that the waiters were throwing the plates out the window because the kitchen couldn't handle the huge number of dirty dishes. Talk about star power. I spent that whole day with Sinatra and his lady, Ava Gardner, who was gorgeous.

As I stood among the ruins I willed myself to envision the famous couple pulling up in their new, baby blue, Caddy convertible in front of the stage door on that rainy day, Frank at the wheel.

Ava wore a tan raincoat and her fantastic, mysterious smile that made you feel self-conscious. Most guys couldn't even look her in the eyes when she was smiling. She mesmerized everybody, including Frank.

I climbed over a chunk of concrete and found the remains of the four, long, curving entrance steps that led to the shiny, brass doors. If these crumpled steps could only talk, they'd tell of the thousands of celebrities who trod or fell there, or of the night that Al the security guard tangled with that seven-foot-two guy. That was some fight. The big guy did not know how lucky he was that the boys with the broken noses missed the fight—he might have left the premises in a hearse instead of a police car.

I could see Tony Martin signing autographs on these steps, looking down on all the gorgeous women begging for his attention. Martin's wife, the beautiful Cyd Charisse, would stand just off to the side and allow the women to fawn all over her husband. "Just business," she would say.

It was chilly at cliff's edge, about a 500-foot drop to the river. I had to watch my step and not slip on the overgrowth. I'd forgotten how cold it could get up here. Back then, we went outside only to shoot raccoons raiding the dumpsters. "Target practice, let's have some target practice," the guys would say, tough-looking characters in fedora hats, pistols in their hands. And they didn't limit their shooting to raccoons. One time they dragged one of the collection guys out and took him on a one-way ride. The poor bastard probably had no idea what he was in for. It took the feds years before they found his body. Someone else was hired to take his collection route.

I spotted, on the ground, a giant arc with a radius of about 60 feet, indicating that the Riviera's footprint measured about 120 feet across on the river side. The crumbling footings I now noticed had held the round walls whose huge windows rolled down to let in the breezes on summer nights. When the roof rolled off, and the windows rolled down, the party was on. That's what owner Ben Marden always said.

I cocked my ear and could hear the music...*dadala, dadala, dadala da, dadala, dadala, dadala da...Mambo Jambo,* that was the song. Perez Prado had the hit, and Pupi Campo's band played it at the Riviera all the time. When those young showgirls—all gorgeous and probably not one of them over nineteen years old (" fresh calamari," some of us would say)—strutted onto the revolving stage, the place was up and running, let me tell you.

Enough of those thoughts. No fool like an old fool.

I sat on a smooth rock and looked through my binoculars at the New York skyline. The George Washington Bridge superstructure was more than a football field away. I remembered this same view from the third tier of the showroom. Some view.

Thanks to me, they got this spot; I handled the negotiations for it. It was probably Meyer Lansky and his associates who put up the money we needed to buy it, but I was the one who made the deal. Marden always confirmed that I played a major role in it.

Everybody used to ask me how I got a job at the Riviera, but I would never tell them the truth. I had sworn to the guy who brought me here that I would never say anything that would connect him to this place, and I never did, at least while he was alive.

I took one last look at the picture in the little box before I buried it with the cameo pin, choosing for their final resting place the spot where the stage door used to be. For years I carried the photo of the two of us in my wallet. She and I had a great thing going. But now it's gone.

Along with all the water gone under the George Washington Bridge since that stranger pointed me in this direction. It seems like about five minutes ago that all of this got started.

I met him in Atlantic City. This guy was some pack of trouble. I have to admit, there was never a dull moment from the time I first met him until the time he cut me loose to go on my own. He always felt that I just wasn't cut out for his type of business and the rough stuff that went with it, but he always backed me up. He had a solution for everything; if there was a buck to be made, he was the first to grab it. The man was a genius...with a giant pair of balls.

Seems like everything that was illegal back then is legal now—what a joke. Booze, bookies, cardrooms, crap games, "numbers." Now we have legit casinos everywhere, especially down the Jersey shore.

I remember it perfectly. The first time I went to Atlantic City was on a weekend pass from the Navy in the summer of 1919. I hitched a ride up from Norfolk, where my ship was docked. I was alone and headed straight for the boardwalk like any other sailor on a long weekend pass. It began to rain early that day, and the next thing I knew, I found myself playing Skee-Ball in an arcade. A tall guy who looked about my age—19—struck up a conversation with me about the Navy, while we each ran the Skee-Balls up the alley, killing time until the rain stopped. Out of nowhere, four tough-looking guys grabbed my new friend, threw him on the ground, and proceeded to kick the shit out of him.

As a crowd gathered to watch the beating, I couldn't resist jumping in to help him. My South Philly (that's where I grew up) mentality kicked in and, before I knew it, I was pulling guys off of him, giving him half a chance to get back on his feet and throw some punches. Together, we started to hold our own, when one of them pulled out an ice pick. Thank God, an arcade employee was nearby, holding a sack of pennies from the machine. Instinctively, I grabbed the sack and swung for the fences. Whammo! I connected with Icepick's squawker, and he went down like a lump of lead, blood gushing from his nose, pennies flying everywhere.

People scrambled all over him, trying to get to the pennies. Moments later, the police came running to see what the commotion was about, and that's when this stranger and I jumped over the ramps and disappeared into the back, looking for a place to hide among the boxes of satin dolls and monkeys. When the cops tended to the guy on the floor, his pals bolted from the arcade.

Minutes later, we lucked out and found the door out the back. When we got a safe distance away, my new friend looked at me with curiosity.

"What's the matter, you're white as a ghost?"

"I think I killed him."

"Come on, pal, dead guys don't bleed that much," he said, like someone who knows all about such things. "But I see you got a soft spot, so you better watch that. If you have to kill somebody, never worry about killing a guy who is trying to kill you. Never forget that…Let's shake, my name is Abe Zwillman—they call me 'Longie.'"

We shook hands.

"I'll tell you what," he continued, "I can probably use a guy like you. If you want, look me up when you get out of the Navy." He handed me a card. "I'm not going to forget what you did for me today."

Those were his exact words—"I'm not going to forget what you did for me today"—and he never did forget me. No one—least of all, me—would have predicted that Longie would turn out to be as big as Al Capone. Those in the know say nobody in Jersey was bigger than Longie Zwillman. Even at that tender age, he was looking to expand his bootleg liquor territory into the Atlantic City area, and he'd made the mistake of not bringing his "friends" to the negotiations. For one lucky instant, I had been his muscle.

I kept his card and was tempted to call him many times after I got out of the Navy several months later. One day, when I reached for my wallet to pay for a haircut in Somerville, New Jersey, Longie's card fell out. The barber stooped, picked it up, and saw the name.

"You know Longie Zwillman?"

"Yeah, he's a friend of mine, why?"

"Okay, pal, this haircut is on the house."

Right then and there, I knew Longie was a good guy to know.

A few days later, I mustered the courage to call him. I had been working as a caddie at the Raritan Valley Country Club, a beautiful spread that was less than a decade old. But I had ambition that went beyond toting a bag of golf clubs.

"Remember me?" I said, when Longie answered.

"How could I forget you? You saved my ass on the boardwalk."
Then, as if he could read my mind, he said, "Are you going to take me up on that job I offered you?"

"I just called to say hello," I lied.

"Where are you working, Gio?"

That's me, Joshua Giorgio Arigo, the Joshua courtesy of my Jewish mother, the Gio my preferred handle among my Italian school chums and neighborhood buddies in South Philly.

And now Gio was about to enter the world of Longie. I was a little ashamed to tell him that I was working at the Raritan Valley Country Club.

"Are you managing the place?"

Not quite.

But Longie wasn't about to put down the guy who'd saved his ass. He spoke to me as if I were already a valued associate.

"I have a drop there [at the country club], Gio." He went on to say that he'd be down with his driver to make a delivery when President Harding came to visit in a couple weeks' time. Longie planned to meet the president. And he did.

That was some day.

* * * * *

I sat on the old, broken steps, and the past paraded before me.

On July 2, 1921, the Raritan Valley Country Club was buzzing with excitement because Warren G. Harding, President of the United States, was due to arrive to sign papers that would officially end the Great War nearly three years after its battlefield action had ceased.

Senator Joseph S. Frelinghuysen, who had helped launch the club on land adjacent to his estate, was going nuts in trying to make sure that everything was just right on that day. We were all ducking for cover, trying to stay out of his way. But I think the senator liked me. He made a fuss over me when I won the caddy golf tournament that summer and received a Hamilton wristwatch as a prize.

When the time came, the President arrived in a cavalcade of big, black Packards with four State Troopers on motorcycles. When the procession stopped, the 10-year-old McKenna triplets ran to the head of the pack, led by their ever-promotional mother. The girls were dressed in outfits that made them look like the American flag. The mother wore a god-awful headpiece that made her look like the statue of liberty.

They said the President's favorite summer drink was ice tea with a sprig of mint, so the McKenna girls brought him a pitcher of the tea as soon as he stepped out of his limousine. When a crowd surrounded the vehicles, the girls broke rank and bolted toward the President.

The one with the pitcher tripped over her sister's shoe, sending the pitcher flying until it splattered on the President's guard riding on the running board. The sound of the stainless steel pitcher hitting the car was like a gunshot. The President jumped out of the car, triggering short-lived panic among his security detail, but applause from the crowd. Quickly composing himself, Harding looked at the McKennas with forgiveness and said, "I think these girls should take a mulligan on this one." The crowd broke up with laughter.

Later that day, just as he'd told me, Longie and two of his guys showed up at the club in an Army surplus truck loaded with bootleg booze. He told me he planned on buying about forty of those trucks to make his "drops."

When he spotted me, he got out of the truck and walked right over to me.

"You're lookin' good, pal, everything all right?" Some of the other caddies suddenly saw me in a new light.

"Get in the truck, Gio, and let's drop this stuff off in the shack behind the caddie pen. This is the good stuff I keep in Reinfeld's warehouse up in Newark. There is a lot more where this came from."

And just like that, my life changed. As we drove toward the caddie pen, we stopped by the first tee, where a foursome was about to tee off. We sat there quietly, waiting for those guys to hit, the engine idling. One of them took endless practice swings, and Longie lost it.

"Will you hit the fucking ball already?"

As soon as I realized that the slowpoke was Judge Nelson, I prepared myself for a few nights in the slammer. The judge stopped swinging and looked up.

"Abner Zwillman, this club is going to pot if they let guys like you in here."

"How you makin' out, Judge, long time no see," Longie said.

So much for the slammer. Everyone at the club seemed to either know Longie or know of him. He cast a big shadow everywhere he went.

When we reached the shack, and Longie's men began unloading the truck, he and I went around back to the pen, where the wooden caddies bench was carved up with initials.

"Some work of art huh, Gio?"

"A lot of asses sat on this bench over the years."

He looked at me. "Are you one of them?"

His message came through, loud and clear.

"Gio, you going to stick around here and be a pack mule for these rich guys, or do you want to throw in with me and my guys up in Newark, and make some real dough and have people look up to you? Your choice, pal; you're a good guy and I owe you one." I didn't need to think about it very long. "What the hell, I guess I'm in."

Longie's face tightened. "You guess?"

"I'm in—no guesswork."

"That's better. Now call whoever you got to call to make your break, and later today we take you back with us to Newark."

I grabbed a ride back to my grandmother's house to pack my bag. She was sitting on the porch when I got there.

"I got an offer to move up to Newark and work in a restaurant," I said.

"Are you sure you want to do that, Giorgio?" She always called me Giorgio.

I told her it was a good chance to make some real money, and she looked at me suspiciously.

"I hope so, for your sake."

I packed my Navy sea bag with the few civvies I had, threw it over my shoulder, and headed back to the club.

When I got there, I was surprised to see a beautiful, young woman talking to Longie—not because she was a beautiful, young woman, but because she was the wife of Dr. Jansen, a club member. Her long, honey-blond hair looked natural—not some dye job. I had heard she was a dancer or something, and thought maybe she knew Longie. When I saw them, I just stood off to the side to stay out of their conversation until Longie saw me.

"Gio, I guess you know Nancy Jansen, right?"

"Not really, but I see Missus Jansen here at the club with her husband."

"Nancy was a Ziegfeld dancer in New York; a big star."

Nancy's expression suggested that she was less impressed with herself than was Longie. "Come on, Gio," she said. "You can talk to me; forget the formalities." She spoke with unmistakably western inflections, adding to her charm. "I see you're a friend of Longie's, so it's okay if you join our conversation."

I could have fallen over. This was the first time I had even gotten a chance to stand near Nancy Jansen, much less speak to her. I had not as much as heard her voice before—this gal definitely wasn't from Brooklyn. Make no mistake, everybody at the club noticed Nancy, especially the guys. We didn't dare make any comments, but she was absolutely gorgeous, way out of anybody's league—at least anybody I knew (except maybe Longie).

Later that day, the President and his entourage left the club and went down the road to Frelinghuysen's mansion to sign the ratification papers. We were told that the President was going to stay at the senator's house for four days, so he could get in several rounds of golf. I realized that I'd miss my chance to caddy for him, but I had other fish to fry. I was going to Newark with Longie Zwillman to start a new life.

The caddy master saw me throwing my sea bag into the back of the army truck, and asked me where the hell I was going. I told him it was none of his business.

"Go find yourself another donkey, pal," I said, acting like a big shot. "I'm done."

But for me, things were just beginning.

Chapter 2

We didn't see another pair of headlights on the backroads at all that night. With the windows in the old Army truck open, I could smell the wonderful scents of the farm country that we were passing through. The stars were bright, and the full moon made it easier to see the ruts in the road. But the sweet air of the countryside quickly changed to the dank odors and factory aromas of the Ironbound section of Newark.

"This part of town is a gold mine for us," Longie said. "Give or take, there are a hundred and fifty speakeasies down here, and we supply damn near half of them. The other half is split between several outfits, and that's where the trouble starts. What those morons can't figure out is that the whipped cream on this cake is piled so high, everybody's piece has some on it. But it seems they don't want to share, so, at times, I have to use a little— you know—friendly persuasion."

"You mean—"

"—I mean, when I grab them by the balls, their hearts and minds usually follow."

As we slowly made our way through the narrow, cobblestone streets in the warehouse district, headed for the North Ward, a chill went through me as I noticed a police car slowly pulling out from an alley and begin to follow us.

"Shit, Longie, we're being followed…Police right behind—"

—"Relax Gio, these are my guys. We've been having trouble with the Mazzochi boys. They figure this is their territory, and have been trying to highjack our hooch. Right now we only have a few trucks making booze drops, but very soon we are going to have the whole fleet in action, and that is when the fun really starts. Those guys are going to be in for a surprise; we're just getting warmed up."

He handed me a $50 bill. "You can stay with me tonight," he said, "and tomorrow we'll find you a rooming house. This'll get you started. You don't get paid a weekly salary around here. You get paid according to how much you collect for me, understand?"

Within minutes, we reached a new hotel, where Longie leased an entire floor. I barely stayed awake during the short trip, but Longie seemed fresh as a daisy, as we pulled up to the marquee. Two guys rushed over to the car and opened the door for him. I got out and stood there, looking at the grand, arched windows. The place had real class.

It was called The Riviera Hotel.

"The joint's brand new, Gio; it didn't even have its grand opening yet. I got plans, baby. Do what I tell you and, who knows, maybe someday you'll own a place like this."

Even at this early morning hour, when Longie entered the hotel, everyone working there vied for his attention. The desk clerk quickly put down the morning paper and came out from behind the counter to take us to the elevator, all the while asking Longie if there was anything he needed. Longie handed him my seabag.

"Have this sent up to my suite, Julius. I want a wake up call around eleven." He gestured toward me with a razor-sharp smile. "My friend here is going to leave in maybe a couple of hours—he's an early bird...But I'm sleepin' in."

"Yes, Mr. Zwillman, of course." The clerk all but bowed to him.

My night, or what was left of it, was spent sleeping on the leather couch in Longie's office.

"Let's go, Gio!" were the first words I heard, at about 6:30 a.m., coming from a stout broad-shouldered man with a Yiddish accent. This guy wore his belt up around his chest, well above his rotund belly. The collar on his slightly stained white shirt was turned up at the tips. He was leaning over the back of the couch, staring into my face, his arms folded. The brim on his grey fedora was turned up, and the smell of the Cuban cigar clenched in his teeth was almost too much for me to handle first thing in the morning.

"My name is Izzie; Longie says you are going to work with me."

"Okay. How's business?" I asked jokingly.

"How's business?" he said, impatience in his voice. "Are you kidding? Longie's got more shit going than Carter's got liver pills. He wants for me to get you a sharp new suit, you know, business clothes, so we can put you on the street to collect for us. Also, we got to see if we can find you a room today. Are you ready to move your lazy ass, or do I have to hang around here all day waiting for you to get your keister off the couch?" He laughed at what must have been my startled expression.

"Sure, sure," I said, as I quickly rolled off the couch and put on my threadbare, suspendered, corduroy pants. "Give me a moment to wash up and I'll be right with you."

I schlepped down the hall to the washroom with a fresh towel over my shoulder, a towel stamped with the name "Hotel Riviera, Newark, New Jersey."

"Hey kid, don't bother shavin'. We're gonna pay off a few merchants who handle the numbers for us. Longie gives them thirty dollars each a week for doing our collecting. Jake the barber is one of them. You can get a nice haircut, shave, the works, from him and put it on the arm. He won't mind; he owes us. Now hurry the fuck up so we can get started."

Izzie seemed friendly enough, but I figured it was too soon to kid him about his hefty stomach. I quickly dressed and headed off with him, carefully locking the door to the office behind me. I could not help thinking what the hell I was getting myself into. Petty shit was one thing, but leaning on people to collect money, and who knew what else, was another story. Longie had a laundry list of stuff he was involved in, from selling protection to the pushcart peddlers to the numbers game, the policy racket…He was working all the angles.

"I thought Longie was just working the booze business," I said nervously, as Izzie and I exited down the steep, back staircase at the rear of the hotel and out onto the street.

"Are you kidding? Longie's got everything covered. He's got more shit going than anybody. He's got brains, personality, and the balls to carry it all off, and everybody loves him for it. Let me tell you something. Street guys who are working for the other bosses are beginning to get the message and come over to our side, mainly because they know Longie is a stand-up guy. Respect, yeah, that's what it is, respect. Longie gets respect from everybody."

The morning in Newark, especially in the third ward, started early. The men with their pushcarts broke the morning mist, as they found their assigned positions on Prince Street. I soon learned that Prince Street was nothing like Raritan. Car horns blared, as impatient drivers tried to get past the throngs of shoppers and pushcarts. Kids were running all over. Horses were getting brushed and washed right in the street, and a man with a garbage can with wheels on it was busy shoveling up the manure left the night before by the horse-drawn carts. The aromas of Newark were nothing like the farm-fresh smell of summer in Raritan. The smell of urine was everywhere,and I wasn't sure if it was from the horses or the men peeing right at curb-side. No one seemed to notice anything wrong with that. When nature called, men would simply face a wall in an alley and relieve themselves.

The cacophonous, cackling sound of chickens in Brownstein's Live Poultry Market rose about five octaves with a bloodcurdling screech from an unfortunate fowl that was set to lose its head.

"Hear that? See what happens when they make late payments to the boss?" Izzie said, as he chugged down the street, while I stopped to watch the action through Brownstein's window.

"Wait a minute," I said, "I want to watch that lady who is feeling up a live chicken over there. You got to see this."

"Come on Gio, we ain't got all day."

But I was entranced by this woman, who'd taken a flailing chicken from the cage, held it upside down by the legs, and examined it from head to tail feathers, even going so far as to lift its wings to check them out.

Finally, she turned the chicken over and put her nose up to the chicken's ass and said indignantly, "This chicken stinks!"

The butcher turned to her and said, "Madam, can you pass a test like the one you're giving my chicken?"

The woman let go of the chicken's legs, and it immediately started flying around the store. She then took her black purse with the brass ball clasp on it, and started swinging it at the butcher. Izzie and I almost fell on the ground with helpless laughter. What a show!

"Keeping it kosher is serious business," Izzie said, trying to compose himself before breaking into a trot down Prince Street.

"Where are we going, Izzie?"

"We're going over to Resnick's—the tailor. This is where we get you that suit of clothes."

When we got to the store, we had to wait a few minutes, as Mr. Resnick was waiting on a laundry customer. He worked feverishly in that hot store, washing the customers' clothes in his own bathtub. He also made and remodeled suits and dresses for his customers. And he wasn't a young man.

As we sat down on wooden, folding chairs and waited, Izzie leaned over to me. "Longie feels sorry for him, huh? The poor schmuck's got five kids, and they all live behind the store. They don't have two nickels to rub together, but they seem to hang in there."

"Five kids in three rooms, and a wife, too?"

"He spends just about every dime he makes on the ponies, and the poor bastard never wins. What're you gonna do? Putting down bets on the nags makes him happy. Who knows, maybe one day he makes it big."

That phrase rang in my ears. My mother always told me that, one day, I was going to "make it big." I wondered if that's what people said to all the losers as a consolation prize.

When Resnick's laundry customer left, it was our turn. Izzie told him I needed a nice suit, maybe something with a vest and pinstripes.

Resnick sized me up. "I maybe got just the thing," he said, a cloth tape measure dangling from his neck, his index finger on his chin, and his other hand on his chest. "You look like a perfect, 46 long. Come back in 20 minutes and see what I got for ya. You're gonna love it."

We waited next door at Kaplan's Deli, where we grabbed a hot, fresh bagel and glass of tea. I could not help but notice the sign on the counter offering a "fat corn beef sandwich" for 10 cents. Izzie, always the anxious one, tapped his fat ring finger incessantly on our table, driving me nuts. I finally got a newspaper from the rack and shoved it in front of him. It was The Jewish Daily Forward.

"Here, read this, calm yourself down," I said. "The guy will be back soon." I went back to sipping my glass of tea and waited.

In about 10 minutes, a kid ran into the deli. "Poppa's back," he yelled, and ran quickly out of the store. That was our signal to return to the tailor's, where Resnick was holding a suit on a hanger with his left hand, while his right stroked it with a whisk brush.

"Here, let's try this on for size," he said, as he handed me the suit. I went into a makeshift dressing area, slipped it on, and stood before a cloudy mirror. The waist needed to be taken in a bit, but everything else, including the vest, seemed to fit perfect. Just as he'd said.

When I returned from behind the curtain, Resnick took one look and was beaming. "You look like a regular Jack Dempsey. How about it Izzie, is that suit him?"

Izzie nodded approvingly. "It's him! Now Should I or shouldn't I ask where it came from? "

"Not to worry—the widow Rosenfeld, you know Moishe's widow, came by and told me she is clearing out her husband's things."

With that, he turned to me and said, very seriously, "Don't give it another thought. Moishe was a very clean man, a first-class banker, you know."

That settled it. I liked the suit and, if it was good enough for Mr. Rosenfeld the banker, it was good enough for me. "What do I owe you, Mr. Resnick?" He was chalking up the back of my pants, while I stood on the small platform looking into the mirror.

"You owe him nothing," Izzie said in a stern voice.

Resnick tended to business. "Here, turn around, I want for you to have a good fit," he said to me.

Moments later, he handed me a brown paper bag with a pair of beautiful, Spectator shoes in it, along with a fine pair of grey spats to wear on top. "Dapper" was the word of the day that described the well-dressed man I soon would be.

When we returned to the Riviera Hotel, and I changed into my new "work" clothes, Izzie grabbed the old outfit and scrunched it into a wastebasket. "How could you wear that shit?" Izzie the fashion plate had spoken.

Now I needed a tie to go with the new suit, and that problem was quickly resolved when Izzie ordered Julius the desk clerk to deliver. With some reluctance, he forked over a maroon-and-white tie that he kept in a desk drawer for special occasions.

The hotel manager, who'd been watching our fashion show, provided the finishing touch: a white handkerchief, which he fluffed up and tucked into my lapel pocket.

"Not bad, not bad at all," said Izzie, as he surveyed me. "Now stop smiling, Gio, we got work to do."

Out on the street, Izzie gave me a crash course, and I was worried that I was going to be the one who crashed. My first job would be to collect the bets from the local bookies, who made money by charging vigorish: hefty interest on a bet or loan. Izzie rattled off terms like spread-betting, money-line bets, proposition bets, parlays, and teasers. I didn't have a clue what he was talking about. When he saw that I was lost, he eased up.

"Okay, just do what I do and keep your mouth shut for now. Let them think you know what you're doing, and just watch what goes on. Nobody is going to try and beat us—that is, until they figure out that you are a little shegagah."

"Come on, Izzie, what the fuck is a shegagah?

Good, old Izzie, fashion plate and professor extraordinaire. He explained that a shegagah is a guy who's unaware of what is going on. "Nothing personal, Gio."

"Thanks, Izzie."

After we'd made the rounds and the day's instruction had ended, he took me to a rooming house next door to the Oheb Shalom Congregation synagogue, where I met the landlady, Mrs. Hurkins. She introduced herself as Florence, the wife of Irving the carpenter. She gave me a room on the second floor, facing the side of the synagogue. Izzie gave it his blessing, saying I couldn't get in trouble there even if I wanted to.

The room consisted of a brass bed with a meager, bamboo nightstand next to it, a tortoise shell lamp, a Morris chair by the window, and a small-but-adequate dresser that had been painted over several times, with a handle missing on the third drawer. A shelf attached to the wall sported a hot plate, an overhead fan was mounted on the tin ceiling, and stretched across the entrance door was an elastic band, where I could hang my ties—or should I say tie. It was the rule of the house that the transom glass over the door be left half-open to alert neighboring rooms in case a fire broke out in one of them. This was to be my home for the next six months

Chapter 3

Joe Reinfeld was the owner and operator of a tavern in the Italian First Ward of Newark, but although Joe was a Russian Jew like Longie, he looked like the quintessential Sicilian: tall and slim with olive skin and dark coloring. Joe and Longie had quite a thing going for them. They would buy hundreds of cases of Haig & Haig from the Bronfmans up in Canada, smuggle them into the U.S., and then store them in Reinfeld's warehouse in Newark. Word was that, if you couldn't pay full price for the good stuff, they could always get you a case or two that had been cut two or three times. A good bottle would cost Longie about two bucks, and he would sell it for $30.00.This looked like a profit of $28 a pop, but anyone with a brain in his head understood that it was costing Longie and Joe a ton of money to buy the stuff and truck it into the U.S. with armed guards, paying off the local politicians and cops, and then distributing it to consumers. Still, there was plenty of room for profit.

What was cool about Longie, though, was the fact that he refused to succumb to the temptation of flashing around his newfound wealth. You would never see him driving fancy cars or wearing big pinky rings or anything like that. Longie would just be Longie, and take care of business neatly, quietly, and proficiently. And he could be trusted to be fair with his partners.

At the end of my first month of paying off the people who were running numbers for Longie, Izzie told me that I had to report back to the Riviera late one afternoon to meet with Longie. He said he didn't know why. I was thinking, "Holy shit, this can't be good."

When I arrived at the hotel, two of Longie's men, Moe and Alley Boy, stopped me near the elevator and asked where I was going all alone.

"Izzie told me the boss wants to see me," I said.

"Oh, is that right? Wait here while I check," Moe said, as he slowly walked to a phone booth, fingering the toothpick in his mouth, all the while never taking his eyes off of me. He flipped up the brim of his Fedora and dropped a nickel into the payphone. Seconds later, he opened the booth's bi-fold door and nodded to Alley Boy. "It's okay. Let him go up."

As I approached the office door, it suddenly opened even before I knocked on it.

"Come on in," said a wiry man wearing a green visor on his head and holding a cup of coffee. Reading specs perched on the tip of his nose, and he was dressed in a white shirt with small ink stains around the breast pocket stuffed with pens and pencils. He wore suspenders, black baggy pants that looked two sizes too big, no tie, and elastic garters that held up his sleeves so the cuffs would not slide down over his hands. He could have used an appointment at Resnick's. I never saw anybody dressed like that before, and wondered who he was.

Longie was leaning back in his desk chair, reading a newspaper with his feet up on the desk. As I approached, he quickly put down the paper and asked for me to sit across from him.

"How's it going, Gio? You doing all right? Bet you like having some dough in your pocket, huh?"

"You're asking me its how's it going? I should be the one to ask you that, Longie," I said. "I don't know how I'm doing. Ask Izzie that question…I'm just doing what he tells me to do."

"Nice suit," he said, as he looked me over.

The phone rang, and he swiveled around in his chair. Reaching for his Western Electric candlestick-model phone, he picked up the earpiece and spoke into the candlestick.

"Yeah,'lo? Hey, Arny! I'll be damned…you're kidding, right?… Of course, I know that! So, what's new?…Look, everybody knows Owney Madden has another year or two before he's up for parole… Yeah, I know he had the broads from his Cotton Club come up to Sing Sing to entertain the inmates. Some balls, huh?

"I'll keep my action, and he can keep his! Look, right now I am not interested in going into business on 142nd and Lenox in Harlem. But thanks for thinking of me, Arny."

With that, Longie hung up the phone and turned to me. "You know who that was?"

"No."

"That is the guy who makes it all happen. That was Arnold Rothstein on the phone. The deals come through here every day. Everybody's got a deal for me. I got no interest in that fucking Cotton Club. Who the hell wants to get involved with a place that has only colored entertainers and help, but all the customers have to be white. That is some crazy shit, right? You watch, somewhere down the road the help is going to be white and all the customers will be colored. Maybe not in my lifetime, but it is gonna happen.

"I got more than my share of stuff to take care of right now. For example, the Dutchman only deals in beer, at least for now, and he gets it brewed right here in Newark. Me, I am not interested in his beer, but if I was interested in taking over his action, we would be shooting it out in the street. You know who the Dutchman is, Gio?"

"You mean Dutch Schultz?"

"That is exactly who I mean. His real name is Arthur Flegenheimer. He's a Jew just like us. Funny, all of us Jews in our business."

Since Longie was sharing all this with me like I was one of his partners, I loosened up. "Yeah, it's crazy, who would have thought that," I said. "When you read the papers, it seems the Sicilians and Italians are taking all the heat. Why is that?"

"Why?" Longie looked like he was ready to spill a secret. "It's because the Jews are satisfied with just making money—no flash, just cash. Hey, that rhymes, don't it? No flash, just cash.

His expression turned serious. "The reason I called you over here was to see if you are interested in working on some other, more important stuff we got going. What do you say, you interested in hearing about it?" He leaned across the big oak desk.

"Sure Longie, whatever you say, I'm a good listener." I, too, leaned forward.

"Okay then. You know, I'm involved with some people in the liquor business. Ever since the Volstead Act was passed, so many schmucks got into this racket by themselves because they think they can make a quick buck and get out. The truth is that these assholes have been brewing their own white lightning in the cellars of their homes, and peddling it on the street for a few bucks to the working stiffs, who are looking to buy on the cheap.

"The fact is that some of these poor stiffs, after drinking that shit, started howling in the night like werewolves and even went blind, and who knows what the fuck else happened to them. You see, the cops never bothered too much with those small-time shot-pushers because there was nothing much to gain either stealing from them or putting them away. Me and my liquor partners, however, get all the attention from the politicians and cops, because they know we are making the bucks, and they want a piece of it. Can't blame them, I guess.

"So what I did was ask the guys who were running their businesses like me, if they would like to have a meeting to iron out some ideas on a working relationship that would benefit us all. They agreed to it, and we all had a sit-down and talked things over. Nobody wanted to infringe on another guy's turf or anything like that. The meeting was just to see how many issues we could agree on.

"So, it turns out that each of us at the meeting was in need of similar things. We needed the suppliers of the good booze, a key person to make the connections to sell it, the trucks to get it to its destination, the muscle to protect our shipments, the police to look the other way when we make our drops and, most important of all, we have to make sure the cops, the judges, and politicians are well greased and see things our way.

"Remember the night we came here in the army truck? Remember how the police rode shotgun for us as we entered Newark? That didn't happen by accident. There's a guy who thinks he owns the whole city: Richie "the Boot" Boiardo. Ever hear of him?"

"No. Sorry."

"Don't be sorry—be smart. He's in the same business as us, except he thinks Newark is all his. He has some tough boys working for him, like Gyp DeCarlo, a guy named Zip, and one of his top guys, name of Johnny Russell. These guys and their boys have been attacking our trucks and drivers. Don't get me wrong, we got our own boys to deal with them and, so far, we're holding our own, but right now we also have an 'in' with the police. Get the picture?"

Once Longie got started talking about business matters, he was like a freight train. He went on.

"So far, all we got is an idea that I guarantee will work, but what is throwing a stick in the spokes are the old bosses, the "Mustache Petes," you know, those alta cockers like Joe "the Boss" Masseria and Salvatore Maranzano. These guys insist that only Italians and Sicilians can make deals with each other. Nobody else is welcome, and that leaves Jews like us out of the action. That means guys like Meyer Lansky and Arnold Rothstein and lots of other guys with good brains are being kept out of the mix." He waited for my reaction.

"Keep going, I am all ears."

"I know you understand. Part of me feels like I must be out of my fucking mind for trusting you so early in the game, but somehow I do. So I am going to tell you some more stuff that I hope I am not sorry for telling you later, understand? Let me clarify one thing for you up front, Gio. What I'm telling you is what they call privileged information. If any of it leaks out, you understand the consequences, right?"

That sent a little chill through me, but I trusted myself to keep my mouth shut. "Don't worry," I said, trying to make it sound automatic.

"Okay, then, for selling the stuff to hotels, country clubs, nightclubs, etcetera, we got Benny Siegel." Longie noticed the look in my eyes.

"You know Bugsy?"

"Who don't? I mean—not personally."

"Never call him that, by the way," Longie said, with a wry smile on his face. "He might do something not too nice, like blow your head off."

Longie spun to the humidor on the credenza and plucked out a sizable cigar, which he cut and lit with practiced style. "Cubans," he said, launching the first few puffs. "The best. Want one?"

"No thanks, Longie, I'm training for the Olympics,"

He laughed behind the smoke. "That's funny, Gio...If you wanna try one, let me know. Now, where was I? Okay, Lepke Buchalter handles the muscle for us and settles the debts, Jake Shapiro also works the muscle, and Frank Costello controls the Italian interests. Lucky Luciano is our ace in the hole, and I mean that sincerely. Unlike most of the Italians, he likes doing business with the Jews. Masseria forbids the Italians to have anything to do with us; he's from the old country. But Lucky has a different point of view; he thinks modern."

"I like that," I said, immediately kicking myself. Who the hell was I to offer such an opinion? But Longie didn't seem to mind.

"Me, too. Now, working out of New Jersey, we had to partner up with Willie Moretti. He is one tough son-of-a-bitch. Loves the bars and nightclubs, and has some terrific connections. Owney Madden is on board, but that's not written in stone right now.

"Our main guy, the one we can count on all the time, is Meyer Lansky. The guy's got brains, he's calm and collected, and he can work both sides of the coin. You can always depend on his word, but the truth of the matter is, if you fuck up and get your ass in a sling, you better not count on Meyer to hold your hand.

"So here's the deal, Gio. I'd like to use you, especially with that new suit you got on, to go around and represent me with my new partners. You do what they need done, as far as visiting nightclubs, taking orders from the purchasing agents for our booze, and stuff like that. How's that sound?"

I felt my cheeks puff out, as I exhaled—I must have looked like an idiot. "Are you kidding, Longie? That sounds great. More than great."

Longie pursed his lips and blew out a couple of smoky circles, then placed the cigar on an ashtray, "You know, that suit looks damn good on you. Tell Izzie to go back down to Resnick's and buy all of Moishe's suits from the widow Rosenfeld—she can use the dough. After he checks them out and has them pressed, get 'em sent over to your rooming house. You're going to need them on your new job. I want you start right away."

Like a dope, I reached my hand across the desk to thank Longie for the promotion. But he just held up his hands, palms facing me in a 'stick-'em-up' position. I knew what he meant: action, not friendship.

"By the way, Gio, I'm going to get you a car to use so you can get around. Hit some of the country clubs and see how you do with the orders. Bring samples of the booze with you, and pass them out to people you think will help you get the orders you need, understand? Spend as much as you think you have to at the bars in these joints. Let them get to know you. Let them get to taste the good stuff."

He told me I'd done a "great job" working the Clinton Hill section of town, that the housewives loved me up there and bought a ton of lottery tickets. He said I gave his operation class. That was like Babe Ruth telling me he liked the way I swung the bat.

Longie informed me that one of my new destinations was to be Fort Lee. "I want you to get the lay of the land over there," he said. "The place is full of movie studios with a lot of thirsty actors. Make your first stop at a place called the Villa Richard. I think it's located on Hudson Terrace. See a guy over there named Jean Richard." Jhan Ree-shard, was the way Longie said it, giving it that French twang bullshit.

"He bought the joint a couple of years ago, and so far he doesn't want to buy liquor from us. See if you can make him change his mind—in a nice way of course. I go up there all the time, and he runs a good place. I am pretty sure he has been buying his stuff from the boys from New York.

"I don't think you'll have any trouble soliciting sales in Fort Lee. Ever since our syndicate decided to work together, everyone is a lot more tolerant. That is not to say we can walk right in and take over things, but greasing the skids and making sure everyone gets a piece of the action sort of smooths things over, if you know what I mean.

"So pack up your stuff, you're gonna take Izzie's car. Drive up to Cella's Hotel; that's where you'll be staying. Get in touch with a guy named Eddie Mannix. He'll take you around and introduce you. He'll probably want to take you to the film studios so you can meet some of the big shots; they always need a case or two." He handed me ten, $20 bills rolled up. "This should last you a few weeks."

That afternoon I packed up, and off I went in Izzie's royal-blue, 1920 Franklin, with the air-cooled engine. (I have no idea what Izzie was driving during my Fort Lee journey.) I had no idea what I was going to do when I got there, but Longie seemed to have confidence I'd figure it out, especially with Eddie Mannix leading the way.

It was about 10:15 p.m. when I pulled up in front of Cella's Park Hotel, a beautiful Victorian place with a mansard roof and a huge, wraparound porch. Everything was quiet, as I parked the car and made my way onto the porch. The sleeping, black, Labrador Retriever woke, but didn't seem to mind my approaching the door. He just put his head back down and resumed his sleep.

"Gettin' much?" asked a spectral figure standing in the dark on the far side of the porch.

"Who the fuck are you?" I responded nervously. Just then, the door of the hotel opened, and a short man in his 50s, wearing a butcher's apron, stepped out.

"Hi, come on in," he said. "I am the owner. Peter Cella is my name. What can I do for you?"

"I believe I have a reservation—Gio Arigo?"

"Oh yes, a Mister Zwillman from Newark made it for you, as I recall. Excuse my apron; my job here is never finished. I was just putting together some beef that came from a farm in Paramus. We have a fireman's dinner here tomorrow night, and they love their beefsteak."

"Who's that guy on your porch who asks if I am getting much?"

"Don't worry, he's one of the unfortunates," Peter said. "He says that to all our guests. We're used to it, but I guess it is a little alarming if you don't know him…Anyhow, Gio, welcome to Cella's Park. We have your room all prepared."

"Thank you, Mister Cella. Let me ask you, do you have a garage on this property with a lock on it? I have several cases of my product in the back seat of my car, which would be easy pickings for anyone who had a mind to steal them."

"Not exactly a garage, but just as good. There's a barn around back where I keep the hotel's carriages with a lock on the door."

"Appreciate that; I will make the inconvenience worthwhile." I handed him a fifty-cent piece.

As we hiked up the broad, plush-carpeted staircase in the hotel, Peter turned to me and said, "We have quite a few celebrities staying with us this week. Barthelmess is filming *The Fighting Blade* over at the Inspiration Studio—the old Universal. Most of the rooms are taken up with movie people. I hope they don't disturb your sleep. They have a tendency to stay up late and party a lot."

My room had a brass double-bed and a soft mattress. There was a Hudson Dispatch newspaper placed carefully on the night table next to the bed. When I picked it up to see what was going on around town, a particular article caught my eye. It was more than just another story about the ban, and subsequent transportation of, alcoholic beverages. These days, instead of just stories on the Volstead Act and the constitutional changes that were taking place, the news stories were openly discussing the impact that Prohibition had on the gangs who transported and sold the booze.

The headline read, "Capone Planning to Leave Brooklyn: Heading for New Home in Chicago."

This was big news. So Al Capone was moving to the Windy City. He would be joining South Side gang boss Johnny Torrio, who had hired him to help fight off rival gangs who wanted to take over Torrio's booze territory.

This could be a big break for Longie, which meant it could be a big break for me. Seemed like a few days ago, I was shagging golf balls; now I was making rounds in the world of big business. I stretched out on the bed and dozed off to sleep.

I dreamed I was captured by a rival gang because I was trying to encroach on their territory. I managed to break free, but they kept chasing me and, when they caught up to me, they just laughed and laughed, and then one of them pulled out a gun longer than a baseball bat.

I awoke in a sweat, my heart racing. The laughter continued, but it wasn't the menacing gangsters who were laughing, but people partying in the hallway outside my door. The alarm clock on the dresser said it was 3 a.m. The transom window above my door was open slightly, so I could hear every word that was said outside. It sounded like there were three women and two men out there. One of the women said, "Now come on, Mister Mannix. You don't think I am going to believe your line of bullshit, do you?"

Eddie Mannix! The guy I was supposed to meet the next day. What was he doing outside my door in the middle of the night? I slipped my pants on and opened the door. Eddie was leaning against the wall in the dimly lit hallway. The broad was plastered.

Eddie quickly straightened and looked at me. "And who the fuck are you?"

This wasn't quite the introduction I'd imagined. "I'm Giorgio Arigo, Longie's guy."

Eddie relaxed. "They call you Gio, right? I didn't expect you until tomorrow. Nice to meet you, I'm Eddie Mannix." He held out his hand out for me to shake, while pushing the tipsy beauty away.

"We got a big day tomorrow; I want to take you around to the studios and have you meet some important people." He took a long drag on his cigar.

Eddie was celebrating that night because he had just returned from California, where he landed a job with Louis B. Mayer at MGM. In those days, the Schenk brothers, owners of Palisade Amusement Park had just about every movie studio in Fort Lee sewed up, and out of respect for the people who gave him his first break, Eddie was in town to check on their interests.

"Hey Gio, how about you let Amy room with you tonight," Eddie said, referring to his female pursuer. "She had a few shooters and missed her ferry back to New York. The next one won't come until tomorrow morning."

"I don't know Eddie—I need my beauty sleep," I said, kiddingly.

Amy, a pretty brunette with finger waves, looked like she was in her early twenties. She had snow-white skin and ample breasts, and she sure looked tempting to me. I was as nervous as a cat to find out if she really wanted to spend the night in my room.

"What's a matter, pal, ain't I good enough for a swell like you?" she slurred in her gum-chewing, Brooklyn accent.

"Of course you are, honey," I said. "Let's keep the party going, what do you say?"

Having handed her off, Eddie bid us goodnight, and she and I stepped into my room.

Amy was wearing a short, green-and-silver, flapper dress and high-heeled, silver shoes with a strap across the instep. As she stood by the window, lifting the side of the shade to take a peek outside onto Center Avenue, I admired her smooth white shoulders and the way her dress fell in a drape to just above her waistline, exposing the flawless skin of her back.

After a few moments, she turned her head coyly to me. "Do you like what you see?"

"Sure do," I said. "Why don't you come over here so we can get to know each other?" Not exactly an original line, but then she wasn't exactly the Queen of England.

She looked at me sternly. "I don't mind sleeping on the floor tonight. I spent the day dodging those lechers at the studio, and now I am stuck here in Fort Lee for the night, so I hope you and I can make believe we are just good friends and keep our distance until morning. Is that all right with you?"

"Sure," I said, changing my tune. "But you take the bed. I'll sleep on the floor."

Then she surprised me. "How about we both try and share the bed—you on your side, me on mine, and never the twain shall meet. Think you can handle that?" I wondered whether her knowing smile was genuine, or a reflex from a movie shoot—Eddie had mentioned that she was an extra in the flickers.

"I'll do my best," I said, still hoping that something more would come of this arrangement.

In bed, her perfume filled the air with hopeful promise. In the twilight of my sleep, I began to feel a gentle hand stroking my shoulder as I lay motionless with my back to her.

I opened my eyes, afraid to move and scare the welcome hand away. It became bolder, reaching around my neck, searching and stroking while we both lay quietly in the spoon position. Finally, one of her long, well-shaped legs—the legs I had admired from the first minute I saw her— reached over my rib cage and gripped me tight as she pressed her body against my back, snuggling closer until I could identify every sensual part of her. I refused to move, pretending I was still asleep, as she began openly to explore every part of my body.

I let an involuntary sigh escape, as she touched what she was searching for, signaling to her that I was awake. When she was satisfied that I was ready, she started kissing and sucking gently on my earlobe and neck. Realizing that I was fast becoming too far gone to wait any longer, I quickly turned over and embraced her, spreading kisses across her face as she willingly opened and accepted me, without a word being spoken.

Now *that* would have made a torrid love scene. Thankfully, no director was in the room to yell, "Cut."

Chapter 4

October was in the air on this beautiful morning; not a cloud in the sky, with a gentle breeze wafting across the front porch of the hotel. I was finishing reading the Hudson Dispatch, sipping a cup of piping, hot, hotel coffee, as I sat waiting for Eddie Mannix to show up for our meeting. About 15 minutes later, Amy came gliding through the lobby in high spirits, bidding a cheery "good morning" to everyone she passed.

"Thank you, Gio, for sharing your room with me last night—I won't forget it." Neither will I, I said with a smile as she sat on one of the white, wicker chairs and peered over the table at my cup. "Where did you get the coffee, inside?"

"Yes, want one? I'll get it for you."

"I would love one. Eddie meeting you?"

As I stood, a folded letter fell from her lap to the floor. When I retrieved it, I noticed the letterhead that read, "Ziegfeld Follies Rehearsal Schedule."

"Hey Amy, are you one of those Ziegfeld girls?"

"Oh, yeah, I have been hoofing it for four years now. In fact, today I have a rehearsal at one, and I better catch an early ferry to New York so I can hustle my ass to the rehearsal studio on time."

"I know someone who was a Ziegfeld Girl. Do you know a beautiful, young woman by the name of Nancy Jansen? Her husband's a doctor."

"Nancy Jansen?…No, I don't think so, although that name does sound vaguely familiar. I knew a Nancy Olsen…Wait a minute, is she a tall blonde with a great figure?"

"That's her."

"Then I knew her before she got married. We called her 'Junior.'"

"Junior?"

"Like a stage name, something different, even kind of sexy—anyway, that was the idea. She was a very troubled woman. She came up on a bus one day from some small town in Texas; that's what she told people. She wanted New York, Broadway, you know—bright lights and high living. She was only seventeen when we danced in the line together. I think she tried to kill herself over the loss of her baby. Something about an abortion with knitting needles, or some other crazy shit she did to herself. Yes, I remember it very well now."

That didn't square with beautiful Nancy from Raritan Valley Country Club, but there was no stopping Amy, as she was intent on continuing.

"The story was that Junior got herself pregnant by some musician, who was married. He never told her he was married, and he dated her for quite a while. She was just a kid back then, and scared as hell. She became so despondent. She tried to kill herself. Oh yeah, that was some story backstage. I think Flo Ziegfeld introduced her to a Dr. Jensen or Johnson, a name like that, and he was supposed to help her."

"Jansen," I said.

"Yeah, that's it! Jansen. I knew it was something like that. Is she a friend of yours?"

"Not really," I replied. "I just met her once."

"…Junior Olsen…Boy, haven't thought of her in a long time."

So that was the story of how Nancy and Dr. Jansen got together. One of these days I hoped to see her again. There was something about her that intrigued me. Maybe it was just her good looks. Maybe it was because she seemed to have such a gentle side. I only knew that I liked her, and thought it was too bad that she was married. If she were not married, I would certainly have made a move on her. Anyway, I figured, this was all good material for the story I might write someday.

Moments later, Eddie Mannix came striding up on the porch, dressed to the nines. For a guy who got his start shaking down patrons with his gang of hoodlums at Palisade Amusement Park, his upward trajectory had been fast. He was soon hired by the owners of the park, the Schenck Brothers, to protect those same patrons from hoods like himself, and was ultimately taken under the Schenck Brothers' wing and introduced to Hollywood society, where he quickly became one of the darlings of the west coast film industry's fast crowd. Eddie was doing all right for himself, and by all indications this was only the beginning for him.

"Hey, look at you two lovebirds," Eddie said. "Have a good night, Amy, or shouldn't I ask?"

"You can't go wrong accepting a gentleman's sleeping accommodations," she said, breaking into peals of laughter.

"Come on, let's get crackin', we have a busy day ahead of us," I said, ending the banter on the porch. "I've got a car in the garage around back with my supplies in it. Should we take it?"

"No, let's take the trolley," Eddie said. "It's only one block north on Main Street.
Amy, you can get one that'll take you down to Edgewater, where you can get the ferry back to New York."

We all left the porch and walked the block-and-a-half north to Main Street to wait for the trolley car. There was optimism in the brisk, fall air and, as if expecting us, the trolley arrived just when we got there. We all dashed across Main Street, and Eddie and I boarded when we saw it was ours. "Yours'll probably be along in a minute," Eddie shouted to Amy. "See ya, sweets."

"You guys really know how to treat a woman," she said, looking up at us from the curb.

"Next stop, Linwood Ave!" the conductor hollered. Eddie told me that our first stop would be at Bill Fox's old studio in Doc Wilet's glass barns. He said the place had closed a few years ago, but he wanted to show me the barns, anyway. That confused me—what was the value in seeing an old, abandoned movie studio? The answer would have to wait, because Eddie scooted off the trolley at Linwood, and I followed. Waiting for us was a man who looked a lot like Eddie, though he was taller and a few years younger. Eddie gave him a quick, vigorous bear hug.

"How's it shakin', Austie?"

"Great Eddie, just fine. How come you don't have time to call Mom and me anymore?"

"Hey, your brother's a busy man these days. Austie, I want you to meet Giorgio Arigo. Longie sent him up here to meet some of our friends."

"Nice to meet you Giorgio," Austie said, as he reached out to shake my hand.

"Feeling's mutual."

He invited me to a weekend "shindig" with "all the mucky mucks" and lots of knockwurst and bratwurst. "All that good German shit," Austie said. "Plenty of beer, too—the Dutchman's finest right out of the tap. We are even going to have some cock-fights. You're gonna love it."

"I'll try to make it, if I am around on Saturday," I said, thinking that these Mannix brothers must have a lot going for them.

"Come on Gio, let me show you around this old studio," Eddie said, as we entered the Linwood Avenue gate. I was still wondering why he was taking me here, but didn't have to wait long to find out. The site watchman greeted us, and Eddie gave me a big buildup.

"Hey Jimmy, meet Gio Arigo, the man who can wet down this town with the finest bourbon and Scotch. He came all the way over here from Newark with several cases of the good stuff. You interested?"

"Shit, yeah!" Jimmy said. "Come with me, and I'll show you where we keep our stash."

We followed him inside one of the glass barns to a large, wooden storage locker previously used to store wood and card-board scenery for movie sets. Jimmy opened the locker and said, "How about this, boys?"

"Holy shit," I said under my breath, as I viewed stacks of beer kegs and mentally counted. "You must have about sixty-five kegs in here, right?"

"Seventy is the count. Hey pal, you got a good head for num-bers…So, what can you get us?"

"Just about any kind of booze you want," I said. "You name it, we probably got it." Eddie and Austie looked at me as I spoke, gauging whether or not I was the real deal. Damn right I was the real deal—I was Longie's guy.

"Okay, then," Jimmy said. "I'll get in touch with my friends. We'll need a couple of days to figure out the order."

Apparently, this was one watchman with a lot of juice.

"What about the law?" I asked.

"What they don't know won't hurt them," Jimmy said. "How are you going to bring it in?"

"Don't worry about that; I'll take care of that myself."

I had already arranged for a family in Coytesville, the next town up from Fort Lee, to make my deliveries. These were the Austin Boys—no relation to Austie Mannix. The six Austin brothers came from the Lower East Side of Manhattan, and settled in Coytesville. Their little trucking company, the Wellington Express, had some of the first motorized trucks in New York. And they could be trusted, and that's what counts the most. The Austins knew the city like their backyard, and most of their business was with speakeasies, which were raided frequently and resurfaced just as often.

The Austin clan's only problem was that they liked to stop and have a few shooters in every joint where they made a delivery. Sooner or later, I figured, they were going to get their asses in trouble, because most of the time they were half in the bag. But, so far, nobody had hijacked any of their loads.

I was excited that my first stop had landed a good order. It was a good guess that the beer stored there must have come from Dutch Schultz's operation. The Dutchman was about to get some competition. Austie looked at me with newfound admiration.

"You got stones, I'll say that," he said. He turned to his brother. "I guess my next blowout will have Zwillman beer, huh?"

Eddie squinted in cautious agreement. "Could be."

He clapped me on the shoulder. "You know, Gio, I promised to take you around so you can check out the studios in town, and I will do that, but to be honest with you, Fort Lee is washed up in the film business. In fact, all of the movie studios on the East coast are finished. The handwriting is on the wall. The action's shifting to California, where they can shoot in nice weather all year long...The village idiot can figure that one out, right?"

It was ironic that, just when motion pictures were taking off, the place where they got their start was about to turn into a ghost town. But one thing I knew for sure was that, movies or no movies, people wanted booze, and that was why I had come here.

As promised, we made our studio rounds. Victor Film Company, Solax, Artcraft, Triangle-Fine, Arts-Keystone, Goldwyn Pictures, Fox—they were all in decline. So was this just a sightseeing tour?

Not quite. Eddie explained that his bosses, the Selznick Brothers, wanted him to keep tabs on the studios they had financial interests in, and that was all of them. I stored away that information and, when we ran out of studios, we again hopped the trolley. This time we were heading for lunch, so we took it east, all the way down Main Street to the Octagon Hotel on the border of Edgewater.

"Next stop is Jean Richard's place, the Villa Richard," Eddie said, as we sipped coffee. He explained that Jean wanted to meet us right away, and that we had to pronounce the name Ree-shard. So that it implied class and didn't sound like a hot dog stand.

"Who is this guy?" I asked.

Eddie explained that Jean (pronounced Jhan) was the head chef at Delmonico's in New York. Prohibition was hitting Delmonico's hard times, as their patrons could no longer be served liquor. "Who wants to eat steak if you can't have a few nice cocktails with it? So the fancy, schmancy, bullshit actors here in Fort Lee—you know, the ones who had some bucks to spend, and hung out at Delmonico's—convinced Jean Richard to come to New Jersey and buy an old hotel just up the road from here. He did just that, but quickly ended up with his ass in a sling. The county cracked down on the operation because of the booze, and also because he had some women on tap, if you know what I mean. But he does run some pretty good shows up there—the place is on the cliffs overlooking the river—with big stars from New York. Top celebrities frequent the joint, and they often bring some of their own babes with them.

"You're gonna like this place, Gio. Jean has only one big problem: he doesn't understand that you have to grease the right wheels to make sure the powers-that-be look the other way."

"Any dope knows that," I said, but in truth, I was just learning.

At that moment, a young couple came into the dining room, and people stopped eating to look at them. It seemed that they were some kind of celebrities, or something. The newcomers stopped at more than a few tables to shake hands and spend a moment chatting. The young woman was doing all the talking, while the tall, skinny guy with her seemed to be very shy. Whoever they were, they were causing a stir, and I was intrigued. When they reached our table. Eddie practically leaped out of his chair to shake the young man's hand, and hug the pretty, young woman.

"Giorgio, meet Mister and Missus Lindbergh," Eddie said, his voice full of excitement. "Anne's Dad and I are old friends, and Charles is a pilot."

I rose from my seat, hand outstretched to greet them.

"So nice to meet you," I said in my best welcoming voice.

It's funny how you change your style of speech, depending on who you are speaking to. This couple, whoever they were, seemed to command the respect that everyone was giving them, so I just followed Eddie's lead.

"Want to join us?" Eddie asked.

"We don't want to interrupt your lunch," Anne said.

"No, no, please sit down. Gio is an old friend from out of town. He's here for a short visit, so I'm showing him around Fort Lee."

"I see," said the young man, looking directly at me. "What do you do?"

"Me? I'm a facilitator." I was smartening up in a hurry in this atmosphere.

"May I ask what that is?" Anne said, smiling.

"A facilitator is someone who makes things happen," Eddie quickly injected. "Gio is a problem-solver. Whatever the problem is, Gio and his company can find ways to come up with the answer."

"You mean…something like a troubleshooter?" Charles asked.

"Yes, something like that," I said, smiling, well aware of the double entendre "How about you—what do you do?" I wondered what the hell this stiff could do that would be exciting in any way.

Before responding, he took a moment to look at Anne, as if to ask her approval.

"Go on, Charles, tell him."

"Well…I'm a pilot. I just fly the mail."

You could have knocked me off the chair with a feather. "Air mail? I've heard of that. Wow, what a surprise. I looked at Eddie, then back at the lanky fellow still standing in front of me. "I've got to talk to you about flying. What the hell keeps it up there?"

Eddie elbowed me kiddingly. "They came here for lunch, Gio— not the third degree."

"Sorry, but flying fascinates me."

"That's okay, Gio," Anne said. "It fascinates my husband, too."

The Lindberghs finally took their seats at our table and, for the next hour or so, Charles graciously answered every one of my questions, while Anne and Eddie held their own conversation. Charles told me that, one day, he would cross the Atlantic in a plane, if he could ever arrange the funding for such an attempt. I couldn't help thinking that, while this skinny soft-spoken guy apparently had guts, he might have been off his rocker.

Just to be polite, though, I said, "If you ever try to do something like that, I promise you I will be there with bells on."

After we said good-bye to the Lindberghs, Eddie and I walked off the big lunch by strolling back to Cella's Park Hotel to pick up my car so we could head over to the Villa Richard and see if I could stir up some business with Mr. Richard. As we walked, I could not help talking about what Lindbergh had told me.

"Don't sell 'em short," Eddie said. "Those quiet guys can surprise you."

Soon after, we were on our way to the Villa Richard, whose owner hadn't yet learned how to "grease the right wheels." Eddie explained that his bosses, the Selznick brothers, had their eye on it. When we reached this restaurant perched atop the steep, craggy cliffs of the

Palisades, my lips parted in wonder. About 500 feet above the river, it commanded a fantastic view of the Hudson River and most of lower Manhattan. After taking a good look at this old, but well-maintained, Mediterranean-style villa, I understood why the Selznicks could see its potential. I was completely taken in by the outdoor, dining terrace that sat on the precipice of the cliff. I had never been to a place that had such a dynamic view of the skyline for miles around.

We were ushered into the kitchen area, where Jean Richard and his master chefs were at work. As I watched him in action—he was like a drill sergeant dressing down his troops—I couldn't help thinking that the chef at the Raritan Country Club could learn a few things from this guy in a hurry.

Despite his intense concentration, Richard loosened when he broke to greet Eddie. "We miss you," he said, wiping his hands on the towel draped over his shoulder before shaking Eddie's hand. "How's California?"

"Great—the weather sure beats the hell out of New York and New Jersey. Jean, meet my friend, Giorgio Arigo."

"Just call me 'Gio,'" I said.

"You can call him anything you want, as long as you call him when dinner's ready at the Villa Ree-shard," Eddie quipped.

"Any friend of Eddie's is a friend of mine," Richard said, as he offered his hand.

I decided to get right to the point. "Jean, I work for a group of people who are interested in helping you get access to the finest liquor available in this country." There was confidence in my voice; even a whiff of arrogance. "Your customers deserve the best, and we got it, as much as you need, whenever you need it."

Words were coming out of my mouth like I knew what I was doing. For the first time, I began to feel like I was important. Maybe Eddie had something to do with that. Everyone respected him, and it seemed to be rubbing off on me. But the question was, when Eddie was not around anymore, would I get the same respect?

My thoughts were interrupted when Richard said, "Gio, please understand that I have been getting my supplies regularly from

New York. They have been very reliable and careful in making sure that I don't get in trouble for selling their bottles."

Just then, we were interrupted by a young, nice-looking fellow who had walked, unannounced, into the kitchen.

"I don't mean to bust up your meeting, but Mister Richard, could you spare a few minutes to talk to me about what acts you want for the weekend show?"

"Bill Miller, say hello to a couple of my friends, Eddie Mannix and Giorgio Arigo," said Richard, who turned back to us with, "Bill books some of the acts for me here at the Villa. And he's not a bad entertainer himself. You ought to see his dance act with this guy named Peterson; they get a standing ovation every time. Excuse me, boys, I will be only be a few minutes. Meantime, please go out on the terrace and order anything you want—it's on me."

And off he went with Miller, leaving us standing in the kitchen with our thumbs up our asses.

"I guess it don't look so good for you at this place, huh, Gio?"

"I don't know," I said. "Maybe I got something that the other guys can't give him."

"What's that?"

"Protection…My guys got connections on this side of the river that the other guys don't have. Maybe it's time to give Monsieur Ree-shard an education on how to run his operation without interference from the politicians and cops in Bergen County. Like you were sayin' earlier, Eddie."

In very short order, I had become a big shot—at least in my own mind. But Eddie had, you might say, a somewhat different agenda. I could see by the look on his face that he wanted no part of what I was talking about. His next words confirmed that look.

"You know, Gio, I have to get myself back, and see my brother and my mom before I fly out of here tonight."

"You're heading back to California?"

"I use the studio's plane. It's down in a grass field in the meadows at Teterboro—a new, Fairchild six-seater. Fantastic machine… Kind of nice working for a big studio."

"I can imagine," I said without a great deal of enthusiasm.

We looked at each other, and understood that our day was over. We each recognized the boundary line between our lives. I admit that, at that moment, I was envious of what Eddie had accomplished already in his life, especially having the opportunity to fly in a plane. Everyone around the town of Fort Lee knew Eddie Mannix, just like they knew Longie around Newark. We jumped back into my Franklin, or should I say Izzie's Franklin, and headed to Main Street.

"Can you drop me off at my brother's up on Linwood Avenue?" Eddie asked.

"You got it," I said, trying to end our outing on an up note. But I realized that his mind already was elsewhere, and no longer on introducing me to people in Fort Lee. Maybe I was out of line when I spoke so smugly about "protection," but hell, wasn't Eddie the one who'd brought it up in the first place? Anyway, Longie and Izzie had schooled me quite well that protection, in fact, was what we were selling. This was no Sunday school picnic.

There was no question in my mind that every time the law confiscated a shipment of our booze, they either sold it themselves, or drank the shit. You would have to have been born yesterday not to realize that. The only time the coppers axed the beer barrels was when the press was around to see it.

After I said good-bye to Eddie, making sure to thank him one last time for his help (and patting myself on the back for my maturity), I went back to the hotel, packed my bag, and drove back to Newark. I still had the feeling that Fort Lee was going to yield good stuff for us in the future. I just didn't know what that might be.

Then that old thought came back to me, the thought that Mom had planted in my head so many years before.

"Someday, you're gonna make it big."

Of course, she figured I'd do it in a way that was perfectly legal. So far, I was straying from that path.

In the years that followed, Longie gave me an education that would last me the rest of my life. He introduced me to ways of making money that I had never dreamed of. I guess he figured he owed me, and this was his way of paying me back.

He would always say that people believed in what they perceived—not what actually *is*. "People will bet on anything," he'd say, "even betting how long it will take for a light bulb to wear out. People bet their money on their dreams, and we are the dream makers. Never forget that."

Chapter 5

Those early years were fast and furious. I went from wearing suits handed down from dead guys, to buying imported suits; the best that money could buy. Borrowing Izzie's car was replaced by owning my first car, a mint-green Buick with black fenders and an emerald-green, mohair interior. The beautiful gold watch that I always wore, the prize I had won at the caddie tournament years before, was, as always, the perfect accessory for my new clothes.

Up to now, nothing I had ever owned could compare with the feeling of owning a luxury car such as the Buick. I no longer felt like an outsider with Longie's boys; now I felt like I was one of them, and I was willing to do anything necessary to take care of my end of our business. But I never forgot to send money to my mother every week.

The years passed quickly and, according to Longie, nothing was unattainable. It took brains to make everything work smoothly, and Longie was the one supplying the brainpower. He always seemed to come up with the right idea at the right time, always knew how to make things happen. The Marines had a slogan that went something like, "lead, follow or get the hell out of the way." From my perch, I chose to be a follower, and somehow that tack seemed to work out well for me. Longie needed a guy who could fit any situation: I was that guy, and he made good use of me.

In May of 1927, he told me to take a little vacation. He suggested I go to Long Island and snoop around Montauk, just to check on the action now that Al Capone was no longer watching the store on the east coast. Although Capone had left his digs in South Brooklyn in 1919, he still had an interest in the comings and goings on the South Shore of Long Island. Rum Row was the destination Longie pointed me to.

On my way there, I decided to take a side trip to Roosevelt Field and watch Charles Lindbergh take off in the flying gas tank he called The Spirit of St. Louis, just as I promised him that day we met back in

Fort Lee. He was on a quest to capture the $25,000 Orteig Prize for being the first person to fly non-stop from New York to Paris. I knew he probably would not remember the conversation we had that day over lunch at the Octagon Hotel, but I hadn't forgotten it. How could I? The newspapers made it front page news and, like everyone else, I was caught up in all the hoopla. So I decided I had to be there at his send-off, feeling sure that the poor bastard was going to kill himself.

Still, I held out the possibility that something historic was about to happen. It was quite a drive out to the Roosevelt Field, where Spirit resided in a hangar. I wondered whether the persistent drizzle would cancel the takeoff. It was about 6 a.m., when I spotted Lindbergh sitting on the passenger's side of the fuel truck that had pulled alongside his plane, which had just been towed out of the hangar.

I pulled the Buick to a stop, got out, and approached him. "Hey, Charles, remember me?"

For several seconds, there was no sign he recognized me, as he looked back and forth from me to the fuel gushing into the individual drums that would be loaded on the plane. Then…"Giorgio, right?"

I was just as astonished as I was when he'd told me, that day at the Octagon, that he flew airmail routes. But I recovered.

"That's me; I'm here on time to root for you all the way to Paris."

"Great, come over here and make yourself useful," he said, passing me a five-gallon, sealed drum of aviation fuel.

"Hand this to the guy up on the wing, and I'll keep 'em coming, if you don't mind."

I complied and, in that instant, had joined Team Lindbergh.

"Are you nervous?" I asked.

"Naw, I practiced the take-off fifty times, using sandbags instead of the extra fuel so I could get a feel of how the plane is going to respond with all this weight onboard. The cool air and rain this morning should help the carburetion. You know, it should respond better to the strain of the takeoff."

Of course, I didn't know. I only knew my Buick didn't do so well with damp weather.

"How did you sleep last night?" I was immediately embarrassed by this dumb question meant to keep the conversation going.

"Actually, I didn't get much sleep last night. I went to see the Broadway show Rio Rita, and then drove back to the Garden City Hotel. By the time I got there, I only got about an hour's sleep, so I am bushed right now. I'm not worried though; it's a long flight to Paris, so I can catch up on my sleep on the plane." His surprisingly hearty laugh broke the tension for everyone within earshot. "Can you do me a favor?"

"Sure," I said, "what's up?"

"You got a car. Would you mind driving down the road— there's a delicatessen in Hempstead—and picking me up a half-dozen sandwiches, some soda pop, and coffee to take along on the flight?"

"Of course not," I said. "What do you like?"

He thought for a moment and said, "I guess I need something that won't go bad. I can't keep it cold without ice; maybe Swiss cheese on rye with mustard. Get two of those, and how about two fresh ham-and-cheese with lettuce and tomato, and maybe a couple of jelly bread on white."

He slapped a five-dollar bill into my hand. Then he asked me to go his locker in the hangar, and take out his gallon thermos jug and fill with black coffee. "Fill it all the way to the top," he said, and then reiterated, "black, it's got to be black and hot as they can make it."

About 7 a.m., I returned with the food and coffee. I still didn't know whether I was looking at the bravest man in the world, or a nut case. What would he have done if I had not shown up to get his food? I asked myself. What else did he forget?

Maybe he figured he was born to be lucky.

By the time I returned, the crew was hooking the front of the plane to an old truck. "Where are you going with that?" I asked one of the crewmen.

"We have to tow it about a mile over to the runway. I hope we don't get this son-of-a-bitch stuck in the mud. "This baby is one heavy son-of-a-bitch, now that we filled it to the brim with fuel." He sounded concerned, but not alarmed. Still, I couldn't resist one of my dumb questions.

"Think it's too heavy to get off the ground?"

"Hell no!" He looked at me, turned away, and paused for a moment. "When a man truly makes up his mind to do something, there is no son-of-a-bitch in the world that is going to change it for him, understand?"

I nodded hard, for I well understand what he meant.

"Follow us in your car, just in case we do get stuck in a rut or something," he said.

The field had been named for Quentin Roosevelt, Teddy Roosevelt's aviator-son killed in action in the "Great War" a decade earlier. Several hundred gawkers looked on, as we pulled onto the makeshift, grass runway. The curious crowd swarmed the plane, quickly surrounding it. The ground crew struggled to keep inquisitive hands away. One idiot even sought to enter the cockpit. I just shook my head.

All of a sudden I was taken aback by a woman in the crowd who bore a striking resemblance to Nancy Jansen, the young woman I'd seen—but had barely spoken to—on so many occasions at the Raritan Valley Country Club. She wore a black scarf, and held an umbrella overhead, the collar of her tan raincoat turned up. I made my way through the crowd and drew closer.

Couldn't be—what would she be doing here? But the closer I got, the more positive I became that it was her. The man at her side also looked familiar to me, but I couldn't place him, either.

Then it came to me. The guy was Ben Marden, a big wheel who I'd met during my Navy days. He'd been a gob just like me, except that he was the go-to guy for anything you needed that you couldn't get on the base. Smooth as silk, in the know, respected by all, and afraid of nothing. Ben was one tough customer, and his broken nose suggested that he'd gone a few rounds with some other tough guys. What was he doing here with the girl of my dreams?

As I was considering my next move, Nancy spotted me from about 10 feet away.

"Well look what the cat dragged in," she said. "What the are you doing standing in the rain?"

Somehow, I maintained my cool. "I could ask you the same question."

"At least I have an umbrella."

"Wait a minute—you were in the Navy, weren't you?" Ben said, taking a good look at me.

"I think we served together for a time down in Norfolk," I said. "We went into dry dock after our destroyer, The USS *Cassin*, needed repairs from a torpedo hit."

I stepped closer to them and extended my hand to Ben. "Gio Arigo."

"That's right...Gio." He took my hand. "Ben Marden."

I looked at Nancy up-close. Her skin was flawless. It had been six years, and she was now even more of a beauty, a new maturity in her features. For someone who'd been through the Ziegfeld wars, she wore it all very well.

"Weren't you the guy who was dating the chief's daughter?" Ben asked me.

I had to tear my eyes away from Nancy.

"She was some looker," Ben continued. "All the guys wished they could get close to her, but you were the top man on the totem pole on that deal...Laverne Timmerman, yeah, that was it. Laverne Timmerman. Oh boy, she was a beaut—in more ways than one."

Nancy gave me an I-didn't-think-you-were-such-a-bad-boy expression, which I counted as a brief flirt. I shifted back to the man at her side.

"What are you doing now, Ben?

"Nothing much," he said, winking at Nancy, indicating that he did not want to answer that question. Though I knew that was hardly the case for Ben Marden, I dropped it there, feeling free to direct my attention to Nancy. Just being polite, you understand.

"Nice to see you," I said to her, "Are you still down in the Somerville area?"

"Not exactly. The doctor and I have split, and I am living in New York at the Pennsylvania Hotel right now. That is, until my divorce is final…You look sharp, by the way." She looked me over from head to toe. "A welcome wardrobe change, I would say. Caddying must be paying well these days."

"That it does, indeed," I said, fully aware that she understood that the clothes I was wearing were not purchased with tips from caddying. For the first time, our eyes met in a manner that was both inviting and assuring, indicating that she was interested in finding out more about me since we last met on the golf course.

"Why did you come out here this morning, Gio?"

"By chance, I had lunch with the Lindberghs a few years back, but I am also pretty friendly with Tom Rutledge, a Jersey guy who built the engine for the plane."

"Really."

"I've always had an interest in flying, though I've never actually done it. I plan to write an article about his attempt to cross the Atlantic."

"You're a writer?"

"Well, I did have a newspaper story published once about the ship I served on that got hit by a torpedo, and that got me hooked. I guess writing is just a hobby, to be honest about it."

She was about to say something, when the airplane's engine roared to life. Ben, who had tuned us out to concentrate on the flight preparations, grabbed hold of his fedora as it flew off his head from the blast of wind generated by the plane's single prop.

"Everybody out of the way," shouted the crewman, as smoke billowed from the revving of the Wright Whirlwind J-5C engine. I thought to myself that my friend Tom Rutledge, who had built the engine in Paterson, New Jersey, was dead right when he said this engine would blow hats off. The plane struggled to move, its wheels sinking into the soft ground due to the load of aviation fuel in the tanks.

"Look, he has no windshield in that thing," Nancy said, pointing at the cockpit. "How is he going to see where he's going?"

"Don't worry," I said, "he's used to looking out of the sides of the plane. Remember he flies his postal plane from the rear cockpit. He can't see out the windshield of that one, either."

Lindbergh's plane lumbered on the ground seemingly forever, struggling to lift itself off the earth and get on with its journey. It kept bouncing and sinking and, just at the moment when we all thought it would run out of runway, The Spirit of St. Louis finally became airborne. A wild cheer went up from the crowd, as the plane ascended to the heavens and into the history books. We stood in the rain and stared at empty sky after the plane disappeared from view. Ben broke the silence.

"I am going to throw that guy one hell of a party if he makes it."

"Where are you going to hold it, Ben?" Nancy asked "In one of your nightclubs?"

"No, sweetheart. Maybe in Yankee Stadium."

We joined the crowd in trudging off the runway.

"Are you two heading back to the city?" I asked. Ben and Nancy looked at each other inquiringly.

"What'll it be?" he asked her. "The big town, or—what's her name?—Aunt Ella's house in Hempstead?"

I wasn't sure what to make of that. Was she staying with her aunt, or was she living with big Ben?

I was rooting for Aunt Ella.

"I think I am going to stay here for a few more days," she said, looking at me as if to explain with her eyes that she was not Ben's girl.

"Okay," Ben said, businesslike. "My car is over there, and my driver is probably anxious to get me back to Manhattan so he can go home to see his family. Give me a call sometime, Nancy; I'm always at my new joint, the Cotton Club on 142nd Street—that's Harlem, darling, if you didn't know."

"You don't have to draw me a map, Ben."

I almost chuckled.

"Either that," Ben continued, "or down at my other place, the Silver Slipper, 48th and Broadway."

He turned to me. "What are you doing now, Gio?"

"I work for Longie Zwillman."

As I anticipated, Ben's demeanor changed instantly once he found out that I was working for the notorious Longie, whose reputation preceded him.

"What do you do for Longie?"

"I meet with people like yourself, and see if we can do business together."

"Of course, Gio. Longie is a friend of mine; we have a lot of common interests and have been working together for some time now. Give him my regards will you?"

"Sure, I'll tell him I met with you on business," I said, only partly in jest.

"Yeah, tell him it was business—monkey business," he said, laughing as he trotted to his car, which had pulled up near us.

"See you two kids around. Nice meeting you again, Gio." He jumped into the back of his Lincoln.

That left Nancy and me standing awkwardly in the light rain. I was beginning to resemble a drowned water rat, which I figured was not likely to improve my chances.

"Can I give you a lift Nancy?"

"I'd like that. I took the bus out here."

For some reason, I felt emboldened. "A woman like you should be traveling by limousine."

She smiled sweetly, and I felt relieved that she didn't appear to think I was feeding her a line.

"My limo is over there across the runway," I said, pointing in that direction.

She laughed. Who knew that I could be this charming?

I was pleasantly surprised that she grabbed for my hand to balance herself, as we leaped across the puddles on the way to my car. When we were inside, she asked, "Do you think that Charles is flying in the rain right now?"

"Not really; he is probably above the clouds and the sun is shining brightly…"By the way"—I was almost afraid to ask—"how do you know Ben Marden?"

"Oh, Ben and I have known each other for quite a while. I first met him when I was in the chorus line at his place on 48th Street. You know, The Silver Slipper?" She took off her kerchief and patted her face in an attempt to dry it.

"Here, use this," I said, handing her a clean towel I had tucked behind the front seat to use when I needed to wipe down the car.

"You've got everything a girl needs, Gio," she said, taking the soft white towel. I wondered if her words had a double meaning.

The traffic on the dirt road was slowed by people stepping across gingerly, trying to avoid puddles. Old, tired cars were stalled on the side of the road, while newer models plunged through the bushes that lined the road to get around those stopped in traffic. Nancy pointed to a clearing beneath the trees.

"Pull over here. Let's wait it out for a while."

"Good idea," I said, although I didn't want to let on that I was upset my new car was now getting covered with mud from the splashing of the vehicles passing us.

"What's the matter, Gio, you look worried. Are you afraid that your car is going to get dirty?"

That startled me. "I guess you can read my mind."

"I am beginning to," she said in a sexy tone.

I looked into her beautiful, brown eyes. Without prompting, she leaned across the seat toward me, her lips parting slightly for our first kiss.

So this was how sophisticated, young women acted. "I didn't expect that, I really didn't," I said.

"Did you like it?"

My expression provided the answer.

"There's more where that came from," she said, putting her head on my shoulder.

For the next twenty minutes, we clung like a couple of teenagers, kissing and hugging and watching the people leave Roosevelt Field in the rain. Then it was time to kick the Buick into gear and make tracks for Hempstead, a pastoral stretch of eastern Long Island. We continued to sit close to each other all the way to the old farmhouse.

"Giorgio, meet my Aunt Ella," Nancy announced, as we stood on the porch.

"Nice to meet you, son," Ella said, welcoming us both into her small, neatly kept home. "Giorgio—that's an Italian name, isn't it?"

"Yes. My dad was Italian, and my mother is Jewish." I felt comfortable with Aunt Ella.

"Nice car you have there," she said. "What do you do for a living?"

"Aunt Ella, please," Nancy interrupted.

"Just trying to make your young gentleman feel welcome; I certainly didn't mean anything by it. Let me make you two some tea. Would you like breakfast? And maybe you should take off some of those wet clothes."

"Sorry, Aunt Ella—can I call you Aunt Ella?" I said.

"Everybody else does," she said, smiling.

"I really can't stay; I have a meeting over in Nominick Hills." The tone of disappointment in my voice was genuine. I already had told Nancy.

"That's all the way at the west end of Montauk," Ella said. The ride is going to take you hours and hours. Can't you stay a while, and at least have a cup of tea and some breakfast with Nancy and me?"

I looked at my watch, and then at Ella's kindly face. Nancy was at my shoulder. My smile broadened. "Where can I hang up this wet raincoat?"

"I'll take it for you," Ella said, snatching it from me. "Make yourself at home; I'll be right back. And you, Nancy, get upstairs, get out of those clothes, and put on my robe—it's behind the door in the hall closet."

Over breakfast, Nancy told me that she had gone to the airfield in hopes of bumping into Ben Marden. She knew that he was friends with Dwight Morrow—Anne Morrow Lindbergh's father—and expected that everyone connected in any way with Lindbergh would be present at the big event. Nancy had worked for Ben in the past, and had heard that he was expanding his empire. She was looking for work as a dancer, which had been difficult since Prohibition had started, as all the legitimate clubs had been shut down.

"Did he offer you anything?" I asked.

She told me that he was working with a new partner, and they were planning to buy several more places around the country. She was hopeful that something would open up for her at one of the new clubs.

I didn't know for sure, but my money was on Meyer Lansky as Ben's new partner. I was told they had business relationships in Cuba and Hallandale, Florida. Lucrative business relationships.

It was almost noon when we finished a breakfast of farm-fresh eggs, pancakes, and coffee. Nancy could really put away that stuff, though I could see that her figure didn't suffer as a result. I offered to help with the dishes, but Aunt Ella wouldn't hear of it. She said that Nancy better take a serious look at me, because a man who is willing to help with the dishes is a rare animal indeed. When I glanced at Nancy to check her expression, she just smiled with a quizzical look that really didn't give you an indication of how she truly felt. She did look wonderful in Aunt Ella's terry cloth bathrobe, though. We agreed to meet in New York for a dinner date very soon. I was excited just thinking about what that could lead to. After I had said my goodbyes, Aunt Ella gave Nancy and me a few moments on the porch alone.

"By the way, I quit smoking," she said with a smile.

"I didn't even know you smoked."

"I used to sneak them."

I took her "confession" to be one more sign that we were getting closer.

"That's good, Nancy, you don't need cigarettes to look like you belong in the smart set. You're plenty smart without them."

I leaned in to kiss her, but, Aunt Ella came bursting onto the porch with my raincoat over her arm.

"Don't forget this," she said, thrusting it toward me. She turned and stepped back inside.

Or *this*, I said to myself, as I drew Nancy close and finished what I had started.

Chapter 6

My next assignment required that I be something of a secret agent. The place was Nominick Hills in Montauk, all the way out on the east end of the island. The mission was to find out about a British ship that had been wrecked in a nor'easter in 1922, with a considerable cargo of whiskey, Scotch, and vodka. It was said that cases of high-quality booze washed ashore in such numbers that everyone in town ran to the beach to claim their share of the booty.

One tough, smart operator somehow took charge of the situation, chased all the locals, and spirited away the entire load to an undisclosed location. My job was to locate the goods and get them into Longie's hands. If I were successful in this enterprise, my stock was bound to rise significantly in the eyes of his organization.

By the time I'd driven out to the little fishing village at Fort Pond Bay, I was exhausted. Three hours from Hempstead on rutted, dirt roads jangled my nerves and flattened my tires. But I did get there, then canvassed the main street for a place to lay my head for the night in that tiny, hick town. I asked anyone in sight for information that would lead me to that hidden cache of expensive booze. No word on that at first, but what I did find out immediately was that this so-called "fishing village" was in line to have a transatlantic shipping terminal built right on its bay. By this time it was 7 p.m., and I was hungry—Aunt Ella's generous meal seemed like ancient history. Thankfully, I spotted a coffee shop at the end of town, and no one was in the place except for the short-order cook, who was reading the Daily Racing Form.

"Hi, new in these parts ain't ya, fella?" asked the cook, who introduced himself as Lenny and poured a cup of coffee without my asking. "You with those shipping terminal people that keep comin' to town trying to screw us out of our land?"

"Yeah, just got finished with some meetings with the engineers," I lied, "and thought I would take a break and get some dinner. Got any suggestions?"

"Sure do," he said. "We got some nice fish, just caught; there's broiled or fried halibut. Or maybe you prefer cod, broiled or fried. And I just made some fresh chips to go with it." He had put down the Racing Form, and brandished a pencil and pad.

Lenny wore a uniform of chef's hat, white shirt, white apron, and white pants. He looked perfect for the part, as if cast by one of the old Fort Lee studios. The only thing that marred his appearance was that he was missing the tip—down to the first joint—of the index finger on his left hand, as if it had been severed by a butcher knife. Probably was. He didn't seem at all self-conscious about it.

"Got anything outside the fish family?" I asked.

"Bacon, lettuce, and tomato sandwich, if you prefer that."

"That sounds good to me—with mayo, please."

"Comin' right up."

Lenny's grill was right in back of the counter, so he did not need to leave the room when he cooked. While he was preparing my order, I grabbed a local newspaper left on the counter. In two minutes, I knew enough about the terminal to hold a conversation on the matter.

"Say, Lenny, do you get many big storms out here?"

"Sure do; don't get caught in a storm in Montauk; it could cost you your life. Look up there on the wall." He pointed his reduced index finger at a handmade plaque memorializing the names of local fisherman lost in storms. "God bless 'em all. Many brave hearts are asleep in the deep."

I nodded in reverence. This was my chance to open up the discussion.

"What happens to those cargo ships that get wrecked and go to the bottom?" I asked.

"Well now, let me tell you," he began. "Sometimes nothing shows up on the beach; but other times, like that time back in 1922 when that British ship went down right before Christmas, the entire beach gets covered with cases of booze. That one let loose maybe 150 cases —it was really a sight to see, but, you know, the guy who got it all—"

He stopped in mid-sentence, and went back to cooking. "Like your bacon well done?"

It was like someone had turned off his switch.

I leaned in and spoke softly. "Is Al Capone the guy you're talking about?"

Rather than send a shiver through Lenny, the name Capone raised a smile. "No, not him," he said, slicing some lettuce. "He left for Chicago to help Johnny Torrio back in 1919. He was a regular customer out here. He loved bluefish; he used to catch them himself, and bring one or two for me to cook...Good tipper, too."

Lenny told me that Capone got the famous scar on his face when he was a bouncer at Frankie Yale's Harvard Club in Brooklyn. He said that Al had insulted a mobster's sister, and the guy pulled out a blade and carved him up. "Yeah, 'Snorky' Al," said Lenny, still smiling.

"What does 'snorky' mean?"

"Means he's quite a spiffy guy, you know, well-dressed and sharp all the way. He's a classy, stand-up guy, too."

In hopes of getting Lenny back to the subject of what happened to that booze-carrying shipwreck in 1922, I offered him 50 bucks for more information.

He lowered his head and looked at me earnestly. "Listen mister, I enjoy living and, if word got out that I ratted out one of the locals, I wouldn't be around long enough to spend your 50 bucks."

"Who's gonna know? It's just me and you here." I waved the 50 held by my two fingers.

His nose twitched a couple of times, as if he'd picked up a scent in the air. Indeed, he had—that of Uncle Sam's currency. He snatched the 50 out of my hand. "All right, here it is...The preacher and a member of his congregation—who, by the way, is a devout prohibitionist—grabbed just about every case of booze before anyone got there. Rumor has it that it that they stashed them in one of those mausoleum things at Nominick Hills Cemetery. It's still there for all I know...and that's all I know."

That was plenty. "You got a telephone here?" I asked

"You did promise not to tell anyone you got that from me," he said nervously, pointing to the phone.

"Don't worry about it—we never met." I winked, but could see that he already was sorry he'd taken the 50. His face paled, as I reached for the phone behind the cash register.

"Hello, operator? I would like to make a long distance call to Newark, New Jersey. Reverse the charges please. The Riviera Hotel."

The sound of crackling bacon added to the static, but a minute later, I was speaking to Longie, barely able to contain the excitement in my voice. "I think I located about two truckloads of that butterscotch candy you like," I said. "I'm going out to see if I can wrap it up and bring it home in a couple of days. Can't talk now, but I'll try to handle this one myself."

"Be very careful, Gio. If I know anything about Long Island, Big Bill Dwyer and Larry Fay have got their fingers in the pie out there, so if you are messing with anything they consider theirs, your ass could be grass."

"Don't worry boss; I've got to get my feet wet sometime."

I hung up and watched Lenny wring his apron in anxiety. "Please don't get me in trouble, pal."

"My word is my bond, Lenny. There's no reason for me to mention you to anyone. You enjoy that 50 and forget the rest."

"I guess you're taking the BLT with, huh?"

"Thanks, wrap it up for me, will you?"

As I drove away, I saw Lenny's trembling hand reversing the sign on his door from OPEN to CLOSED.

About two hours later, after picking up a bottle of aspirin and taking two to fight the headache I felt coming on, I was checking out the scenery from the window of my room in the Cutler Rooming House. The following morning, no trace of a headache, I made my way to Nominick Hills Cemetery in a light rain. I looked out toward the horizon from the hill, and wondered if Lindbergh had made it across the pond. I wondered, too, if he had liked the sandwiches I got him. I remembered that he hadn't paid me for them.

As I walked through the old tombstone rows, I could see the dates on the stones reading back to the 1700s. I noticed that most of the stones were for men lost at sea and, according to the engraved dates, most of them had died at very young ages. I spotted a gravedigger at work across the field and approached him. "Hey mate!" I shouted.

He stopped his digging, peered up from the waist-deep hole, and said "Morning, sir, can I be of help?" I figured I had an obliging sort here, one who might help me find the liquid treasure.

"I was told to see you about some bottles that might have been left here."

He wrinkled his brow. "Bottles?"

My smile was sardonic. "I think you know what I'm talking about."

The digger removed a handkerchief from the pocket of his bib overalls, lifted his newsboy cap, and wiped his forehead. "Did the preacher send you?"

"That's right."

"You tell him for me that if I don't get my dough on time, I'm not going to keep watch for him anymore."

"Are you sure you really want me to tell him that?"

The digger thought about it for a moment. "Nah, not really, better left unsaid."

I knew then that this guy was scared, and figured I could take control of the situation.

"I'm going to send some trucks out here to the pick up the booze," I said. "Where is it?"

"You're standing on it," he said, as he pointed a crooked index finger down toward the earth.

"Right here?" I asked, shuffling backwards and almost tripping over a tombstone.

"Yep, right under you, buried just like everything else here. If you're going to get this stuff out of here, you are going to have to bring the men to dig it out, because I'm not going to do it for you. You have to dig one big hole here, and we don't have any of those newfangled power-diggers. And how about you giving me the back pay the preacher owes me?"

"Sure, I've got it right here," I said, taking out my wallet and handing over a $50 bill.

"Fifty? Are you shittin' me? Sumbitch owes me for three months—that makes it 150."

"Okay, listen," I said. "I'll pay you double that if you stay on as foreman during the digging. Consider this a down payment."

He brightened considerably.

"Let's keep this under our hats," I said. "The name is Gio, by the way. I work for the archdiocese." If I worked for the archdiocese, Longie worked for the pope. "What's your moniker?"

"Newton T. Fuller," he said proudly, "son of Captain Fuller of the barque Esmeralda. The Captain is buried right over there." he added. He pointed to an obelisk about 20 feet away.

"He must have been a brave seaman," I said, a reasonable guess. "Now, for this little project, I can get two trucks, but I need you to find the diggers."

"That ain't no problem at all," he said, "We got us one batch of lazy ass boys around here that calls themselves the Boy Scouts, and alls they do is run around rubbing sticks together and poundin' their pudding. Why, them shits would jump at the chance to make some money diggin' a hole in the ground. You should see them uniforms they wear; you'd think they were doughboys from the Great War in that getup."

The digger had quite a vocabulary, once you got to know him.

"When was the last time anybody contacted you about the… you know, the cases of booze?" I asked him.

"About three months ago. All they did was drive out here and ask if everything was all right."

That suggested there were several people in on this. Now that I'd found it, I wanted this stuff out of here as fast as possible.

"Only one problem," the gravedigger said.

Was he going to hold me up for more money? "What's that?"

"Trucks is a foolhardy way to go. Better to get it to a boat in the harbor, or maybe a freight train to take it all the way to the city just like the farmers do out here. Didn't that preacher tell you nothin'?"

"That's good thinking," I said, skipping over his question. "A boat would attract too much attention, but the train is a damn good idea. How do we work that?"

It was almost like he was reading my mind, because almost before the words were out of my mouth, he said, "We got ourselves access to four hearses out here, and I'm in charge of all of them. I maintain them myself, and keep them up and running. The hearses can take the stuff to the siding, where we can load it on the train... O' course, that's gonna cost you extra."

An enterprising gravedigger, to be sure.

"Leave it to me," he continued. Now he was really warming to the task. "We got to figger out whether to use the Long Island City to Montauk, the Bushwick branch, or the Montauk branch at Fresh Pond. I'll find out which one is best. You just show up on Saturday morning at about six, and I'll have everything ready. But I want to get paid on the spot. Okay?"

That Saturday morning, I awoke at about 3 a.m., wondering if this whole idea was going turn itself around and bite me in the ass. Could I trust this guy Newton? Suppose, after all, he did work for Big Bill Dwyer.

These thoughts ran through my head, as I dressed and headed out to the cemetery. Just as I made my turn off the main road, I saw smoke billowing out from above the tree line, and realized it was coming from the cemetery. What in the hell was going on out there? I couldn't believe my eyes, as I made the last turn into the cemetery. Campfires were burning, and about two dozen Boy Scouts were cooking breakfast.

"Attention!" shouted one of the boys. Instantly, all the rest, in full uniform, snapped to attention.

"Scouts, at ease!" commanded Newton, who had stepped forward and saluted me. "This here gentleman is a federal agent, and he is here to carry out a secret mission for the government of the United States. He has chosen you young men to be deputized to be his assistants on this particular assignment. Each of you will now begin digging, as I described to you."

Shovels were piled nearby. Four hearses waited on the access road. Eye-twitching, grave digging Newtown Fuller was making like D.W. Griffith.

"Bugler, sound the work call!" the scout leader commanded, and the scouts grabbed the shovels and attacked the earth. The fucking Boy Scouts of America, for chrissake, digging up a shipment of illegal booze for Longie's fearless man, Gio. This was one for the books.

Fuller ambled over to my side, as I stood there, transfixed. He was waving a thick newspaper. "Hey Gio, you see the headlines in The New York Times this morning?"

"Are you, by any chance, talking about Lindbergh?"

"Yeah."

"Did he crash?"

"Hell, no. He made it with flying colors. He thrust the newspaper in front of my face, and I stared at the headlines for May 21, 1927.

LINDBERGH DOES IT! TO PARIS IN 33½ HOURS: FLIES 1,000 MILES THROUGH SNOW AND SLEET—CHEERING FRENCH CARRY HIM OFF FIELD

"Well, I'll be a monkey's uncle," I said. "Sonofabitch really did it!" I grabbed Newt by the shoulders and shook him, the paper falling to the ground. Behind us, the Scouts were shoveling to beat the band.

"Take it easy will ya!" Fuller said, as he bent down to pick up the paper. "Fer God's sake, you act like you know this guy."

I wasn't acting.

Meanwhile, I could not believe the energy of these kids, as they dug like gophers, never stopping. One-by-one, the cases came out of the ground and were loaded into the hearses. One hundred and twenty full cases in all. We broke open a case to inspect the condition of the corked bottles, and most looked liked they had survived the shipwreck just fine. The bottles were separated from each other by a heavy insulation of straw, and packed so tightly that they were immobile.

I turned to Newton. "Aren't you afraid that the parents will find out that their boys were duped?"

"Of course not; they believe they're doing something for the government, so what's not to like?...Now where's my money?"

"Will you take a check?"

"Are you out of your mind?"

"Then you'll have to wait until I get the cash. As soon as I have it, you'll have it."

His eyes went dead. I didn't make this guy to be a stone-cold killer, and I figured I could handle myself if he picked up a shovel in anger, so I wasn't too worried. And I did mean to come back and pay him his end, as soon as the booze was safely transported, and Longie settled up with me.

"You didn't tell me this yesterday," Fuller said in a flat tone of voice. His eyes wandered and locked on the prized, gold watch on my wrist, the one I'd won as a caddie. It had sentimental value, and also was a damn fine timepiece.

"That there's a very nice watch," Fuller said.

I waited.

"How about me holding that for collateral until you get me the cash," he continued.

I looked around, wondering if Dwyer's boys were about to come rolling into the cemetery. Better play it smart. I took the watch off my wrist and handed it to him.

"Wise decision," Fuller said. His strange, mirthless smile suggested that this enterprising gravedigger had some muscle behind him, and not just some local preacher.

By the time the boys had finished loading the cases, it was 10:30 a.m. Throughout, the hearse drivers had just stood around playing grab ass as they jabbered about who knows what. My instincts told me these guys could be trouble. Unlike the scouts, they were mature enough to know a scam when they saw one, and I was anxious they might turn on me and grab the booty. My last order to them was to make sure that all of the drapes were closed tightly so no one could see inside the hearses.

They followed Newton and me in my Buick, as I drove west toward New York. After second guessing myself, I did not like the idea of taking this stuff to a railroad siding and shipping it via rail—too many question and prying eyes. About five miles away from the cemetery, I turned to Newton and told him there was a change in plans.

"We're gonna drive straight to New Jersey, partner."

He was not overjoyed with the new strategy. "Let me out of this car," he shouted. "I am not going to New Jersey with this stuff, and neither are those drivers."

"Would you like to get out while the car is still moving?"

The gravedigger buttoned up, one eye darting, the other twitching.

I decided to lobby the drivers, promise them a sweet reward if they cooperated. I pulled my car over to the side of the road, but by the time I got out, a state police cop had stopped right behind me, his motorcycle raising a racket.

The jig was up.

The trooper cut the engine of his Harley Davidson twin cylinder, and dismounted. I tried to appear relaxed as he approached, but I was anything but. Fuller stayed in the car.

"Any problem, sir?" New York's finest asked, as I stood shivering in my boots.

"No, officer, we are just heading back to New Jersey, that's all. We have an entire family here who died in a horrific fire, and we have to take them all home for burial. It's a real mess—they haven't even been embalmed."

"Sorry for your losses. Can I be of any assistance?"

Yes, you can refrain from inspecting our vehicles.

"Thank you, officer, I would appreciate that," I said, with the look of a bereaved funeral director on my face. He wandered over to the back of the first hearse.

"Why'd you stop?"

I cleared my throat. "Oh, just wanted to check directions with my drivers." He was looking into the rear window, as I stepped closer to him. "Would you like me to open the hearse for you?" I reached for the rear door handle and produced a handkerchief that I held to my face. "Horrible smell, officer."

He immediately stepped away from the hearse with, "Let's take this poor family home." He fired up the Harley and proceeded to lead us toward the Promised Land.

After a while, I noticed that the gas gauge in my car was practically down to empty, and assumed that the hearses were in the same predicament. Thankfully, a filling station appeared before too long, and the caravan turned off the road to refuel.

When the first hearse pulled up to the pump, the driver jumped out and charged at me, shouting, "What the hell is going on here? We were supposed to go to the railroad siding." To calm him down so he didn't blow the whole deal, I reached inside my jacket pocket and with an outstretched index finger, made it look like I had a gun.

"If you open your fucking mouth one more time, I am going to stick the barrel of my Smith and Wesson down it, and blow your fucking brains out." Without a word, he turned and got back in the hearse, as I told the attendant to fill 'er up.

One by one, the hearses were filled, while I told each driver that there was a huge government bonus in it for him, if he drove all the way to New Jersey. When all the vehicles, including my Buick, were filled with gasoline, the state cop explained that he couldn't escort us any further, as he had to head back to Montauk. I said goodbye and thanked him for his trouble, then instructed the hearse drivers to take off while I paid the tab of $7.50—75 gallons at ten cents a gallon.

"You guys sure burn a lot of gas," the attendant said, wiping his sweating brow with his sleeve.

"Here is a sawbuck; keep the change," I said, as I left the station, breathing a sigh of relief that the cop had departed, and that we all had enough fuel to make it to the 125th Street Ferry Terminal. Before leaving the station, I used the pay phone to call Izzie and tell him to bring a truck and to meet us at the ferry terminal in New York. The plan was to switch the cargo, so the drivers could go back to Montauk. I told him to bring money so I could pay off the drivers, and also to bring along Rita, a girl who hung around the bar at the Riviera Hotel.

"Are you fuckin' crazy, Gio? I got to ride all the way to New York with that nutsy Rita. She never shuts her mouth."

"Just bring her," I said. "It will take her five minutes to perform a service, and then we all can go home...And don't forget the money."

"Will a C-note be okay?"

"Yeah, that's good, in small bills." I said. "But that's just for the drivers. I need another two seventy-five for the gravedigger."

"Two seventy-five? You're costing us a lot of money, Gio."

"The guy set it up, Izzie. Compared to what we're gonna make, that's like tip money."

Rita's "service" was to take care of Fuller beyond his regular invoice. The whole trip, he groused to me about missing out on a "fantastic piece of ass" in order to help me transport the booze. And I didn't even need him to make the trip, he complained further, since we didn't transfer to the train.

Okay, Fuller, I figured. Since you're such connoisseur of the ladies, I'll deliver a fine New Jersey piece of ass to you as a bonus for your fine work on my behalf.

As we drew near the terminal, I saw Izzie standing in the street, waving.

"It's about time you got here, you schmuck," he yelled. "I made arrangements to use this garage to make the switch, and we don't got all day. He pointed to an abandoned, brick warehouse facing the water. The hearses pulled into the dank garage, followed by Izzie and, yes, Rita in the old army truck.

Izzie quickly took out the cash from his pocket and waved it in front of the drivers' noses to inspire them to put their backs into the job of off-loading the booze. Meanwhile, Fuller kept asking me when he and Rita could be alone. She was sitting in the cab of the truck, looking petulant as she waited for her John to climb in.

"Okay, Newt, she's in the truck over there; go to it, ol' buddy."

"She knows?" His facial tic began to flicker and spasm.

"She ain't here to pose for pictures, Newt."

"But nobody is gonna watch, right?"

"I can't say that, Newt. Who knows? But once you're with Rita, I think you'll forget about everyone else." I elbowed him in the side and smiled lasciviously.

"I don't know if I can do this," he said in a whiny voice. Now the nerves in his cheek went into frenetic spasm, and his head snapped back and forth. I grew alarmed, and tried to calm him.

"Look Newt, we went to a lot of trouble to get Rita over here for you, and she is a beautiful lady. I truly wanted to show my appreciation. Now, if you want to pass her up, that's your business, but let's settle up now. Izzie brought the money I promised you, 275 smackers." I handed him the dough. "Here you are, paid in full."

He greedily counted the cash I had handed him. With money in his pocket, he seemed to regain his composure and confidence.

"I guess I am ready to knock off that little piece now," said the debonair Newtown Fuller.

"And for all I care, I really don't give a shit if you all watch me."

"That's the spirit, Newt," I said. "One thing—how about you give me back my gold watch before you climb in the truck with Rita."

Chapter 7

By the time 1928 rolled around, my success at coming up with good ideas that worked kept me in the forefront of the "thinking department" in Longie's operation. One day in October of that year, the Boss informed me that my old acquaintance, Ben Marden, was interested in purchasing the Villa Richard. Longie hoped that he and Ben could get together, and maybe open up a swanky "carpet joint" on the Jersey side of the Hudson River.

My first thought was why guys like Ben and Longie would want to buy an old hotel (built in 1904) that had seen better days—especially in a town like Fort Lee, whose fifteen minutes of movie fame was quickly fading, just like the silent films made there. The answer to that question came when I revisited the Villa Richard to see if I could make some headway with Jean Richard on the booze front. In those days, we had to be very careful about making deals with booze or anything else. On the other hand, Capone, who was never known for being careful, seemed to have things going his way in Chicago, and was spending money hand over fist. Longie said that Al had just purchased a fourteen-room mansion down in Palm Island, Florida, his favorite winter hangout.

I could only shake my head. Here was a guy as crude as they come, and he was making all kinds of dough, thanks to Prohibition. Johnny Torrio, Al's mentor, had been out of the action since Hymie Weiss and Bugs Moran had shot him in front of his home in 1925; Johnny was one lucky sonofagun that day, after taking two bullets, one in the hand and one in the groin. Bugs had put the gun to his head for the coup de grace, only to have it jam. Al had come a long way since the days when he was working as a bouncer at the Harvard Club in Brooklyn, but I wondered why he and Deanie O'Banion continued to shoot up the town and each other. Maybe it was the old Irish versus Italian thing; the two factions had been battling it out for dominance forever.

In New Jersey, we spread cash rather than spray bullets. And after those hoogles had learned to like the taste of a few C-notes now and then, everything seemed to work out fine for us.

What I didn't know was that Izzie had arranged to sell Richard 125 cases of booze very cheap. Then he arranged through local politicians to have the Villa Richard raided by the county cops, who confiscated all 125 cases. The raid had put such a financial strain on Jean Richard that, for him to stay in business, he had to borrow money from us to keep going.

The source of Izzie's booze? My cemetery haul, of course. He offered Jean Richard such a bargain price that the innkeeper couldn't resist. The best part of the caper was that Izzie switched most of the good stuff out of the expensively labeled bottles and replaced it with some cheap stuff that Reinfeld had in his warehouse. Nobody could tell the difference. Izzie said the cops would break up the bottles anyway, except for the ones that they grabbed for themselves. It was easy, he said; Reinfeld always kept the empties with good labels so he could just fill them with cheap shit whenever he wanted to short-change someone. His reputation was for the good stuff.

The raid also sent Rita and her girls to county jail for a night, on charges of soliciting for the purpose of prostitution. Who knew that Rita was working a side job out of the Villa Richard? So that's why she was always borrowing Izzie's car, and had been leaving Newark at all hours for the past few months. She always used the excuse that she had to visit her sick mother, who was dying in Englewood Hospital. According to Rita, they had been giving her mother last rites every Friday night for the last two months; her mother would always make a miraculous recovery on Monday morning. Everyone liked Rita, so we all looked the other way. She was so pissed off about the bust that, immediately upon her release—after she had put up bail herself—she phoned Izzie and threatened to put a contract out on him. He just laughed it off, and told her she couldn't borrow his car anymore.

The fallout from the raid seemed to quiet down when a meeting took place with the Fort Lee Police Chief, Andrew McDermott, and Jean Richard. Chief McDermott always found a way to allow cooler heads to prevail. Coytesville once again returned to its docile existence when the neighbors stopped gossiping about the "harlots" taking over the town. The Chief was a very tough customer, though, and if you made a big deal about "knowing your rights," he wouldn't hesitate to use his *left* to settle an ugly situation. Appeased by the raid, local women were once again allowing their husbands to frequent Rambo's, El Rancho, Club Bali, and the Parkway Inn, all taverns near the Villa, in the north end of town. Very colorful joints; I was always eager to hear the latest scuttlebutt coming out of them.

One night at one of the joints, a couple of rummies got into a fight over a woman nicknamed "The Seal" because she always wore an old, sealskin coat. One of the combatants was blind as a bat—he was known as "Owl." The other, a gent with snow-white hair, was "General Lee." The general could not walk without the aid of crutches. Both of these guys were in their 70s, and neither was married to The Seal. When Owl called General Lee out to fight, the general could not get off the bar stool because someone had taken away his crutches. Owl, on the other hand, kept feeling people's faces to determine which one belonged to the General, who sat quietly and waited, sipping drink upon drink that the locals bought him.

Later that evening, when the Owl was in his cups, the owner put a finski on the bar and said, "This goes to anyone who is willing to take the Owl home in a wheelbarrow." It must have been a great sight to see old Owl being carried home in a wheelbarrow; I wish I had been there.

When I got to Fort Lee, the first thing I did was phone Eddie Mannix to invite him to dinner, so I could get the lay of the land since the last time I was here. But Eddie was in California for meetings with the Schenck Brothers, who were after a girl they thought would make a big movie star. The girl's name was Harlean Carpenter. She was from Kansas City and was about to change her name to Jean Harlow. She had just finished a bit part in the silent comedy Moran of the Marines, but she lit up the screen with her platinum-blonde hair, attitude, and exquisite figure. The Schencks were knocked out by her on-screen presence and were trying desperately to sign her before someone else did.

Minus Eddie, I was on my own to make the rounds in Fort Lee. The drive up Hudson Terrace to Myrtle Avenue, where the Villa Richard was located, was beautiful on this sunshiny day. As I turned into the driveway between two bluestone columns, I was taken aback by the beauty of this old, Mediterranean-styled villa. Sure the exterior décor was ostentatious for this part of the country, but this was a movie town and demonstrating ostentatiousness was de rigueur. I stopped the car when I spotted a team of surveyors placing monuments on the far south end of the property. After parking the car, I walked down a wooded path and approached them.

"Hey guys, nice enough for you today?"

"Yes sir, we should be done in about two hours," one of the men said.

Again, feeling my way through the opening of the conversation I asked, "Did you get all of it?"

"Well, we're just getting started working on the top of the cliff; we finished all of the work down where the footings for the bridge will go."

Then it came to me. Now I knew why Ben Marden was hot to buy the Villa. There was going to be a bridge built right here, right next to it. I wanted to learn if it was going to connect New York and New Jersey.

"Did you calculate the length of the bridge yet?"

"We didn't, but the designer, did, and he said it would be about a mile long. The Hudson is narrowest right here." The surveyor pointed to the other side of the Hudson.

"Hey, what are you doing here?" called a voice from out of the woods. I turned, and it was none other than Ben Marden, walking with Jean Richard.

"Holy smokes, Ben, I never thought I would see you again so soon."

"Nice to see you, too, Gio. What brings you to this neck of the woods?"

"I was hoping to see Mister Richard and talk over some business."

"Well, here I am," said Jean. "What can I do for you?"

"Wait a minute, before you guys get started with shop talk, let's go inside and have lunch on me," said Ben.

Jean waved him off. "Your money is no good here, Ben."

I stepped up. "How about I buy lunch and send the bill to Abner Zwillman?" They both laughed, as we headed onto the Marine Terrace to enjoy the sunshine and fresh river breeze, and have some lunch. Jean excused himself, saying that he had to check something in the kitchen. Ben and I studied each other for a moment, like chess players. He spoke first.

"See much of Nancy?"

"As a matter of fact, I do. She is doing fine; her divorce went through, and now she is a free lady."

"How come it took so long?"

"Who knows—something about a community property settlement."

" I can tell, you have more than a casual interest in her don't you Gio," he said.

The abruptness startled me. I don't think my mouth came unhinged, but in that moment, I must have worn a dumb expression.

"She used to dance in my chorus line at the Palais Royal," Ben continued. "When she had her war paint on, she was stunning. I don't mean to say that she wasn't already a knockout, but when she put on that theatrical makeup and dressed that statuesque body to the nines, she was beauty personified. People used to go wild when she walked onto the stage with the line. Even though the other girls were beautiful, too, there was something about Nancy that knocked 'em dead.

"You should marry her."

"Her ex was a research scientist at Greystone."

"Yes, I knew," I said, familiar with the name of New Jersey's state mental hospital.

"So you know that she tried to commit suicide over the loss of an illegitimate child. Those were awful days for her. Thank God she's still very much with us."

Had he just wanted to sound generous with his suggestion that I marry Nancy, or did he regard her as a personal liability? He didn't give me time to ponder it further.

"So what's new, Gio? Other than Nancy, that is. And your plan to put the arm on Jean."

My eyes narrowed. "It's not like that, Ben."

When it's Longie Zwillman, it's like that."

I inhaled the river-cooled air and took in the panoramic view. "What's new with you, Ben?"

"I want Jean either to take me in as a partner, or sell the Villa to me outright."

"Makes sense, Ben. If you get the place, are you thinking of taking on some partners or are you going to go it alone?"

He folded his arms. "That's up in the air right now. If I took on anybody for financing, it would be some of my old cronies from Brooklyn. But then again, they got more than they can handle right now. You know about their Cuban ambitions, right?"

"You mean Meyer?"

"Yep."

"I heard things are loosening up under the new president, the Liberal Party guy."

"You heard right. Zayas was involved with graft and everything else, but the bad part of that was that the dumb bastard was sloppy and got caught. Can't trust those conservatives to get it right, huh?"

"If you buy this place, Ben, are you going to have a spot in here where the boys can get a little action now and then?"

"Not so fast, Gio, I didn't get it yet. Jean Richard is no dope either, and now that Othmar Ammann, the architect for the new bridge, is coming here almost daily for lunch and dinner, and bringing his friends to fawn all over Jean, he is beginning to realize what a star he is— at least behind the stove—and also what great potential this joint has since the bridge is going to be his neighbor."

"I know what you mean. Why should he give up a good thing just when it's going to turn itself around and make him some real money?"

"The one thing I do know, Gio, is that Jean is scared to take the big risks. We tested the waters, or I should say that Longie's guy Izzie tested the waters, when he arranged to have the Villa raided by the county cops."

"Who told you that, Ben?" The possibility of a leak within Longie's crew bugged me. But Ben Marden didn't need leaked information to get the lay of the land. He offered me a broad smile.

"You think I was born yesterday? We all know that Izzie made that move. Just like we know that Jean Richard hasn't got the stomach for trouble…That's how we're going to force him to sell."

I looked at him, then beyond him. "Here comes Jean with the food."

"Delmonico steaks, only the best for you two," said Jean, accompanied by his waiter holding our tray of food high above his head.

"Beautiful Jean, you really outdid yourself," said Ben, admiring the large tray of food fit for a king. The four steaks were cooked to perfection, each of them at least an inch-and-a-half thick and covered with mushrooms and onions. My god, did he think we could eat all of this? String beans almondine, baked potatoes with sour cream, freshly baked rolls, on and on it went. Ben grabbed his napkin, unfurled it with one big snap of the wrist, and placed it upon his lap, sliding his chair closer to the table.

Jean turned to me and bent slightly from the waist. "One steak or two, Gio?"

"One is more than enough for me." Ben passed a bowl of string beans almondine to me.

"Come on, boys, dig in and enjoy the meal," said Jean, as he joined us. The lunch went without incident, the conversation limited to news topics and such. The only clue that Ben was beginning to put the pressure on Jean came toward the end.

"Jean, who does your bookings?"

"I have been using a young fellow named Bill Miller."

Ben whistled softly in recognition. "No kidding. Miller books acts for me, too." Ben looked away from his host and said casually, "So when can we begin negotiations for me to buy this place?"

Jean jumped up from his chair like he was hit with a bolt of lightning. "What do you mean 'negotiations,' Ben? I haven't even said I'm looking to sell."

Without saying another word, Ben rose from the table. "Thanks for the wonderful lunch, Jean. I'm anxious to phone my partners and tell them what a fine host you are."

After Ben had left the Marine Terrace dining area, Jean turned to me with a look of surprise mingled with irritation. "He's got some nerve, trying to strong-arm me like that. I don't care how big a big shot he is; I'm not some bug he can just step on."

"He's used to getting his way," Jean. Soon enough, I knew that Ben Marden and his—or I should I say, our—guys were going to own the Villa Richard.

About two months later, Longie got a call from Ben Marden inviting us to a dinner and show at the Cotton Club. Ben asked Longie if I could be there, too, that he wanted me—with Longie's permission, of course—for some deal he was working on. Knowing that whatever Ben touched turned to gold, Longie was thumbs-up all the way. Besides, who would want to miss a chance to see Duke Ellington and his orchestra playing swing tunes?

After Longie had told me that I was to be in on that dinner-and-show meeting, I asked him if I could bring a date.

"Suit yourself. If you want to bring a 'frail,' that's your business, but I want to tell you there is going to be a lot of chocolate candy up there, so you may want to come by yourself." I just smiled and said I'd rather bring an old friend with me. I told him her name was Nancy, and we had been "keeping company" of late.

I called Nancy and told her about the invite, and she was excited to see the show (and I hope, go with me). She was living in Harlem in an elevator building with a doorman, which was a very nice way to live in 1928. The night of the meeting, I put on my best suit and tie, had my shoes shined, and took a haircut from Carlo Vitetta, a real artist in my book. Izzie booked a limo, and with him at the wheel, and Longie and his date Gloria in the back with me, we were off to Harlem to pick up Nancy at her apartment at 145th Street and Edgecombe Avenue. From there, it would be only a few blocks to the Cotton Club.

As we pulled to the curb, I noticed that Nancy was in the center of some sort of commotion outside of her building. The doorman was trying to push two men away from her. They seemed to be drunk and were grabbing at her. They were apparently Latin types, and were yelling something in Spanish to the doorman. I was out of the car door before we stopped at the curb. I grabbed one and hit him squarely in the face, breaking his nose. I could tell that it was broken because of the way it moved to the far left of his face. With him out of the action, I turned to the other guy, and saw Longie stomping on his hand, which held a switchblade. The blade folded in on itself, putting a large gash in the guy's outstretched hand.

In seconds, it was all over.

"Best workout we've had since that day in Atlantic City," Longie said to me.

The two drunks wobbled to their feet, with a little help from Longie and me. Just then, a taxicab pulled alongside us, and I opened the back door and pushed them in, as the cabbie yelled, "Hey, get those guys out of my cab. They got blood all over them!"

Longie took out a fist-sized wad of cash, peeled off a sawbuck, and handed it to the cabbie. "Will this cover it, pal?"

The cabbie changed his tune more deftly than Ellington shifting the key signature. "Sure will, sir. Where should I take them?"

"Take them down to the river and throw them in." Longie was smiling.

"Gotcha boss, will do," the driver said, as he put the cab in gear and drove off.

"You okay, Nancy?" I asked, putting my arm around her and leading her to the limousine.

"Fine," she said, "let's just get out of here." She grabbed my arm. "Wait! Wait a minute. I want to thank the doorman for protecting me."

"Don't worry about him; Longie is thanking him now." Sure enough, Longie was freeing more dough from his thick wad.

"What was that all about?" I asked.

"Those guys wanted me to go with them. One of them was trying to take my purse out of my hand...I guess I'm a popular girl." She looked at me sheepishly.

"It's okay, don't worry, you're safe now," I said.
As we entered the limo, Gloria took Nancy's hand and helped her. "Nancy, say hello to Gloria, a good friend of ours," I said.

"Hi, nice to meet you," Nancy said, as they both gave each other a welcoming smile.

As we drove the few blocks to the Cotton Club at 142nd and Lenox, Gloria and Nancy seemed to hit it off quite well, chatting away like old friends, neither trying to outdo the other, each of them—of a fashion—in show business.

As we pulled up in front of the Cotton Club, electricity was in the air.

Chapter 8

As soon as we entered the club, Longie gave his name and slipped the colored waiter captain a tenski. The captain immediately snapped his fingers, and a host of attendants led us to Ben Marden's table.

"Nice joint you got here, Ben," Longie said, before he was even seated. "Looks like you are doing land office business."

"You might say that," Ben said, rising to greet us. "Things have been really cooking here since we opened back in twenty-three. Wait 'til you hear the Duke and his band— they are really gonna knock you out."

The rest of us exchanged hellos with Ben as we sat; I paid close attention to his reaction to Nancy and didn't see anything telling. "Cigars, cigarettes, mints," echoed a dulcet call from behind us. I turned toward the sultry voice. A gorgeous, black woman in a French maid's outfit was carrying a tray with a ribbon around her neck.

"Could I have a pack of Old Gold?" I asked.

"Why don't you try a pack of Gitanes, the new French cigarettes that just came out?" Gloria said. "I just love them; they make your throat feel cool."

Longie turned to her. "Glor, will you let the man buy what he wants?"

"Ten cents," said the beautiful cigarette girl, placing the Old Golds on the table. I handed her a fifty-cent piece and told her to keep the change.

Our table was practically on the dance floor, and although Ben and Longie plunged immediately into subdued conversation, I overheard most of what they were saying. Ben told Longie that the Cotton Club formerly had been called Club Deluxe. Jack Johnson, the first Negro heavyweight boxing champ, had opened it in 1920 and, three years later, Ben changed the name after buying it with the backing of Owney Madden, the prominent bootlegger and gangster now imprisoned in Sing Sing.

Under Ben's management, the club's interior had been entirely reworked to double its capacity to 800, and its spectacular décor was designed as a glamorized "plantation environment." Although the entertainers and most of the staff at the club were black, the audience was limited exclusively to white patrons, who flocked to innovative nightly revues performed by a scantily-attired chorus line and talented musicians. The dancers were carefully selected— they were required to be 'tall, tan, and terrific,' light-skinned, and under twenty-one. The Cotton Club soon became the most popular cabaret in Harlem.

More recently, Ben had moved his business operations downtown, first to the Palais Royal and then to the Silver Slipper. Speaking to all of us now, he said he was working on plans to open a downtown Cotton Club in midtown, hopefully in the old Palais Royal building at Broadway and Seventh Avenue, the very heart of the Great White Way. But Ben's "dream," he said, was to buy the Villa Richard in New Jersey, so he could start a new joint of his own outside of Manhattan.

"Wanna throw in with me?" he asked Longie, as if asking him if he wanted to order dessert. "You could run a helluva card room."

I knew that business was going to be discussed on this night, but I didn't think it would begin so fast. But then, these guys loved action and figured why waste time in beating around the bush.

Ben and Longie kept up their conversation all through the opening number, a jungle scene production number. Fourteen gorgeous women, 'light, bright, and damn near white,' were dressed in skimpy material that showed off their luscious bodies. Their skin seemed to be covered with a light coating of oil that made them glisten under the lights. One of the girls in particular caught everyone's attention; she was young, tall, light-skinned, and absolutely stunning.

"Who's that?" I asked. "She's gorgeous." As if the others were chopped liver.

Ben smiled knowingly. "Lena Horne—remember that name, Gio. She does more than dance. You should hear her sing. Someday she is going to be a big star."

I watched Gloria and Nancy, while keeping one eye on the show; they were digging through Gloria's purse to find some salve to apply to a scratch that Nancy had received on the side of her face during the scuffle outside her apartment. Gloria produced a tiny vial and put a dab of cream on the back of her hand. She then took Nancy's chin in her other hand and, like a mother with a child, gently rubbed the cream into Nancy's cheek. I watched transfixed, as Nancy sat motionless, her eyes closed, letting Gloria slowly rub the oily substance into her gorgeous face, slightly smearing her lipstick. To me, the intimate movements of Gloria and Nancy were as sexy as the dancers' gyrations. Something was going on here, I thought.

Ben interrupted my concentration. "Gio, listen, I want to buy the Villa, and Longie says you're the guy to make a deal with that stiff, Richard. Do you think you can pull that off? I don't care how much it costs, but ask him if he could hold a note for us. We can negotiate the vig, but see if he will hold some money. Open negotiations with an offer of 250 big ones.

"If you can't set the hook with that, call me and I will up the ante. Remember, two hundred and fifty 'K,' that's the offer; see what you can do with it. And, by the way, if you put this deal together, from here on—with Longie's permission of course—you work for both of us. How's that sound?"

Sounded damn good to me.

Ben raised his glass, and the rest of us followed. "A toast to our new joint, the one that Giorgio Arigo is going to get for us. As Lucky Luciano and the boys would say, 'Ah, salute!'"

To which I quickly supplied the appropriate response, "Gendon!" the New Jersey pronunciation of the Neapolitan cent'anni—may you live for 100 years! We all drank deeply as hopes and dreams were set in motion. Funny, but again I noticed that Nancy and Gloria, while they were toasting, seemed to be looking at each other instead of looking at the rest of us.

During the lull between the opening production number and the next act, Ben told us that Ellington came aboard after Andy Preer, leader of the Cotton Club Orchestra, had died suddenly.

"We wanted King Oliver," he explained, "but the money wasn't good enough. You mark my words, the Duke will be the king of the music business in no time at all." Ben loved to talk about business, the people making the moves, and the moves they made. "Owney is— was—a tough bird," he said. "You either did things his way or no way. Duke had to agree to play for the floor show and also for dancing later in the evening. And he not only does two shows a night here, but also a radio show on WHN. You can hear him all over the country."

I had heard of Duke's band and even had some of his Victor records. I loved the music of the day, and took pride in knowing the names of the musicians in his band. I boasted to Ben and Longie that I could name all the people in the band.

"I got twenty that says you can't," Longie said.

Ben chimed in, "Give me a twenty on that, too."

"Okay guys, you're on." I gave them the rundown. "There's Smith Ballew, who handles the vocals, Barney Bigard on tenor sax and clarinet, Wellman Braud on bass, Chick Bullock also on vocals. Let's see, Teddy Bunn on guitar, Harry Carney alto and baritone sax, Duke on piano, of course. Sonny Greer on drums, Fred Guy on banjo, Otto Hardwick alto sax and soprano sax, the great Johnny Hodges on clarinet, alto and soprano sax, Rudy Jackson clarinet and tenor sax, Freddie Jenkins on trumpet, 'Tricky' Sam Nanton on trombone, Lou Metcalf trumpet, Billy Taylor tuba, Juan Tizol valve trombone, Cootie Williams trumpet and vocals, and Harry White on trombone."

I took a gulp of air. "Hand over the money, gentlemen."

I then posed a question. "Can anybody tell me the name of Duke's band when he first came to New York back in 1923?"

"What, do you want to bet another twenty on that, too?" Ben kidded.

"His band was called the Washingtonians," I said quickly with a smug look.

Ben looked at Longie. "Holy shit, who is this guy? You brought me an encyclopedia on music."

"Ben, you ain't gonna believe what this guy can do," Longie said. "So far he has not let me down on anything. We got a winner on our hands." They each tossed balled-up, twenty-dollar bills across the table.

The Ellington band created the perfect sound for the "jungle music" needed for the dances. The hot, sultry, growling technique of trombonist Sam Nanton's, aided by Johnny Hodges sensuous tenor sax, and Harry Carney's opulent baritone sax, added unmistakably dark inflections to the erotically charged dance moves that captivated the audience.

I was both captivated and distracted. Gloria continued to fawn over Nancy, who seemed to invite her casual touching. And Marden, though he was the consummate gentleman, did not take his eyes off either of them all evening. When he asked Nancy to dance, I felt a surge of jealousy. I was Nancy's date, but I felt like an outsider, watching Gloria snuggle up to her, and Ben vie for her attention.

Longie brought me back to business. He was amazed that Ben would even consider buying the Villa Richard, considering that the stock market was reaching an all-time high and, sooner or later, was likely to plummet.

But Ben saw even more prosperous days ahead—at least for himself. He was certain that, in the next few years, Prohibition would be repealed because it was a failure as social police, and was benefiting only the gangsters. He predicted a bright future beyond the Roaring Twenties. "Just wait and see," he said, like a man with inside information.

We stayed for two shows that night, the first beginning at midnight, and the second at 2 a.m. By the time the nightcap was over, the sun was just about coming up. While Ben took care of the bill, Nancy and Gloria giggled like schoolgirls all the way to the cloakroom. Gloria grabbed Nancy's coat out of my hands and lovingly wrapped it around her new girlfriend. As I took my own coat from the attendant, I was suddenly aware of a silence behind me. I glanced at them, and saw Gloria's arms inside Nancy's coat and wrapped around my girl's slender waist. Part of me was in shock, but another part felt that I didn't want them to stop. When Nancy's eyes met mine, she gently pushed Gloria away.

Izzie was waiting in the limousine in front of the club, sound asleep with a Sunday paper covering his face. Four, young, black men were leaning on the car, just killing time. Longie told them to get the fuck off the car, which they promptly did. Then he walked around to the driver's-side open window, reached inside, and blew the horn in repeated, short blasts. Izzie was so startled that he reached inside his coat to his shoulder holster and grabbed for his heater.

"Hold the phone, Izzie; it's only me."

"Are we okay, boss?"

Longie noticed a brown paper bag with an empty pint of Scotch in it. "Move over, I'm driving," he said, nudging Izzy aside. "Jews aren't supposed to drink, numbskull." He gave him a well-deserved rap on the back of the head.

"Are you coming back to Jersey with us, Gio?" Longie asked.

"No, he's going to stay with me at my place tonight," said Nancy, cuddling up to me in the back of the limo.

"Gloria, you ride in the front with Izzie," said Longie. He was onto something. Gloria turned sullen, as she lit a cigarette and looked out of the window. As we drove to Nancy's apartment, Longie reminded me that I had better get cracking on meeting with Jean Richard. "Lot of chips ridin' on this one," he said. "You need any cash?"

"I can always could use a little extra 'dough, re, me' to get things moving, Longie."

He withdrew a plump envelope from his breast pocket and handed it to me. "Spread this around. We want what we want when we want it."

This was the first time Longie had handed over such a large sum of cash to me. I felt like I was really moving up in the world. Longie dropped us off on the corner at an all-night grocery. The time was 6:40 a.m. The sun was just about up, and both Nancy and I were exhausted. We picked up a quart of milk, some coffee, eggs, and the Sunday papers. The two blocks to Nancy's apartment felt like a marathon. The daytime doorman was already on duty. I asked him if he had any news about the scuffle outside the previous night, and he said he knew nothing about it. All's well, I thought.

I couldn't wait to ask Nancy what was with her and Gloria, so as we got off the elevator and out of earshot of the elevator operator, I just came out with it. "Nancy, what was going on with Gloria and you all night? I couldn't believe what I was seeing."

"Come on Gio, you know that there was nothing to it, Gloria was just having some fun with me. Did it turn you on?"

Nancy unlocked the door, and we went inside. I was shocked that she was turning the whole thing around on me. Now I had to answer her question. My hesitancy set her in motion.

"It did turn you on, didn't it?" she asked, as she took off her dress and stood there in her bra and half-slip. "I bet you would have loved to see Gloria and me together—all the way, huh?" She reached down to take off her pumps. "Think about what might have happened if we had invited Gloria over here to spend the night." She laughed and grabbed my face with both hands, trying to force me to look into her eyes. I struggled to turn my head in an attempt to prevent her from reading my feelings. Her racy words overloaded my circuits, prompting me to grab her by both arms and push her down on the bed, where her laugh turned hysterical. The evening was ending on a high note as I took what I wanted. She went right to sleep after the lovemaking, and I stayed up, listening to the radio.

On WMNCA out of Peekskill, New York, a man being interviewed was a wealthy investment banker from Tuxedo Park. His name was Alfred Lee Loomis, and he had great credentials, having attended Yale University and Harvard Law School. What kept me listening was the fact that this guy Loomis, by all accounts a really smart guy, was considering liquidating most of his personal holdings. The stock market, he advised, was on the brink of disaster. As I heard what he had to say, I thought of Ben Marden's forecast that "change was coming."

I had only paltry investments, but Nancy had told me that her community property settlement with the doctor consisted of a huge amount of shares in AT&T. I had to warn her what this guy on the radio was saying. I drifted off, but awoke at noon, thinking about Loomis and how he was going to lighten up on his Wall Street portfolio. I felt I better call Longie, too; he would know what to do with this information.

Maybe he would think I was a nut, but to me, this Loomis could be right on the money. He was a rich guy and, as mom always said, "If you can't hang with people better than yourself, stay home." Well, I wasn't hanging with Loomis, but I sure trusted what he'd said on the radio.

About an hour later, I called Longie and woke him up. He wasn't too thrilled with that.

"What the fuck are you calling me on a Sunday for?… "This better be good."

It was, I thought. "I just heard disturbing news on the radio. This big investor—name's Loomis—says to sell your stock now before it's too late."

"What's his angle?"

"Angle? You tell me, Longie. He's a self-made multimillionaire; lives up in Tuxedo Park with all the robber barons—"

"Tuxedo Park! That's the place that won't let us Jews in. Harriman is buying up all the land he can get so he can build us a kibbutz right in the middle of those bastards…This is why you're waking me up, Gio?" And with that, he slammed down the phone.

About three hours later, Longie phoned me at Nancy's apartment and congratulated me for "being on the ball," as he put it. He had called the "Little Man" in Miami and relayed what I'd told him. Miami said he shared the same suspicion, and was going to lighten his holdings on Monday.

"Our friend sends his regards and says that he can't wait to meet you," Longie added. "He told me to tell you that he thinks you got the stuff to make it big in the organization."

I couldn't believe those last words. Nancy wondered why I seemed to be smiling all that day. I had to keep the meaning of the Little Man's words to myself, but I did advise her to sell at&t. Later that day, I took the ferry back to New Jersey and then a bus home to Newark, and all the way I kept thinking of Nancy. Even after that strange night at the Cotton Club, I began to think that, sooner or later, we might consider getting married. At least that is what I hoped for. But for now, I had to keep my mind on the prize: convincing Jean Richard to sell his Villa Richard to Ben Marden.

Chapter 9

Tuesday morning, after making an appointment with Jean Richard, I hopped in the Buick and headed north. Jean and I had decided to meet at the Rustic Cabin, a roadhouse in Englewood Cliffs. It was located in the woods about three miles north of the Villa Richard, and we counted on not being disturbed there. Jean was right on time, and brought with him a man he introduced as his accountant, Warren Chase from Hackensack.

At a table in a quiet corner, I opened the discussion by telling Jean that this country was in for a dramatic change, something that would make the impact of the Volstead Act look like peanuts.

"The stock market is going to crash," I said.

Jean looked at Warren and turned back to me. "Are you nuts? You ask me to come here today to discuss the sale of my Villa, and you come up with some harebrained bullshit that the sky is falling?"

Warren piped up, "Just a minute, Jean. I've been watching the market, and from what I see, this whole country is carrying too much weight on the solvency of the government. I don't think it can last, but who can tell when it's over? As they say, you never know when you're at the top of the market...or when you hit bottom."

Wise words. I pressed my advantage by reminding Jean that he must have been hit hard when the Villa was raided.

"I know, I know," Jean said dejectedly. "But I was set up...and I know who set me up."

I felt a chill run down my back, but sat silently and waited.

"It was those goddamned, county politicians," Jean said. "They thought they could come to the Villa whenever they felt like it, and ask for takeout food and dessert for themselves and their wives. Those cheap shits wouldn't even leave a tip for my help... I know it was them. Finally, I had enough and told them to take a hike, and that is when they sold me down the river."

I restrained what otherwise would have been a sigh of relief. "I know. That must have been awful for you."

"It was, but I got over it...Now tell me, why would Ben Marden, who owns the Palais Royal and the Cotton Club in Manhattan—and God knows what else he's got up in Saratoga—want to buy my place? Is it because the politicians decided to throw our money away building a Hudson River bridge so people can come over here and feed the chickens? This place needs a ton of work that'll cost him a bundle. And believe me; I am not going to cut my price to accommodate him."

"What is that price, Jean?" I asked casually.

"One seventy five."

"One hundred seventy five thousand?"

Jean looked at his accountant and said, "Boy can count."

I chuckled, aware that he had revealed his asking price for the first time. I was getting somewhere.

"Let's suppose you and Ben agree on a price—"

"—One seventy five."

"All right, one seventy five. When do you think a closing can take place?" I had my best poker face going for me.

"It doesn't matter to me," Jean said. "Just come up with the money, and I will hand over the keys. We can negotiate the inventory later."

"Wait a second!" Warren said. "Why sell?"

I was taken aback. "We've been over this, Warren," Jean said.

"I don't mean that...Why don't you give Marden and his investors a five-year lease on the property instead?

Shit, I thought. Now this fuckin' accountant is going to kill the deal.

"No, seriously, a lease is better for you, Jean," he continued. This way, if Marden makes a big go of it, you can always take it back after five years. You can bet he'll pour a ton of money into the place, and all the improvements will stay with the building when he leaves."

"You got a point there," Jean said excitedly. "Sure, why should I give these guys my joint? I make money either way, and could be a big winner if I lease. Why didn't you tell me this before, Warren?"

"I just thought of it."

Jean looked at me, a twinkle in his eye. "They will never out-smart this Frenchman."

My smile was both bewildered and derisive. Didn't they understand I was there to smooth the way for Ben Marden, that I was basically his guy?

Shifting strategy on the fly, I returned to my opener. "I was listening to a guy on the radio last Sunday morning. Al Loomis is his name. He was talking about the financial markets, and he said—"

"—Wait a minute…Loomis…Are you taking about the big investor?" Jean asked.

"Yeah, that is exactly who I'm talking about."

Jean sat forward. "He comes here all the time. Would you believe, he drives a Rolls Royce and comes down every day from Tuxedo Park to get the Edgewater Ferry; his office is on Wall Street, of course…Nice guy, and smart as hell."

Warren chimed into the conversation, saying that Loomis was some kind of a physics genius, who had set up a laboratory in Tuxedo Park to do experiments with guys from the Massachusetts Institute of Technology.

"I'll tell you something else, too," said Jean, "he has a girlfriend that he brings to the Villa sometimes. From what I hear, she is his best friend's wife! Can you believe that? Leave it to the people with money to do whatever they like."

My patience was starting to wear—what did all that have to do with the price of tea in China? Or, more to the point, the price of the Villa Richard.

I sat back in my chair as lunch was served and, throughout the meal, watched intently as Jean fidgeted, making small conversation but not touching on the subject at hand. Finally—

"Gio, I want to be straight with you. I have made up my mind— I am not going to sell to Ben or anyone else right now. If anything, I am going to lease. Sure the place could be doing more business and, when the movie business comes back to Fort Lee, as it probably will, business should get healthier, no? After all, who in their right mind would think that California farmland has anything to offer sophisticated actors and bon vivants? I would be nuts to sell right now. I am going to give it some more time. What do I have to lose?" To my ears, he had a false air of confidence. I stretched my arms and tried to look relaxed.

"You know, Jean, Ben is hoping to take on some partners in this venture."

He narrowed his eyes. "What do you mean, partners?"

"You know, strong connections with a real interest in financing the transaction. I think those guys are going to be so disappointed if they don't get what they want."

"Are you trying to scare me, Gio?"

"Not at all, I am just trying to wake you up to the fact that there are some powerful people out there who are interested in your place, and that fact can bring you a harvest of some serious money. And like I say...timing is everything. If you can't see that, I can't help you."

"I didn't ask for your help, " he said in a tight voice.

Warren cleared his accountant's throat. "Maybe, Jean, you should take this offer a little more seriously."

Jean glared at his numbers-cruncher. "Warren, you change direction more often than the wind coming off the Hudson River. I thought accountants were supposed to be consistent, steady as she goes."

Warren seemed unfazed. "What I mean is, you're still in the black right now, but if our friend Mister Loomis is right, you may soon be swimming in deep water... with no way to get to shore."

The tide of the battle seemed to be switching in my favor at this point. I thought I'd churn the water even more. "Incidentally, Jean, some people are a little upset about you having Rita and her ladies from Newark at your Villa." I looked at him with a suggestive expression. "They wanted me to tell you that."

Jean's face reddened. "I didn't get a piece of that," he shot back.

"I had nothing to do with that; I was surprised to hear that they were operating out of my hotel. You got to believe me." Now, there was a note of fear in his voice.

I straightened and squared myself in my seat. "Look, Jean, let's face facts. Fort Lee is done as the movie town it was. You are hard-pressed for cash to keep things going here. The stock market is going to tumble, and now you've got the Villa tied to illegal activities." I was trying hard to keep my language polite.

"Ben Marden wants to offer you one hundred thousand even for the place—lock, stock, and barrel. What I mean is all inventory and furnishings are included." I watched his eyes dart about. "There, I've said it," I picked up. "One hundred large. Are you in?"

I extended my hand across the table, hoping he would shake it and seal the deal.

He had an impulse to grab my hand, then seemed to change his mind in an instant, leaving my paw out there like a dead fish.

"Not so fast, Mister Smart Guy. You can tell that boss of yours that Jean Richard is no pushover. I don't have to sell this place, no matter what you think."

I let his words float between us for several seconds, then smiled reassuringly. "It's more important what Mister Marden thinks, and he thought you had a mind to sell. And I can tell you that he has never seen you as a pushover."

My words seemed to appease Jean, but he was still a long way from signing on the dotted line. Now my mind was racing trying to come up with another solution to the stalemate. I quickly found myself talking without having any idea what I was going to say.

"You know, Jean, maybe you are right in not selling the place, with the bridge and all coming through. Who knows, this real estate could become a lot more valuable. But why would you want to stick it out here running this place until that point? It might be years away."

I sensed that I was heading in a manageable direction. "Why don't you allow Mister Marden to lease the place from you until that time?" I looked at Warren, for his reaction, and his nod boosted my confidence. Then he turned to his boss.

"Jean, if you want my opinion—"

"—I don't."

Warren buttoned it up like a guy accustomed to put-downs. After a few moments of silence, Jean appeared to have reached a conclusion.

"How about we give Ben the right of first refusal—that's fair isn't it?" He looked at Warren, then me, and assumed we were with him. "I won't take anything less than thirty thousand for the business, which will include everything that is not nailed down—as the Jews say, the 'whole megillah.'" He looked in my direction, a wry grin on his face. "In addition, I want a thousand a month triple net… Can you live with that?"

I wasn't going home with no fish in the basket, so I said a simple "yes." Longie had taught me to say yes a lot during a negotiation—I could always change my mind.

And, on the face of it, this didn't seem like such a bad deal. I figured Ben Marden could make hay out of it.

Once again, I reached my arm across the table to Jean Richard. "Are you going to shake my hand this time?"

Jean and Warren both laughed. "You got yourself a deal, sonny boy," replied Jean, as his hand clasped mine.

On my drive back to the Riviera Hotel, I decided that I wasn't going to call Longie. Instead, I would give him the news in person. Too bad Ben couldn't be there, so I could see his face when I made the announcement. To me, putting this deal together was big-time, but to Ben and Longie, it was old hat, and I guessed they would be disappointed, but not upset, to learn that all I could get was a lease deal. I stopped to call Nancy and tell her that I had put my first night club deal together. She seemed to be as excited as I was. Maybe this was the beginning of "making it big."

It was about four o'clock by the time I got to Newark. Moe was at the elevator as usual, and as I stepped right past him, I said, "Don't give me any bullshit. I got to go up and see the boss."

Moments later, I burst into Longie's office and yelled, "We got it! We got the Villa Richard!" He grabbed a bottle of Scotch from his credenza, and poured me a stiff shot. "Drink this before you pass out. What's all the noise about, Gio?"

I gave him the complete rundown and, when I got to the part about how you offered $100,000 cash to buy it, I was turned down flat, and so the best I could wangle was a five-year lease. The deal is thirty grand for the business everything included and a thousand a month triple net. Longie smacked his forehead with the palm of his hand.

"What the fuck did you do that for? You know you were supposed to call me or Ben before you made any decisions like that."

My heart sank. I slumped back in my chair, spilling Scotch out of my shot glass onto my lap. Longie leaned across his desk and stared at me for what seemed an eternity, and then broke into a big smile.

"Got ya that time, Gio. Great work. Ben and the boys are going to be thrilled at your success. Here, you call him with the news." He dialed Ben's number on the phone.

"Wait a second, there's more to it, Longie. Richard says that he will not give Marden any renewals when the lease runs out in five years."

"Don't worry about that, Gio. Jean Richard will never see the day when Marden's lease runs out." He handed me the receiver. "Now talk to Ben."

Will never see the day? That didn't bode well for Jean Richard.

"Hello, operator," I said into the phone, "I would like to place a long-distance call to the Colonial Inn in Hallandale Florida, person-to-person to Mister Ben Marden." I looked at Longie, who had a kind of predatory smile.

"Hello, Ben, this is Gio."

"Gio, how the hell are you?"

"Good, Ben. I have some news for you on the Villa Richard. I did the best I could, but all I could get was a five-year lease with no renewals, and we shook on the deal."

I held my breath.

"Let you in on a secret. I never really expected him to sell, anyway. In fact, I figured a lease was a long shot…You did great work, Gio. Great work."

I could let my breath out. "Thanks, Ben, hope it pays off."

"Oh, it'll pay off. Don't worry 'bout that."

Longie got on the phone with Ben to discuss the details, but I was flying too high to hear much of their conversation. The next thing I knew, Longie was gripping me by the shoulders.

"Ben will meet with us in a few days, when he gets back from Hallandale. He has some money down on a couple of ponies running at Gulfstream; says Rothstein told him to bet the ranch on those two nags. I just hope he doesn't bet the down payment on Villa."

He smacked me playfully on the shoulder. "Can you imagine Jean Richard running a kitchen with a staff of 53 when he was at Delmonico's? Ever there, Gio?"

"I was in the Navy, then," I said. "All I could afford was a couple of hot dogs and a beer."

"Delmonico's was quite a joint," Longie said. "They had private banquet facilities, ballrooms… Prohibition really killed their business."

"You think Ben wants to turn Villa Richard into another Delmonico's?"

Longie smiled. "Bigger…better."

The following day, I read in the paper that the stock market had hit an all-time high. Maybe Loomis had it all wrong, I was thinking. Maybe now was the time to grab even more shares. It was easy enough to do so—you could purchase on margin by putting up only ten percent.

My broker, Kenny Margolen, had always told me not to invest any more money than I felt comfortable doing. But in this case, with the market on such a roll, and all the banks getting in on the action, I was feeling comfortable at any cost, and told Kenny to grab as much as the cash in my account could handle. Whatever stocks he picked were fine with me. I told Nancy to do the same.

So much for the counsel of Al Loomis.

Kenny was always in his office before the market opened. I called him at 7 a.m.

I grew up with Kenny in South Philly and like me, he moved to New Jersey as a kid, settling in Fort Lee when his father took a job at an embroidery company in West New York. I trusted his judgment. When I called, he was in, as usual. I always wondered why he felt he should be in his office before the sun came up, but that's the way he did things. He was a creature of habit, and that is what I liked about him. You always knew where he was and where he stood on a matter: no bullshit. I asked him what he thought about putting up all the chips, which were really not that many, maybe three thousand in cash that I managed to squirrel away from the bonuses that Longie would hand me under the table.

"Are you crazy?" he said.

"No, last time I checked. But, for your information, I am ridin' a hot streak."

"Bully for you. Lesson number one: Only schmucks buy at the peak."

I said that I had told Nancy to jump in heavy, too. He told me to call her back immediately, and tell her to forget the whole thing.

"I'll tell you what," Kenny said, "if you want some action today, sell what you got, and then in a few days when the market settles, buy your shares back."

This seemed to be a good idea at the time and, in retrospect, it was great advice. Nancy also cleaned up on that move. After all was said and done, I was relieved that I didn't tell Longie and the boys about my misguided "insight" on stock market matters. Better to let my reputation rest on my Villa Richard negotiating laurels.

Still, I read that noted economist Irving Fisher proclaimed, "Stock prices have reached what looks like a permanently high plateau." It was so hard for me not to go along with my hunch on the market staying strong.

On October 24, 1929, which was to become known as "Black Thursday," the market lost 11 percent of its value at the opening bell. In an effort to stop the slide, a New York Stock Exchange vice president placed bids to buy large amounts of U.S. Steel at a price well above the current market. He did the same thing on other Blue Chip stocks, which seemed to stem the tide, at least for that day.

Neither Longie nor Ben seemed concerned. They both said they did not pay too much attention to the stock market, because all the money invested was traceable, and that would be the last place they would want to sock away their dough.

Over the weekend, the public grew more and more nervous, and the following Monday, the Dow Jones Industrial Average lost another 13%. The next day, it declined by 12%. At this rate, Wall Street was going to wind up in the Hudson River before the week was out.

Within days, the Rockefellers bought huge amounts of stock to demonstrate faith in the system, but the public had lost its faith, grabbed what they could out of their portfolios, and headed for the hills. I wondered if the financial climate would jeopardize the Villa Richard deal. I felt confident that the Villa's ideal location made it a choice spot in any economy.

Eddie Mannix had told me that the Interstate Park Commission did a study back in 1919, when Jean Richard bought the place. Apparently, on the contiguous Carpenter property, an old stone stairway led down the steep cliffs to the river. These stairs were used by the Carpenter Quarry people way back when and were still used to access Hazard's Bath House at the bottom of the cliff. A simple head count of people using the stairs determined that about 50,000 people climbed down each summer to swim at Hazard's Beach on the Hudson River.

Maybe, all things considered, Ben would go through with the deal anyway. It remained a question on my mind for the rest of the day. The answer to that question came a few days later.

Ben's thinking was that the bridge coming to New Jersey would, in itself, spur business growth. What's more, he was in tight with the "Broadway guys," who wanted to see him make good at his new venture. The Villa Richard deal was going through, on schedule.

Who were the so-called Broadway guys? They were a group of friends, most grew up in Brooklyn together, and now they were making their mark outside of the legitimate methods of doing business. They included Charles "Lucky" Luciano, originally from Sicily; Frank Costello and Albert Anastasia, each from Calabria; Joe Adonis and Vito Genovese, from Naples. Meyer Lansky and Benny

"Bugsey" Siegel were Jewish. The fact that there was such a wide diversity in the backgrounds of these guys seemed irrelevant, given that they were able to work together, for at least a while, and share in the common fortune connected to their alliance. On the other hand, Joe Masseria and Sal Maranzano, rival heads of the New York Mafia, felt that those not of Sicilian heritage could not be trusted. To them, the Broadway guys, were outsiders, except for Luciano, who happened to be an outstanding earner with a keen intelligence, and for whose allegiance Masseria and Maranzano vied. The caveat was that if Luciano had any ideas about joining either of them, he would have to sever his association with Meyer Lansky and others not born in Sicily.

Lucky, however, considered Lansky a tremendous financial brain, and there was no way that he was going to forgo a lifelong friendship to join with either the Masseria or Maranzano factions, at least for now. The "M boys" were so immersed in the Castellammarese War—the bloody power struggle for control of the Italian American Mafia—that they couldn't see the handwriting on the wall, which spelled out that a change in ethnic relationships was inevitable.

Of course, it was no secret that these guys operated outside the law. When business disputes arose, they could hardly take those problems to court. They were obligated to settle their differences themselves and, typically, their method of settlement proved fatal to the loser of the dispute.

As far as Ben Marden was concerned, his owning so many successful nightspots could not keep him insulated from his patrons, who frequently operated outside the law. Ben had a benevolent way about him. He was always first in line to make a charitable donation, or pay a bill for someone down on his luck. Both criminals and law-abiding citizens loved the guy.

Chapter 10

While the new bridge was being built, the Villa Richard was being transformed into "Ben Marden's something or other." Ben was at a loss for a new name. Ben Marden's Villa? No one liked that name. "Villa Marden" didn't fare much better.

After the leases were signed, and the business had changed hands, Longie and I took a drive up to the Villa on Ben's invitation. Standing on the outside dining terrace overlooking the river, the three of us struggled to find a proper name for the place.

Then Longie got that look in his eyes, like he had just spotted a truckload of booze ripe for the plucking.

"Why don't you call it 'Ben Marden's Riviera,' like the Hotel Riviera in Newark? At least here, you have a river to connect the name to."

We looked at each other high over the Hudson. "That's it," Ben said excitedly. 'Ben Marden's Riviera' it is."

At this time, Longie was making trips to Hollywood every chance he got. He told me he was dating Jean Harlow, and they were crazy about each other. He said he never felt this way about a dame before. I wished him luck, but told him to be careful.

"Me, be careful?" he said. "Are you out of your mind? I didn't get this far being careful, and I am not going to start now... with anything."

My plate was full, taking care of details for Ben. He was in constant touch with me, and would always tell me not to leave town without calling him. I wondered whether he expected me to call him when I went from Fort Lee to Cliffside, only two miles away.

When the business changed hands and Ben took over, he called the corporation "Riviera Catering Company" and, for the next several months, the building received a serious face-lift: a new kitchen, fresh paint for the corridors, wallpaper in a fantastic floral pattern and new carpeting in the rooms. The ballroom took on a new air of sophistication, too, as its tired, Victorian trappings yielded to Art Deco.

At the outset, Ben's new investment didn't measure up to what he had in mind, but the disappointing cash-flow reversed course when the basement's Marine Room, and the real party, started. All the wheels were in motion by the spring of 1934, when the records showed that the Riviera was doing business on a large scale, mainly due to the Marine Room's popular, if illegal, activities.

"By special invitation only" was the watchword for the Marine Room. Unless you were previously vouched for as being "good" for any losses incurred, you were persona non grata at the downstairs casino. Players were picked up in a private cars and driven to the Riviera for a lavish dinner and show, topped off by a spin of the wheel, the roll of dice, or hands of poker, whichever suited their fancy. There was no shortage of qualified patrons begging to get on Ben's private invitation list. With his elite clientele at the Cotton Club and Palais Royal, he could pick and choose whom to invite across the pond.

So Ben finally had a joint on the Jersey side of the Hudson with access from the city via the Hudson River Bridge. He was pleased, sure, but wanted it to be much more than just "another joint." He envisioned a "classier" place, like Lou Walters' new Colonial Inn in Hallandale, Florida. One day, when he was feeling particularly frustrated, he drew me aside.

"Gio, I want you to find out who owns that parcel of land here on the cliffs closer to the bridge. I don't want anybody buying that except me—got it?"

All told, Ben spent $150,000 to spruce up his Riviera. Day by day, week by week, the Union Hall sent the very best carpenters to tear down the old interior and put up the new. Painters, plumbers, electricians, tradesmen of every stripe and specialty attended to Ben's every whim. I often thought that those union guys had gotten the word from the powers-that-be that they'd better make it right the first time, because this was a Ben Marden project.

If Ben was a taskmaster, he was also a generous host. The skilled workers were treated to terrific meals. And you would think it was a Port Authority Police commissary the way the cops would stand at the kitchen door out back and nosh on the free sandwiches that Ben insisted were theirs for the taking. Fort Lee cops did the same thing. Ben Marden's Riviera was a magnet for any public employee who wanted a free lunch. To Ben, however, it was just the price of doing business and a small amount to pay to have the law look the other way.

On October 25, 1931, the day the George Washington Bridge was opened to traffic, General Ben threw a bash at the Riviera. VIPs strolled or drove across the new bridge. No one seemed to remember the new span being referred to as the Hudson River Bridge, when it was in its design stage. Othmar Ammann, the chief engineer, and Cass Gilbert, the lead architect, of the 4,760 linear-foot suspension bridge, were the stars of the day, as everyone crowded onto the Marine Terrace to behold the beautiful structure.

Originally, the bridge was to be encased in concrete and granite, but due to Depression's impact, steel got the nod. To some, the naked look of the silver-colored superstructure was a glorious sight to behold. There was no sign of depression on the Marine Terrace, as the Veuve Clicquot champagne flowed like water. Locals crowded the free, clams-on-the-half-shell table to watch Iggie Simpson devour 16 dozen of the tasty mollusks, a local record never to be broken. Iggie's wife was on hand to cheer him on, and explained to his new fans that her celebrity-husband was a "G-Man." People nodded and arched their eyebrows, figuring Iggie was a secret agent of some sort, but his true vocation was less glamorous: that of Coytesville's garbage man. Up on the Marine Terrace, all things were possible.

I learned that, what the Coytesville citizens lacked in affluence, they more than made up for with kindness, humor, generosity and, most of all grit. Ben Marden would not turn his back on their needs, and made it a practice to prepare 500 lavish food baskets on Thanksgiving to be distributed to the residents of the town.

Gaiety was in the air on the day that the George Washington Bridge debuted. Discussion about the astronomical sum of $75,000,000, which had been spent to build this titanic structure, seemed to chase the clouds of despair that hung over most families' homes. They were relieved of their woes, at least for one afternoon. "Things should get better soon," said the optimistic, especially those high on the free drinks. Charlie Luciano, Benny Siegel, and Joe Adonis, known as "Joey A," showed up later in the day, as the crowd finally thinned. Longie, Izzie, and I were just finishing some excellent Chinese fare, when they came out onto the terrace, accompanied by Ben Marden. Siegel was in awe of the huge bridge's steel construction and filigree enhanced by the sun bouncing off exposed columns reaching toward to the sky.

"How much does a ton of steel cost?" he asked everyone within earshot. We just looked at each other, wondering why it was so important to him. Before he could get a satisfactory answer, he and Charlie drifted from us to mingle with the remaining crowd.

Ben Marden wanted to introduce me to Sophie Tucker. "Sophie and Joe E. Lewis are going to open for me next week, and she came up here early. She's a real pip; she came back from England just so she could be here to celebrate with us today. Will you and Longie be here for her show?"

"I don't think Longie would miss it for the world," I said. "Same with me."

"Don't forget to bring Nancy."

Here we go again, I thought; he just won't quit on Nancy. He waved me across the room.

"Three guys I want you to meet are over there at the bar. The little guy with the broken nose is the boxer Tony Canzoneri, and the guy with the cigar is Gus Becker. The other one, with the gray jacket, is Ed Sullivan, who happened to be a pretty good boxer before he became a sportswriter for the Evening Graphic. I think Ed is going places. He spends so much time at my clubs you, would think he was a show business columnist. Maybe someday he will be.

"Tony is a great fighter. He fights anybody, anytime; he don't give a shit. Last November, he knocked out Al Singer at the Garden. I think he's one of the few guys in the world to hold two or three titles at the same time. Becker is a huge fight fan; won't miss a fight, and always gets ringside seats. I think they got seats reserved with his name on it at St. Nick's and the Garden."

As we approached, Gus spotted us. "Great party, Ben, you out-did yourself this time. Now I don't have to go over to Harlem to get a good show and a meal; I can do it right here in my hometown of Coytesville."

"That's a helluva compliment coming from you, Gus." Hey, meet my main guy, Gio."

"Pleased to meet ya," Gus said. Canzoneri grunted, and Sullivan smiled, as I shook their hands.

"Gio, Gus here owns Rambo's Tavern on the other side of town," Ben said. "Everyone calls it Gus Becker's. I love to stop in there and have a few shooters…You got a baseball team, too, right Gus?"

"Well, it's not exclusively mine, but we call it the Coytesville AC. We play at the Linwood ballfield on Sundays. You know, Ben, Babe Ruth promised to bring over his barnstorming team to play us in the spring. Why don't you see if you can make it?"

"I don't know if I can make it with all the shit I have going here, but I would like to put down a C-note that says your team can whip Babe's All-Stars."

"I'll take the other end of that bet," Sullivan said. "I never go against the Bambino."

Gus chomped on his cigar. "That's just like you, Ben—always putting me on the spot. How the hell can I bet against our own team? That's why you're the guy with all the money; you're always one step ahead of the rest of us."

We moved toward Sophie Tucker's table, where she was seated with Walter Winchell, the *New York Daily Mirror's* abrasive, syn-dicated columnist, who also had his own radio show on WABC, a CBS affiliate. Winchell always found a way to weasel himself into situations to get his stories, sometimes placing his health in jeopardy. His close friendship with Cotton Club honcho Owney Madden put him on the track of potentially explosive, inside infor-mation. For a while, Winchell practically lived at the Club, and learned things Madden didn't want him to know about.

Before we reached the table, Marden said, "Owney says that Winchell has a big mouth, and it's gonna get him in trouble. I think Winchell got the message, because he hasn't been to the Cotton Club for at least a few weeks.

"Sophie! So, how is my baby girl?" Ben exclaimed, as we arrived at her table.

"Couldn't be better, Ben," she said in her distinctive contralto. "Just got back from England, and I have to go back there again and eat mutton with all those limeys." Her laugh seemed to rise up from her stomach.

"This girl is all over the place; she never sits still for a minute," said Ben. "Meet my friend, Gio."

"Hey, good lookin.'" Sophie said. I don't know if I blushed—I may have. Winchell just fixed me with his stare.

"Easy does it, Sophie," Ben said, giving Winchell a slap on the back with the reminder, "Don't forget to give the Riviera a good write-up about our party today, okay, Walt?"

"Don't worry, you'll get what you deserve," Winchell said in his customary, clipped tones.

Just then, Meyer Lansky and two men strolled onto the Marine Terrace, and Ben steered me in their direction. A moment later—

"Meyer… Glad you could make it. I was hoping you could find your way out here to the sticks to celebrate the opening of our beautiful new bridge." Ben shook Lansky's hand with his right, and patted the shake with his left. "This is my new assistant, Giorgio Arigo."

Meyer did not offer his hand, but offered me a piece of hard candy in a cellophane wrapper. "Good for the throat," he said. He gave another one to Ben. Odd "gifts" from this surprisingly unprepossessing man whose brainpower was crucial to the Outfit's success.

"I see Charlie Luciano is here to celebrate with you," Lansky said.

"Yes, and Ben Siegel, too," I said, trying to sound like an insider, and hoping that I wasn't offering that information out of turn.

"Nice place you have here, Ben; what a great location," Lansky said.

"Well there are a lot of friends who helped me get this place, right Meyer?"

"No Ben, you make good choices, and this is only one of them. This place is going to be very successful. The investment is safe here. Mazel tov, Ben…Word has it that your man Gio, here, did an outstanding job with negotiating the purchase and, as I recall, he gave us the right dope on getting out of the stock market just in time. Am I correct, Ben?"

"You're right, Meyer, he is outstanding at handling business matters, and gets it done without mistakes."

"For an Italian kid, you're doing just fine, Gio," said Lansky with a thin smile.

"Wait a second, Meyer, he's only half Italian. The other half is just like us. And if you don't believe me, have him drop his pants and you can inspect the evidence."

But this was not a joking matter to Lansky.

"I don't think that's funny at all, Ben," he said. "When I was a kid, some Irish guys in Brooklyn said the same thing to me—I should drop my drawers and show them my circumcision. Instead of doing that, I grabbed a broken dish and cut the throat of the leader of that pack of rats. That was my first brush with the law."

Ben and I both gasped at the deadly serious manner in which Meyer told us the story.

I quickly changed the subject. "Did you see Larry Fay over there, watching that guy eat the clams, Ben?"

"I sure did. Which reminds me, I have to say hello to him."

Luciano and Siegel made their way over to Meyer, their expressions signaling a desire for privacy, so Ben and I excused ourselves, and headed in the direction of Fay and Big Bill Dwyer. After a few steps, Ben noticed I wasn't with him, he stopped, and turned around with a puzzled expression.

"You go ahead, Ben," I said. "I'm sorry, but I can't meet those guys right now.

"How come, Gio? They're good friends of mine. You were the one who just mentioned Larry's name."

I couldn't tell Ben, but how could I face them after taking off with their 125 cases of booze in Montauk? I didn't want my face to give anything away. If they ever found out it was me, I might be trying to swim in a cement kimono.

"I gotta call Longie about something," I said.

"Go ahead, call your other boss." For a moment, he acted as if he were hurt, but then broke into a smile to show he was only kidding. "Listen, Gio, before you go…When are you going to get me that piece of property next to the bridge?"

"It's coming," I said.

"So is Yom Kippur."

"I been working on it. I found out it's owned by a Missus Kelly; Mary, I think. I called her, and she said she might be interested in selling. She said she is going through her agent a company called Michael Realty"

"Nice work, Gio. Just don't drop the ball, make sure nobody else gets that property okay? Set something up for me."

He went off to talk with Larry Fay and Texas Guinan, who were enjoying themselves at a table off to the side, out of the wind.

I knew quite a bit about Larry Fay. He was a bootlegger, and a big one. He made his mark bringing in the good stuff from Canada and controlled a lot of the action on Long Island. Because he made no secret of his business, he'd been arrested about 50 times. But they never pinned a thing on him. All the politicians frequented his joint, the El Fey on 47th Street, and consequently, the press hounded him and hostess Texas Guinan for scoops. Fay had worked his way up the bootlegging ladder and made half a million bucks. He wanted to be a nightclub owner, so he bought the El Fey in Manhattan, where Texas Guinan would hold court, sitting on the piano and insulting guests, who felt privileged when the insults were directed at them.

As fellow club owners, Fay and Ben knew each other very well, and frequented each other's establishment. Maybe Ben bought from him a while back, who knows. All I knew is that I didn't want to meet anybody who I had stolen from. On the other hand, maybe those 125 cases were small potatoes to Fay. Not to me, however. In any event, I was taking no chances on being found out.

Texas Guinan, hostess extraordinaire, got more publicity than Jimmy Walker, the fashion-plate Mayor of New York. She had a Major League mouth on her; you didn't have to be within 10 feet of her to hear that loud, raucous voice spewing funny, exaggerated quotes. She had come a long way up the ladder, and done lots of different things to earn a living and her colorful reputation. She'd even made a silent movie in Fort Lee: The Wildcat. In 1920, Texas had opened a speak called the 300 Club on W. 54th St. in Manhattan. She had a knack for attracting the socialites of the day. At the smallish 300, her scantily clad dancers practically rubbed up against the customers. In 1929, she had made a movie appropriately titled *Queen of the Night Clubs*. Walter Winchell was writing a play about Broadway for her. Texas Guinan was all about bright lights and brassiness. On the Riviera's Marine Terrace this day of the GW Bridge launch, I saw her capture the crowd with her signature line, "Hello Suckers!" Ben was beaming because the great Texas Guinan was entertaining his guests, and they were lapping it up.

I had not needed to make a call to Longie—that was a ruse. I stayed largely out of sight until I saw Fay and Dwyer leave the premises. The party went on until about six o'clock, with Ben and his waiter captains anxious to shoo the guests in time for the place to be readied for a nine o'clock floorshow. Locals still on hand pocketed tasty morsels from the buffet tables wrapped in Ben's finest napkins, as they left. Some even grabbed whole dishes of condiments to take with them. A captain asked Ben what to do about the pilfering.

"Give them what they want," Ben said. "They are our friends and neighbors."

The evening show would feature Ed Wynn, an endearing comedian whose rubbery face had made his mark in vaudeville a decade earlier. As the sun went down on the grand opening of the George Washington Bridge, the bridge's lights lit up the entire cliffs, all the way up to Ben Marden's Riviera, a setting that was somehow both tranquil and dramatic, with the promise of more serious drama to come.

Chapter 11

I rejoined Ben a few minutes before Lansky and Siegel approached him. "I got a logistics problem," Lansky said quietly. "...Miami."

Before he could elaborate, Fort Lee Mayor Louis Hoebel and Police Chief Andy McDermott came over to say goodbye and thank Ben for his hospitality.

"How are people faring since the Depression hit?" Ben asked.

Mayor Hoebel responded first. "We have real serious problems, Ben. Many of them don't even have enough food to eat. Forget about jobs, because there are none. Most of them, young and old alike, are moving back in with each other. You know the movie business in Fort Lee is not what it used to be. California is taking away all that revenue that we used to get from the studios. In fact, some of the studios have literally gone up in smoke already. Can't say the owners were looking for insurance money to bail them out, but it sure looks suspicious."

"We got an idea who the torch man is, and it won't be long till we put him away," said Chief McDermott. We all looked at each other.

Ben said that he had spoken recently with young Elliott Roosevelt, the son of Franklin Roosevelt, who was planning to run for President the following year. Elliott explained that his father had a plan to establish work projects for the "employable unemployed." That would be part of the existing Works Progress Administration that had been on the books for some time, but was inactive.

"Maybe, Mister Mayor, you could look into that," said Lansky. "I get the feeling that Roosevelt is just what this country needs right now."

"Who knows?" said Hoebel. "Anything would help the situation. Lord knows we have to come up with something to get these people back to work. I suppose I could try something like that on a local level."

After Hoebel and McDermott left, Ben turned to me and said, "Give it a few more years and all of this Prohibition stuff will be over, and we can sit down with good guys like those two, have a drink, and relax."

"Hey, Marden," Siegel said, always a hair-trigger away from an explosion. "We're all good guys here."

I saw a flicker of anger in Ben Marden's eyes, but he quashed it. "Just a manner of speaking, Benny. Of course we are."

The four of us, on Ben's invitation, began an evening walk along the cliffs, single-file on the narrow dirt path leading north. Like four Boy Scouts exploring the terrain.

"You know, this guy Elliott Roosevelt might come in handy for us someday," Lansky said. "He's outgoing, and wants to be part of his dad's bid for the presidency."

"You think we can convince them not to repeal the 'Eighteenth?'" Siegel said. "'Cause that's definitely in the works, and would really throw a stick into our spokes. Right, Meyer?"

"Listen, Hoover's commission did an investigation on the pros and cons, and advised against repeal. So there is nothing to worry about yet, Benny."

We had walked only a hundred yards or so before we found a clearing near the corner of Washington Avenue and the cliffs. Lansky said to Ben, "Someday this would make a nice place for a park, don't you think?"

"Yes, helluva view from here."

Indeed, it was one helluva view, the glorious new bridge creasing the sky, and the towers of Manhattan—including the Empire State Building completed earlier this very year—seen through the girders. Lansky took it all in with an eye that seemed to see the future as well.

"The reason I wanted to talk to you, Ben, is because—I don't know how you do it—you never seem to have trouble finding competent help in running your establishments. You have a knack of picking out good help, I admire that. How do you do it?"

"Well, all I can say is that I mostly try to hire people who really appreciate the jobs I offer. They need the money to support their families. Simple as that, comprende? I got the idea of using

Cubans for help five years ago when you and I were on a trip down to Havana, remember? One day I was walking alone in the city and got to speaking with some guy who owned a small café. He told me about the impoverished people called the Ciboneys who were the real native Cubans. He said they needed work desperately. So I thought to myself, New York is just the place where these people will fit in perfectly. The men have this wonderful charm about them and handsome looks that my customers will go for, so why not bring them up here." "So that is why you have so many Cubans working here. Marden, I got to hand it to you, you truly do have a handle on all the details."

Ben's smile was more of a twitch. "I do lay many of them off in the winter, when things get slower around here. Remember, many of them do not have their papers and legally shouldn't be working here in the first place, so they appreciate me paying them off the books. I'm happy with the arrangement because, as you know, some of our income is on the Q.T. So it all works out fine for me."

Lansky continued to gaze at the horizon. "I take your point, Ben. Now consider this: since my busy season in Miami is the winter, how 'bout you send your people to me when it gets cold up here?"

"Funny you should say that, Meyer. I was actually thinking of closing the place down in late October and then opening again in April. Does that make sense to you?"

"It makes perfect sense." He turned to look Ben in the eye.

"Okay, I think we can handle that, Meyer, but you got to promise to send them back to me in April."

"You have my word on it, Ben."

We all resumed our walk. Siegel and I had been taking in the conversation without saying a word.

Suddenly Siegel piped up. "Hey, you guys are supposed to be catering to a sophisticated clientele, right? Surely, sophisticated people would find it more appealing to have their food served by beautiful waitresses. How come you guys don't see it that way?"

"First off, Benny, it's traditional to have male waiters in posh places," Lansky said, sounding like a professor up from the streets.

"Secondly, sophisticated people, as you call them, have wives and girlfriends who don't like to be served by babes better looking they are." He glanced at Ben, then back at Siegel. "Comprende? Cuban guys are just fine with American women, and are no threat to American men. By the way, fagellas also like the Cubans."

"If you say so," said Siegel, looking puzzled.

Lansky was the first to turn and start heading back to the Riviera. We followed a step later.

"See that tree over there?" Ben Marden asked, as he pointed to a large pin oak tree, which stood just off to the side of the well-trodden, dirt path. "Several years ago, they found a guy wired to it and burned to a crisp. Cops said he committed suicide."

Benny's laugh had a guttural spite to it. "Now that is some shit. I love this town if the cops think that some guy can wire himself to a tree and then light himself up like a Roman candle. What if they find a guy with ten slugs in him—is that suicide, too?...Tell you what, this sap screwed somebody out of some money."

"Or made nice with someone's wife," I said, happy I found an opening to make a comment.

"Could be that, too, kid," Siegel said.

"I don't know," Ben said. "I just know that they had to cut him down from that tree."

Siegel shrugged his shoulders. "Don't know why—this is a kind of nature trail, wouldn't you say? That's all part of nature." No one laughed.

Now that Lansky apparently had concluded his business, Benny—Only My Enemies Call Me Bugsy—Siegel was in a talkative mood, which was his normal state. "You guys are missing out on a fantastic new invention," he said. "It's called a 'jukebox.' My money says that every shot-and-a-beer joint in this country is going to own one. I have been following this thing, and it can't miss. I told you about this, Meyer, right?"

"What the hell's a jukebox?" Ben asked.

"You put coins into it, and it plays music."

"Like a music box?"

"No, not at all. This thing is as big as you are, and it has dozens of songs on it, and when you put a nickel in, it plays any popular song that you choose. It lights up with wild lights that get you juiced up right away."

"Doesn't take much to get you juiced up, Benny," Lansky said, laughing, then turning to Ben Marden. "Let's stick to talking about how we're going to get your experienced Cuban waiters, Ben, down to our neck of the woods in the wintertime to help us out. Sure, we can get all the Cubans we need, but the problem is none of them have any experience working a first-class operation, and since you have already trained them…You know, Ben, I have my eye on a joint down in Hallandale, right down the road from Gulfstream Park. It might be a good idea if you and I considered a partnership sometime soon—think about that, Ben. This place is called the Colonial Inn. Great spot, great shows, all the gambling you want and, in addition, the ponies are just down the road."

Ben had mentioned the Colonial Inn to me in the past. He knew the place well and had been there several times. "I will, Meyer," he said. "I will."

"Gio, you remind Mister Marden here about what I just said. In a few years, Lou Walters might sell the Colonial Inn. He has too many joints right now—plus the track—and I think he can be persuaded to sell us one."

When we got back to the Riviera, Ben invited the two of them to stay for dinner and the show, but Lansky said he needed to return to New York. Ben left us out front, where fine women emerged from the passenger side of automobiles that had entered thorough the bluestone columns.

"Just look at these cars," Siegel said. "Duesenbergs, Auburns, Cadillacs, Lincolns, and even a Hispano-Suiza. Where the fuck do these people get all that money?"

Lansky sniffed the evening air. "Who cares, as long as we can take some of it and put it in our pockets."

"I second that, Mister Lansky," I said.

"From now on Gio, you call me Meyer. I came up through the ranks just like you are. Someday, if you keep your nose clean, you can make it big."

Those words again, like a repeated refrain: "make it big." As Lansky's driver pulled up to the curb, we said our goodbyes.

"Are you sure you don't want to stay for the show?" I said, a final courtesy. "Paul Whiteman's band, Ed Wynn—"

"—Maybe next time." Lansky's hand was raised like a traffic cop, and I knew I'd better not overstay my welcome, even though he'd placed us on a first-name basis. "Say hello to Longie for me, and tell him he owes me money," he said, and winked as he entered the back seat of the black Chrysler.

Just as Siegel was about to enter the car, he turned to me and said, "If you ever get a chance to come out to California, look me up. I got a black book full of phone numbers of Hollywood starlets who would jump at the chance to meet a good lookin' guy like you. Who knows, maybe I could even get you a screen test."

"Enough of that bullshit, Benny," Lansky said from the car. "Let the man go; he's got work to do."

I went back inside the ballroom and saw Paul Whiteman on the bandstand with his lead vocalist, the popular Mildred Bailey. Mildred and Paul were on a roll with their new hit record, When It's Sleepy Time Down South. I decided to go backstage and watch the show from the wings. Moonfaced with a thin mustache, Whiteman wore a black tuxedo and brandished a white baton. Seven years earlier, he had premiered Gershwin's Rhapsody in Blue, with the composer himself on piano. Whiteman had become perhaps the leading ambassador of popular American music. His band's jazzy scores were a hit with college kids, as well as their parents. He was associated with Tin Pan Alley's best tunes, and a top draw on both the ballroom and nightclub circuits. The Whiteman organization seemingly was always on the road, playing in venues like Karzas's Trianon Ballroom in Chicago, the Vanity and Grande Ballrooms in Detroit, and all the major hotels throughout the country.

And here he was at Marden's Riviera, the hottest musical act in the country. Some said it was payback for Ben giving him a steady gig years earlier at the Palais Royal in Manhattan. Ben had an eye for talent and an instinct for treating people right.

Paul and the orchestra played their version of *Willow Weep for Me*, a song they would soon record for Capitol Records. Couples took to the dance floor for favorites such as *Whispering, Song of India, Japanese Sandman, April Showers,* and *Wang-Wang Blues.* The women, in their finest flapper dresses, with their tuxedoed gentleman, spun round and round through the night.

Downstairs, invited guests gambled in the full-scale casino called the Marine Room, which boasted four roulette tables, a bird-cage, several craps games, and three blackjack games nightly. It didn't take long before investigators from the New Jersey State Assembly made repeated visits to the Riviera for the sole purpose of observing the goings-on downstairs. Seeing this, Ben went into disaster control mode. Fearful that the Riviera would be shut down, he called me into his office.

"Those sneaky bastards have been taking notes on everything we're doing," he said. "They could shut us down if they wanted to."

He turned away from me and stared at the wall behind his desk, pounding his fists on the arms of his leather chair. It was distressing to me that all the work and dreams that gave birth to an enterprise like the Riviera could be so easily thrown off the cliff.

"Isn't a club supposed to be a private place?" I asked Ben.

He stopped his pounding.

I walked to the side of his desk. "What if we made the Riviera a private club, and kept the public out?… No, wait a minute—what if we only make the Marine Room private?"

He turned toward me.

"We say it's a non-profit thing, you know like the golf courses do," I continued. "We convert the Marine Room, on paper, to the Marine Club. We become a private organization formed to promote the civic welfare and to provide recreation and amusement for our members…It's kosher, Ben."

A light came into his eyes. "You could be a fuckin' genius, Gio! Right now, the only people we let in there to gamble are the ones we approve of, anyway. So, in a way, we are already operating like a private club. We pick up our clients with our own fleet of cars, give them some drinks, and let them lose their money…I love this, Gio. You are one smart son-of-a-bitch."

The following morning, Ben called his attorney and set the wheels in motion. After the paperwork was completed, the Marine Room was renamed the Marine Club, and the G-men desisted. We were back in business.

The boy genius had saved the day.

"Business as usual" became our battle cry, as we moved the Riviera forward. Ben redoubled his work for local charities. At one point, we all kidded that Ben would be chosen the local Man of the Year.

No detail was too small for the Riviera in its attention to clientele. If a young lady needed a dance partner, while her husband or beau was downstairs trying his luck at craps, the Marden policy sprang into action, and a suitable male would be sent over to her table to converse or even dance with her. It was a lead-pipe cinch that an older woman dancing with a young stud meant her husband was rolling the dice downstairs. Led gracefully around the dance floor by one of Ben's handsome "lady sitters," she couldn't have cared less when her husband returned.

Ben took pride in hiring people who had an air of sophistication, good looks and, most of all, fine manners. One of his greeters in the Marine Club, a young man named Irving Mandel, also collected checks for gambling debts owed to the club at the end of the night. Irv had the kind of job that no one wanted, but he seemed to be happy doing it. He did have muscle on his side in case it was needed, but his orders from the top were to avoid confrontation. He had a nice but firm way of, shall we say, embarrassing the clients into paying up. His sure touch worked even with "the boys" who had a streak of bad luck at the tables and were unable to pay up. Irv somehow would find the words to convince disgruntled hoods into honoring their obligations.

Stars like Bing Crosby entertained at the Riviera. Month after month, the customers came, liquor flowed like water, the gaming continued, and everybody was happy. Winchell, Sullivan, Hedda Hopper, Louella Parsons, and their fellow gossip columnists all had favorable things to say about Ben Marden's Riviera.

Politicians raved about the generosity showered upon the locals in need. Everybody who was able to work, and keep their mouth shut, could find a job there, providing they were sober and had a modicum of good looks and decent manners. Ben would "give you the shirt off his back," many folks agreed. His one flaw was his reputation as a philanderer. But always with a touch of class. He was seen around town and everywhere else with the most beautiful women imaginable.

His marital commitments did not slow the pace of his escorting beautiful women all over New York. It was no secret that he showered his lady friends with expensive gifts with the same energy he displayed in his philanthropic initiatives for those in need. Money was merely a means to fulfill his worldly desires, to have fun, and to stay ahead of the curve in business. It was interesting to me that, from his point of view, the Riviera, which became one of the premier showplaces in the nation, never seemed to measure up, even after he'd sunk an additional $150,000 into it to refurbish it. He would walk around the ballroom, waving his arms and almost talking to himself, looking up at the ceiling and with his arms as if he were estimating dimensions, or trying to determine a way to push out the walls and make the ballroom bigger. One time, I asked him why he never seemed satisfied with his "creation."

"Gio," he said, "this place isn't bad, but it's not what I have in mind as being truly representative of me. You've got to realize that guys like Lou Walters, Jules Podell, and I are all in competition with each other as to who has the best joint, and here I am stuck with an old-time building that, no matter what I do, can't meet the standards of the twentieth century."

Of course, he had chosen to be "stuck" with the place, but I didn't point that out.

"Did you ever get to that Kelly lady who owns the property down the road from where we are now?" he asked me. "I need that location, before Rockefeller remembers he's forgotten to buy it. Offer her anything reasonable but get it for me."

I had been doing my homework. "Ben, her lot is less than two acres, and it's long and narrow, and lies in between two parcels owned by the Palisades Interstate Park Commission. Are you sure you really want it?"

"I want it—that's all you have to know."

A few months later, in the spring of 1932, I got a tip from the produce delivery driver, who happened to be the brother in law of the a guy from Michaels Realty that Mrs. Kelly was about ready to sell.

Ben was ecstatic with the news. He relished the idea of building a new Riviera, one that would set the standard for all nightclubs to follow.

"If I can build on this lot, which is much closer to the George Washington Bridge," he said, "it will give me a backdrop of lights and sky that no other place in the world has."

I thought it was a pipe dream, but Ben was an unstoppable force. Ben told me that he went into contract for the property. I was shocked to hear that the deal was going to close for as little as one dollar and other valuable considerations. As for the "valuable considerations," I left them to Ben and Mrs. Kelly to figure out.

But the national stage took precedence over Ben's grand plans. If Franklin Delano Roosevelt were elected President—and he was the odds-on favorite—the good times we had going for us, the bootleg hooch and the tax-free profits, were likely to become a thing of the past.

Chapter 12

On the evening of March 1, 1932, the Lindbergh baby was kidnapped from his crib at the family home near Hopewell, New Jersey. Radio news flashes bombarded the airwaves about the kidnapping. Newspapers printed pages with screaming headlines, day after day. Even the Depression took a backseat to this heartbreaking story.

On that night in March, Coytesville resident and New Jersey State Police motorcycle patrolman Joe Rutter sped to Hopewell to aid in the investigation. He was immediately assigned to assist in collecting evidence and getting involved with the case. Talk was all over Coytesville and Fort Lee that one of their local boys was on the job to hunt down the kidnappers.

"Nicky" was Rutter's nickname, given to him by Coytesville kids when he was growing up. He graduated from Fort Lee High School before joining the Troopers. Ben knew Nicky quite well, because, when he wasn't on duty with the state police, Nicky made routine deliveries of seltzer in pressurized bottles from his family's bottling plant, located on the front lawn of their home in Coytesville.

Zoning requirements were looser back in those days.

When I read the story about the kidnapping, I immediately called Longie.

"Remember when I went to Roosevelt field to watch him take off for Paris?"

As tough as Longie was, the image of a baby kidnapped from its crib unnerved him.

"I am going to put up ransom money," he said. "Find out what I have to do, and I will do it right away. I'm also going to call Lucky and Meyer and all those guys, and see if they will throw in some dough."

Longie seemed to make it a one-man-mission to catch the kidnapper. Of course, Ben Marden offered to throw in some cash along with the rest of them. The following week, when Nicky

Rutter was off-duty and had returned to Coytesville to resume his seltzer deliveries, I saw him arrive at the Riviera in a white Dodge "Huckster" pickup.

"Hey Nicky, you guys got a minute?" I asked, as he and his helper began offloading a dozen cases of seltzer.

"What's up, Gio?" he asked.

"I hear you are working on that Lindbergh kidnapping case."

"Yeah, I was down there the night of the kidnapping. Nothing much to tell yet." He said as he began stacking cases of seltzer on his hand truck.

"What happened that night, when you were sent over to Hopewell?"

"It was about ten o'clock, when the family discovered the baby was missing. They said they put the little tyke to bed around nine, and went downstairs to read. I was on patrol on my motorcycle, when I got the call. I had just got the bike out of the shop after getting my headlight and some wiring fixed. I was cruising around Morris County testing it, when orders came in to hightail it down to Hopewell and give some backup to the guys already on the scene."

Though far from a braggart, Nicky was eager to talk about his experience.

"My job was to set up a roadblock and cordon off the winding road leading to the Lindbergh property. It was hard as hell to find the place that night; I was stopping every quarter mile to take out my map while trying to read it with my flashlight. I finally got there, though."

"It was cold that night," I said. "You must have froze your balls off on that bike."

"I'm used to it…So anyway, I park the bike down the road from the house, and almost trip over a homemade ladder thrown to the side of the road. We figure the kidnapper used the ladder to get the baby out."

"I bet the place was humming with police and newspaper people."

"Are you kidding? Hundreds of people showed up when the news broke. Ninety-nine percent of them were just nosy." He placed his last case on the hand truck, and caught his breath. "Funny thing, the Lindberghs were supposed to go up to Dwight Morrow's house on Next Day Hill in Englewood that night. It was a Tuesday, but the baby came down with a cold, and Anne did not want to take him out of the house. That's why they stayed in Hopewell. If you ask me, somebody had to know the movements of the family pretty damn well, because Charles and Anne did not have a set routine for anything, and no one knew they were scheduled to be home that night, other than maybe family members up in Englewood."

He put the hand truck back onto the tailgate of the truck. "That's about it."

"Are you going to work anymore on the case?"

"Maybe. Chief asked me to get involved with the ransom money." The "chief" was H. Norman Schwarzkopf, superintendent of the New Jersey State Police, who had been offered the assistance of the FBI by J. Edgar Hoover himself. "I hope I get to do that; it will look good on my record."

One minute, at the center of world news; the next, delivering seltzer to the Riviera.

The newspapers told of a $50,000 ransom note left on the windowsill of the baby's room that night. On March 6 came another ransom note, upping the demand to $70,000. Two days later, a third ransom note arrived. At this point, New Jersey Governor Arthur "Harry" Moore called a conference, which was attended by prosecutors, police authorities, and other government officials. Lindbergh also hired his own team of investigators through his attorney, a retired Bronx schoolteacher named Condon—Dr. Condon, if you please. The good doctor was largely a blowhard, who offered to act as an intermediary to negotiate with the kidnapper on behalf of the family. Condon was in charge of the $70,000, and it was he who began negotiating in coded messages with the kidnappers through the *Bronx Home News* daily newspaper.

In all, thirteen ransom notes changed hands. The sixth was delivered by taxicab driver Joseph Perrone, who was hazy about the description of the man who gave it to him. The note stated that the next in the series—number seven—could be found beneath a rock at a vacant newspaper stand near an elevated subway station. That note promised that a sample of the baby's clothes would be given to Condon at Woodlawn Cemetery near 233rd Street and Jerome Avenue. When Condon went to the cemetery that night, he met a man waving a handkerchief to attract his attention. At this meeting, the payment of the ransom money was discussed.

On April 2, Condon found the twelfth note under another rock in front of a greenhouse at 3225 East Tremont Avenue in the Bronx—exactly as described in the eleventh note. The ransom had been reduced to $50,000. The thirteenth, and final, note claimed that the little boy was on the fishing boat Nellie in Martha's Vineyard, Massachusetts. Condon gave the $50,000 to a man who called himself "John."

More than two months after the kidnapping, the tiny body of the Lindbergh baby was accidentally found, partially buried and badly decomposing, about four-and-a half-miles away from the Lindbergh home and along the highway near Mount Rose, New Jersey. The skull had been fractured on both sides. The ransom money had been paid in marked bills, as the FBI had instructed. Now, all anyone could do was to wait for that money to start showing up.

About a month later, a waitress in the service of Mrs. Dwight Morrow, Anne Morrow Lindbergh's mother, committed suicide by taking poison, which only added to the mystery. All of the staff who worked in the Morrow and the Lindbergh households had been questioned numerous times concerning the case, and this young woman's movements on the night of March 1st were carefully checked, but it was determined that she had no connection with the baby's abduction.

A month later, over the July 4th weekend, Longie called me at Cella's Hotel, where I was staying in Fort Lee. He told me that he was coming to Fort Lee with an associate, Willie Moretti, who had just returned from Italy to help with business. We decided to meet in my room the next day to discuss the Riviera's prospects. All night long I listened to Lindbergh news updates on the radio in my room. They came every half-hour.

Longie arrived the next morning at eleven, and immediately brought up the kidnapping. He seemed even more upset with the horror of it all than Ben had been—two tough guys not lacking in humanity. He told me that Schwarzkopf had asked for his help in gaining any information on the matter—maybe someone in Longie's circles had some inside dope.

When we got down to business, I told them that Ben had his eye on another piece of property for a new club just down the road from the Riviera. "He said he would build the Taj Mahal of night-clubs," I said. Longie just snickered.

"Marden thinks just like Bugsy Siegel—nothing is good enough for him," said Moretti, full-faced with a receding hairline. "Can you imagine spending a shit-house full of money at a time like this, investing in a new and bigger nightclub? He has one big set of balls. He has a great club now with this Riviera, so what's his problem?"

Longie had something else on his mind. He said that Roosevelt was a cinch to be the next president, and had "his ducks lined up" to repeal the 18th Amendment. "The party might be over for us."

"It ain't gonna happen like that at all," Willie said. "So what if they repeal Prohibition? We're still gonna sell bootleg booze, and we're gonna do it under the table—without the fuckin' tax. How do ya like them apples?"

Longie looked like he smelled rotten eggs. "Do you really think that people will go out of their way to buy untaxed booze when they can get it easily and legally at a local joint?"

"Of course they will. Only a dumb shit would want to pay taxes on his booze. The only reason those guys are getting drunk in the first place is because they are so depressed about the government taxing them to death."

Longie and I burst out laughing at Willie's logic, but he was right-on-the-money with that one. No one would want to buy a taxed bottle of booze if there was another option.

"Okay, let's get down to business," Longie said, looking at Moretti. "We've got to grease some palms to keep our business on the Q.T. I brought some dough with me"—he turned to me— Gio, I want you to make some campaign donations in equal amounts to both the Republicans and the Democrats. Although the election is several months away, there's no time like the present to get things started. I want you to go to their political rallies and make nice with the bigwigs and you know, let them know you support them, and then spread the campaign money around. That way, they will remember us when we need a favor."

"Sounds good, Longie, I'll take care of that," I said, as I put five hundred dollar bills in my wallet.

"Holy shit! Did you see those moths come flyin' out of his wallet, Willie?"

"I ain't seen no moths."

"If you would give me a bigger piece of the action, the moths wouldn't have any room," I said to Longie with a broad smile.

"We'll see, we'll see," said Longie, patting me on the shoulder. "Right now we have to take care of business, and let's keep Marden out of this. He is doing enough for us already. Maybe if we can buy ourselves a few more politicians, it'll help this new place he wants to build sail on through."

"That's heartwarming," Moretti said acidly. "Give 'em a kiss for me, will ya?"

"Hard to figure what drives Ben," Longie, said. "He already has enough going on for ten men...Maybe he's never stopped thinking about the Fifty-Seventh Street jinx."

"Fuck's that?"

"Remember, he got the downtown Cotton Club started there, but that was short-lived. And there were a bunch of other places that started up in that spot, but they all went under. Remember back when Paul Whiteman opened at the Palais Royal?"

"I was still shagging golf balls back then," I said.

"Well I was there with a date," Longie said. "Whiteman, who was known as the King of Jazz, hired George Gershwin to write something for him… So, you know what he wrote?"

"No, what?"

Longie sat back and let the suspense build for a few seconds. "Rhapsody in Blue, that's what."

"Yeah, so how was it?" Willie said, sounding uninterested one way or the other.

"Not bad, Willie. You would have appreciated it."

Willie tried to figure out if Longie was sincere or just putting him on.

Longie turned to me. "So, Gio, we clear? I want you to orchestrate—get it?—the political payoffs. Give 'em your best 'Whiteman.'"

"Regular comedian, Longie," Willie said. "You oughta go onstage."

By the time 1932 rolled around, I was up to my eyeballs with trying to juggle all the things Longie had on my plate, and the real estate deal for Ben to acquire that parcel of land closer to the bridge. For the latter, I had met with the attorney for the listing agent, Michael's Realty, and carved out a deal. By this time, all that remained was a title search, because it was an all-cash transaction, so I thought. Our attorneys had given us the green light, so all that was left to do was show up at the closing with an amount yet to be determined because there were other unspecified considerations that I was not privy to.

About this time, everybody was asking Longie questions about the death of MGM executive Paul Bern, who happened to be Jean Harlow's husband. Although Bern's death from a gunshot wound to the head had been ruled a suicide, suspicions were running rampant because Hollywood's most famous platinum blonde had been Longie's squeeze before getting hitched. Longie didn't appreciate the chatter, and called none other than Eddie Mannix—by then an exec at MGM—to get the skinny on what had happened. Longie told me that Eddie reported Bern had left an apologetic suicide note for Harlow, but the press wasn't buying the note, and preferred sensationalizing the story by characterizing the death as cold-blooded murder. There was always some excitement or danger surrounding my job—maybe that's why I loved it so much.

On a more respectable note, Ben wanted me to handle the distribution of his traditional Thanksgiving baskets of food to local families down on their luck. The fire companies agreed to help with their pumper trucks, as did Izzie—on Longie's say-so—with a convoy of cars supplied by his "boys." I was clearly a young man with connections.

Speaking of which, that week I attended no less than five political gatherings, handing out cash to those in charge so they could purchase campaign signs and flyers. When I hired local kids to put up signs, a couple of them asked me why they were given both Republican and Democratic signs. "It's always good to hedge your bets." I explained, but I don't think they quite got it. As a show of appreciation for others on my "team," I sent several bottles of Hiram Walker's Canadian Club Whiskey to houses where campaign workers were holed up making phone calls to get the vote out.

Election Day, November 8, 1932 in Fort Lee and Coytesville was a big deal. Those who worked at the polls made a day's pay. Those working the phones at home were fueled—sometimes too much so—by bottles of Haig Scotch and Canadian Club that were my treat.

By the end of the day Roosevelt had won. The New Deal was at hand and the ladies working to get the vote out were plastered.

On the evening before Thanksgiving, everyone who had volunteered to help with the distribution of Ben's 500 food baskets arrived at the Riviera's kitchen door to pick up their deliveries. Coytesville resident John Barrymore—the Great Profile himself— drove one of the fire trucks; it was common to see the stars of the silver screen pitching in with such activities around town. Firemen painstakingly loaded every basket on the back of their trucks, as if they were stacking fresh eggs. The baskets were filled with fresh turkey, corn, rutabaga, potatoes, turnips, and freshly baked bread. There was even a small pumpkin pie atop each. The volunteers formed a chain to pass the baskets out of the Riviera's kitchen door to be loaded onto the Fort Lee and Coytesville fire trucks.

Ben's friends and associates—tough guys with broken noses—worked alongside little ladies of the Dutch Reformed Church's "Friendly Circle" to get the job done. I thought it was cute to watch the little ladies steal glances at Barrymore, as he engaged in manual labor. When the trucks were finally loaded, the workers were offered huge turkey sandwiches and cold bottles of beer supplied by Ben's buddy, the Dutchman. Of course, the church ladies declined the offer of beer, but gladly accepted nice tall glasses of fresh lemonade provided by the kitchen staff.

That night, the baskets were distributed throughout the boroughs of Coytesville, Fort Lee, and Palisade to any family not too proud to accept one. Although everyone at the Riviera was exhausted by the time the place was cleaned up, Ben would always find time to shake everyone's hand.

The year ended the same way, with hope for better days ahead. You could feel the enthusiasm in the air, as everyone waited for FDR's inauguration, for him to grasp the reins firmly and guide the country out of its dismal situation.

Chapter 13

For the Riviera's 1933 New Year's Eve celebration, maître d'hôtel Jack Arkin—elegant in a black tuxedo—had everything running full-tilt, and all of the 400 regular employees were dressed in their uniformed finery. The waiters wore red, double-breasted jackets with well-starched white shirts and ties, cream-colored pants, and white shoes. Female staff wore cream-colored dresses with red accents and white pumps. Arkin, newly hired by Ben, dispatched silent orders with snappy hand gestures and finger waves from his lectern at the entrance to the ballroom. Everyone was in a state of full alert, as a cool 650 customers piled in when the doors opened at 8 p.m.

A fleet of private, luxury limos and cars—Packards, Chryslers, and Cadillacs— formed an impressive caravan as they approached the entrance to drop off well-dressed charges. These cars had been sent over the bridge to New York to pick up high rollers, who were expected to drop a few farthings in the Riviera's secret casino during the evening. Champagne at the club flowed like water, as popping corks, clinking bottles, and the splash of the vintage beverage delighted everyone. The waiters, always professional, narrowly avoided bumping into each other as they sped between tables in an effort to leave no champagne flute empty. The girls passed out noisemakers, hats, and party favors to the throng of revelers. After couples were settled at their tables, those husbands and beaus who were lucky enough to have been invited to gamble, and chomping at the bit to try their luck at roulette or craps, were signaled by the cigarette girl to go to the cloak room and wait to be escorted downstairs to the Marine Room, where the action was beginning. The ladies left alone at their tables were joined by gentlemen "team members" who kept them company, while their men were occupied.

The show began exactly at 10 p.m., with an announcer intoning, "Ladies and gentlemen, Ben Marden welcomes you to the Riviera nightclub high atop the Palisades, just up the terrace from the magnificent George Washington Bridge, to ring in the New Year. To start the evening off on the right note, the Riviera Latin Band, direct from Cuba is onstage and ready to play for your dancing and listening pleasure."

Nancy and I had a ringside table right next to the dance floor, as the band opened with its theme song. Nancy was impressed with the attention I was getting from the waiters—"Is there anything you need, Mister Arigo?" was a phrase heard at our table throughout the night. Even Ben himself came over to our table, more than once, to ask if everything was okay. The band kept cooking, and the revelers lapped it up.

Unnoticed by just about everyone but me, Meyer Lansky and Benny Siegel arrived a little around eleven accompanied by a group that made up a full table of ten. They were ushered to a choice table off to the side of the bandstand as an army of waiters and captains surrounded them attentive to their every whim. Soon after, Charles Luciano, Joe Adonis, and Frank Costello arrived with their stunning ladies.

The infectious, Latin music was piped out to the parking lot, where freshly fallen snow twinkled along with the lights on the nearby bridge into early morning. Button men, the bodyguards and drivers of some of the club's most notorious guests, stood in the cold, waiting patiently and sipping coffee supplied by Marden. At the stroke of midnight, when Nancy and I were dancing to the uptempo Siboney, I deftly reached into my pocket and took out a small, neatly wrapped box with a delicate, white, ribbon tied round it. I handed it to Nancy.

"What's this?"

"It's for you…open it."

We stopped dancing and stood still in the middle of the dance floor with confetti raining down all around us. She held the box tightly in her hand, while looking into my eyes. Her gaze at that moment was different than I had ever seen before. For several seconds, she just stood there, looking up at me clutching the box and not saying a word.

Finally, I broke the silence with, "Well open it, already."

"I'm afraid to…Are you sure you want to do this?"

I was *damn sure*. "I wouldn't be giving it to you if I didn't want to spend the rest of my life with you."

She carefully opened the box and held it up for me to take the ring out. I removed the diamond from its deep blue-velvet nest, as she lifted the delicate third finger on her left hand so that I could—with trembling hands —slide the one-carat ring on it. By this time, other couples had stopped dancing and encircled us with their "ooohs" and "aaahs."

Nancy sighed, and her eyes misted. "We've come a long way since the Raritan Country Club, haven't we?"

I tugged her closer. "Does that mean 'yes?'"

She threw her arms around me, and gave me a squeeze worthy of Strangler Lewis. That was more than enough of an answer for me.

"If it weren't for you constantly telling me I was something special, sweetheart, I would never have made it this far," I said.

Nancy released me and stared into my eyes. "Someday you're going to make it big, just like your mother always said."

When we went back to our table, Ben was there, popping a bottle of champagne. He poured a round for everyone within earshot, held up his own flute, and said, "Here is to one of the nicest couples I know. Congratulations on your engagement. Mazel Tov!"

Nancy did not renew the lease on her Harlem apartment, and we set up housekeeping in a one-bedroom apartment on the second floor of a two-family house, close to trains and bus service in Hackensack, New Jersey. Several weeks later, to celebrate my engagement, Longie decided that he and I and some of the guys should go down to Union Hill and see Sam Cohen, manager of the Hudson Theater, a burlesque joint where we could go backstage and meet the ladies. He called it "the boys night out." We all piled into Longie's Cadillac with Izzie at the wheel and motored to Hudson County for the festivities. The booze flowed like water, as we hit joint after joint on the way, ending up at the Show Spot, next door to the theater. A ramp connected the two sites, so that acts could jump back and forth between numbers. Ben told me that

Fred Astaire had performed here years before. It must have been about 4 a.m. by the time they dropped me off at our new apartment. Nancy was furious with my appearance, as I tiptoed in.

You can't beat married life.

The rest of 1933 was a blur, as I plunged into the day-to-day business of running the Riviera. I was responsible for everything, from accompanying Ben on business trips to handling issues that Longie brought up—he was the type of guy who did not let anything slide, and was always on the lookout for problems that might disturb the smooth running of the Marine Room, so it was my job to keep vigil on the comings and goings of certain people he had fingered on his list of potential troublemakers.

My skin grew new layers of thickness, as I survived storm after storm of infighting between the club's silent partners. Fear of Prohibition ending was the source of the money worries that bugged the boys. Sure enough, late in the year, the 21st Amendment repealed Prohibition, and sent a collective shudder through those whose fortunes, or at least livelihoods, depended on the restrictions of the previous decade. Where would they find another means of easy revenue to dip their thirsty beaks into?

The new year opened with news that General Carlos Mendieta had become president of Cuba. Ben was excited to hear that the revolutionary junta had requested the resignation of his predecessor. He predicted that Lansky would love this turn of events. Ben anticipated new business ventures in Havana, where Lansky's Oriental Park Race Track already was a success.

In July, I was called to go to a meeting at the Arrowhead Inn in Saratoga Springs New York, where Lansky had conducted business ever since he'd boosted cars and ran whiskey for Arnold Rothstein. Rothstein came to recognize the maturing Lansky's intelligence and ability to get things done without leaving a bloody trail. The Arrowhead Inn was one of the first investments Lansky had the opportunity to get in on. Just like his teacher, he preferred to use brains, rather than brawn, to negotiate deals. Lansky always felt that if each party left the negotiating table feeling a little bit dissatisfied, then it was a good and fair deal.

The Saratoga Inn and the Piping Rock were both highly recognized "carpet joints" open only during racing season. Before Rothstein got knocked off in 1928, he was a fixture at the Inn, holding court there every season. His main interest was to satisfy his never-ending urge to gamble, provided that the odds were in his favor. Word was that he had most of the jockeys in his pocket; either that, or his knack for choosing winning horses was beyond uncanny.

Hotels such as the Grand Union, the Gideon Putnam, and the Excelsior Springs catered to tourists. The Arrowhead, on the other hand, was a place where those in the know would try their hand at craps and roulette. If you asked anyone, including the mayor of Saratoga Springs, Henry J. Schrade Jr., he would tell you that "no such thing is happening in my town." Although Lansky and his people always managed to run an operation in clear view of the public, nothing was ever regarded as illicit.

I asked the Arrowhead bartender a lot of questions, mainly why the place had been spared by the authorities. He told me that, since the Depression took hold, politicians and police had looked the other way, as the Arrowhead provided jobs for local people who needed work.

I realized that the same reasoning held true for the Riviera. In a sense, the guys running gambling operations were geniuses: They were doing the country a favor by opening their gaming operations in big-time nightclubs, where the action brought in big-money customers, who, in turn, demanded first-cabin service, thus forcing the clubs to hire lots of people who needed jobs. Gambling may have been illegal, but it certainly was beneficial to the public interest during the Great Depression, as it was coming to be known.

Of course, operating outside the law meant that the law couldn't be asked to intervene and resolve disputes; therefore, conflicts were resolved in a clandestine manner. When the outcome of a "settlement" did not meet with either side's approval, the shooting started.

I now had a fundamental understanding of how and why my business functioned as well as it did.

After checking into my room at the Arrowhead, I lay down on my bed to take a catnap before lunch. I had just closed my eyes, when the phone rang.

"How's it going, Gio?"

"Great Ben, I just got here."

"Listen, I just found out that the state assembly formed a committee to look into our gambling operation. I don't know all the details yet, but my source is going to keep me posted."

He hung up. I lay back on the bed and tried again to catch a nap, but this time a knock on the door had other plans for me.

"Mister Giorgio Arigo? I have a telegram for you."

When I opened the door, three guys pushed their way into my room. They weren't selling bibles.

"Who the fuck do you think you are, pal, coming up here and asking a lot of questions of our man at the bar?" said the big guy with the fedora hat pulled down over his forehead. The next second, I was flying across the bed and onto the floor.

"Who sent you up here?" said the short, balding guy. The third guy looked on with quiet menace—as if they needed a third guy.

I stood, caught my breath, and tried to chase the stammer from my voice. "I work at the Riviera in Coytesville, New Jersey."

"You mean you work for that sonofabitch Zwillman, don't you?"

Dumbfounded, I was searching my brain for a wise response, when Fedora incongruously broke out in a smile. "You were sent up here by Longie, weren't you?"

"You got that right," I said, shooting the works. "What the fuck is with you guys anyway?"

"Fucking Hoover is sending guys up here all the time," said number-three, who introduced himself as the manager of the card room. "Private dicks—not his Fed boys. They spy on our operation and harass the hell out of us. "We understand you have been sent up here to take a look at our operation."

"Well, if you understand that, why the rough stuff?" I patted one shoulder to be sure it was still in its socket.

"Think that was rough?" said Fedora. "Just testin'."

"We were told that Marden has the best roulette tables money can buy, and we would like to know how we can upgrade ours," said card room manager, almost apologetic by this point.

"Our stuff was sent out from Detroit," I said, breathing normal now. "Our roulette tables were manufactured by H. C. Evans, and the decorative wheels are made by B.C. Wills. Nothing beats the B.C. Wills wheel. Anyone who has seen one can tell by the lines that run around the cone and lower ball-track, and the small rounded ball-stops. You can even have them put the name Arrowhead Inn on the turret. Most joints do that, they add their own name." I was babbling, I realized. "We have three of them."

"So B.C. Wills in Detroit is where we can get them, huh?" the short guy asked.

"No, you can't buy them yourself; they are too traceable and the Wills Company is on J. Edgar's hot list. You order them through me, and I have Wills ship them to Cuba. Then we bring them back to the USA on a booze boat and get them up to you."

The three of them looked at each other and nodded approval. Card Room held out his hand. "It's a deal. We want three of them."

"We get paid up front." I was feeling my oats now.

"Not a problem. What's the damage?"

"Twenty-five hundred each, and that includes the tables. However, we gotta figure in that it costs another three grand apiece to get them here from Cuba—you know, a lot of prying eyes along the way that need to be paid off. The grand total is sixteen thousand, five hundred smackers—for three." Arithmetic had been my best subject in school. "Cash on the barrelhead."

Card Room had cooled his deal-making hand by his side.

"Fuck that," Fedora hooted. "We can buy them direct from the Wills Company!"

"You could try that, but the wheels won't do you much good if you are not around to use them," I said.

"Listen you prick, are you threatening me?"

"No, asshole, I am promising you." I balled up my fist to punch the guy's lights out, if I had to.

Fedora was about to lunge at me, when Card Room, obviously the one in charge, said, "Enough," then without missing a beat, "You got yourself a deal, Mister Arigo."

After a moment of silence, other than Fedora gnashing his teeth, Card Room asked me, "Did you have your lunch yet?"

"I was just about to."

"Let's go down to the taproom and settle up over lunch. My treat, he said excusing himself as he left for his office."

And settle up he did, handing me sixteen-five in a stack of bills, which filled all of my pockets. After lunch, I was escorted all over Saratoga Springs, ending up at one of the spas for a mineral bath which my new friends insisted I take. It was invigorating, but one time was enough for me.

I felt stupid when, before stepping into the bath, I put the money in a glass "Ball" jar that was left on top of one of the lockers, wrapped a towel around it, and set it right next to the tub I was in. (The attendant kept trying to remove the towel, and I kept grabbing it back—it was like Laurel and Hardy. Afterwards, I hurried back to my room, grabbed my unpacked suitcase, and made a beeline out of the hotel and into a waiting cab.

"Take me to the train station...and hurry."

"How about that news," the cabbie said, once he reached cruising speed.

"What news?"

"You know, about Dillinger."

"What happened?"

"They shot 'em to death. G-men caught him outside a place called the Biograph movie theater and blew his ass off."

"Chicago?"

"Guess so."

"I'll be damned." I thought about the difference between Dillinger and the guys I worked for. Dillinger seemed to dare the Feds to catch him, while guys like Lansky and Longie took great care to stay out of the limelight. Brooklyn guys were smarter.

The Riviera was in its heyday in 1934. Star-studded performances, show after show, ensured that audiences kept the house packed, almost pushing the walls out. When it came to booking acts, Marden was no slouch. He brought the best to the Riviera, including the incomparable Hildegarde, the incomparable cabaret chanteuse. Hildegarde Loretta Sell was born in Wisconsin, but became an international star due to her ability to sing equally well in several languages. Her magnificent gowns were the best that money could buy. It was said that she would spend at least $10,000 per year on her wardrobe. Her fee could be above $10,000 for a weekend's engagement, and she performed for kings and queens all over the world. Hildegarde gave an outstanding performance at the Ritz Hotel in London in 1934 at the Duke of Kent's wedding, and again for King George V's Jubilee, so it was no wonder that Ben had to have her at any cost. Nothing was too good for Ben Marden and his Riviera, and he routinely booked Hildegarde.

I recall being with Nancy, at Ben's invitation, at one of Hildegarde's Riviera shows in the spring of '34. That night, she sang *Lili Marlene* and *Darling, Je Vous Aime Beaucoup*, two of my all-time favorites. That evening we shared a table next to the dance floor with Hollywood stars Franchot Tone and Joan Crawford. The place was so packed that Tone, a classy guy, had insisted we join them for dinner. It never ceased to amaze that I constantly rubbed elbows with the rich and famous as part of my job.

But I was neither rich nor famous—I had just sold my car to put food on the table, since Prohibition had ended and the fast bucks had stopped coming in. If Tone sensed that I was scrabbling, he never let on. After inevitable talk about Bruno Hauptman being indicted for the kidnapping and murder of the Lindbergh baby, the conversation at our table turned to Crawford and Bette Davis having a quarrel over Joan dating Franchot. Joan made light of it, but Franchot was deeply concerned that he was portrayed as having "dumped" Miss Davis.

The romance between Nancy and myself was less hectic, and to hit a hopeful note, we told our Hollywood "hosts" of our plans. In May, we tied the knot. The reception was held at the Riviera, of course, and Longie served as best man. Nancy's maid of honor was dancer Dottie Lang, who was, by this time, featured in the chorus of George White's Scandals. She was a stunning brunette; Ben could not take his eyes off of her, and he wasn't alone.

Of course, my bride wasn't exactly a ham sandwich, either. The occasion was further burnished when none other than Joan Crawford and Franchot surprised us at the church, presenting us with a gold cigarette lighter suitable for a coffee table. It came with a tray inscribed, "To Nancy and Gio. May the world be your oyster: Fondly, Joan and Franchot."

People made friends fast in Hollywood...and at the Riviera.

Ben had bankrolled our wedding reception, and only the finest of everything was served. I was indeed making it big, but it was on Ben Marden's dime.

Chapter 14

On Christmas Eve of 1934, Nancy and I were Ben's guests at the 21 Club on W. 52nd Street in Manhattan. Ben wanted my "good ears" present for his meeting with noted architect Louis Allen Abramson. When we arrived at 21—late, due to snow-snarled traffic—Nancy and I were shocked to see Dottie Lang there, also as Ben's guest. I guess it hadn't taken Ben very long to get acquainted with her. We were introduced to Abramson, and ordered our supper of prime ribs and champagne.

It was unusual for Ben not to be in Havana or Miami at Christmas time, but this meeting in New York seemed to be of the utmost importance to him. For the past several months, he had been focused on Cuba; I knew that he and Lansky had been trying to gain a foothold with the political leaders down there, seeking their protection and endorsement. These relationships had to be firm for Lansky to build the world-class hotel and casino that Ben always talked about. It was essential that their investment be protected, and the accounting procedures handled with a great deal of creativity. But on this night in New York, Ben's top priority was to meet with his architect. After a round of pleasantries, I asked the two of them if they had the recent New York Times article about Japan renouncing participation in the Washington Naval Treaty, which limited the number of warships it could have in its navy. Neither had. As navy men, Ben and I shared that additional bond.

"Those Japs can't be trusted," Ben said. "But right now, it's the Germans that worry me; I hear rumors about this guy Hitler, who is harassing the Jews. He's the one we have to watch out for."

Dottie interrupted the "downer" talk. "Okay, boys," said the stunner, "it's the holiday, so let's not talk about this stuff, and get down to the vo-dee-oh-doh." After the meal, cigars came out, Nancy and Dottie chatted away nicely, and Ben got down to business.

"Lou, I have been following your work for some time now," he said to the architect, "and I am especially fascinated at the way you work Art Deco into your designs. I attend temple meetings on occasion in Brooklyn, and a friend of mine pointed out that you designed the East Midwood Jewish Center. It bowled me, knocked me out completely. Then I found out you did Longchamps on 59th Street, and also the one on East Broadway. I took a ride down to look at both and, Lou, I'm telling you right now that you are the guy to design the greatest nightclub the world has ever seen: my next nightclub."

Abramson didn't say anything, just listened.

"I want everyone who sees it to understand that it was built as a nightclub, and not converted from an office building," Ben continued. "I want it to be the Taj Mahal of night clubs, nothing short of getting the world to recognize it as the best of the best."

Ben described the Riviera, and then the new piece of land he'd just acquired, brimming with energy as he spoke of its "fantastic view." Thanks to the new bridge, he contended, people of substance would be moving out of the city to New Jersey. Entertainment was not exclusive to New York City. Ben wanted to build his club on the new tract—"the finest piece of property in the northern hemisphere."

Abramson smiled. "That covers a lot of ground."

"Rockefeller wanted the land—what does that tell you?"

"Not much. He wants everything."

"Well, he wanted this, and I beat him to it. You are not going to believe this, but we paid only a dollar for it, though we had to throw in some 'valuable considerations,' which I am not at liberty to discuss." He looked liked a cat that had just dined on a canary. "We've closed on the property, and the planning board in town has tentatively approved on the idea…Now it is up to you to come up with the plans so I can get final approval."

I could see by Lou's expression that he was excited at the prospect. He took out a pencil and notepad from his breast pocket, and jotted some notes. Nothing could hold Ben back at this point: He wanted a place that could seat 1,200 people, with a bar and lounge that could accommodate 200 more. He wanted the building to take up the entire width of the property at the edge of the cliff. He wanted it to reflect his taste in abstract art. He went on and on, sketching out his vision, his dreams. Then he quickly turned to me. "Are you taking all this in, Gio?"

"Got it, boss." I would let the architect take the notes.

Ben's description of what he envisioned seemed to come out of a preplanned symphony of ideas: Rotating bandstand, rotating dance floor, a roll-off roof, huge windows that would disappear into the floor. As he unfurled all aspects of his "Taj Mahal," he never strayed from the basic idea of using the George Washington Bridge and the lofty Palisades as accents for his grand-scale project.

"One thing Lou, I want you to design a plush, soundproof, very special, hidden room built into the roof that no one can detect it being there. It has to be at least 50' long by 35' wide and don't ask me what it is for. I don't even want you to show that room on the plans if you know what I mean."

Abramson didn't even flinch throughout Ben's dictum, but when it concluded, he raised his eyes above his reading glasses. "Do you know who Arshile Gorky is?"

Ben smiled and said, "Now you know what I am looking for, don't you?"

"Indeed, I do. In fact, I happen to know him; I met him about nine years ago when I was redesigning the lobby of the Hotel Belleclaire up on West 77th Street."

"I have been such a fan of his, Lou; I can't tell you how much I enjoy his work. I'm especially impressed with his 'Biomorphic Abstractions.' I think he is following the works of Miro, don't you?"

I scratched my ear. Biomorphic Abstractions?

"Maybe so," Abramson said. "But I know for a fact that Cezanne's works are Arshile's first love, because he told me so."

The ladies and I just looked at each other, as if we'd be listening to a conversation in a foreign language.

"You know Arshile Gorky is not his real name," Abramson said. "His real name is Vosdanik Adoian. He came to this country after his mother died, as a sixteen-year-old refugee from Turkish Armenia."

Abramson explained that, while he was working on the Belleclaire, Arshile showed up one day and told him that world-renowned Russian writer Maxim Gorky had lived in the building in 1910. Thrilled that the Russians had saved the Armenians from the Turks, Arshile had taken the name Gorky as a kind of testimonial, and told everyone that he was Maxim's nephew. "Some balls, huh?"

Ben and I all but snorted, and even the girls laughed.

"Who gives a damn what he decided to call himself," said Ben. "The guy is a genius, and I want to put some of his works in my new club. It is about time that we introduced our customers to the finer things in life, don't you all agree?"

"What is your time frame?" Abramson asked.

Ben glanced at me and sat back. "I haven't figured that out yet. Give me some time to talk with my associates. In the meantime, please get started drawing me up some sketches of your ideas."

He turned to me. "Gio, you are going to coordinate the construction of this place?"

I almost choked on the ice cube I was sucking. "Ben, I don't know a damn thing about architecture."

"You didn't know a damn thing about real estate, either, until you landed the property we're going to build on."

He turned back to Abramson. "Louis, I'd like you to report to Gio on this project."

"Sounds fine to me," the architect said. "I can tell that Gio is the kind of guy who underestimates himself, and I like that. People like that have a lot more in the tank than they want you to know about." He turned to me with, "I'll have a written proposal for you in a week."

That's how Ben conducted business—he knew what he wanted, and who he wanted to get it done for him. Afterward, he said to me, "I really like that guy, plus he comes highly recommended from my pals at the temple. Let me tell you something, Gio, this club will set the standard for all nightclubs that follow—mark my words. No more second-floor jazz like the Cotton Club. This new place is going to be 'all club,' from the ground up; no more candy stores on the grade level and the nightclubs upstairs. Prohibition is over, and now we will bring our good taste center stage. We are going to have more fun and make more money than we ever dreamed of."

It was impossible not to get caught up in Ben's enthusiasm. His demonstrated confidence in me was a godsend, as, with Prohibition no more, I was no longer a hotshot pushing illegal whiskey. I'd become a mere foot soldier in Longie's and Ben's operations and, to some extent, they'd been propping me up financially. Ben's promising, if high-risk, project seemed like my ticket back to the "elite" in their worlds. My bank account needed that, and so did my ego.

Still, this was unfamiliar territory. What did I know about architecture and construction? I learned a long time ago, however, that it is okay if you don't know the answer to something as long as you know where to find the answer. I was willing to do the spadework to find answers.

When we left 21, Nancy insisted that we see the Christmas tree at Rockefeller Center. Ever since she'd read a newspaper article about workmen putting up the tree in 1931, she would insist that we visit it every Christmas. We had joined tens of thousands of families in that tradition.

The streets of New York have never recognized clocks. At 2 a.m. on a Sunday, crowds of people bathed in the glow of the Christmas lights, many having attended Midnight Mass at nearby St. Patrick's. The night felt magical to me. Nancy became very quiet, as we stood there and gazed at the tree.

"A penny for your thoughts, Nan."

She blinked away her reverie. "Oh, nothing much, I was just thinking, are you sure you really want to get involved with these people, Gio?"

Her question puzzled me. "What do you mean, Nancy? These people? You know how good Ben and Longie have been for me. For us, when you get down to it."

Creases of doubt at her eyes and on the bridge of her nose made her look ten years older. "I worry that it all might catch up with us. There are some bad hombres that you have to do business with when you work for Longie and Ben Marden—you don't have to tell me. Just because I don't see the other side of the business doesn't mean it doesn't exist."

I place my hands on her shoulders, and squared her up with me. "Listen to me, Nancy. I don't have to deal with the 'other guys.' That's Ben's department. Or Longie's."

"I'm not so sure of that, Gio. The 'other guys' put up the money for all these ventures you get yourself into."

"You don't believe me—?"

"—Of course I believe you, but—",

"—The way I see it, Nancy, is that the Jews run things, and the Italians provide the muscle to make sure they run smoothly. Me, though I am half-Jew and half-Italian, I seem to fit in better with the Jews, so there is nothing to worry about." When I winked at her, her smile was a reflex that lasted less than a second.

"The day is going to come, Gio, when you will be sorry that you ever got involved with these people. Ben seems to be a very nice man, but he rubs elbows with some big-time hoods, and if you play in the mud, you are bound to get dirty. That's all I'm going to say about it for now."

"Good, because I don't think I can support you by being a waiter."

With that, she lightened up. "If you really hustled, you could make enough in tips."

On Christmas morning, it was about noon when Nancy and I finally got out of bed. Our radio was tuned into WJZ, and we were listening to Fred Waring and his Pennsylvanians doing a set of Christmas favorites. The coffee was on and, because Nancy was not working at the time, she had created probably the greatest Christmas present I ever received. She handed me a sealed envelope with my name on it. When I opened it, it contained 10 slips of paper. On each was a note promising a gift in kind. The first slip said, "This certificate is good for one sexual favor of your choice anytime you request it." The next one said, "Good for one trip to the store to get ice cream for you." The next, "Good for one back rub," then,

"Good for bringing you breakfast in bed every Sunday for the month of February." Her list went on and on; Nancy's creativity—and sweetness—really made our Christmas a good one.

When it was my turn, I reached into the pocket of my flannel bathrobe, took out small giftwrapped box, and said softly, "Merry Christmas."

"Come on, Gio, you know we don't have the money to buy fancy gifts."

"Who said this is fancy?"

She opened the box and found a cameo pin mounted in a gold frame.

"Where did you get the money to buy this?"

Reflexively, I covered my wrist, naked without my gold watch on it, the watch I had won at the caddie tournament years before, the watch I had sold to buy the cameo pin. I caught myself in time, and yanked the hand away.

"Hustled tips."

When the Waring band finished its final set broadcast on the radio, the news came on. The biggest story of the day was that the FBI had found a suspect in the Lindbergh baby kidnapping case. His name was Bruno Richard Hauptmann, a German immigrant. Nancy labeled the Germans, especially Hitler, "nut cases."

"That guy is really going to be trouble," she said. "And I hear his puppet—that pipsqueak Mussolini—is making the Italian school-teachers wear military uniforms. What a world."

"Let's get back to *our* world. What did you think about our meeting with Marden and Abramson last night?"

She replied, "I think it is a great opportunity for you, but I am a little scared that you are getting yourself in too deep. I don't care what you say, nobody has the money and connections that Ben does who is not linked up to something that smells rotten."

"Come on, Nancy, Ben is a businessman, and he's involved with other big investors who invest in nightclubs, that's all."

"Look," she said, "don't tell me for one second that Longie and his boys are lilies of the valley. I've been around the block a few times with people like them, when I was a dancer, and you would have to be as dumb as a one-day-old monkey to think that they're legit."

"Well, *I'm* legit—that's all I know."

"Really? So the bootlegging was fully approved by Uncle Sam?"

I drew closer, my eyes matching the undercurrent of anger and frustration I saw in hers. "That's over with, Nancy. This is all above-board. I am not stealing anything; I work hard for my money, and this is only the beginning, Ben tells me."

She inclined her head downward, but I tilted her chin so that she was looking at me again. "Hey," I said with a small smile. "You knew you weren't marrying an Ivy Leaguer."

Her eyes misted. "I worry, that's all." She reached her arms around me, and tucked her head between my neck and shoulder.

It was dark before evening, and we walked along snow-covered Summit Avenue to look at the houses festooned with Christmas lights. It was a wonder that, on Christmas, you did not sense that the country was in the midst of an unprecedented, economic depression. We came upon a boy who looked about 10, as he pre-pared to sled down the slope of his front yard.

I shouted to the kid, "Let me see you do a belly whop."

"Okay," he said, "watch this." He backed up onto the side lawn, ran as fast as he could, and leaped onto his sled, propelling it down the slope with impressive speed.

"Hey, you're good at that," I said. He picked up his sled, and walked over to us.

"Nice sled you got there," I said.

"Just got it for Christmas." I could not help but notice that the sled was not new at all. It had a fresh coat of red paint on the boards, but one of the runners was slightly bent, indicating to me that it was a hand-me-down.

The lad was all smiles, as he handed me the rope and said, "Want to try it?"

I shook my head. "Thanks, but I'll leave the sledding to an expert. You have yourself a merry Christmas."

"Sweet kid," Nancy said, as we continued along Summit. "Why'd you pass on the sleigh ride? I would have loved to have tried that thing, lying on top of you."

"Wanna get us arrested?"

A floating cloud compromised the half-moon, but the decorative lights all around guided our path. I had my girl at my side, and I felt expansive.

"You know, Nancy, this morning I got to thinking that I should not give up on my idea of becoming a writer. Maybe I could get a job at a newspaper, or even write short stories... Maybe I'm just dreaming, but you don't know until you test yourself, right?"

She took my hand. "You have so much potential, Gio, and that's what Ben and the others see in you. You have always been their voice of reason; they know that they can trust you. Now. I worry that, one day, they might get a bug in their ass that tells them that they can't trust you anymore."

"What bug is that?" I said, trying to make light of the matter.

"It's a bug you don't want to bite you."

It seemed liked we walked for over an hour before we found ourselves in a newspaper shop, which was about to close. We ordered hot chocolates to sip on our walk back home. By the time we made it back to our rental, our feet were just about frozen off. How different this night was from the previous night, when we had dined at 21. Reality tends to set in, when your feet are cold. But at home, the feet thawed, and visions of sugar plums danced through our heads after we finished off a bottle of cognac, that Izzie had sent up to us. Nancy made each of us two cocktails with fresh lemon juice added. So this is family, I thought: Nancy and me, happy as two bugs in a rug.

Different bugs than the one she feared might bite my bosses someday.

Chapter 15

There was no rest for the weary. Ben called me from Havana soon after New Year's in 1935 to tell me he had some more ideas that he wanted me to pass on to the architect. Foremost, he wanted a serpentine bar that would accommodate a whopping 65 people, and a lounge area that could handle about 140 more with couches and cocktail tables.

When I called Abramson, he was a bit put off by how quickly Ben wanted to make things happen. He was designing a new wing on Bellevue Hospital, and the Riviera job would have to wait a few weeks, he said.

This is why Ben had me on the job—to deal with situations such as this, to bring a "voice of reason" (in Nancy's words) to the task.

At his invitation, I arrived at Abramson's 10th-floor studio very early the following morning. The architect had not arrived yet, so I waited outside the door, a touch uncomfortable lurking in the hallway as the secretaries arrived for work in other offices. As they got off the elevator, they could not miss me. Leaning against the wall and reading the morning Herald. I would smile and tip my hat as they passed. After about 45 minutes, Abramson materialized with his own morning paper under his arm, and a cup of coffee in his mitt. Without saying a word, he walked right past me, even though I said, "Good Morning, Lou." When he unlocked the door and pushed it open, he turned to me, and said, "Well, are you coming in or not?"

An inauspicious start, but I didn't rattle—especially when big money was at stake.

After he got his office up and running, he motioned for me to sit down at his desk. "Let's have it, Gio?"

"You know how it is, Lou. I'm the middleman. I do their bidding—to some extent, anyway."

"What do you know about building?" He was neither imperious nor irritated.

"Only that the roof better not collapse, and both sides are in it to make money."

He smiled and laughed under his breath. "Very good. Maybe you and I can get this thing built, at that. Provided they leave us alone long enough to do it right."

I knew then that Louis Alan Abramson did not get where he was by being stupid. He knew his business, and he knew something about people, too. I was anxious to learn everything I could from him.

"What's with this bar thing you're talking about?" he said.

I interlaced my fingers. "Ben explained it this way: a bar that winds around the lounge like a snake."

"A snake, huh?"

"That's what he said."

"Mister Marden is getting ahead of himself. First, we put up the building. Then we bring in the snakes."

"Maybe not, Lou. Ben is talking about making the walls of the room rounded, too, so that everything flows together."

"Did he tell you what he thinks the shape of the building should be?"

"Rounded on the river side, so that all windows in the ballroom have spectacular views of the Hudson and the New York skyline."

He looked beyond me, as if spying a vision. "Like the bridge of an ocean liner waiting to be pushed off the cliff and into the Hudson." I didn't know whether he was joking or serious. His eyes returned to mine.

"You know what, Gio, I like that. Ben is a true visionary, but I don't want to start working on a sunken ship. How 'bout you go over to Fort Lee and have a talk with the mayor, and make sure this project is kosher with him. If he says it's okay to launch this thing"—he was having a ball with the maritime theme—"then I can recommend several excavators who worked on the bridge. I'll give you their names in a minute. They have the equipment and know-how to blast the whole cliff apart. Used to be that, to excavate the bluestone on the Palisades, you had to build raging fires for days on the rock to be broken up and, when it was hot enough, dump gallons of cold water on the stone. You should have heard those boulders pop... Today, it's a bit more sophisticated.

"I'll figure how much rock needs to be removed. Meanwhile, you get quotes on how much they would charge, per ton, to blast and remove it."

And that was our game plan, clean and uncomplicated. The following day, when I called the town of Fort Lee, I learned that Mayor Hoebel had completed his last term in office, but was still my best bet because he was making the big decisions until the new man got the lay of the land—or the cliffs, as it were. I called Havana to tell Ben about my meeting with Abramson, and also to see how he felt about me contacting Hoebel, whom he knew well. He took my call in a damn fine mood.

"Guess who I ran into down here?"

"No idea," I said.

"Dottie Lang."

I smiled to myself. "Not hard to take, Ben."

"I ran into her at the Hotel Nacional. She's down here on a modeling assignment, and she has the whole place buzzing."

"Including you, sounds like."

"Watch it, buster," he kidded. "You could be talking about my future wife—you never know. I just bought her a diamond wristwatch."

"Not bad."

"Did you tell Lou about the serpentine bar?"

"I did. We came up with the idea of having the building look like the bridge on a cruise ship, portholes and all." I waited to be shot down.

"You know what that might not be such a bad idea. Did you think of that?"

"He brought up the idea, and I expanded it."

"Thinking of going into architecture, kid?"

"Only if the pay is better."

"That's not going to happen, once we get this thing underway. You stick with me, kid."

"I plan to."

"When will his plans be finished?"

"Don't know"—I didn't mention Abramson's Bellevue Hospital gig—but Lou has asked me to arrange a meeting with the mayor to get the pulse of the town…Fort Lee…Wanted to bounce that off you first."

"I took care of that myself six months ago, Gio. Everybody in town is onboard; all we have to do is file for permits when the plans are completed. What I'm concerned about is those fuckin' Rockefellers from across the river. If they find out that we bought that little piece, they will be all over us like a cold chill. He could contact the New Jersey Highway Department and make them condemn the property immediately. That would kill the project. My contact in the highway department says Rockefeller has no idea our piece of land even exists, so, for now, I've got to rely on him. But that's why time is of the essence, understand?"

"Got it. He'd really bust it up that way if he knew?"

"Absolutely. In thirty-three, this guy Bill Welch proposed a plan to build a parkway along the Palisades from the George Washington Bridge all the way up to the Bear Mountain Bridge in upstate New York. So far, those fuckin' Rockefellers have given them three hundred acres of the land they already bought around there. I'm scared stiff that they could make it three hundred and two with our little piece. Roosevelt's Civil Works Administration would back it in a heartbeat—they love highways and bridges."

"Here's the way this thing works, Gio. The Palisades Interstate Park Commission probably will be forced to pay Rockefeller fair market value on the land he's turned over to them. Once we build on the new property, if they want to take that, too, they would have to pay us every dime that it cost us to build. There's no way they're gonna do that—too much dough for a public agency to spend on a little piece of land. Plus, our attorneys would give them fits. But the key is that we've got to hold on to it, and build the damn thing before anyone's the wiser."

Ben Marden, wheeler-dealer. His knowledge extended well beyond showgirls.

"So it's like you have a built-in insurance policy, Ben."

"It's called hedging your bets, son. But, in a way, you're our insurance, Gio. We trust you and, as a demonstration of that trust, we will be adding a bonus of fifteen hundred dollars to your next paycheck. With that, maybe you and Nancy can put a down payment on a house, and fire your landlord."

That was wonderful timing for me. I searched for words, and managed only, "Thank you, Ben, I really appreciate it."

"No need to thank me...you earned it."

I felt richer and, more importantly, proud. "Ben, one question. What are we going to do with the old Riviera, after we build the new one?"

"That's Richard's problem, my boy—we only lease it from him... Funny you should ask. The State has already made Jean an offer—a damn good offer, I should add. Of course, he has to pay us to move our business out of there. The attorney says we should hold out for more money, so that is just what I am doing. All is fair in love and business, Gio.

"And the action is not only at the Palisades. I might have a deal on the Palais Royal. Lou Walters and I have been talking about making a little swap: He gets the Palais Royal, and Meyer and Jake Lansky get the Colonial Inn in Hallandale, Florida. Lou Walters says he wants to change the Palais all around, and call it the Latin Quarter or some name like that. He thinks the Mambo craze will sweep the country.

"How would you like it if I send you and Nancy down to the Colonial for a vacation? Beats a sharp stick in the eye, doesn't it, Gio? And who knows, someday you might be running the place."

As Ben kept dropping all this good fortune on me, I was thinking about Nancy recently sounding the alarm on working with him. "Ben, I could use some time in the sun."

"Good, consider yourself booked. Now, one more thing. I don't know if he ever mentioned this to you, but Longie would like to run a casino upstairs in the new place. I can't think of anyone better than him and Moretti for that. What do you think?"

"A hundred percent for that, Ben."

"Good, because I have no other choice in the matter." His gritty laugh told me Longie had *given* him no other choice.

It had been one zinger of a phone call. My stock had just risen sharply. At a time when the average workingman in America was making between $25 and $50 per week, I was in line for a $1,500 bonus. Wait until Nancy heard that.

When she did, she prepared a more extravagant dinner than any offered by the most expensive restaurants in New York, Paris, or anywhere else. The girl was a looker, and she could cook, too. What a bargain.

A month later, I went to New York on a snowy day to pick up my bonus at the Palais Royal and, instead of a check, I was handed a small, zippered, leather, bank envelope with the words "Hotel Nacional" embossed in gold letters. When I opened it, I found the $1,500 in small bills.

I ran down to the subway, the leather envelope tucked tightly under my arm, and quickly caught the 'A' train up to 168th Street, where I jumped on the 86 bus to New Jersey. I got off at the Bridge Plaza, on the Jersey side, and caught the 82 bus back to Hackensack. All the way home, I considered what to do with my bonanza. Should I buy a car? Lord knows I sure needed one, since my nine-year-old Buick, the car that had served me well since 1926, was sorely in need of a valve job and kingpins. With my new responsibilities, I really needed to be available at all times for all the crazy stuff Ben was having me do, and I could sure use my own wheels again.

In an absolute coincidence, as I got off the bus in Hackensack, there was Walter Stillman, of Stillman and Hoag Buick in Englewood, offering bus riders a demonstration ride in one of his new automobiles. I could not believe that this kid, the son of the owner, would be out in this weather to pitch test rides. He told me later that he had taken his campaign door-to-door just to keep his dad's business afloat.

Maybe this was an omen for me to buy a Buick. The price: $1,610. I could swing that, now that I was in Fat City.

"Want to take a spin?" Walter asked me.

I played it coy. "Not really."

"Come on, the ride is free, and I will drive you home. What's the point of walking in the snow when you don't have to?"

I got behind the wheel of a Buick "straight eight," and drove the few blocks to my home on Summit. I liked the ride, and the fact that it had a great heater made it all the more appealing.

"You take trade-ins, Walt?"

"Absolutely."

I made sure not to leave my treasured envelope behind. As soon as I walked into the house, Nancy, who never missed a trick, asked, "Where did you get that?"

"I have to call Longie right away; then I'll explain everything."

I was excited to tell Longie all about my action, but as soon as he answered my call he preempted me.

"I haven't told Ben Marden this, but from now on, you'll be working with him exclusively."

It took my breath away. It was as if a bomb had gone off.

"Too much knowledge is not a good thing," Longie continued. "I am going to make my move to get the card room at the new Riviera, but frankly, you're not the kind of guy who should be involved at that end of the business. You're a nice guy, Gio, and the people I am working with are a little rough around the edges…Hey, that's no surprise to you, some of the jamokes I have to deal with."

"I know what you mean, Longie," I mumbled.

"Gio, you did some great work for me, and we had some good times together. And this doesn't mean we're strangers, or even that we might not work together again."

Just like that, I had slipped out of gangsterdom, probably forever. It was a sad moment for me, though I knew immediately that Nancy was going to be elated to hear this news.

First, she had to give me the latest news on the Hauptman trial that had begun in Flemington, New Jersey. The whole country was glued to the radio for updates on the trial, and we were no exception. Nancy felt that the prosecutor had been out of line in badgering the defendant in an effort to gain a confession out of him on the witness stand. "You can't stop the tide," I said to her—the whole country had made up its mind before the trial that Hauptman was guilty and should be executed.

I put the leather, bank envelope on the kitchen table and looked at her. After opening the zipper, her eyes grew large, and she put her hand over her mouth.

"How much is in there?"

"Fifteen hundred smackers."

She dumped out the neatly banded bills onto the kitchen table. As was the envelope itself, each band was labeled "Hotel Nacional, Habana Cuba."

"Oh, my God," she said. With that, she dropped everything and rushed toward me, almost knocking over a pitcher of tomato juice, spilling a little in the process. Cat-quick, I shepherded the bills to safety.

"Watch what you're doing!" I yelled, but undiscouraged, she released a fusillade of hugs and kisses on me. Tomato juice kisses come fast and furious.

"See, it's about time you're making it big," she said, licking tomato juice off of her fingers. I might have reminded her that, not long ago, she seemed less optimistic about my—our—future, but I kept my mouth shut.

Later, as I was reading the Palisadian newspaper in bed, I told Nancy about the ride home in the Buick. "Nice car," I said.

She read my mind. "Let's think about it."

The following morning, I awoke to her staring at me. "What?" I asked.

"Let's go right down to that dealer and buy the best car we can get."

Days later, when I was brushing snow off of our new Buick, Nancy called me in to take a telephone call from Ben. I stomped my snow-covered galoshes on the inside mat, and grabbed the receiver in the hallway.

"Can you make lunch at the Villa Rosa in Coytesville?" he asked, a note of urgency in his voice.

"Myrtle Avenue, right up from the Riviera, right? Yeah, sure, Ben."

"Meet me there at noon. The plans have been completed; I got a set from the architect."

When I arrived at the Villa Rosa, I saw Ben walking up Myrtle Avenue, clutching a rolled-up newspaper. I waited for him to reach me. It didn't take long.

"We might have a problem—a big one."

"What's up, boss?"

"Remember that committee I was telling you about a while back, you know, the so-called Honorable House of Assembly of the State of New Jersey?"

"Not so honorable?"

"Well, I have been told that they have concluded, after interviewing a lot of people that we are running a full-blown gambling casino. They call us a "roadhouse of distinction" in their report. In addition, some bastard they interviewed said we were making up our own blackjack rules in favor of the house. Here, read this."

He thrust his copy of the *Herald Tribune* toward me and, when I unfurled it, I saw the article encircled by thick, black ink. It read, in part:

> *The most plush and platinum of New York's sin palaces isn't, as a matter of fact, in Manhattan, but across the Washington Bridge on the New Jersey Palisades. But the real feature of the establishment is the game room downstairs. Only Bradley's Palm Beach Club is more formally luxurious and, while we had no way of estimating the stakes the evening we were present, they were said to be very high.*

I looked up at him. "So, what's this mean, Ben?...Trouble?"

"Maybe."

Chapter 16

Since the day Ben handed me the set of plans in the spring of 1935, my workload only increased in volume. To our delight, the state assembly investigation went nowhere (thanks to perhaps a payoff or two?), and it was business as usual in the Marine Room. I didn't ask any questions; I just put in sixty- and seventy-hour work weeks, claiming most weekends. Nancy was proud of me, and pleased with our improved lifestyle, but our time together during this period was limited. I was always dealing with masons, carpenters, plasterers, plumbers, and electricians; not to mention numerous architectural changes in the plans, to satisfy Ben's latest brainstorm. He did not, however, interfere with my calling the shots when it came to construction; his focus was the design.

Overseas, Hitler was causing increased havoc within the civilized countries of the world. He had defiantly violated the Treaty of Versailles by authorizing the founding of the Reich Luftwaffe, the aerial warfare branch of the German Wehrmacht, and soon afterward, approved the manufacture of a dozen U-boats. He was a madman, but a smart cookie. He had ordered Germany's commercial airliners to build aircraft—in secret—to military specifications, so when the time was right, it was a simple matter to have them converted to bombers. Although Ben and his Jewish friends were alarmed by the situation, there were many German sympathizers in Bergen County who belonged to social organizations that honored the Deutschland. Indirectly, many Jews felt satisfaction when Bruno Richard Hauptman was electrocuted for the kidnapping of the Lindbergh baby on April 3, 1936.

My life was consumed by the jobsite beginning each day at 6 a.m. The superintendent on would review the work scheduled for the day. The oilers would show up in suits and ties, and change into coveralls before starting the compressors that ran the clattering jackhammers. Not one day's work began without the customary "boilermaker," which consisted of a shot of whiskey and a glass of beer—the men regarded it as an essential part of the project. The Italian masons, most of them living in Fort Lee, kept to themselves, puffing their De Nobili cigars while arguing that it was a far better idea to build a roaring fire upon the stone to be removed, and then douse the rock with cold water so it would break up, than to use dynamite and weaken the surrounding stone strata, especially around the edge of the cliff where the foundation was to be placed. These Italian craftsmen worked slowly and steadily, taking great pride in what they accomplished for the day.

Ben sometimes would visit the site and, on this particular day in September, he came into town to meet his new singer, Ruth Denning, who was appearing in the Riviera's last show before the club would close for the annual migration to Florida and Cuba. Ben had spotted the 21-year-old beauty in an episode of Radio Rascals, in which she performed her hit, Don't Keep Me in the Dark. Ruth was about to be recognized by her college sorority as the member who had accomplished the most since graduation. Ben saw this as a good publicity hook, and came to town to pump it for all it was worth.

The revolving stage and bandstand, the panoramic windows that lowered into the floor, the 60-foot-diameter roof that retracted on warm summer nights…All were being painstakingly installed by workers who had never seen the likes of such a structure. One day, with work nearing completion, the "finishers" arrived. A Cadillac pulled up and disgorged four, well-dressed men, who were quickly joined by a crew of six, tough-looking ironworkers. The super was ordered to dismiss his workers for the day. When everyone had left, replacement equipment operators fired up the cranes and began hoisting into position additional truckloads of steel that had arrived on the site under cover of darkness.

I stood in awe, as column after column was bolted into place in a remote area on the northeast side of the roof, nowhere near the roll-off portion of the structure. The beams formed a grid for a separate 70-by-50-foot, rooftop room next to steel support columns designated to hold a huge sign. In eight hours, the steel work was finished, and the entire new, secret addition was cloaked with metal sheathing, making it look like part of the roof, and the base for the sign. The workers received envelopes of cash, and departed quietly.

Now that was efficiency. And it bore Longie's fingerprints. Guess, in a way, I still worked for him.

Dining manager Jack Bruno, a favorite of Ben's, was working overtime to design the seating layout for the dining room in the new club. Bruno had performed similar chores at both the Colonial Inn and the Palais Royal. I was told to give him carte blanche, including access to architect Abramson, and the team of highly skilled carpenters, who were constructing the ramps that would encircle the room for ease of food distribution. This was a finely tuned operation, and all I had to do much of the time was stay out of the way.

Meanwhile, every day through the new construction, the old Riviera was packing them in with great shows, featuring stars such as actress-dancer Carmen Miranda, comics Joe E. Lewis and Myron Cohen, and bandleader Ted Lewis.

The week before Thanksgiving, Ben was in town and all excited about preparing his traditional 500 food baskets for the needy in shall we say "the old Riviera?" As usual, his volunteers were up and ready in a party-like atmosphere in the Riviera's kitchen. Baskets were loaded into the fire trucks, cabs, and private cars, as soon as the food preparation was finished. After every one of the volunteers had left, and the paid help had cleaned the kitchen, Ben departed for New York and, exhausted, I drove my Buick back to Hackensack, where Nancy was planning to have a few friends over for a pre-Thanksgiving cocktail party. For me, it was lousy timing, and she chewed me out for being a rotten host. Well-deserved, I have to admit. I fell asleep in the living room, which was just as well from Nancy's point of view, though I suspected she'd get over it.

At about 5 a.m., I was awakened by the loud, insistent shrill of the telephone. It was Police Chief McDermott telling me to come right down to Fort Lee because the old Riviera was on fire. He said that the fire had started sometime in the middle of the night. My first thought was that the new building was not finished yet, and we needed several more months to complete it. I was sick thinking about it, especially in my exhausted condition from all the days and weeks of working two shifts on the jobsite. I quickly threw on some clothes, and told a groggy Nancy what had happened. Moments later, the Buick was racing down Route 4. By the time I passed Grand Avenue in Englewood, I could see the predawn sky to the east lit up by the flames. My God, what had happened?

When I arrived at the Riviera, Hudson Terrace was blocked with fire trucks from Coytesville, Fort Lee, Cliffside, and Englewood. I parked on Myrtle Avenue and ran down toward the fire. Fire hoses were everywhere, but no amount of water could quell the raging fire that was shooting flames 50 feet in the air. Before hundreds of onlookers, dozens of firemen fought to beat down the flames. Through the crowd, I saw Ben rushing forward in consternation. Frank Schmidt, the Coytesville fire chief, recognized him.

"What's happened, Frank?"

"I don't know, Mister Marden, I think the fire started in the cellar and made its way up through the balloon-type structure."

"What do you mean 'balloon-type' structure?"

"That just means that there are no fire separations between floors. This place is just an old, wood-frame building; I think it was built about 1904, if I'm not mistaken."

I had drawn near and was following their conversation, when a deafening blast shot through the building, knocking down walls and caving in the roof. The refrigeration unit exploded, and the smell of ammonia was everywhere. We quickly took our handkerchiefs and covered our faces with handkerchiefs or whatever was handy. Just then, I saw a fireman being carried out, away from the flames.

"Who's that?" asked Ben.

"That's one of my men, John Tierney," said Frank, as he ran toward the downed fireman.

"Gio, this is one big fucking mess," said Ben. "If anybody asks questions, don't answer anything until you clear it with me, understand?"

We stared into the hellish, orange glow. "I can't believe this," Ben said, needing to talk. "When we closed this place for the winter two weeks ago, everything was fine, and yesterday when we opened it to get out the food baskets, everything looked all right. How the hell could this happen?"

By this time, newsmen from around the entire New York area were on the scene.

"Are you Ben Marden?" asked a reporter from the Brooklyn Daily Eagle.

"Yes, I am."

"How do you think the fire started?"

Before Ben could answer, a hail of burning cinders showered the crowd of onlookers, forcing everyone to scatter in all directions. By the time, the reporters around Ben had regrouped, the questions were coming like punches.

"When did the fire start?"

"Was anyone hurt?"

"When was the last time the place was inspected?"

"What's your insurance coverage?"

"Was anyone looking to settle a score with you?"

Ben was overwhelmed. "Excuse me, gentlemen. I have to find out what happened myself."

He took my arm and led me over to a wooded area away from the crowd.

"Most everything we use, we got from Jean Richard in our lease, so it's possible our loss is minimal at best. I don't know what kind of insurance Richard had, but that's his business. The main thing is that nobody gets hurt." He gazed back at the destruction. "Too bad it had to end like this."

We walked another few paces into the woods. "Richard should get either his condemnation money, or he sells to the Rockefeller group," Ben said, his voice lacking its normal inflection. "Our new building should be finished in six months. We have to look to the future, Gio."

Come the morning, the fire was still burning; smoke and ammonia fumes permeated the air. People sought souvenirs among the steaming ashes. Firefighter Tierney had been resuscitated, and was recuperating at Englewood Hospital. The fire inspector determined that defective wiring in the cellar kitchen had caused the blaze, and had discounted any notion of arson. Public opinion, however, considered the fire to have been deliberately set, and cast aspersions on Ben, given his known association with a few less than upright citizens. Fire had been a common occurrence in recent years in Fort Lee, plaguing movie productions and suspiciously destroying film industry property. People naturally suspected the torch. Ben stayed in town for a while to settle related insurance matters, commiserate with Richard (not that Jean needed it) and, in general, give the old girl a decent burial.

And it was back to the project at hand: the new Riviera. The spring of 1937 found me in a panic, as I was swamped with details. Ben insisted on having a barbershop and a tailor's shop built in the basement. We were only weeks away from the grand opening, when Ben decided that we needed something special to decorate the rounded walls on both sides of the stage. The problem was what, and who would handle the job on short notice. A bunch of us were standing on the dance floor and discussing the matter in loud, frustrated voices, when we heard an electrician shout from the back of the room, "Hey, I can paint something for you."

Our heads swiveled in his direction.

"I do contemporary paintings as a hobby," he said. "I bet I can make you something that will look like the real thing."

Ben, who had laid out big money for the Gorky pieces, took a couple of steps toward the eavesdropper. "You must be kidding, right?"

"Hell, no, just give me a shot at it. When it comes to contemporary abstract art, nobody knows what the hell it is anyway." He drew more laughs than did some headliner comedians.

Ben shrugged. "Unless anybody else has a brilliant idea, let's see what this guy can do."

For the next few days, the electrician was up on the scaffold, brush in hand. Muted shades were matched with soft pastel colors, winding and twisting their way into a beautiful mural that framed the stage. But when the mural was completed, the electrician was nowhere to be found. Just like the Lone Ranger, he had ridden off into the sunset and into Riviera lore. "Who was that masked man?" we all kidded for weeks after the painting was finished.

Painters and electricians, chorus girls wearing short shorts, arrangers and composers, press people, waiters looking for jobs, chefs in white coats and hats, intermingled every day, all day long, in the weeks leading up to the grand opening. Ben had me join composers Fred Ahlert and Joe Young, orchestra leader Bunny Berrigan, and singer Sue Mitchell for a run-through of their arrangement of *The Image of You*, one of the featured songs in "Ben Marden's Riviera Follies of 1937." I sat in delight and awe, as Bunny's band previewed that tune and other showstoppers such as *Blue Rhythm Fantasy* and *I'm Happy, Darling, Dancing with You*. At the end of the day, Ben motioned for me to follow him out of the showroom.

Longie and Moretti had arrived. Things had changed between Longie and me, but we hugged and exchanged backslaps like the friends we continued to be. Ben led us down a darkened hall and into a janitor's closet, all very mysterious. As we stood crowded together, he picked up a power cord connected to a large pedestal fan, and we all watched as the wall in front of us opened up to a staircase with bright, red carpeting and glass handrails. It was like entering a fairy-tale palace, as we climbed the stairs to the hidden gambling casino.

As we entered the rooftop casino, Ben turned to us and said, "What do you think, gentleman?"

Complete with roulette, craps, blackjack, baccarat, cashier's booth, and an undeniable elegance, the room reduced us to silence for what seemed like half an hour. Finally—

"Not bad," Willie said.

"Fuckin' fantastic!" said Longie.

Ben beamed and spread his arms as if to encompass his creation. "It's everything I promised, right boys?"

"More," said Longie, not one given to excessive praise.

"One more thing," Ben said, pointing to an unlikely door behind us. "Open it, Gio."

I complied, revealing a small anteroom with a single beam of light coming through a peephole.

"This is our lookout on the dining room. Just in case some uncharitable people show up."

"We don't want any of those kind of fuckers," said Willie. "Smart move, Marden."

An eye-opener with its blue-and-yellow color scheme, its art deco inspiration, and part of its foundation cantilevered over the edge of the cliff, the new Riviera opened on June 8, 1937. Ben was all jitters throughout the afternoon. The press hounded him the entire day, like puppies following their mother, looking for milk. In the Marden tradition, he had hired as many locals as he could, even after he'd filled all the budgeted jobs. He was a one-man welfare operation.

In the parking lot, Ben's young daughter, Gertrude, was practicing her single line, "I christen thee 'The Riviera,'" which she was to recite for the press an hour before opening, as she broke a bottle of champagne on the front steps, as dignitaries do in launching a new ship. As the evening drew near, cars came in from everywhere. Nine carhops sprinted about to handle the crush of vehicles waiting to get into the circle in front of the main entrance. Once the overflow crowd was inside and seated, the lights dimmed, and a voice leaped from the state-of-the-art sound system: "Ladies and gentlemen, welcome to Ben Marden's Riviera. The Riviera is proud to present, for the first time on this opening night, Ben Marden's Riviera Follies of 1937."

Luminaries of all stripes showed up that night: politicians, judges, socialites, Fanny Brice, Jack Dempsey, Russian Prince Mdivani, the not-so-regal mobsters...you name it. Lansky, Siegel, Moretti, and Longie sat at a ringside table, and when Marden stopped by to greet them, he leaned over to hear Bugsy's semi-confidential remark.

"Remember I told you I wanted to build a place just like this, Ben? Well, I found the perfect spot."

"Where's that, Bennie?"

"Town out in the Nevada desert. It's called Las Vegas."

Ben and Bennie: visionaries, one of them ruled by violence.

In the following morning's *Journal-American*, Frank Cotton wrote, "They merely chuff across the George Washington Bridge, and there they are, at Ben's place. It has a shoeshine stand, barbershop, a masseur, and electric-eye doors; everything the old Riviera had done without, except the rumors." A week after the opening, a reporter from the *Times* wrote, "There is a door which opens, so they say, to the right people, who are curious to know how the wheels go around."

The roulette wheel and the social whirl, indeed, went round and round. Ben Marden had done it. He had built his impenetrable castle of entertainment on the picturesque Palisades in Fort Lee, New Jersey.

Chapter 17

Throughout the summer of '37, headliners such as Bing Crosby, Bob Hope, and Myron Cohen played the Riviera in its inaugural season. Ben wanted the big names, and managed to recruit them.

One day in August, Willie Moretti came up to my second-floor office at the club and asked if I could convince Ben to book a young singer from Hoboken, a winner on radio's Major *Bowes Amateur Hour*. He'd been a singing waiter at the Rustic Cabin in Englewood Cliffs, and had sung on the *Town Hall Tonight* radio show.

"You oughta hear this kid sing Exactly Like You," Moretti croaked. "He knocks it outta the fuckin' park."

Yeah, sure Willie. The next Crosby, I suppose. Because of all the hoopla that the new Riviera was generating, everybody was looking for an "in," and I was the guy they approached. Why me?

"Hey, *stunad*," Moretti said, following that utterance with a half-speed slap of my cheek. "Everybody knows that Marden trusts you, and you—you big dope—you don't have a fuckin' clue."

Moretti may not have been a Rhodes Scholar, but he knew the score. From that point on, I began to think that maybe I was put in this job for a reason, instead of thinking I was just lucky to have a job at all.

"All right, Willie. What's the name?"

"I wouldn't steer you wrong, kid."

"You sold me. What's his name?"

"They're called Frank Sinatra and the Sharps."

That sounded as enticing as a swarm of mosquitoes. "Who? What?"

"Forgeddabout the Sharps—they're just the backup singers. The kid's name is Sinatra. He weighs about ninety pounds soakin' wet, but I'm tellin' you, Gio, he's the next big thing."

When I mentioned Sinatra to Ben, making sure to bolster the pitch with Moretti's endorsement, he brushed it off.

"I don't care how good he is; right now, we need established stars with a following that can pack the place, so I can pay the freight around here."

Moretti was not pleased when I told him, but held his tongue at first. I promised that I would bring up the subject up again later in the year, and maybe get his boy in as a production singer.

"Marden might not be able to afford him by then," Moretti said.

He insisted that he and I take a ride to the Rustic Cabin to see what he was raving about. About a week later, we went there on a Friday night and grabbed a quick dinner. Sinatra was scheduled to sing with Bill Henri and the Headliners, for the direct broadcast of the WNEW radio show. When this short, skinny guy with a shelf of slicked hair and piercing blue eyes sang into the mike, the women in the audience all but went into a trance. Even more impressive, his styling and sincerity seemed to impress the men as well. Moretti looked like a new father ready to hand out cigars. On the way back to the Riviera, he kept punching me high on the arm, saying, "Can I pick 'em or what?" I felt I should go back to bat with Ben, but then what the hell did I know about singers?

Nothing more happened in the weeks that followed. I seemed to be spending most of my time reporting the goings-on at the club to Ben, wherever he happened to be. Almost like magic, the club seemed to be running itself. Upstairs in the casino, the action was brisk and clean; sometimes I would be called upon to go up there and relieve one of the spotters. Although the casino quickly achieved notoriety, politicians and police left this "carpet joint" untouched.

In the fall of '37, Nancy and I were invited to the 21 Club to celebrate the engagement of one of her friends. It was a resplendent affair. Barbara Addicks was a school chum of Nancy's, and had asked her to be the maid-of-honor when she wed socialite Robert Bartley. Nancy kidded me that I would be dining in the presence of high society this night.

"We all piss in the same urinals," I said dryly.

She gave me a swift elbow. "Class all the way."

Barbara had grown up with Nancy, with both of them attending Maude Lawrence School for Girls in El Paso, Texas. During their freshman year, they cut school to go to Dallas to see some country music show with a bunch of local boys. Barbara's family eventually tamed the hellion (she was the instigator, according to Nancy) in time for her trip to New York and her coming-out party at the Waldorf, which paved the way for her introduction into high society. I have to admit that I was surprised when I saw the rock on her finger. It must have been about six carats; it dwarfed the one-carat ring on Nancy's finger. But after sizing up Robert Bartley, I thought that although Barbara married oil money, Nancy got the better deal. The dinner was more of a cocktail party with finger foods than the sit-down dinner I expected, and I was starving by the time it was over.

Party socialite Elsa Maxwell, a close friend of the Bartley's, invited us to stop by afterward at the Embassy Club for supper and a show. I knew the Embassy, on 57th Street, to be a haunt of Dutch Schultz. In fact, word had it that the Dutchman was the owner of the place at one time or another. So I was surprised to see Bill Miller, Jean Richard's old—and Ben Marden's current—booking agent, greeting some of the guests like he was the owner.

"Hey Bill. My God you get around."

"Welcome to the Embassy, Gio. What brings you here tonight?"

"We just came from an engagement party at 21. Bill this is my wife, Nancy. I think you've met before."

"Of course, I know Nancy. You look lovely."

"Thank you," Nancy said with a warm smile.

"Always," I said to Bill.

Nancy looked at me. "And thank you."

"Can I interrupt this love fest for a moment?" quipped Elsa. "I'm here, too."

"Of course you are, my dear," Bill said, as he leaned over to give the heavyset woman a kiss on the cheek. "We never forget you, Elsa. If it weren't for you, there would be no 'Café Society' in New York. Are you all staying for supper, or just the show?"

"Both," I said with a little too much emphasis. "I'm starving. Hey, Bill, what's going on here, are you the owner of this place?"

"Yes, I bought it recently. I also have been working with the Danziger Brothers at Luna Park. You know those two guys Gio? Eddie and Harry?"

"Not really."

"Talk about two guys who got the tiger by the tail."

"How did you get involved with them?"

"Harry's an orchestra conductor, and I met him through bookings. Let me get you a waiter, so we can feed you bunch of hungry folks." He motioned a waiter to come right over.

After Bill left Elsa said, "Mister Miller is a true gentleman."

"He is every bit of that, Elsa," I said. "I know him quite well. He does a lot of bookings for my boss. His word is his bond."

"Do you think we should have dined at Luchow's?" Nancy asked.

"Why do you say that, Nancy?"

"This place looks too fancy."

"Forget about that. These people are just a bunch of bums who clean up good," said Elsa, laughing at her own joke.

After we'd polished off the main course, I was sipping a snifter of brandy, when a young woman approached our table like a character right out of a movie. "Elsa darling," she said, "so good to see you. What brings you here tonight with this good-looking couple?"

"Oh Dorothy, it's great to see you, too. We just stopped in for supper after attending an engagement party at Twenty-One. Meet my friends, Nancy and Giorgio Arigo."

"Giorgio Arigo? Aren't you the guy who works for Ben Marden in his Xanadu Pleasure Dome operation, over in New Jersey?"

Taken off-guard, I spluttered, "Ah, you know my name."

"Everyone does, my friend—at least in my business. They say 'if you want to get to Ben Marden,' it's you they have to go through. Is that true?"

"Not really, I just take care of some stuff for him, that's all."

"He's being modest," Nancy said.

"And what *is* your business, if I may ask?" I said to the newcomer.

"Why, information… sprinkled with gossip. I write for newspapers."

"This is Dorothy Kilgallen, Gio," said Elsa.

"My column is called 'The Voice of Broadway,' and it appears in the New York Journal American," said Kilgallen, who looked too sweet for gossip. "Tell me, is it true that one must receive a special invitation to enter the gaming casino hidden in the roof of the Riviera?"

I smiled obliquely. "Gaming casino? I have no idea what you are talking about Miss Kilgallen."

"Dottie, Giorgio is my guest," Elsa said, "and if he tells you he doesn't know of any gambling casino in some roof, then there must not be one, right?" She laughed uproariously. "Now, what are you drinking, Dorothy?"

"You know me Elsa, just some seltzer with a lime in it."

"My God, you are a cheap date, aren't you girl?"

As I warmed up to Kilgallen, I mentioned the young singer, Sinatra, who had captivated the crowd at the Rustic Cabin. She already knew about him.

"A secretary at our paper fell in love with that kid, just by looking at him. I have to see what the fuss is all about."

Bill Miller joined us for a spell and asked me about the Riviera. "I read something in *Architectural Digest*," he said. "Praised Ben Marden for his taste and style."

"What the hell are you doing reading *Architectural Digest*, Bill?"

"I don't know. I found a copy in the men's room."

We talked about nightclubs around the country, and compared them to the Riviera. We agreed that nothing could compare to the engineering complexity of the Riviera. Bill reported that Meyer Lansky and Vincent Alo had teamed up to run a land office business in Hallandale, Florida. "They're like two peas in a pod," he said. "Both quiet, almost introverted guys who love to read. "The law looks the other way down there."

"Sometimes, up here, too," I said.

Kilgallen did not have to take notes. Everyone knew that Lansky was on top of his game, when it came to milking the last buck out of any enterprise.

Our party went on until 3 a.m., when the Embassy closed.

When we got up to leave, Bill offered to get us a ride, but my new Buick was waiting to do the honors.

"Bill, you're moving up pretty fast in the ranks, aren't you?"

"I've been lucky so far. Some nice people out there have done me a good turn."

"Doesn't hurt to have friends in high places. As long as one of them doesn't throw you off the roof."

"Enough of this gangster talk," said Elsa. "It's time to take the women folk home."

Just then, a waiter came over and said to Bill in low tones that I picked up, "Boss, there is a phone call for you." Bill excused himself and rushed off.

As I picked up the check, Elsa grabbed my arm and said quietly, "I took care of this, Gio."

"Elsa, I didn't want you to—"

She shushed me. "It's my pleasure. Hey, how about Dorothy asking you about Ben's gambling casino? You're getting to be big stuff, Mister Arigo."

After Kilgallen and Elsa left for the ladies room with Nancy, I shook the hand of the waiters' captain, slipping him a double sawbuck.

"Sorry," said the captain, "Mister Miller told me your money is no good here."

"Take it," I said, "and tell Bill his money is no good at the Riviera from now on." I said, in hopes of forming a bond with my new friend, Bill Miller.

As we waited for the valet to fetch the Buick, I told Nancy about my exchange with the captain. "Well you can be damn sure that your money is good with me, pal, so give me whatever you got whenever you get it." In the car, she drew my right arm across her shoulders, cuddling up as close as possible as we drove across the bridge to New Jersey.

Over breakfast the next morning she said, "Bill Miller is a guy on the way up, isn't he, Gio?"

"He sure is. I think it's because everyone likes him so much. That goes a long way."

"Where is he from?"

"I think he's from Brooklyn, He told me that he was born in Russia, though. When I told him I was half Italian and half Jewish.

He said he was Jewish, too, and his name was not really Miller. He changed it when he came here."

"That's a guy you should get to know, Gio. His star is on the rise, and he's a gentleman—not a mug. Even Ben has too much 'tough guy' in him."

"Stop it, will ya? Ben has given me a sweet job, and he's been like a father."

She gave me a skeptical look.

"Well, at least a big brother," I said. You gotta understand that Ben believes that gambling and entertainment go together, just like every other major club owner in this country does. Who's to say that the government is right by creating laws that make gambling illegal? Look what happened with Prohibition. They repealed that law and made booze legal, so you see, the people were right—not the government. Someday, gambling will be legal in New York and New Jersey; mark my words."

"However that goes," Nancy said, "I think your friend Miller is going places. You should arrange to go *with* him."

"I wouldn't call us fast friends just yet, honey. He needs me like a hole in the head."

"Don't be so sure of that Gio. He might be in deep water one day, and need a guy like you that he can trust to help keep one stroke ahead of the sharks."

My eyes locked onto the morning paper's headline: HOWARD HUGHES SETS NEW AROUND-THE-WORLD RECORD. After following the Lindbergh adventures so closely, I was awestruck when I read about Hughes making it around the world in three days, 19 hours, and eight minutes in a Lockheed Super Electra. It seemed like only yesterday that Lindy had made his flight across the Atlantic; now, here was Hughes circling the entire planet.

Nancy didn't appreciate playing second fiddle to a newspaper. "Put that paper down and get dressed; you promised you would drop me off to go shopping in Englewood, while you take care of whatever you need to do at the Riviera."

In truth, there didn't seem to be much need for me at Ben's palatial nightclub. The Riviera was running under its own power, like a Swiss watch. The only exciting thing for me was watching the action coming and going. You could tell who won and who lost in the casino by their expressions.

One night, the hair on the back of my neck bristled, when one of the Cuban bus boys came to me, panting and out of breath. He said that, while he was outside taking a smoke break, he saw our casino greeter, Irving Mandel, being forcibly led to a waiting car.

Perhaps Irving had become ill and was being taken home or to the hospital? Fat chance.

We never saw him again. But we all knew that it was in everyone's best interest to mind our own business, so we kept mum about Irving and his unexplained disappearance. Cost of doing business.

Nancy had a point about the "tough guys."

In the world beyond the Riviera, the year was winding down with fears about Germany, especially its treatment of its Jewish citizens. November 9, 1938 was a day that chilled the hearts of all Americans, especially those who had ties to Germany. Nancy and I were glued to our Westinghouse radio, as Martin Block kept interrupting his Make Believe Ballroom program to provide updates on the latest aggressive action taken by the Nazis. The most recent outrage, an event that had occurred the previous night, was called "Kristallnacht" (Night of Broken Glass). Block described, to his spellbound and appalled listeners, how the Nazis had burned synagogues, destroyed Jewish shops, seized property, and killed Jews at random. Hour after hour, the radio reported such atrocities.

"Oh, my God, this calls for war!" I said to Nancy over dinner, as I tried to explain the ugly, grisly events to her.

"Did that really happen?" Nancy asked. "Or is it another hoax like that Martian invasion?"

She was referring, of course, to the Orson Welles radio broadcast that had panicked many listeners two weeks earlier by reporting that the Martians had landed in, of all places, New Jersey. I set her straight.

"Unfortunately, this has been happening, sweetheart. No one would attempt a hoax this cruel. The newspapers have been writing about what's going on in Germany. Now it's come to this."

Like most non-Jews, Nancy did not share my emotional reaction to this horror. I could not wait to go to work the next day to see how some of my Jewish co-workers were taking this. I sensed that this awful event was not the last of it; something unspeakable was happening overseas.

Ben called me at the Riviera from Florida to tell me that he was beginning to worry about how this international turmoil might affect business. He said he could not figure how the U.S. could stay out of the problem for very long. I no sooner got off the phone with Ben, than the Ritz Brothers—Al, Jimmy, and Harry—walked into my office. From the horrid to the ridiculous.

The boisterous Ritz boys were headliners wherever they appeared. Ben would always find a spot for them if they were available, and right now it appeared they were here to wreck my office and, in general, wreak playful havoc at the Riviera. It was about 4 p.m. when they came barging into my office, insisting that they speak to Ben in-person, but I explained that he was in Florida.

"Ring him up," Harry demanded.

"For you, anything, Harry," I said, slapping Jimmy's wrists, as he opened drawers in the file cabinets.

Al took the water pitcher from my desk and began watering a pot with plastic flowers. Once they saw that I could not control their antics, they suddenly stopped and broke into their rendition of the Tony Martin hit *I Get Ideas*. The Ritz Brothers did not play contrasting characters, as the Marx Brothers did, but would act like clones of each other, which made it hard for the audience to tell them apart. These guys could do just about anything: sing, dance, crack jokes, impersonations of Tony Martin, Ted Lewis, Peter Lorre, Alice Fay, and even Katharine Hepburn. Nancy and I loved their act, and would try and catch them on stage whenever we could. At this time, the boys had just finished a major movie, The Three Musketeers, though in this film, they were not quite the dashing swordsmen of epic literature. They were looking to get back into the nightclub circuit with a week at the Riviera.

Ben wanted to speak to them immediately. Jimmy grabbed the phone and touted their new flick that was breaking box office records. I thought about how easily emotions could change, moment to moment. Twenty minutes before, Ben and I were enraged about Kristallnacht, and now Ben and Jimmy Ritz were bantering about a nonsensical movie. Then again, without humor, life was a grim proposition.

Yes, the year 1938 seemed to have a split personality. Few in the United States, still licking the wounds they had suffered during the Great Depression, could imagine that another world war was looming. But I believed that the U.S. could not ignore the brutal lawlessness underway in Europe. I had served in the Navy, remember, and understood the moral fiber of this country.

For now, though, there was no response from Washington. Throughout the following year, business was booming at the Riviera. The casino was operating in full view of everyone, including the law. Ben and his partners truly knew how to run things. It seemed that nobody could do anything wrong. Billboard magazine ran articles about the Riviera, praising it for being the "Show Place of America." The Riviera was on a roll, as they say in craps games; show after show packed them in. The club became the watering hole for big spenders, and Ben the darling of the Smart Set.

As 1939 wound down, a friend of mine who lived in Philly sent me an article from the nearby *Reading Eagle*, which explained what had happened to our departed casino greeter, Irving Mandel.

READING EAGLE
Reading, Pennsylvania
December 12, 1939
Murder in Jersey Linked To Rackets: Police Say
Missing Victim Missing Buchalter Witness
Atlantic City, NJ, December 12, 1939: A man whose brutally beaten body was dumped in a shallow, quicklime

grave was identified today as Irving Mandel, 44, described by Atlantic County Prosecutor Joseph Altman as a missing witness in a Federal inquiry into the racket charge against Louis (Lepke) Buchalter.

Altman said Mandel disappeared late in 1938 from Ben Marden's fashionable Riviera nightclub, atop the Palisades across the Hudson River from New York City. Mandel's body was identified by his brother, Benjamin Mandel, who told Altman that the missing man had traveled throughout the nation and seemed to be running from something.

Had "mouth of gold"

The bullet-ridden, stabbed, and skull-crushed body was unearthed by hunting dogs last Wednesday. Its identity was ascertained, Altman said, when New York Detective Johnny Broderick took a picture of the reconstructed face and circulated it throughout sporting spots until the brother, a ticket broker, recognized it. Benjamin Mandel told Altman that he sold sporting tickets to Lepke and "all persons of that ilk."

The victim's "mouth of gold," a $1,000 dental job, aided the search, Altman added. Irving Mandel had been employed in Ben Marden's nightclub, and Benjamin Mandel said he knew his brother was under FBI subpoena in the Lepke investigation.

Benjamin explained that his brother's job at the Riviera was "to appear well-dressed and greet people. If anyone owed checks, it was his duty to contact the people and get the money. Benjamin told Altman, "The boy never had a police record. He was honest and never gambled. He was a retiring fellow and never in trouble."

Altman would not say what Irving Mandel's connection was with the Lepke case, but remarked: "This fellow worked for Ben Marden. Marden was subpoenaed to testify before the Grand Jury in the Lepke case, but refused to talk. Now, suppose somebody was afraid this man would talk?"

Marden was called before the Grand Jury in New York on August 16th, when the Jury sought to find how Lepke escaped through the underworld. Afterwards, Marden said all nightclub operators in the metropolitan area were called to tell whether Lepke visited their places, to say who was with him, and what they talked about.

Lepke has since surrendered to police, and is on trial at present in New York before Federal Judge John C. Knox on narcotics conspiracy charges.

At first I couldn't wait to tell someone, anyone, working at the Riviera about the article, but my better judgment took hold, so I just rolled up the newspaper clip and put a match to it. Silence is golden, I thought.

Chapter 18

Singer Billy Daniels had a modest hit called *Diane* on Bluebird
Records, and another one in *Penthouse Serenade*. Ben wondered if
"colored" entertainment would work at the Riviera, and Billy had
become a crossover artist, so he was a logical choice to break the
color barrier at the club, even though he had a reputation of being
hot-tempered and, in fact, had been in several brushes with the law.
He had been introduced to Ben by Bill Miller, who had booked him
at a few spots in the early 1930s. His first big gig was with Erskine
Hawkins, before going out on his own as a solo act working in clubs
such as the Onyx Club, the Ebony Club, and the Famous Door.
Daniels's popularity was on the rise, and Ben was in a quandary
about hiring him for the Riviera.

The Will Mastin Trio was another colored act that appealed to
white audiences by early 1941. Mastin himself had been a success
on the "chitlin' circuit and vaudeville's Orpheum circuit, which was
where he met Bill Miller, when Bill was hoofing it with partner Nat
Peterson. On occasion, Mastin would bring along his nephew; the
indefatigable Sammy Davis Jr., who had been performing with the
trio since he was a young child. Sammy was quickly becoming the
mainstay of the act. Ben saw them and loved them, but again questioned whether this was the right time to bring in colored entertainment, when huge white stars were readily available?

Since switching musical homes from Harry James to Tommy
Dorsey, Sinatra had indeed become huge. He was doing so many
recording dates that he didn't have time to do anything else. Hits
like *In the Blue of the Evening* were running up the charts. Axel
Stordahl was handling the arrangements for Dorsey at that time.
Nelson Riddle, who played trombone in the Dorsey band, and
Frank were becoming friends.

Moretti kept kidding me that Ben had missed the boat with
Sinatra. "I told you that Marden wouldn't be able to afford Frank."

"That's not it, Willie. It's Dorsey's cut he doesn't wanna pay."

"One of these days, this matter needs to be straightened out, and I just might be the guy to make it happen."

"I trust with no broken bones, Willie."

He looked scandalized. "This'll be all peaceful, kid."

While we kept one eye on business, the other one fixed on world news. The country was so horrified about what was taking place in Europe, that no one seemed to be paying much attention to our relationships in Asia. As usual, we closed the Riviera for the winter, and most of our people headed for Cuba to work at one of Mr. Lansky's places in the tropical climate. I stayed put to plan for the 1942 season.

The United States had been at odds with Japan since 1931, when Japanese forces invaded Manchuria, which, at that time, was part of China. Ultimately, Japan had been unsuccessful in conquering the rest of China and, in 1940, allied itself with Nazi Germany. By the following year, the Japanese occupied all of Indochina. Admiral Isoroku Yamamoto, commander of the Japanese fleet, devised a plan to immobilize the U.S. Naval fleet with a surprise attack on Pearl Harbor. In October 1941, as we were preparing to shutter the Riviera, the Japanese high command gave final approval to Yamamoto's plan, which called for the formation of a taskforce commanded by Vice Admiral Chuichi Nagumo. The "task" was to wage war against the United States. The plan called for the deployment of six aircraft carriers accompanied by 24 supporting vessels. In addition, a group of submarines was to sink any American warships that escaped the Japanese carrier force.

But the real action was in the skies. Early on the Sunday morning of December 7, the world pivoted on its axis, as the Japanese unleashed a surprise attack on America's slumbering Pacific fleet at Pearl Harbor. Instantly, the recovery from the Great Depression ceased to make headlines, as President Roosevelt declared war on Japan. Many people in the entertainment world enlisted in the armed forces or Merchant Marine. Mickey Rooney, Jimmy Stewart, Henry Fonda, Clark Gable, and Ronald Regan were the biggest movie stars to step up to the plate for their country.

Moretti, told me that Sinatra had tried to enlist, but was declared ineligible due to an eardrum puncture that he had suffered as a kid in Hoboken. Glenn Miller and several members of his band joined the Air Force, and made front-page news by parading on Pennsylvania Avenue to a marching version of Saint Louis Blues.

"Maybe I should sign up, too," I said to Nancy. "I don't want anybody to think I am a slacker."

She laughed. "They don't want old guys like you, who already served in the First World War."

I thought maybe I could be like Julia Child, a great chef who was a dear friend of Ben's. Rumor had it that she was working as a spy with the Secret Service. Some spy—how come I knew about it?

With war underway, the national mentality changed. There was a sense of shared sacrifice. Cans were recycled, gas was rationed, cooking fat was saved and stored for reuse.

Nightclub closings throughout the country became a daily occurrence. Ben instructed me to hold off on preparations for the Riviera's 1942 reopening until further notice. My paychecks were uninterrupted, as the war raged on. Then, in the summer, Ben decided to call it quits and relayed instructions: empty all freezers and storage shelves, donate the meat and the mountain of canned goods to the war effort, change all the locks, arrange for the Fort Lee Police Station to watch the building. All of the tables, chairs, kitchen equipment, office furniture, paintings, and even the liquor supply were to be left on-site. He wanted me to show up unannounced at the building at least four times a week to check on the security guards we'd hired. I exceeded that quota, usually making a Riviera run twice a day. I was happy to feel useful and to get out of the house.

The inactivity depressed me.

One night, when I came home with a paper under my arm and a long face as usual, Nancy told me that she had just gotten a job at the Ford Plant in Edgewater. Ford had received a contract from the War Department to build more than a thousand Jeeps; Nancy and many others were hired for the assembly line. At first, I was not happy with the idea of my wife toiling on an assembly line, but I quickly realized that she, too, welcomed the chance to get out of the house, and wanted to do her part to help the war effort. Countless others—men and women—felt the same way.

As the war deepened in Europe, stateside we were still trying to pull ourselves out of the Depression. Fortunes began to change in the fall of 1943. As I was making my usual rounds at the Riviera, Bill Miller dropped by the vacant building on a beautiful, autumn Saturday morning. I happened to be outside, getting some files out of my Buick, when he drove up in a Cadillac convertible that I didn't recognize.

"Hey pal, what time does the show start?" shouted a male voice. I could not see who was in the Caddy due to the bright sunshine bouncing off its windshield.

"What are you, a wise guy?" I shouted back.

With that, the door of the car opened, and out stepped my old friend, Bill Miller. "Remember me?" he said, smiling and offering his hand.

"Oh, my God, Bill Miller, how the hell are you? What are you doing up here?"

"Just taking a ride and checking out some early fall foliage. I had to get the women out of the house, and we were planning on going up to the Milestone Restaurant in Englewood Cliffs for lunch. Got time to go with us?"

Another man and two women stepped out of the car.

"Gio, this is my brother-in-law, Abe Vine, and his wife, my sister Molly, and this is my girlfriend, Mary. Everybody, meet my old friend, Giorgio Arigo. He works for Ben Marden."

"Pleased to meet you folks," I said. "I can't make lunch, Bill, but would you like to come inside for a little while and see what the Riviera looks like, now that it's been closed up for three years?"

"I would love that, Gio," Bill said without hesitation, almost as if he'd been anticipating the invitation. "Are you sure it's all right?"

"Of course. Ben would be thrilled to know that you stopped by." The others seemed to be very interested, too.

Surprisingly, the yellow-and-blue exterior still looked sharp, even though it hadn't been maintained during the three years since the place had been shut down.

"Do you come by here often, Gio?" Bill asked.

"Yes, that is part of my job. Sometimes I have to run up here from where I live in Hackensack in the middle of the night to turn off all the lights during blackouts. I was just signed up to be an Air Raid Warden two weeks ago. My responsibility only takes in one place, and you're lookin' at it."

"Well, I guess there are some big-time targets up in this neck of the woods, like the Ford Plant and the George Washington Bridge right over there," Bill said, pointing to the bridge. "My girlfriend here refers to it as the 'Bridge to the Riviera.'"

"Easy to spot from the air," I said. "Come on, follow me; we'll go in through the stage door."

Bill said that, when he was booking acts for Ben in the late '30s, he had been at the Riviera several times but never toured the building. "It's a little spooky in there these days," I warned them. After I opened the stage door, we entered a little vestibule. To our left was the employee time clock, with the time cards still in their rack. As we glanced at the names, I noted that several of these men were currently serving in the military. We climbed the four steps to the backstage dressing rooms.

"On your right is Tony Martin's dressing room—when he is here, that is," I said, like a tour guide. "We call it the 'Star's Dressing Room.'"

I opened the door with a cut-out star hanging on it. "Note the full bathroom, complete with shower," I said.

Molly picked up a notepad and flipped through it. "Look—here's Jimmy Durante's phone number."

"Where?" asked Mary, all excited.

As we left the Star's Dressing Room, we walked past the rear of the revolving stage. The silent bandstands looked ready for action, random musical arrangements still in place. I plucked one from a heavy, red, music stand. "*The More I See You*—Harry Warren. He wrote *At Last*, too."

"Pretty talented guy," said Abe. "What's this over here?" He opened the door to his left.

"That's the chorus girls' dressing room. Go in, don't be afraid—no one is in there."

The room had clothes hangers everywhere. A few costumes were still dangling, where the girls had left them in 1941.

"This gives me the creeps," said Mary. "Let's move on."

"I'm with you Mary, let's walk around through here, and if you want to go upstairs and see more dressing rooms, I will be glad to take you there."

They followed me, as I made my way through the black stage curtains surrounding the revolving bandstand.

"And when we're dancing, and you're dangerously near me... I get ideas... I get ideas," sang Abe, dancing around the oval stage. He held a rolled-up piece of paper in his hand as if it were a microphone, while the two women placed their bodies in the most provocative positions, emulating assertive showgirl poses.

"Who needs Tony Martin?" I said. "And look at Mary. Sell it, baby."

"You happen to be looking at the former captain of the line at the Latin Quarter in New York," said Bill. "That's where we met."

"I can believe it." But Abe's antics and the onstage frolicking stopped suddenly, as each of us felt the sadness that plagued the 1,200-seat room. Sadness caused by the terrible war that seemed as if it would never end.

"Come on, I want to show you how to get into the secret gambling casino in the roof," I said, attempting to change the mood. I stepped down the two steps at stage left, from the revolving dance floor to the dining room level, and took a quick left turn, leaping up the three steps that led to the serpentine bar and lounge. The walls were covered with Arshile Gorky paintings, which we admired as we walked the 15 paces to an intersection where the men's and ladies' rooms were located.

"Let's take a right here," I said, excited at what awaited us. "Down at the end of the hall is a janitors' closet."

"Just what we came to see," said Abe.

"We're going to get some brooms and clean up the place," said Bill.

"Like hell we are." I couldn't tell if Mary was kidding or offended.

"This is the way to the secret casino, " I said reassuringly, as we all squeezed into the closet, closing the door behind us.

"Why are you closing the door, Gio?" said Molly nervously.

"The mechanism won't work unless the door is closed."

"Mechanism?"

"Watch this." I picked up the cord to the pedestal, floor-model fan and handed it to Mary. "Would you plug this into the socket?"

She took the cord, giving me a serious eye-to-eye look, and then plugged it into the wall socket. Immediately, the nondescript panel in the wall to the left of the fan slid sideways into a pocket, revealing the thickly carpeted staircase with its glass handrails.

We weren't in a janitor's closet anymore.

"Oh boy, will you look at this," said Abe, the first to enter.

"Upstairs we go," I said, leading the troupe up 15 steps to the casino.

The craps tables were covered with white tablecloths; the same held true for the roulette wheels. Everything stood ready for the action, but no action was in the offing. We returned to the main level, took five bar stools off the bar, and sat on them.

While the ladies and Abe chatted about this unique nightclub I had just showed them, Bill leaned over toward me. "Do you have any idea what Ben wants to do here when the war ends?"

I had been thinking about that for some time. "I don't have a clue, Bill. I believe he wants to sell his interest in the Palais Royal in New York, and I heard that Lou Walters is interested in buying it. I think Ben feels he is carrying too much weight now that the war is on, and the joints are shutting down and not bringing in any money. Do you want me to see if I can get some information for you on this place?…Are you interested?"

The light that came into his eyes told me he was. "Maybe, who knows? Sure, see what you can find out for me; I'm always interested in a new venture. Thanks, Gio."

We all left the building and went outside, and I locked the stage door behind me.

Bill and I looked at each other, and I could see the wheels turning in his enterprising brain. "You amaze me, Bill."

He smiled. "What's so amazing?"

Molly jabbed him in the ribs. "The Amazing Mister Miller— now there's an act worthy of the Riviera." She turned to me. "Bill still thinks he's a kid. Enjoying himself takes precedence over everything else. He was like that even when he was a kid."

Before he got back into the Caddy, Bill thanked me for showing them around, and said casually, "Ask Ben if he wants to sit down and talk."

I sensed that there was nothing casual about his intent. I saw new life for the Riviera.

If this damn war ever ended, that is.

Chapter 19

Coincidences do happen, and a few days later I got a call from Longie, who asked me what was going on with the Riviera. He said that he was in the dark as to why Ben decided to shut it down.

"Why the hell did he lock up the joint?"

I tried to explain that, without gasoline to fuel their cars, people have no way of getting there. In addition, government sanctions on food supplies had restricted the club's menu.

"We've always provided transportation for people who want to gamble a little, so what's the story?" Longie said. "Get hold of that boss of yours, and find out what the hell is going on."

I wondered why Longie seemingly was in the dark about the Riviera.

Moments later, I called Ben to convey Longie's puzzlement, and summarize the visit with Bill Miller. Ben was surprised that Miller had interest in the Riviera.

"Where would he get the dough?" Ben said.

"Maybe from Longie," I said, only half-kidding.

"Now *there's* food for thought," he said.

I hesitated, not wanting to seem too familiar, then asked, "Ben, what are you working on right now?"

He answered as if it were a natural question for me to ask. "I'm thinking about investing in a place in Manhattan called the Playhouse Theater. It's not like it's the next big thing, but you know what—I've lost interest in the nightclub business. Too much heartburn. Remember when they subpoenaed me to testify about gambling at the Riviera, all because that bum had squawked about losing his ass in the casino? What was that—thirty-nine?"

"Think so."

"It's never been the same since then. I am not getting any younger, you know, and all this shit going on with the Nazis and Germany, along with everything else, is really getting to me. All I am interested in right now is lightening the load, getting rid of some of the extra business weight I'm carrying. And some of the mashugana assholes that go with the turf."

"So, should I tell Bill Miller you might consider selling if the circumstances are right?"

"Couldn't hurt."

"Tell me about Longie again. What exactly did he say?"

"Ben, didn't you explain to him why you were shutting down?"

"Yeah, I told him. Of course, I did."

"Didn't seem that way when I talked to him."

"Well, it's no secret, Gio. For chrissake, Longie knows the score. What are you getting at?"

"I don't know. He said there is no reason that the card room should be shut down just because the nightclub is dark. He feels that the card room is the perfect spot to continue bringing the money in."

"He don't give a shit about anything but making a fast buck," Ben said. "My ass could end up in the hoosegow, while he struts around like a peacock. No fucking way. Tell you what: Call Miller up and ask him if he wants to talk in person. Yeah, do that."

He sounded so emphatic, it was as if he were talking himself into unloading the Riviera.

"I'll take care of it, Ben."

"And, by the way, Gio, call Moretti and Zwillman, and ask them to remove all their stuff from the upstairs room. Tell them that we heard we are going to be raided. Got that?"

"I got it, Ben, but don't you think that it would be better if it came directly from you?"

"Maybe you're right, Gio. Those guys put a lot of weight on respect. I better handle it myself."

The two of us hung silently on the phone, sensing that our conversation needed something more before ending. Finally, Ben said, "All right, so call Bill Miller and ask him when he can meet with me. Tell him he can name the place. I will be back in New York next week."

I tried to reach Bill for two days, but could not get through. The secretary who answered the phone at the Embassy Club asked me if I wanted to leave a message, so I did—at least six of them. Finally, Bill returned my call and told me that he was in Miami trying to close a deal on a club he owned. He said he expected to be back in New York by the end of the week, so anytime after that would be fine to meet with Ben.

When Bill returned to New York, he called right away to ask if I could set up that meeting with Ben. When I asked him why he wanted to buy the Riviera, as he already owned the Embassy, he explained that the Embassy was a "small spot" that held maybe 150 people—I knew that the Riviera could handle more than a thousand. As the owner of Luna Park in Coney Island, Bill liked the big crowds. But it wasn't just size that attracted him to the Riviera.

"Let me tell you something, Gio. Maybe I shouldn't be saying this, but, since I am the guy who has to put his ass and his wallet on the line to get these places, I will tell you unequivocally: I would trade all of them for that Riviera you guys got."

"Really? Why's that?"

"It's got...*style*. No nightclub in this world can hold a candle to it, and you can take that to the bank."

He was right. For some men, there was more to business than just money.

"Ben has been in Cuba for about a month," I said, "but he's due back in New York next week. He seems as motivated as you, Bill. I'm pretty sure we'll set a meeting for the two of you as soon as he gets back."

I was more than *pretty* sure. I reached Ben later that same day, and he immediately flew to New York via Miami, landing at Idlewild Airport just before midnight—on a Sunday, yet. I was waiting at the Pan Am Terminal, when he arrived. Rather than irritable after two night flights, he was in high spirits. I grabbed his tan, leather suitcase with the gold monogrammed letters "BM" from the porter.

"How was the flight?"

"Terrific. We flew in the new Boeing 307 Stratoliner—it's the first plane to have a pressurized cabin. Very comfortable, no matter how high we went. I guess we got lucky; Roosevelt commandeered just about all of those planes for the military."

Dressed impeccably in a seersucker suit, blue shirt, and a pink-white-and-baby-blue tie, he was tan and rested. As usual, he had a bright white handkerchief folded neatly in his breast pocket. After all those hours on the planes, Ben still looked neat as a pin.

"Did you hear from Miller?"

"He'd like to meet with you in the Embassy Lounge on Tuesday night. If you have time, he wants you to stay for dinner and a show."

"Good work, Gio."

"I'm just the messenger."

Come Tuesday, Ben asked me to join him for a drink a couple of hours before his meeting with Bill Miller. We met at the Metropolitan Club, one of Manhattan's most exclusive private clubs. By the time Ben arrived, I had been waiting at the 60th St. entrance for about 10 minutes. We were seated at a table in the lounge area; Ben ordered a Macallan single-malt Scotch, and I asked for a simple Johnny Walker Black with soda. Ben got right to it.

"What do you think, Gio? Should we hold some paper on the Riviera, or should we say we want cash?"

"What does your accountant say?"

"Haven't discussed it with him yet. You know, I wasn't born yesterday. When Miller lost Luna Park in the fire, he just about lost his whole stake in the place. I heard that he hadn't taken out much insurance on it. Not so smart, but what had really impressed me was the fact that he put together a deal with Coca Cola, and got them to put up huge billboards branding Coke with Luna Park. That little deal put Luna Park on the map, and Miller created that whole scenario himself. That fire was a damn shame. Best laid plans, huh, Gio? Miller's got a lot of creative talent, besides having the balls to take on such a huge project. From all that I hear, he's a pretty nice guy, too, and that's how I remember him, when he booked some acts for me. Right now, I think he might be a little short on the do-re-me since the fire."

When we finished our drinks, we grabbed our coats and walked the three blocks to the Embassy. The line was thick with well-dressed patrons waiting patiently to see the dinner show.

"Come this way, Gio," Ben said, as he led me around to the side door and down a dimly lit alley. "We can get in through the kitchen."

Ben Marden knew about angles and shortcuts. By the time we got to the lounge, Bill was waiting there. The two impresarios exchanged compliments.

"You look great, Bill," said Ben. "Glad that you decided to become an entrepreneur, instead of limiting yourself to booking acts."

"Trying to follow your big footsteps, Ben. Hey, before we get rolling, do you guys want to stay here and catch the show, or would you rather go over to the Waldorf and see Frank Sinatra's show in the Wedgwood Room?"

"Now that sounds terrific, too," said Ben. "Six of one, half-a-dozen of the other."

"Let's do the Wedgwood," said Bill. "It is probably quieter over there."

We all hopped in a cab and made it to the Waldorf just as Sinatra was finishing a sweet version of *Sweet Lorraine*. As he began singing *Paper Moon*, applause filled the elegant room. Feeling a bit nervous about being here in the first place, I fidgeted with a table card that said "supper cover charge from 10:30: $2.00. It noted that, in addition to Sinatra that night, Volkoff & Milada of the Ballet Russe would be performing with the Leo Reisman Orchestra. The crowd noise didn't stop Ben from cutting to the business at hand.

"Bill, we've known each other a long time, and I trust you, just like I trust Gio, here. You have never given me any reason to think otherwise. When you told me that you could book a certain act for me, you always came through as promised. Now Gio tells me that you are interested in buying the Riviera. *How* interested?"

Bill looked at him for several seconds without saying anything.

"Very…Right now I am running the Embassy and another club, and I plan to take my shares out of both of them."

That surprised me; Bill hadn't mentioned it to me. I felt like he'd just answered Ben's main question: Where would Bill find the dough?

"Is that other club the Florida Copa, Bill?" asked Ben.

"Could I pass on answering that question, Ben?"

Ben sat there with a big smile on his face. "These are not the kinds of operations I am interested in running for the long term," Bill continued.

"What's so great about the Riviera?" said Ben, playing devil's advocate.

"The crowd."

"What about the crowd?"

"It's big."

"Most of the time."

"And it's...*electric.*

Ben sat forward. "You shoulda been my press agent—not just my booking agent."

"Ben, whether you know it or not, over the years that I have observed the way you do business, you have taught me that your people come first. I have always thought of you as a live-and-let-live guy who always leaves a little on his plate for those less fortunate, and that is the way I would like to pattern myself in this business, too. Sure, I have taken advantage of a few opportunities that opened up for me, but right now I have some backers who would like to strike a deal on your place. When I lost Luna in the fire, I was devastated, as you probably know, but I did make good with the Danzigers. I don't owe them a penny."

Ben nodded appreciatively. "That's a good way to stay in one piece." We all laughed at that one. A seriousness crept into Ben's eyes. "Tell you what, Bill, take that napkin in front of you and write down your offer, fold it, and shove it over to me. If I like it, I will call you in a few days. If I don't like it, you won't hear from me, okay?"

"Sure, I understand, Ben, thanks." As Bill sat back in his chair, we picked up the beat and Sinatra's distinctive vocal from the bandstand. "Great singer, huh, Gio?" Bill said, poking me on my arm and asking if I had a pen.

For several minutes, it seemed, Bill cloaked the napkin with his left arm. Writing his dollar offer took two or three seconds. He slid the napkin facedown to Ben, who lifted one edge like he was peering at a stud poker card. "Oh, so you want me to hold three-fifty large on paper for you, is that it?"

Bill's expression gave nothing away—poker, indeed. "That's the only way I can do it, Ben. And I will say this, too: I won't close on it until the war is over. What good is closing if I can't open and make the money to pay you back?"

Ben's lips curled and opened into a broad smile, as he appraised his suitor. He turned to me. "Your boy has a little sechel, doesn't he?"

"If you say so, Ben. I don't know all those Italian words."

We laughed again. As if on cue, the waiter came over to our table with an unexpected round of drinks.

"Excuse me, sirs, the group over there sent these drinks over."

As we all turned to see who sent the drinks, Ben said, "Bill, that's Willie Moretti sitting at that table with those people. They're huge Sinatra fans."

"Sure, I've seen him around."

Ben hoisted his glass in a gesture of thanks, while turning and facing the other table. When he turned back, he said, "Bill, Longie Zwillman, and Willie run the card room at the Riviera. You know that don't you?"

"Of course, who doesn't? Ben, I've got to tell you something. When, and if, our deal goes through, there will never be any more action in that card room." Bill paused to let that sink in. "I would have no way to pay you back if the place was raided and the club shut down."

Ben scratched at his temple and smiled derisively. "I understand, Bill, but let me tell you something: There will be hell to pay when you tell them that you won't allow them to operate upstairs."

"I'd rather pay hell than not pay Ben Marden."

That got a laugh that sounded more like a cough. "Can I write that on your gravestone? We're talking about Zwillman and Moretti. They don't take things lying down."

"Here's the thing, Ben. I think you should be the one to tell them. After all, those guys are part of your operation—not mine... As for the business itself, I'm sure I can make it just on the entertainment and the atmosphere; I really don't need the gambling aspect to make it work. When you opened the place during the Depression, it took everything—including the gambling—to meet the nut on the place, but it's a different world today."

"You know, you're going to miss out on quite a bit of extra income if you shut that room down," Ben said,

"That's nothing compared to what I would lose if I got shut down by the law."

Ben folded his arms and smiled lightly, as if he had just been surprised by some news. "All right, Bill, it's your—"

"—Don't say *funeral.*"

"If I accept your offer, I will speak to them...What should I tell them?"

"Tell them that if my mother, Lena, ever found out that gambling were taking place up in that room, and I had something to do with it, she would die on the spot. It would break her heart. She got us out of Pinsk—me and my brothers and sister. She always says that she is so proud to be here in the United States, where it is safe to live, so I am not going to do anything that would change her image of me. I owe her that."

Ben looked at him. "Maybe she should talk to them."

You couldn't help but laugh at that one.

As we were leaving the Wedgwood Room, Moretti approached us with the look of a proud uncle. "So Ben, now do you see what I was talking about with Sinatra?"

"You were right, Willie. He's really got it."

"Better than Crosby, right?"

"Well, he's gettin' there." Ben turned to Bill. "Among his many talents, Mister Moretti knows his music."

"I know broads, and I can see how they go silly over this skinny paesan. How about you book him right away, when you open up the joint again?"

Ben and Bill exchanged glances. "Who knows, maybe I am never going to open up the joint again," said Ben, leaving Willie with his mouth half-open. When we walked to the cloakroom, Moretti followed.

"What am I missin'?"

Ben and Bill picked up their fedora hats. "Willie, you know Bill Miller, don't you? Used to do my bookings, speaking of bookings."

Moretti looked suspiciously at Bill. "Pleased to meet ya."

"Likewise, Mister Moretti."

"Willie, we'll talk soon," Ben said, and we left Moretti standing there, wondering what was in the wind.

During the cab ride back to the parking garage at the Manhattan Club, Ben repeated his promise that he would speak to Moretti and Longie about the gambling operation if he agreed to sell the Riviera to Bill.

"But I'll tell you what, Bill—that offer you wrote on the napkin really doesn't cut it for me. You're not even in the ballpark."

Bill shifted subtly in the backseat of the cab. "Just a second, Ben, the Riviera has been closed for a few years now, and it is going to need a transfusion of cash to get it up and running again. I have that to look forward to before I can even open the doors."

Ben fixed him with a hard stare that seemed to take forever to loosen. "Okay, I guess we both have to walk away from these negotiations a little bit disappointed to make it a fair deal."

He held out his hand. "Do we have a deal?"

Bill grasped Ben's hand. "You can count on me to pay back every cent of the purchase-money mortgage."

"I guess we got a deal then" said Ben. "I'll file the napkin."

"Does Gio come with the deal?" Bill asked, only half-kidding.

Ben looked at me with a mixture of admiration and affection. I felt 10 feet tall. "Gio takes care of most things around here that don't fall into a category," he said to Bill. "He even negotiated the purchase of the land for me. He's been like a right-hand man." He turned back to me. "What about it, Gio? You interested in working for Bill?"

I felt a little choked up. "Sounds good to me."

"Me, too," said Bill. "How 'bout if your first assignment is to go to Willie and Longie, and tell them that I will no longer permit gambling. How would that be that for starters, Gio?" Ben broke up with laughter, but he stopped quickly when he saw how serious I looked.

"I've known Longie a long time," I said, "so I know how to talk to him. But Moretti is another story."

Chapter 20

At 7:03 p.m. on August 14, 1945, the New York Times zipper in Times Square spelled out five words: PRESIDENT/ TRUMAN/ ANNOUNCES/ JAPANESE/ SURRENDER!

From the street crowd's reaction, you would think the Messiah had come, and maybe he had. Strangers hugged, people congregated by the tens of thousands in the square in a joyous scene repeated across the United States. Within days of that announcement, a sign in Macy's window announced nylon stockings for sale, and women lined up for blocks, awaiting their turn to purchase the prized hosiery. No more painting their legs to give the appearance of nylon stockings. The real thing was back.

A few weeks later, newspapers reported a different sign of the times: people were going to restaurants again, now that wartime food rationing was no longer in force. This was the signal for which Bill Miller had been waiting. Since he and Ben Marden had come to terms for the Riviera sale, Bill had formed a small consortium of investors, who willingly bought into his dream. Each one was ready to pony up the necessary cash to supplement Ben's mortgage loan of $300,000 to close the deal.

Each of his new investors, although neophytes in the restaurant business, was squeaky clean by reputation, which was the only prerequisite that Miller required in his partners. Bill explained to me that staying clear of mob investors gave him a fighting chance to make a go of it. However, he recognized that the other side of that coin was that the casino profiteers would not go away quietly.

That premonition rang true at Christmas time, as we were organizing the office, following the closing of the property a month before. Some "visitors" came by to pressure Bill to reopen the gambling room they didn't all have crooked noses; it only seemed that way. As well-prepared as we were with reasonable explanations to counter their demands, Bill had to resort to his last-ditch argument: He could not possibly run a casino room because it would kill his mother to think that he was involved with something illegal. He hoped that would penetrate their tender hearts.

They responded eloquently.

"What kind of bullshit are you handing us, Miller? Who do you think you are, breaking our shoes and telling us you won't open the casino because it will offend your mother?"

"All I can say is that it's the truth. If you force me to open that room, I will throw in the towel and walk out of here with my brothers and my partners, and then you will have nothing. You know you have other interests, other than that room upstairs. So take it or leave it. I don't have a choice in the matter."

They looked at each other. "This is not the end of it, Miller. You will open that casino in the spring…*or else.*" With that, they shouldered their way out of his office.

Both Bill and I sat quietly for what seemed an eternity.

"Did you really mean what you said, Bill?" I asked, breaking the silence.

"Most of it…I guess. I don't think we have heard the end of it yet, but for now, maybe we can come up for a little air. I felt all along that they would feel left out when Marden sold the place to me, but he forgot to tell me that those guys are under the impression they come with the deal."

Despite such threats, we were gearing up for opening. We had detailed our inventory of restaurant items, and reviewed the proper functioning of the mechanicals in the building. The books concerning the purchase of liquor and food, however, were incomplete, leaving everyone, including the accountant, in the dark regarding what and how much was ordered.

Bill had me schedule interviews for people he'd identified to fill key positions in the office, and on the floor and bandstand: publicity agents, booking agent, security, concessionaire, beverage supplier, barber, wardrobe mistress, makeup artist, waiter captains, orchestra leader, a pair of Latin bandleaders, two trumpeters, and a drummer. The new Riviera was on a roll.

For weeks, the club was busier than Grand Central Station. Bill brought in his brother, Joe, to restart the kitchen after a five-year layoff. New hires filled out paperwork. Unsolicited applicants arrived in droves, begging for jobs. Vendors waited for hours to pitch their products. Dancers rehearsed on stage with master choreographer Donn Arden. To me, the whole scene seemed like the greatest show on earth.

Arden and theatrical producer Ron Fletcher designed the show, insisting on a dozen showgirls in the line, instead of the half-dozen Bill had planned. Fletcher refused to continue without the full complement. Bill took me aside.

"Who do you know that's got a pocketful of dough to pay the freight for all these people?"

Bill contained himself when others were around, but in private, I could see that anxiety was chewing him up.

"The nut on this place is crushing my skull," he said. I tried to calm him as best I could, as hour after hour passed with tons of money going out and nothing coming in. The club needed a paint job and new carpet. What didn't need to be replaced had to be cleaned and freshened. It was an enormous task. Tradesmen hired to do the work expected their money in short order. Union reps began coming around, asking why their people were waiting for checks. Bill somehow kept the lid on the boiling saucepan, telling everyone that he was right on track, and was even considering adding a swimming pool to make the place a mini-resort. Of course, I knew that he had no such intention—he was merely putting up a brave front to stave off the onslaught of bill collectors.

Though he had serious money at risk in this venture, Ben Marden—to his credit—applied no pressure. To the contrary, he was in Bill's corner all the way. Of all people, he understood what Bill was going through.

But numbers rarely lie, and Bill had needed the Riviera's grand reopening to be a blockbuster. He did have one trick up his sleeve, and that was to hire Bea Kalmus of radio station WHN. Bea was a singer, as well as the first female disc jockey in the U.S., and she had a terrific fan base. The fact that she was a looker with personality didn't hurt. During her program, she often sang right along with the records she played, told jokes, and did impressions of famous people.

When I called Bea to discuss the Riviera, and the possibility of her broadcasting live from the club, she said, "If Miller needs publicity, I'm the gal that can get it for him."

"I was hoping you'd say that."

"By the way, why don't you see if you can get Frank Sinatra to do the Grand Opening?"

"That would be fantastic, but after seeing the draw that Frank had at the Paramount, I don't think Bill could afford him right now."

"All right, so much for the bobbysoxers. So concentrate on a more mature audience, people who have money and are willing to part with it to see a classy dinner show."

"Tony Martin," I said, letting the name hang out there.

"Yeah," Bea said. "Love it. Love him. I heard he is being approached by WMCA to take over a spot."

"Really? "

My next call was to our publicity guy, Seth Babits, who already was thinking Tony Martin. We got Bill on the extension phone.

"Bill, I think we can get Tony Martin," Babits said.

"Fantastic!" I hadn't heard Bill's voice reach that level of enthusiasm for weeks. "You're the best, Seth… Grand Opening?"

"That's what we talked—me and the booking agent, Nat Goldstone."

"What's the nut going to be for Tony?"

"Podell, at the Copa is paying him five grand a week, so Goldstone says you'd have to up the ante for him to switch over."

"You tell Tony that I'll pay him ten."

I swallowed hard when I heard that.

"Double?" Babits sounded as if he were in a mild state of shock.

"You got it."

"Okay, Bill. I'll call Cy."

"That's George with me. Seth; get it done pronto!"

As Seth hung up, Bill asked me to stay on the line.

"Bill… wow."

"This is going to be like Sinatra's song, *All or Nothing at All.* We'd better pray that we can pack the place. Meet me downstairs, Gio, and we'll see how the dancers are doing."

As soon as we entered the showroom dining area, Abe Vine, Bill's brother-in-law, who was in charge of purchasing food and beverages, charged in, shouting, "Bill, Bill, tell this son-of-a-bitch I am not accepting this horse meat he is trying to push on us." Abe was red in the face, with the meat vendor on his tail.

"What are you talking about Abe?" said the vendor, holding two steaks in wax paper. "These steaks are Grade 'A' prime. Here, look, Mister Miller." He held out the steaks.

Bill glanced at the steaks, then at Abe, then back at the man with the beef. "Looks like they ran at Aqueduct two days ago. Now saddle up those steaks of yours and send them to the glue factory." Everyone within earshot cracked up. "If you can't bring us the best that money can buy, I can't use you."

When the vendor left, Bill turned to Abe and me. "Ran in a stakes race, I believe."

"Bad joke, Bill, bad joke," said Abe, as he walked away, too aggravated to enjoy the moment.

Bill's rule was that only the best would do, and everyone at the Riviera had better subscribe to that thinking.

Walter Nye, the orchestra leader, was onstage and upset that his musicians were going into overtime with rehearsal for the show. The basis for his complaint was that Donn Arden was still in the process of selecting the twelve girls he wanted for the chorus line, while weeding out the remaining ten that had come for the audition. By the time Donn finally made his final choices, it was obvious that the girls were virtual clones, each of them standing about five-foot-seven (in bare feet, of course) with firm rear ends, small breasts, and faces that could launch a thousand ships—or, at least, a thousand husbands. It also appeared that not one of them was even one pound overweight.

"Thank you girls, thank you," said Arden. "Those of you who received slips of paper should be here tomorrow morning at 11:45 to meet with Mary Smith, who will help you with your costumes."

"Some costumes," said one of the chosen girls. "They're probably nothing more than a G-string and a couple of pasties."

"Not to worry," said another. "I worked with Donn before, and he was good about letting us keep our dignity."

On the second day of rehearsal, Tony Martin entered the show room dressed in a casual gray shirt and black pants, looking as handsome as ever. The shoes he wore looked more like slippers—I had never seen anything like them before. He was accompanied by Nat Goldstone.

"Hey, Bill, I hear you are looking for me," said Tony, as he sauntered into the room. Bill hurried to greet him, and they hugged like family. I had never seen Tony Martin up close before—much less met him—so when Bill called me over, I felt like a little kid.

"Gio, this guy and I have been around the block together a couple of times. I feel like I have been booking him since he was twelve." Tony just smiled and shook my hand.

"Nice to meet you Tony," I said. "You Italians have it sewed up when it comes to singing." I immediately worried that I had acted too familiar.

But Tony Martin seemed to have the same unflappable personality offstage. "No, no, Gio, I'm not Italian; I'm Jewish, just like my buddy, Bill, here. My name is really Alvin Morris, but I changed it to Tony Martin after college, when I was playing tenor sax and singing with Tom Guren's band in California. And that's the way it's been ever since."

He turned back quickly to Bill.

"So, I hear you're going to pay me ten grand to open the club for you, huh, Bill?"

"Well, that's just for the newspapers. Okay?"

"And here I thought it was for my bank account."

They each were teasing a bit, but suddenly the air had become charged. Tony threw an arm around him.

"You did say double what Podell is paying me, am I right, old pal?"

Bill looked like he was experiencing momentary indigestion. "Guilty as charged, Tony. But I need two shows a night, and maybe three on Saturday night. Okay?"

"You got yourself a deal," said Tony, as he held out his hand.

While star and club owner were negotiating, onstage activity had stopped, the chorus girls just stood there ogling the star singer. Within a few minutes, Nye came down off the revolving bandstand and walked over to Tony to chitchat. Meanwhile, Goldstone opened a fat, leather bag, and took out music charts, which he handed to Nye. The bag sported aviator wings and the Air Force star—Tony had served in the Army Air Corps.

"These are our arrangements, Walt. Check them over, please."

"Tony, great to see you out of uniform," said Nye, the debonair, violin-playing orchestra leader. "The last time I saw you, you were singing with the Miller Band at Yale."

"Yes, that was with 'Captain Glenn Miller and the Army Air Force Band'—I must correct you, sir."

"You know, Gio," Bill said, "Tony got the worst deal in the world when he enlisted in the Navy. He was assigned to this guy Maury in California, who bought Tony's Studebaker. The papers made a story out of it, saying Tony was buying preferential treatment."

"Let's not talk about that—it's over and done with," said Tony. "For the record, I sold the car for top dollar. I didn't give it to him, like the newspapers said. I knew Maury from Hollywood for years. When I signed up for the Navy, I was assigned to work in the same office as him. He was a lieutenant commander and needed a car, so I sold him one of the four I had at the time."

Bill looked at him, deadpan. "Only four?"

Tony smiled his stage-bright smile. "He wanted a Cadillac, what can I tell you? There was nothing more to it than that. But then the press got hold of the story, and made me out to be a guy who was looking for special treatment by giving Maury the car instead of selling it to him. So I needed a change of scenery, and Glenn arranged for me to get reassigned to the Army Air Force, and sing with his band. But the Navy squawked that now I was really getting preferential treatment, and the Army finally sent me to Calcutta, India, where I ended up in charge of booking entertainment for the troops over there."

"Hearing this," said Bill, "I don't know how we managed to win the war."

We laughed, but Tony kept going. "Those guys in India had nothing—no USO shows, nothing. So I rounded up as many people as I could find who had a modicum of talent, and put together some shows. Those amateurs really put their hearts into it. After all was said and done, they gave me a bronze star."

Tony looked around with his irresistible smile, as if waiting for applause, but Bill just stared him down.

"I'm glad you didn't want to talk about it, Tony."

We laughed harder this time and, yes, offered a round of applause.

All this time, Nye had been reviewing the music charts. "Where is the second tenor part on *I Get Ideas*? Let's get moving. We've got union musicians here, and overtime costs an arm and a leg. Let's run through the arrangements."

Onstage, Arden announced to his dancers, "Okay, girls, the final four will be Dusty Reale, Pat Cotton, Joy Skylar, and Judy Tyler. Thank you all for coming today, and good luck."

When Tony got up on the bandstand, Nye gave a moderate-tempo four-count to the band. The four-man sax section delicately opened the four-bar intro to Begin the Beguine, a song that Tony had sung with the Glenn Miller band. His deep, romantic, baritone filled the room, even without the microphone.

"My God, he is so good," said Bill. "Now if we only get Jackie Leonard to open for him, we are in business."

His headliner secure, Bill Miller went back upstairs to face the music.

Chapter 21

Cars filled the main parking lot and the dirt lot across Hudson Terrace, and spilled onto the Terrace itself for about a mile up the road, almost to the next town of Englewood Cliffs. Inside, from the kitchen to the stage, opening-night jitters abounded at the Riviera. The showroom, soon to be beyond the fire ordinance, was abuzz with excitement throughout the sets of Pupi Campo and his Latin Band, who spun exotic arrangements of *Que Rico El Mambo, Que Te Parece Cholito, Quizas, Quizas, Quizas,* and plenty more hot rhythms. Dolled-up women in satin dresses and, of course, new nylon stockings with the vertical seam running down the backs of their shapely legs, were shakin' it on the dance floor, their tailored men in tow, quick-stepping the latest mambo moves.

"Photography girls," their Graflex Speed Graphic cameras flashing, took snapshots all over the room. Eli Quain, the concessionaire, had given them instructions not to photograph anyone who did not request a photo, as the crowd surely included businessmen escorting women who were not their wives, and politicians consorting with gangsters. Newspaper people were taking notes on their breast-pocket pads, noting important items for the gossip columns. Winchell, Sullivan, and Kilgallen were all on the scene.

"Cigarette girls" circulated with trays of Old Golds, Pall Malls, Camels, Raleighs, Chesterfields. and cigars such as the fine Cuban brand, Partagas, plus less pricy Bearings, Muriels, and Robert Burns. They provided packets of Sen-Sen to those wishing to freshen their breath after a smoke. The tables sported squeaky clean crystal, glistening silverware, white linen napkins, and black, Bakelite ashtrays imprinted in white with the name Bill Miller's Riviera. Alongside each ashtray was a sky-blue book of matches with an artist's image of the Riviera printed in yellow.

The ever-popular Asian Food section of the Special Menu for opening night read:

- Special Barbecued Spare Ribs $ 2.00
- White Meat Chicken, Chow Mein with Mushroom, Water Chestnuts and Bamboo Shoots $4.00
- Shrimp Chow Mein with Mushrooms $3.50
- Chinese Pepper Steak with Mushrooms $4.00
- Subgum Chow Mein with Almonds $3.50
- Chicken Chow Mein with Mushrooms $3.25
- Chop Suey with Mushrooms $3.50
- Shrimp Cantonese $3.50

Not only Asian food, but every imaginable American specialty: steaks, chops, chicken—all cooked to perfection, boasted the menu. The April evening was too cool for the round roof to be open, but through the huge windows facing the river, the George Washington Bridge provided a glittering backdrop, the twinkling of thousands of lights making it seem like the room was bathed in stars.

Bill nervously appraised the house, as he stood near a table shared by his sister and fiancé, and my wife. Abe Vine and I also stood nearby, trying to get a ballpark count, as people entered the showroom.

"How does it look, Abe?" Bill said, without turning his head.

"I bet we have seated over a thousand right now."

"We shouldn't even bother counting, boss," I said. "Whatever capacity is, just add ten percent and that'll be the crowd."

"Your lips to you-know-who's ears," said Bill. "Look over there at 'Captain' Gallo. That guy moves people like he's lining up toy soldiers." Indeed, Gallo was leading a column of people around the third tier of tables, farthest from the stage but closest to the huge, exterior windows.

"Is that Frank Costello over there?" Abe asked.

"Sure is," said Bill. "Look who he's with…His cousin."

"Who's his cousin?"

"Willie Moretti."

"Yeah and there's my buddy Longie with them," I added. "Should we send a round of drinks over, Bill?"

"Sure, why not." I was surprised that Bill didn't seem apprehensive, though there had not been any further pressure put on him to reopen the casino, which slumbered above us.

"Who are the broads?" Abe said.

Bill shushed him with a glare. "No broads tonight—that's their wives."

I signaled headwaiter Jack Osterdahl to take care of that table.

"I'm still worried about those guys," Bill said.

"Don't worry about it tonight, Bill," I said. "Looks like they have all they can handle with their wives."

"Let's send orchids over for the women," said Bill, in a flash of inspiration. "Get Eli to bring them over himself. We'll keep the women on our side, know what I mean?"

"I'll get him, Bill."

He pointed to a table right in front of the stage. "Look over there, ringside. That's 'The Crow'—Frankie Crosetti, New York Yankee shortstop. And I see he has his buddy, Charlie Keller. 'King Kong' Keller, the left-fielder, with him."

"Where's Babe Ruth?" Abe asked.

Bill frowned. "He retired more than ten years ago."

"Yeah, but he lives in New York."

"You got a point, Abe. Good thinking. We should send a special invitation."

"What about DiMaggio?"

"Same thing…Gio?"

"I'm on it. Bill, look, I think I see Jake LaMotta over there, talking to Jack Bruno and Lou Gallo. He just lost a decision to Sugar Ray Robinson six weeks ago."

"Yeah, but he beat the crap out of Robinson before that," said Abe.

"We're lousy with celebrities tonight, huh fellas?" said Bill.

As Pupi Campo's band reached the last handful of measures of their final number, the lights dimmed and the revolving stage receded into the shadows, fading out their sound. Walter Nye's sixteen-piece show band already had kicked off a hot version of

Mambo Jambo, as they came into view when their side of the band-stand rotated onto the stage.

"Break a leg, Bill," said Abe, as he put his arm around Bill's shoulders. "Ditto from me, boss," I said, as I put my right hand in my pocket and crossed my fingers.

The musical dynamic of the Nye orchestra dropped ten notches, as a deep, unseen voice came bursting through the speakers: "Ladies and gentlemen, Bill Miller's Riviera is proud to present, the Donn Arden Dancers." Applause shook the room. Clark Granger, the production singer, let loose with *Bless All the Beautiful Girls*, and twelve gorgeous chorus girls in brief, feathered costumes stepped out onto the stage in a slow, hip-thrusting manner that electrified the audience. The girls stood motionless, as the raised dance floor in front of the revolving bandstand began its slow circuit, carrying the girls on a full rotation around the dance-floor stage. Their faces displayed the faintest of welcoming smiles, adding to their allure.

The showroom went dark, other than the stage. The food had been distributed on huge, round aluminum trays prior to showtime. Small courtesy lights at the foot of the steps leading to the second and third tiers guided the waiters through their beverage deliveries. As the line of girls exited the stage to a Nye "chaser," the orchestra broke into an arrangement of *The Lady in Red*, and Tony and Sally DeMarco, perhaps the most accomplished ballroom dance team in the country, appeared from behind the black curtains at the side of the stage. The audience responded to their dips, lifts, and swirls, as Sally was hoisted in the most graceful manner, only to settle back down in absolute sync with Tony. They glided and danced to the Latin beat and the enthusiastic reception of the crowd. When the DeMarcos finished to enthusiastic applause, the announcer said, "Here is a guy who needs no introduction, but he is making us give him one anyway...Ladies and gentlemen, here he is, coming to you directly from the kitchen, the fat man himself, Mister Jackie Leonard!"

The crowd responded in an uproarious manner, one man yelling, "Hey Jackie, you tell em!"

Wearing his trademark, black, thick-rimmed eyeglasses and a black suit that looked two sizes too small for him, Leonard bounded onto the stage. When the crowd stopped applauding, he grabbed the microphone and took a handkerchief out of his pocket to wipe his brow.

"Good evening, opponents"

The crowd belly-laughed, as Leonard merrily delivered a plethora of individualized insults. One by one, he picked his victims and proceeded to destroy them, to everyone's amusement. The nervousness that Bill experienced while waiting for the show to start disappeared, as Fat Jack rattled off zinger after zinger. After concluding his "routine" and exiting the stage, he was called back three times to take a bow. The third time, Nick the doorman weaved through the audience, and motioned Bill and me over to the entrance.

"What's up?" asked Bill, slightly annoyed that he was called out of the room.

"We got a problem, boss," Nick said. "We got a guy on the ground outside. He's wearing a lumberjack outfit. He's over seven feet tall and drunk as hell. He tried to push his way into the club with two bottles of Schaefer beer in a brown paper bag. I called Al—"

"—Where's Al now?"

Nick led us out the front door, where we stood at the top of the steps and looked down on security chief Al Austin sitting on top of the allegedly seven-foot-tall lumberjack between two cars. The big guy was face down on the asphalt, with Al's knee pushing down on the back of his head.

"You missed a hell of a fight, Mister Miller," said Nick. "This monster picked Al up and threw him over that Cadillac. Then the fight really started. Al took out a blackjack and whacked the guy over the head. The guy asked, 'Are you trying to hurt me?' Then he up and threw Al over the car again... It was like, you know, Dempsey-Firpo or somethin'. Ever seen that one?"

"Long time ago, Nick."

According to Nick, Austin came back for more punishment, and Jerry Bakunis, the Riviera's soft beverage supplier, jumped the big guy from behind, grabbing his arms as Austin landed a hard right to his jaw. They both took the giant down to the ground, and that's when Austin put a chain around the guy's wrists and began cranking it up, causing the guy to scream like a banshee, which attracted a lot of attention. A tight knot of onlookers was still there, waiting for resolution.

"Okay, folks," Bill said, coming off the steps. "The show inside's a lot better—I guarantee it. Go ahead back inside and have a drink on me."

Moments later, the Fort Lee Police arrived.

"Book this fucking bum," said the sergeant. Two officers managed to drag the giant to the squad car—a 1941 Ford, two-door sedan—and stuff him inside.

Bill looked at his security chief, head to toe. "You okay, Al?" He brushed dirt and cinders off of Austin's uniform.

"One piece, I think," Austin said, as he took out his handkerchief and wiped blood from a scalp wound off of his face.

"I want you to see Doc Shapiro right now; he's upstairs in the office, filling out some paperwork. Nice work Al; you too, Jerry. Bonuses in order for you boys."

As Al and Jerry walked down the ramp to the kitchen on the south side of the building, Bill said to me, "We got ourselves a couple of guys there we can really count on. That Austin is one gutsy guy."

"Should've brought his slingshot," I said.

"Hey, Arigo, you're funnier than Leonard."

"I don't think so, Bill. He was damn funny tonight."

I followed Bill, as he trotted up the five steps and through the brass doors, moving quickly through the serpentine bar area and back to the captain's station. As we approached the showroom, all was dark and quiet. The audience was in a trance, as Tony's rich voice rendered the Piaf classic *La Vie En Rose*:

AND WHEN YOU SPEAK
ANGELS SING FROM ABOVE
EVERYDAY WORDS
SEEM TO TURN INTO LOVE SONGS.

"What's up boss?" whispered Jack Osterdahl, the waiter captain.

"Nothing much Jack just a little disagreement outside. So, what's the head count?"

"So far we squeezed 1,100 into the room. For the second show, we have at least a thousand more reservations so far. Not bad, huh, boss?"

"Could be worse," said Bill, smiling.

Tony Martin had the audience mesmerized, his straw hat tipped jauntily over his left eye, his black tuxedo impeccably tailored. He raised his left arm as if he were dancing, holding an imaginary partner's right hand, while his own right hand rested just below his stomach. This bit of fantasy drove the women in the audience wild, as did the rest of his sensuous movements as he continued singing:

HOLD ME CLOSE AND HOLD ME FAST

THIS MAGIC SPELL YOU CAST

LA VIE EN ROSE.

He followed with the romantic ballads *You Belong to My Heart, It Had to Be You,* and *I'm in the Mood for Love,* and was ready to go into his next song, when Jackie Leonard ran back onto the stage, wearing nothing but a towel wrapped around his privates and the lower portion of his rotund midsection, yelling, "Where's the soup? They promised me soup!" The antic comic halted Tony's singing, as he scooted around the stage, his fat belly jiggling. After he made his way off the stage, through the audience, and out of the showroom, and the crowd's laughter and wild applause settled down, the baritone resumed with two more beauties: *I'll Be Seeing* You and *Don't Take Your Love from Me.*

An appreciative roar rose from the audience, even before Tony reached the end of his final song. The audience grew exhausted from applauding.

Afterward, Bill's face hurt from smiling. Somewhat battered, but recuperated, security chief Al Austin sat calmly in the chorus girls' dressing room, as Mary Smith, the wardrobe mistress, sewed a torn sleeve on his uniform, and Dr. Shapiro attended to the cut on his forehead.

In the kitchen, Joe Miller and the twenty other chefs were cleaning up, while having a few beers to celebrate their role in Opening Night: 2,200 fresh dinners. Bill, Abe, Eli Quain, and I waited in the lounge to say good-bye to some of Bill's friends. We were all taken aback when we were approached by Frank Erickson, said to be a bookmaking associate of the late Arnold Rothstein, and now Costello. Although the press always connected Frank to the mob, Bill knew him as one of the most charitable guys around.

"Bill, I just wanted to stop and tell you what a great evening we had tonight," Erickson said. "You got a winner on your hands with this place." Turning to me, he said, "You're gonna make it big here, buddy."

There were those words again: you're gonna make it big. I was now 54 years old, and thought that maybe he was right, maybe my time had come, my ticket to writing the book I promised myself and Nancy.

Then Erickson spoiled the party.

"Too bad you won't open the casino upstairs, Bill."

"Sorry Frank, I just can't open that room," Bill said, without hesitation. "It's personal more than it is business."

Erickson picked up his fedora and put down a five-spot for the hatcheck girl. "I respect that, Bill," he said, fitting the hat on his head. "I just hope no one takes it too personal."

Chapter 22

The antics Jackie Leonard brought to the stage that night did not go unnoticed beyond the Riviera. The inner circles of the entertainment business quickly noted, in the press and on the radio, that his antics were the ticket to something new for cabaret acts. They were the ingredients to connect the ridiculous with the sublime. Prior to Leonard's impromptu invasion of Martin's space at the Riviera, romantic baritone singers were all held in reverence by the audience, as they sang lyrics that soothed the hearts of the gals at home, while their husbands and lovers served overseas during wartime.

Jackie Leonard and Tony Martin just may have been the catalysts that began a new trend in nightclub performing, and maybe, at New York's Belmont Plaza Hotel, word of their shenanigans may have triggered the teaming of two other cabaret performers: Dino Crocetti and Jerome Levitch, who became known as Dean Martin and Jerry Lewis.

Jerry and Dean were both appearing at the Glass Hat lounge in the Belmont Plaza Hotel, when they first decided on the possibility of teaming up. In March 1946, they were billed separately, at New York's Havana Madrid nightclub. Only this time, they started to fool around onstage, as Jerry launched a wild comedy routine or two in the middle of a Martin song. In July, the pair was booked into Skinny D'Amato's 500 Club in Atlantic City, and scheduled for two nightly shows. The show was well rehearsed and tightly staged, but on their first date, the first show fell flat. Between shows, Skinny called them into his office.

"You guys went over like a lead balloon. Where's the funny stuff you promised?"

When Martin and Lewis returned to the stage for their second show, all bets were off.

"Let's just do what we like to do when we kid around with people," Jerry urged his partner. "We got nothing to lose."

Except sanity. When the second show started, Dean took the mike and eased into a love song in his smooth, inimitable way,

Jerry came barging out, dressed like a busboy, and looking crazed. He proceeded to smash dishes all over the stage, and set the band's sheet music on fire. For a while, Dean continued to sing…then he joined the madness, throwing dinner rolls at Jerry, and chasing him around the stage. The audience, which included Abe Vine and his wife, Molly, shrieked.

When Abe arrived at the Riviera the following night, the first thing he did was to tell Bill all about the mayhem at the 500 Club. I was in Bill's office at the time.

"They made Jackie and Tony look like a snooze-fest, and that already was pretty crazy," Abe said. "I'm telling you—they actually wrecked the place. I thought the audience would pee their pants, Bill."

"Does that include you, Abe?"

"You're damn right it does. We got to get these guys here."

"I'll look into it," Bill said. I was surprised at his seeming lack of enthusiasm. Maybe it was because Martin and Lewis were a new act, and Bill considered the Riviera to be a premium place—which it was.

"I already did," Abe said, still excited. "I went backstage and talked to them both, and they said they would like to appear at the Riviera sometime, but would have to clear it with their agent, Abby Greshler. Dean said they were booked solid for a while, and even had some movie possibilities."

That seemed to open Bill's eyes. "That's pretty fast work. I know Abby. He's president of the Diamond Agency and has been a friend of mine for a long time. He's right out of Central Casting."

"Call him," Abe said.

"You running entertainment now, too?"

"I just don't want us to miss out."

"I know." Bill smiled to indicate he was teasing. "Did Martin sing a real song, or did they just horse around?

"Tell you the truth, Bill, I forget."

"'Cause that boy has a nice, smooth, singing style that I happen to love—he's had some recordings. And, more importantly, the ladies love him."

"Now that you mention it, Dean was telling me he adopted that style from the Mills Brothers. Did you know that, Bill?"

"Sounds like you and Martin got pretty chummy. Know what? You've got hidden talents, Abe."

"I'm going to tell you something else. You know who was in the audience, roaring with laughter along with the rest of us?"

"No, who?"

"None other than our buddy, Willie Moretti."

"Oh shit. Did he see you? Does he know who you are? "

"He was having such a good time with the group he was with, he wasn't paying any attention to the rest of us."

"You know, I think I am beginning to get this entire thing figured out," said Bill, looking like a man who'd come to terms with a thorny problem. "We're constantly worrying about the 'boys' and what they might do. We even try to keep them out of here. Let's forget about all that, and make an effort to welcome them into the Riviera, invite them here as our special guests. I know one thing for sure: our audiences love to be around them. Those guys are celebrities, right along with the stars we put onstage. Think about it, every day the newspapers are full of stories about them."

"I can see it in lights," I said. "Bill Miller's Riviera presents 'the Gangsters.'"

Bill and Abe looked at me like I was nuts.

"From now on, the welcome mat is out to everybody on both sides of the law," Bill said.
"Gio, tell the captains, whenever one of the 'boys' comes into the club, make sure his group gets a good table, and treat them with the same respect and dignity that everyone else gets, maybe a little better. After all, their silver dollar is as round as everyone else's."

Bill Miller was a beautiful guy to work for and, by the end of 1946, it looked like I had a job for life, or at least as long as the Riviera was in business. Over the holidays, it was very obvious that many of the mob guys, whose numbers had been increasing since Bill had instituted his Open Door policy, were noticeably absent for some reason. Not that they were the main group of patrons in attendance by any means, but their presence, and their heavy tipping to the captains and waiters was sorely missed over the holidays.

Late in the year, Bill learned that Lansky and Luciano were to host a major conference in Havana, which every major crime family would attend. The "Havana Conference" at the Hotel Nacional took place during the last week of December, starting just before Christmas, and was seen as the most important mob conference since the famous gathering in Atlantic City seventeen years earlier. It intended to survey the postwar landscape for organized crime. Cuba had become the mob capital.

Up north, the newly launched Riviera only gained in popularity, as the club hosted all comers—high school proms by spring, charitable luncheons in the fall. Bill made sure there was something for everyone. For the Hebrew National Orphans' Home, for example, he booked pianist-humorist Victor Borge and ventriloquist Jimmy Nelson, the latter a regular on Milton Berle's television show.

But while the Riviera earned a respectable civic profile, it breathed dynamic nightclub entertainment for adults seeking heat and glamour. Its reputation solidified during the next two years, as the strengthening economy brought in the customers, and the Riviera showroom attracted the hottest headliners in the country.

In February 1949, Bill scheduled lunch with Martin-Lewis agent Abby Greshler at Jack Dempsey's on Broadway. As usual, he asked me to drive him into the city and join him for lunch. By the time I entered Dempsey's after parking Bill's car, Bill and Abby already were at the meat of the matter.

"Abby, we get first dibs on them, right?"

"Of course," said Abby. "They go to your place before they go to the Copa—you can take that to the bank. Look, Bill, you have always treated me like a king. How could I let any other club owner scoop you? You know that would never happen, sweetheart."

They shook hands on the deal, and Abby made a trip to the men's room before our meals arrived. Bill looked at me, his expression halfway between angered and amused.

"I don't trust that sonofabitch."

Sure enough, in the spring of 1949, Martin and Lewis signed for an engagement at Jules Podell's Copacabana. Bill countered by booking Jackie Gleason along with the June Taylor Dancers.

"How come we've got the June Taylor Dancers, and not the Donn Arden Dancers?" I asked.

"Well, I heard that Jackie is crazy about June's sister, Marilyn, and so he demands a package deal. That Gleason has not hit his full stride yet, but in a little while, he is going to be the biggest thing out there."

"He's pretty big right now," I said, extending my arms in front of my stomach to signify Gleason's girth.

Bill had booked a new singer named Eddie Fisher for New Year's Eve, 1949. Fisher was fresh off the Catskills circuit, and did not quite have his act together yet. The response he received from the Riviera audience was lackluster. However, the following June, Berle gave him a spot on his TV show, and Fisher was suddenly a smash, getting rave reviews for the two songs he sang. But could he maintain that appeal live, and in a full nightclub show? That was the question in Bill's mind.

A few days later, after the Berle TV show, Bill asked me to find out if Fisher could fill in for Fran Warren, who was the supporting act for Danny Thomas, the current headliner at the Riviera. Fran had taken sick and was unable to make the date.

"Are you sure you want Eddie?" I asked him. "Remember last year?"

"That was last year, Gio. Watch what happens this time."

When Fisher arrived for a 3:15 rehearsal, he had only a handful of arrangements with him. When Walter Nye asked him what he was supposed to do for the rest of the show, Eddie said, "Don't worry about it. We can fake it."

Nye stared at Fisher like a schoolmaster about to discipline a student. "Young man," he said, "my orchestra is not in the habit of 'faking it,' as you call it."

"Well, if you can't fake it, I will sing a cappella, so don't worry about it."

Fisher had a bright, almost childlike way about him, and we all had to realize that, though he was just a kid, he was rising quickly to the top of the entertainment ladder. He did not even have time to buy a tuxedo or hone his act. But he did have a couple of hit records: Anytime and *Oh, My Papa*. When Eddie Fisher took the Riviera stage that night, the crowd responded. The appearance on the Berle show and the radio airplay had registered. But his repertoire was thin, and after doing the arranged half-dozen or so songs, he turned to Nye and said, "Guess I have to go it alone now." Looking up at the musicians, he shouted, "If you guys can fake it, let's do it. They are screaming so loud I don't think they can hear me sing, anyway."

I was standing next to Bill at his usual spot by the kitchen door, when he turned to me and said, "See, what did I tell you? Look at them. They are going wild—what a difference a show on TV makes, huh?"

As the Riviera surged, Bill's financial situation improved. In July, he made the final payment on the purchase money mortgage that Ben had been holding. From then on, I noticed that Bill had even more zip in his step. He had passed the test, and finally started believing that he was making it big as a restaurateur-showman.

So when Greshler showed up at the Riviera in the fall to pitch Martin and Lewis, Bill felt no need to accommodate him.

"You sonofabitch—you told me last year that we would have the first shot at Martin and Lewis, and then you book them at the Copa! I am going to kick the shit out of you, you little weasel!" It was the worst temper I had ever seen come out of him. Gentleman Bill could also be one tough hombre.

Greshler responded like a true agent. "So Bill, I guess inviting you and the wife over for dinner on Saturday night with Vi and me is out of the question, huh?"

At this, Bill's enraged face dissolved in laughter.

"Look, sweetheart, I want to do you a favor—what can I do to make it up to you bubby?" Greshler asked plaintively.

"What can you do for me, you fuck? I'll tell you what: If you ever want to book an act in my club again, you will have to get Dean and Jerry to show up for my nephew's bar mitzvah in December. How's that for what you can do for me?"

"Consider it done Bill. Just tell me where and when…What's the kid's name?"

"Barney."

"What's the address?"

"Give me your pen, Gio." Bill wrote the address on a Riviera envelope: 198 Lee Avenue, Brooklyn. He handed the envelope to Abby and turned to me. "Let's see if your friend Dreshler makes good on his promise this time, Gio."

"On my mother's grave," Dreshler insisted, pressing a hand to his heart, Pledge-of-Allegiance style.

In early December, on bar mitzvah Saturday, Dean and Jerry rang the bell on the door of the apartment over the grocery store, where Barney Miller and his mother Dorothy and his dad Joe lived, the same apartment where Bill Miller grew up. When Joe opened the door, Jerry leaped into their small apartment and proceeded to sing, "Take my hand, I'm a stranger in Williamsburg." After about four bars of that, Dean asked, "Does anybody have a drink for a thirsty prospector?"

From there, the decorum of the religious celebration plunged into chaos, as Dean and Jerry ran around and moved anything that wasn't nailed down, including pictures hanging on the wall. And there was "Uncle Bill" shaking his head in amusement. Conniving Dreshler had come through. Not too many kids would have as memorable a bar mitzvah as Bill's nephew experienced: a living room seat on the hottest act in America.

The next stop for Bill and wife was Miami, which they reached after a three-day drive in their new Lincoln Continental convertible. Abe Vine asked me if I wanted to drive down to Miami with him, so we could bring the Lincoln back to New Jersey, as Bill had chosen to fly back up north to attend an important meeting. But this was not the time for me to head south.

"Al called me the other night—in the middle of the night," I explained to Abe. He said he was camped out in the 'star's dressing room' as usual, about 15 feet from the stage door, and heard a knock on the stage door 'bout two a.m. When he went to the door and looked through the small window at the top, a man was standing there, with his face covered in blood, or what looked like blood."

"The guy cries, 'Let me in! They're trying to kill me!' So Al keeps the door closed, calls the police, and asks them to send an ambulance and some backup. When he goes back to the dressing room and picks up the house phone, there was no dial tone. So now he's a little nervous, and he grabs the 12-gauge from the stall shower—you know, the one they use for shooting raccoons that raid the dumpsters—and he rushes out of the dressing room, across the revolving bandstand, and down onto the stage. Then he goes through the bar and into the lobby, crawling on his hands and knees in case bullets are about to come pouring in."

"This was right after the snowstorm, don't forget. Al said it was hard trying to see through the fogged windows and the windblown snow, but he could make out four men crouching off to the side of the stage door."

"Shit, we got tens of thousands of dollars' worth of liquor left in the building over the winter," Abe said, as if that had just dawned on him.

"No shit, Sherlock…So, Al pumps a round into the chamber of the 12-gauge, opens the lock on one of the doors with his master, and fires off a round of buckshot into the air, in their direction. Then he sees those four guys running down the parking lot and jumping into the back of a box truck. Al locks the door, goes back to the dressing room, and turns off the radio. For the rest of the night, he sat in a chair, holding the shotgun his lap. When the sun came up, he carefully opened the stage door and looked around outside. No drops of blood on the snow; only the tracks of those four guys coming and going."

"So, after that, Al wants me to check on him once in a while. By the way, Abe, the telephone wire had been cut."

"Mob guys?"

"I don't think so." They found a new place to run their gambling operations: the old baby-carriage factory on Lemoine and South Marginal, right in the middle of Fort Lee."

"No kidding—I know that place," Abe said. "All right, Gio, I'll handle the car. You take care of business up there. See you soon."

Little did I realize that fate had drawn me a lucky hand.

Although the Riviera traditionally closed in late October and opened again in April, New Year's Eve was the one night the club opened in winter. Joe Miller joined Abe for the trip to Miami, where they spent a few days relaxing before driving back up north, Abe in his car, Joe in Bill's 1948 Lincoln Continental. It was Christmas Eve 1951. As they approached Jacksonville, with Abe's car in the lead, a drunk driver sailed across the highway divider, hitting Joe's Lincoln head on. Abe careened to a halt, ran back to the mangled Lincoln, and pulled an unconscious Joe from the smoldering wreck. Two days later, the day after Christmas, Joe was dead.

Bill always blamed himself, because it was he who had asked Joe to drive the Lincoln back from Florida. The tragedy cast a pall over the Riviera, just as it was becoming perhaps the premier nightclub in America.

Chapter 23

The effect of Joe Miller's death on the morale at the Riviera was only exacerbated by the Korean conflict, which was raging in the Far East. President Truman kept telling the people that it was "only a police action," but we sensed that those words were a cover-up of the truth. Many of the young guys who worked at the Riviera—car-hops, waiters, kitchen staff—as well as some of the celebrity per-formers, were volunteering to join the action.

I was drinking coffee one morning with an electrician named Eddie, who said, "This Korean thing is taking away all the good singers."

I looked at him, somewhat amused. "All of them?"

"A guy I knew back in Brooklyn, named Vito Farinola, just signed up. We were in the same class at Lafayette High School. He is one great singer."

Vito, huh? "If he's so great, how come I never heard of him?"

"Oh, that's because he changed his name to Vic. Vic Damone. I think Damone was his mother's maiden name or something like that. You've heard of him now, right?"

"Of course," I said. "In fact, I know the boss wants him to appear here, when he gets out of the service."

"Really? I can't wait. That will be terrific." Eddie almost spilled his coffee.

The Korean "conflict," as it was called, had everyone in despair, thinking that the U.S. was heading for another war on the scale of WWII. Many believed that Truman's use of the term "conflict" was nothing more than stage management to stem a national tide of dis-trust of his administration. Meanwhile, in 1951, skilled stage man-agement was a key to the Riviera's continued success. The perform-ers who graced that stage—Danny Thomas, Lena Horne, Peggy Lee, Red Buttons, Jimmy Durante, the Will Mastin Trio (featur-ing Sammy Davis Jr.), Joel Gray, Tony Arden, Martha Ray, the Jack Cole Dancers—locked up our audiences, heart and soul. And we anxiously awaited the time when "The Voice," Mr. Frank Sinatra, would be here, too.

In the last week of September, we finally hosted the madcap Dean Martin and Jerry Lewis show. The week of their appearance, Dean and Jerry had a tremendously hectic schedule. Although they were booked at the Riviera for two shows a night, they were also booked at the Roxy Theater in New York to do five shows a day. And in-between shows, they kept their act going. These boys, it would seem, had superhuman stamina.

They arrived slightly early on their opening at the Riviera, and were hanging around outside the stage door about 75 feet from the parking-lot attendant's bench. As the evening's first few cars pulled up to the entrance, Jerry said to Dean, "Let's go over and sit on the bench with those guys and have some fun."

After kibitzing a while with the young carhops, Dean said, "Hey Jerry, you go over and park that nice man's car, while I talk to that good-lookin' lady getting out of it." So, Jerry grabbed a bottle of window cleaner and a rag, ran over to the car, and went to work on it, Jerry Lewis-style, while Dean helped the guy's wife out.

Jerry then said to the poor guy, "All right, Buster, out you go. You're holding up the works here. I need this car to practice on...I just got my learner's permit."

"Hold on, son—you're new at this," Dean shouted.

The car was a new Oldsmobile with standard three-speed transmission, and the owner just stood there, dumbfounded, as Jerry jumped behind the wheel, pushed the clutch in and out, grinding the gears into first. What happened next was right out of a Ringling Brothers Circus, as the new car bucked wildly around the parking lot, thanks to Jerry's expert handling. Everyone watching the parking lot performance, including Bill Miller, was in stitches, as Jerry and Dean greeted the arriving guests with one comic bit or another, zaniness that somehow prepped, rather than tired, them for an impeccable comedy performance in the showroom. Many people in the audience had seen the antics of the two outside in the parking lot, and were doubly primed for their hilarious performance.

"Ladies and gentleman, Bill Miller's Riviera is proud to present the comedy team of Dean Martin and Jerry Lewis," said the voice over the sound system. Before the announcer could get his words out, everyone in the room was screaming and on their feet.

Dean came out first with, "Oh, my God, this looks like the Last Supper. That guy over there looks so old, I bet his social security number is two." After a few one-liners by Dean, Jerry came bounding onto the stage, looking like a juvenile escaped from an insane asylum.

"Dean, you're a very talented guy."

"Yeah, my talent is exceeded only by my alimony payments."

Back and forth they went for an hour, making it up as they went along, to the hysterical delight of the audience. Dean sang *Almost Like Being in Love* from the Broadway musical *Brigadoon*, then reached into his bag of tricks and tested out a new song written by Harry Warren. Although it wasn't yet scheduled for release by Capitol, Dean felt this was the song that would put his vocal career on the map. What could be better than to début it at the Riviera? The song was called *That's Amore!*

When Dean had finished, and the applause died down, Jerry asked the crowd, "How do you like Dean's new nose?"

Dean responded, "At least it's a lot smaller than Durante's."

They simply tore up the Riviera stage, leaving the audience, and the musicians on the bandstand, exhausted from laughing. As I stood in the audience, watching reactions, I saw Willie Moretti motioning to me to approach his table. I hadn't seen him or Longie enter the club, so I was surprised to see them sitting at a second-tier table. As I approached, Willie grabbed my arm and said, "Hey Gio, sit down. Great show, huh?"

Longie rose from the table, put his arm around my shoulders, and said, "See kid, didn't I tell you? Stick with me and you're gonna make it big." He turned to Moretti. "Willie, did I ever tell you how this kid saved me from taking a beating?"

"Come on, Longie, that's old news," I said. "Can I get you guys anything? I asked.

"No, not now," Moretti said, "but let me tell you something, Gio, Longie here tells me that your boss has been gettin' some heat to reopen the casino upstairs. Is that right?"

I hesitated, and my eyes turned to Longie, my safe port in a storm.

"Hey Willie, lay off the kid…he's got nothing to do with our room upstairs."

"What do you mean *our* room? Ever since Miller took over this joint, we have been on the outs. Listen, Longie, and you, too, Gio: If Miller thinks he can—"

"—Enough, Willie," Longie said sternly. "Gio, before Willie has a stroke, get him a fresh Johnny Walker black, will you, please?"

"How about if I send a whole bottle over to you guys," I said, rising from the table.

Moretti broke out into a wide smile. "Tell your boss to relax," he said. "I was just teasin'. Nobody is going to bother him anymore regarding that room upstairs."

I was surprised to hear his words. "Okay, I'll tell Bill what you said."

Then Moretti said, "My friend, here," nodding toward Longie, "was shocked to hear that you have been bothered by certain people." He stared into my eyes. "Now you go and tell Bill, 'no more problems.' Be sure to tell him that." He patted me on my cheek, as if to send me on my way.

I thought he was laying it on a little thick.

"So Willie, what you are saying is, from now on, nobody is going to care if we go up there, right?"

"Fuck do I care?" His words to the contrary, Moretti didn't sound so accommodating anymore. "Nobody has used that room for years now, am I right?"

"That's right. Bill always insists that we stay out of that room." I looked at Longie, then back at Moretti. "Mostly out of respect for you."

"Nothing is up there anymore, so you can suit yourself," Willie said dismissively.

When I saw Bill later that night, I relayed Moretti's pronouncement. He smiled.

"That was big of him, huh Gio? Kefauver's got all those boys on their best behavior...for *now*."

Indeed, Senate hearings being conducted by Tennessee's Estes Kefauver, had put the clamps on organized crime. Both Longie and Moretti had testified at those very hearings, and neither was anxious to step out of line.

On a late afternoon in early October, intrepid security chief Al Austin rushed into the upstairs office, looking for Bill and me.

"Did you hear the news about Moretti?" he asked, out of breath.

"Who?" secretary Dorothy, Joe Miller's widow, asked.

"Willie Moretti."

"Is he a singer?"

"He didn't get a chance to. He was murdered around noon today at Joe's Elbow Room Restaurant."

"Across from Palisades Amusement park?"

"Yep, that's it."

I came out of an inner office and drew close. Bill was not on the premises. Al looked at me and, by my expression, he knew I had heard him.

"One of the Fort Lee cops told me that Willie went there for a late breakfast with some friends," Al continued. "Before he even had his coffee... This is unbelievable. He was here to see the show this past weekend. Backstage, I heard him ask Jerry and Dean to meet him for lunch today. He was kidding around with Jerry."

"Obviously, Jerry Lewis never made it to lunch with him today," I said.

"Jerry called the office, early this morning," said Dorothy. "He said he had the mumps, and the doctor told him he was quarantined. But I thought he was kidding."

"Thank God they missed that breakfast appointment," said Al.

A cold chill raced down my back when I heard the news. Up to now, even though I knew that guys like Longie and Willie were in the type of business that played for keeps, knowing them on a personal level made them seem like everyday characters to me. The talk around the club was that Willie met his end because his underworld associates felt he was much too accommodating in his answers to Kefauver's committee. According to them, he had violated their code of silence, known as omertà—he should have simply invoked the Fifth Amendment, as virtually everyone else did.

If the Moretti rub-out were not enough excitement for the Riviera and Fort Lee, two days later, Fort Lee Police Chief, Fred Stengel was found dead, with a bullet wound in his head fired from his own service revolver.

The official police report read this way: "On October 6, 1951, the body of Police Chief Fred Stengel was found dead from an apparent suicide. Stengel had been awaiting trial on charges of protecting gambling joints for the underworld czar, Joe Adonis. Stengel shot himself in the head with his service revolver a few days after bigtime gambler, Willie Moretti, was gunned down in nearby Cliffside Park, NJ. Moretti was 'rubbed out' for talking too much. He had been expected to testify in Stengel's trial."

Sometime after Moretti's demise, word reached Bill and me that Ben Marden had just pulled off the coup of the decade. He and his partners had purchased, from Amado Trinidad, the Radio Habana Cuba (RHC) *Cadena Azul* radio and television network. The new president of the RHC "Blue Network," which consisted of 12 stations located in all six provinces of Cuba, was Edmund Chester, former vice president of the Columbia Broadcasting System. Clarence Alexander, of the Dumont Television Network, was appointed its manager. As part of the deal, Ben obtained permits to construct and operate television stations in Havana, Matanzas, Santa Clara, Ciego de Avila, Camaguey, and Santiago.

"At first," Bill explained to me, "the broadcasters in Cuba did not want anything to do with foreign entities coming in and taking over their networks. But Elliot Roosevelt, FDR's son, stepped in and smoothed things over to allow Ben and his partners to execute the deal."

I found that fascinating. "How did that happen?"

Bill had that look in his eye: Sit back, 'cause I'm gonna tell you a good story.

"Elliott Roosevelt was first called in to do a survey that would establish a value for the whole thing. The Cubans were asking for a million-and-a-half, but Elliott's survey estimated the actual value to be closer to one million even. Then, when Cuba's president, Prío Socarrás, balked at having Marden buy it all up, Elliott offered to step in as a negotiator—as long as he was released from his position as the appraiser."

"And he negotiated pretty smoothly."

"Looks like. Tell you what: I think the old man had his back."

As I say... fascinating. "Well, one thing is for sure; Marden won't let any grass grow under his feet."

Bill looked into the distance, as if he could spot his fortune on the horizon. "Gio, someday I am going to build a hotel in Cuba. It's anything goes down there."

While wheeler-dealers maneuvered on the island of Cuba, government wheels were turning in the Riviera's backyard. A new highway project entailed New York and New Jersey jointly seizing the land on which the Riviera sat. Not even a Jerry Lewis could navigate around high-speed traffic.

The actual planning for the highway—called The Palisades Interstate Parkway—had begun in 1933, and was overseen by a man named William A. Welch. Ben Marden had perceived the threat, when he purchased the land for the new Riviera. During the 1940s, John D. Rockefeller renewed the concept of a parkway along the New Jersey Palisades and into New York State, and teamed up with the ultimate planner for the project, the powerful Robert Moses. Work on the roadway, which was to run along the west bank of the Hudson, had begun in New York in April 1947, and on the Jersey side the following year. At that point, the Riviera property was not in the crosshairs, but since the New Jersey portion of the Parkway had started about a half-mile to the north, the writing was on the wall that, sooner or later, the Riviera was going to be gobbled up, just like all the other properties along the Hudson.

For the greater good.

In 1951, nothing seemed to be going right, not only for the Riviera and the people who made their living there, but also for the stars who performed there. Sinatra had divorced his first wife, Nancy Barbato, the mother of his three children and married the ultra-glamorous, tempestuous movie star, Ava Gardner. Their star power and volatile tempers were the talk of the town. That Sinatra seemed restless, even in performance, was not surprising. His career had been tailing off, as his label, Columbia Records, saddled him with songs and arrangements that did not do his style justice. His marriage was sapping his energy. Still, he packed them in at the Riviera. The famous voice, which had deserted him not long before, was back in top form, and those who listened closely discerned a growing maturity in the sound.

The legions of bobbysoxers, who had cemented his legend in New York, also had grown up. No longer were they teenagers, taking the bus and Eighth Avenue Subway to the Paramount Theater, only to wait in line for hours for tickets. Now they made reservations at places like the Riviera. They had exchanged their bobby sox for nylon stockings.

Perhaps his biggest and, early on, most influential fan had been Willie Moretti, who had never missed a Sinatra performance at the Riviera. At one time, each lived in the same neighborhood Hasbrouck Heights, New Jersey. It was said that, prior to Sinatra's getting divorce, Moretti had urged him to stay with Nancy. On this trip to the Riviera, Sinatra felt Moretti's absence.

Sinatra had just finished filming *Double Dynamite*, and had signed to do the picture, Meet *Danny Wilson*, each destined to fall flat. A role that could catapult him to stardom was elusive. We all believed that he was a sleeping giant, whose career would take off again, like a second-stage rocket.

As a singer, Sinatra was becoming a master interpreter of lyrics, rather than just a heartthrob. "Frank could sing the names in the telephone book and make it sound good," Bill liked to say. But what he really could do was sing a name in a way that clued the listener into that person's feelings. For a popular singer, that's an achievement.

Aside from Sinatra's fan base of maturing bobbysoxers, he also had fans from the dark side: the most notorious mobsters this country has ever seen. Like every other young performer, Sinatra's exposure to the mobsters in the early stages of his career was as normal as blueberry pie, because these guys owned or influenced the joints that hired him. That was not the case at the Riviera, of course, but whenever he appeared there, the Chicago-based Fischetti brothers would meet with him backstage. His friendship with Charlie Fischetti had begun in June of 1946, when Sinatra was making the film *It Happened in Brooklyn*, and accompanied the mobster when he visited his mother in Brooklyn during the shoot. Later, Sinatra was invited to stay at the Fischetti family home in Miami and, from there, he went to Havana, where he was seen in the company of Lucky Luciano at Meyer Lansky's place, the Casino Grand Nacional. This launched a spate of malicious rumors about Frank being connected to the mob.

At the Riviera, we discounted the newspapers' playing up a supposed Sinatra mob connection. The nastiest press had been coming for years from *New York Daily Mirror* columnist Lee Mortimer, who went as far as to provide Clyde Tolson, number-two man at the FBI, with a picture of Sinatra in Havana, and cited the singer's close friendship with Willie Moretti. Mortimer frequented the Riviera to glean stories for his column, and we all wondered if the two would come to blows, as they had outside a Los Angeles restaurant in 1947, resulting in a lawsuit. No such fireworks happened at the Riviera.

That was good news for Bill, who wanted fireworks confined to the stage. And Frank Sinatra and many other entertainers were capable of generating them.

Chapter 24

In April of 1952, Bill Miller called a private meeting with his attorney, Mort Learner, his accountant, Al Kevelson, and myself in his office to discuss the condemnation of the Riviera property by the New Jersey Department of Transportation. He explained that the Rockefeller Foundation had purchased almost all of the New Jersey Palisades land, stretching from the George Washington Bridge in New Jersey, north across the state line to the Bear Mountain Bridge at Stony Point, New York. While most of the Parkway property was acquired amicably, two significant pieces needed to be acquired through eminent domain, otherwise known as condemnation. These were the Burnett estate in Alpine, and Bill Miller's Riviera nightclub in Fort Lee.

"Bill, I think we are running out of time with holding off the inevitable," said Learner.

"Don't worry about the compensation; it will be taken care of, as I told you," Kevelson said, then asked Learner to explain how all of this had come to pass. It was a tale of Life in the Big City.

"In the early nineteen-twenties," Learner began, "John D. Rockefeller quietly bought up as much land as possible along the summit of the New Jersey Palisades. By nineteen-thirty-three, he had acquired several hundred acres, and he donated that to the Interstate Park Commission, with the stipulation that it be used for a scenic parkway from the George Washington Bridge to the Bear Mountain Bridge. He added the caveat that all man-made structures had to be removed. I have here a list of all properties acquired during that process."

Learner looked around at everyone. "Did you people know that the property along the cliffs was known as 'Millionaire's Row?'... Dr. Ernest Cadgene was a French chemist, who operated silk mills in Paterson; his property was located in Englewood Cliffs. Manuel Rionda was known as the 'Sugar Baron,' because he owned sugarcane plantations in Cuba. He built Rio Vista in Alpine—the largest of the Palisades estates. I wonder if he knows Meyer and the boys?"

No one laughed.

Morty went on with his list. "Rionda's nephew built Glen Goin, which was located on the old Nordhoff estate. Rockefeller also acquired John and Mable Ringling's place, Gray Crag... Yes, *that* Ringling—from the circus.

"Then there was the estate owned by John Clawson and Cora Timkin Burnett, a scientist and an artist. Cora was heiress to the huge Timken Roller Bearings fortune. The two of them designed a weird, secluded place in an isolated section at the edge of the cliff in Alpine. Lord knows what they were up to when the oil lamp went out"

This time, we laughed. All except Bill.

"Let's save the comedy for Joey Bishop," he said, nervously tapping a pen on the desk.

"Only trying to lighten things up a little, Bill," said Learner.

"Lighten up your ass," Bill spat out. "We're losing the Riviera. And I've got all my marbles in this game."

"Can't fight city hall, Bill."

We all looked at each other. Learner had it, right on the money.

"Tougher than the mob," I said.

"That's about the size of it," Learner said. "...I'll go on. Let's see, we have Cliff Dale, a summer home owned by George A. Zabriskie, a flour merchant and amateur historian. And lastly, Penlyn, the Oltmans' estate. All these owners 'capitulated'—at a premium, I might add— and their estates have been demolished. Just two properties resisted: the Burnett place and...the Riviera. Now they will be condemned."

"Makes it sound like I'm a leper or something," Bill said. He stood, walked around the desk, and faced all of us like a football coach ready to deliver a pep talk. Except none was forthcoming this day.

"So, that's all of it," he said. He looked at me. "Gio, you have been involved with this place since the early days...I'm sorry."

"So am I, Bill. Not your fault...Is the property already gone?"

"As a matter of fact, it is," said Morty. "That's how eminent domain works. After they take it, they begin the settlement process, which includes the consideration of cash that they are willing to pay for it." He was looking at Bill now. "They establish the amount they are willing to pay you, Bill, through an appraisal process, and when that is settled, you move out and they move in. It's as simple as that."

"Don't we have anything to say about the amount of money they are going to pay us?" asked Bill.

"You can hire your own appraisers, and have them give you their opinion of the value, and then both sides can fight it out."

"What about the business? I'm going to lose my income and everything else I've worked for, and these bastards are not going to pay for that?"

"I've been trying to tell you, Bill—they *will* pay for your business. They have to. And I expect they will also make an offer to pay for your relocation."

"That's big of them. You know, I am so damn disgusted with this, it makes me sick to my stomach. I've worked all my life toward making this place the greatest night club in the world, and now look at what's happening. I stuck my neck out for this place, time and time again, to make it a clean operation, and they just walk in and take it away from me?"

Bill was never one to lap up the credit, but now that his back was to the wall, he wasn't bashful.

"Look Morty, I don't care how much it costs; I want to fight them all the way."

"You know, Bill, Marden went through the same thing that you're going through right now," I said. "They took his place through eminent domain, too."

"I don't think that was eminent domain," Gio. "I heard that, after the smoke cleared, it was Jean Richard who bellied up and sold it to them without a fight. No, that place was not taken by eminent domain, no matter what anybody thinks. From what I hear, our place and the Burnett place are the only two holdouts, and at least we are making them fight for it...So Morty, you think I'm crazy or what?"

Morty's smile reflected his admiration of Bill's tenacity. "Look at it this way: If you build the business even more from here, they will have to pay more for it."

Bill turned to me. "Okay, Gio, that settles it. I am going to put together the greatest shows money can buy, and we're going to pack this place every friggin' night, and we are going to make the people understand what they are losing." He turned back to Morty. "How much time do we have left before they take it?"

"Six months, a year, maybe a little more if we stall them."

"That's not much time at all, especially to sign the top acts and schedule them to come here. I think it is in our best interest to have a meeting with our entire staff and lay it on the line. We need to tell them truth. Maybe they will understand or maybe they won't, but I will be damned if I am going to keep them in the dark."

And that was what Bill Miller was all about.

"Gio, maybe this is your chance to write that book you have always talked about."

"I might just do that Bill, I might just do that," I said, with conviction.

"I mean it Gio, you have a big story in you and it needs to come out, so why don't you write that novel about the Riviera, from start to finish. You got a real story here, and it's not over yet."

"You really want me to do that, Bill?"

"Hell, yeah! Why not? Show the people what this place was all about. Now let's see if we can get this place to go out in a blaze of glory."

"I hope you don't mean a blaze, as in 'fire,' like with Ben's first place here."

"I told you guys, leave the jokes to Bishop and Durante."

Four days later, per Bill's wishes, I called a meeting of the entire staff. There must have been about 200 people in the showroom that day, and Bill provided a nice buffet. Rumors had been flying around for weeks, but except for Bill and myself, no one knew exactly what the score was. Bill asked me to open the meeting, so I got up on the stage and tapped a spoon on a glass in front of the mike to quiet the house. Then I played MC for a moment on the great stage of the Riviera.

"Our boss wants to say a few words about the future of the Riviera" I promptly turned the microphone over to Bill. You could have heard the proverbial pin drop. He adjusted the microphone stand to his height, while the speaker screeched in pain for a harsh second.

"Hi everyone. First, I want to thank you for taking the time to come to this meeting. I know I did not give you much time to prepare to be here, but I have to tell you something that is happening beyond my control. You see, the Palisades Interstate Park Commission has decided to build a highway right through here, where we are standing, and they have told us we have to leave."

A collective groan came up from the audience, as the words settled in their heads.

"I can't tell you exactly how long it will take for them to move us out—maybe a year, maybe a little longer—but I can tell you that we have no choice in the matter. We are ordered to go, so they can tear the building down. I know that some of you have dedicated your lives to this place, and it will be hard for you just to pick up and move, but keep in mind that, if it wasn't for each and every one of you, the Riviera would never have become what it is today."

"To those of you, who feel that they must leave right now, I can only say that I understand; for those who want to stick it out 'til they bring in the wrecking ball, I love you for it. Either way, I can only thank you all for being such a big part of all of our dreams. I want you all to know that we are in the process of trying to find you work in other clubs—after all these years in this business, I have a lot of contacts and, I believe, friends. So we'll see if that helps... Good luck and God bless you all."

There was no applause, as Bill left the stage. His listeners were in shock. When Bill, Abe, and Dorothy left the building, and a murmuring rose to a din, I picked up the microphone.

"I have an announcement," I said, quieting things down. "On that long serving table, by the doors to the kitchen, is a signature sheet for those of you who wish to stay on until we close the place. I will ask you to sign it, if you wish to remain on until the end."

A line formed immediately and, one by one, people signed to commit to staying. Later that day, I called Bill and told him what a surprise it was to see almost everyone pledging to stay until the bitter end.

"I had a feeling that might happen," he said. "What a terrific bunch. Make sure Dorothy puts a few bucks extra into each of their paychecks next week: twenty-five for the waiters, and fifty for the captains. Gio, I want you to take a drive up to the Rustic Cabin and see our man, Eli Quain. I think Louie Prima and his Big Band are up there this week, and you might as well take Nancy along with you to see the show and ask El if he has any spots to put our people."

That Saturday, Nancy and I headed up to Englewood Cliffs for the late show. We drove north along the desolate wooded highway, passing the Old Salt restaurant, a well-known chophouse frequented by elite clientele. As we neared the Rustic Cabin, we could hear music piped outside from huge speakers mounted high up on the telephone poles. We pulled off the highway and turned onto the gravel driveway leading to the huge, log-cabin-styled roadhouse.

The parking attendants were scrambling to handle the traffic. "I guess Prima is really drawing a big crowd," said Nancy.

"Yes, he has this new singer with him, Keely Smith. Remember meeting that kid who sang with the Saxie Dowell Band, when we went down to Norfolk for my shipmates' reunion at the Naval Air Station in 1947?"

Nancy squinted, as if to prod her memory. "Oh yeah, I remember her. She was just a kid."

"She was sixteen, but she sang like a pro. That was Keely Smith, only then her name was Dorothy Keely."

"Are you serious?"

"I believe she comes from an Irish and American Indian background."

Eli Quain provided all the concessions at the Rustic: photography girls, darkroom staff, cigar and cigarette sales, souvenirs, hatcheck, bathroom vending machines, and valet parking. As we entered the door, he was waiting for us in the lobby, and ushered us into the bar, where we sat and ordered drinks.

"I've reserved a table for us upfront in the showroom," Quain said, "but first I want to talk a bit about seeing if we can plan to find some jobs for your Riviera people. What's the timing on that?"

"I'm not sure, but by the way things are going, probably a year. They said we can stay until they are ready to start building that section of the Parkway."

"Well, I'll do what I can, Gio. Most of your Cuban waiters will go back to Cuba and work at the hotels down there, right? Ben can help with that."

Our conversation was interrupted, when we heard the show starting in the main showroom.

"We'll take our drinks inside," Quain said, motioning toward the bartender. "Let's get to our table; we can't miss Prima. He's great."

Louie was onstage with a ten-piece orchestra, and opened with one of his favorites, *Robin Hood*, followed by the old chestnut *When You're Smiling* and the irresistibly Italian *Che La Luna*. Keely, who had been standing off to the side, then walked into the spotlight, singing Cole Porter's classic *Night and Day*, followed by *A Sunday Kind of Love*, written by Louie himself.

In my opinion, the highlight of the show came when Louie introduced Sonny Geroni, his drummer, to play the solo on *Sing, Sing, Sing*, a piece written by Louie back in 1937. Sonny's showy solo sent the audience into the stratosphere, people yelling and running out of oxygen. Two waiters ran through the audience to help a man who was slumped over his dinner plate, his wife screaming, "Help him! Someone, help him!" Quain quickly left our table and rushed to the aid of the stricken man.

"Is there a doctor in the house?" shouted Prima, over the microphone. In seconds, the man was carried bodily through the audience and into the office near the front door.

When the audience had quieted down, Louie continued with his show, playing favorites like *Banana Split for my Baby*. He ended his set with a rousing version of Way Down Yonder in New Orleans, stepped down off the stage, and made his way through the audience, all eyes following him as he trucked along, while laying down a wicked chorus, Dixieland style.

As if by coincidence, just at that moment, we saw the coroner exit the office, with the corpse of the dead man lying on a gurney covered with a blanket. A collective gasp filled the Rustic. We all stood up to watch, as Louie and the band strut right up behind the gurney, and burst into the most sanctified version of When the Saints Go Marching In I had ever heard.

As the gurney was pushed out the front door and loaded onto a hearse, Louie and the band continued to march around the somber vehicle, playing a funeral dirge in a pious, respectful manner.

"For Christ's sake, what a way to go," I said when Quain came back to our table.

"I guess we need a drink after that one. The doctor said the poor man died instantly, probably before he even reached the office."

Louie had given him quite a sendoff, but the image of what had happened clung to Nancy and me during our drive home. Understandably, she was shaken. So was I, for that matter. I didn't say it, but I was thinking, "Louie Prima can really knock out an audience."

Chapter 25

The days and weeks that followed brought worry and indecision to the employees at the Riviera. No one had any idea when the plug would be pulled. Still, they put on their best face in front of the customers, and things appeared to proceed as normal.

By 1953, change beyond the walls of the Riviera was accelerating. After being straight-armed for months, Frank Sinatra finally landed the role of Maggio in the big-budget war movie, *From Here to Eternity*. Burt Lancaster, Montgomery Clift, Deborah Kerr, and Donna Reed also starred in the movie, but it was Frank who stole the show. At the club, it was no secret that Ava Gardner—at the height of her powers in Hollywood—had spoken to Joan Cohn, the wife of Columbia Pictures boss Harry Cohn, who relented and gave Sinatra the role that would change his life. The two women were quite persuasive in this matter.

Meanwhile, Sinatra was scrambling to find another record company after having been dropped by both Columbia Records and his talent agent, MCA. When his recording contract was picked up by Capitol Records, his career resurrection began in earnest. Teamed with innovative arranger Nelson Riddle, another Jersey boy, he cut sides that created a new style of singing, and popularized the long-playing record format. And his work in From Here to Eternity was poised to earn him an Oscar.

Bill wanted a return Sinatra engagement at the Riviera. And Sinatra saw it as the perfect venue for him to prove to the world that he was back and better than ever. I was in the office when Bill called Bill Allenberg at the William Morris Agency to see if he had any weeks open in his client's schedule. Sinatra's return would come sooner than expected.

Lena Horne was just finishing up her stint at the Riviera, and Eddie Fisher already had been booked to close out the year. So the deck was clear for Sinatra right away, and Allenberg grabbed the time slot for his resurgent singer.

Instantly, morale at the Riviera began to improve. In-house barber Rocky Vitetta cut everyone's hair. Bill had all the carpeting shampooed throughout the club, even though we all knew that the carpeting was going to be ripped out soon enough. Mary Smith, the wardrobe mistress, mended the girls' outfits, which—not a huge undertaking, given their skimpiness. Indeed, every last stitch was checked to make ready for Sinatra's upcoming show of shows. Al Austin removed all the old furniture from the Star's Dressing Room, and replaced it with new. The brass doors upfront were painstakingly polished with Brasso by the maintenance men. The parking lot was swept clean. You would have thought the Queen of England was coming, and who knew, maybe she was.

I shared this intense focus on our soon-to-be-extinct nightclub, as if such dedication might delay or even cancel the inevitable demise. But I was well aware of the events and headline-grabbers of the day. Young Massachusetts congressman John F. Kennedy been elected senator of that state, and was about to wed an elegant, upper-class woman named Jacqueline Bouvier. I had heard of him because Longie once told me that the father, Joe Kennedy, was a friend of Franklin D. Roosevelt. Joe Kennedy had gone to Scotland with FDR's son James, and made a fortune by becoming the exclusive American agent for Gordon's Gin, and Dewar's Scotch. In addition to buying distribution rights for Scotch whiskey in the U.S., Kennedy also purchased spirits-importation rights from the Canadian importers Schenley Industries. That was the kind of business clout that made Longie pay attention.

The biblical epic *The Robe*, released by 20th Century Fox was the first feature film using Cinemascope technology, and many of us—including me—took a break to see it at the new, air-conditioned Lee Theater on Lemoine Avenue in Fort Lee.

There was electricity in the air on September 1, 1953, the day Frank Sinatra was scheduled to open at the Riv. Nothing was left to chance in preparing for a reservations-only, packed house for the two shows scheduled for that night. The phones had been screaming for weeks with fans begging to be on standby, but not one reservation had been cancelled.

Comedian Joey Bishop, the opening act, arrived early on the afternoon of the show, in plenty of time for the 4 p.m. rehearsal, and grabbed a sandwich in the kitchen. As I escorted him to his dressing room, he told me that Sinatra had asked him to be his opening act when both were appearing at the Copacabana the previous year. Bishop said he was impressed with the fairness with which Bill Miller handled his contract. "Is Bill Miller always that nice?"

"That's the kind of man he is," I said. "I worked for Ben Marden before Bill—Ben bought the place, and was also a fair man. And a dynamo."

Bishop looked at me, wide-eyed. "You're the guy."

I was puzzled. "What guy?"

"The one who fixed the slots upstairs."

We both laughed. "Those days are gone," I said. "And soon, all this will be gone."

After settling Bishop in his dressing room, I went to the stage door, where Austin told me that he'd just learned that the notorious Fischetti Brothers—Rocco, Charlie, and Joe—had come in from Chicago and had asked to come backstage to see Sinatra after the show.

"What did you tell them?" I asked.

"What could I tell them—you know who they are, don't you? Al Capone's cousins."

"Well, our boss insists that everyone is welcome here,"

"Yeah, but are they welcome to come backstage?"

"As long as they don't shoot up the place."

Bad joke, and Al didn't laugh. "Hey, Al," I quickly interjected, "don't get confused, but Frank Sinatra's pianist and conductor is also named Bill Miller, so if you get phone calls backstage, make sure you get a hold of the right Bill Miller."

It was mid-afternoon when Sinatra pulled up to the stage door in a dark-blue, Cadillac convertible with the top up. He was driving, and Ava was by his side. In the backseat was Sinatra's pianist/

conductor, the "other" Bill Miller, and, I later learned, New York radio show host William B. Williams, who had been singing early praises for the Sinatra comeback. Al and I were standing by the stage door, and greeted them when they arrived.

"Here Frank, let me take that suit bag for you," said Al, as Sinatra, wearing a sport coat and open-collar shirt, opened the trunk. Ava, who was sitting in the front, opened the door herself before I rushed over to grab it and offer my hand as she got out. As she exited, her tan raincoat opened slightly to reveal her gorgeous legs—just like a movie scene. "My God, she is beautiful," I thought to myself, as she got out of the car, giving me that slightly teasing, mysterious smile that she was so well known for on screen. No wonder Frank was so crazy about her. I pulled the front seat forward so that Miller could exit, and he removed a fat, black valise from the trunk—stuffed with musical arrangements, I learned later.

"Where is the bandstand?" Miller asked, as he trudged through the stage door.

"Right this way Bill, four steps up, make a left, and you will see it behind the curtain," I said, directing him to the revolving bandstand.

"You don't have to show me where my dressing room is," Sinatra said to me with a grin.

"We're glad you're back, Mister Sinatra," I said, and carried his two bags to the dressing room. Gio, the porter, in action.

Seconds after Sinatra arrived at his dressing room, waiter captain Lou Gallo gently knocked on the door, carrying a tray with Frank's favorite drink, four ice cubes and two fingers of Jack Daniels with a splash of water, alongside a tall iced tea with a sprig of mint for Ava.

"Right on schedule," Sinatra said. "By the way, what time is Walter Nye going to get here so we can start the rehearsal?"

"He's probably here already," Miller said. "I spoke with him yesterday. He's bringin' the cream of the crop: the best musicians from Local 526, coming up from Hudson County."

"Do we have Russ Russo on drums?" the singer asked.

"We sure do, Frank; fact, I'll bet he's setting up now."

"Good, let's get this thing over with."

They both left the dressing room and headed for the stage.

The revolving bandstand was facing backstage, so when Sinatra climbed onto the stage, the engineer's voice came through the speaker: "Hang on, guys, I'm going to rotate the bandstand, so you end up out front."

Sinatra shot back, "Hey, did you jokers ever fly this thing before?" sending up a round of laughter from the musicians, as the bandstand, with conductor Nye and his full complement of musicians, rotated toward the main showroom.

Sinatra leaned on the baby grand piano, sipping his Jack Daniels, while Nye passed out the sheets for *I've Got the World on a String*, written by Harold Arlen and arranged by Nelson Riddle. Sinatra had just recorded this version for Capitol—his first cut for the label, and Riddle's first arrangement for him—and the song already was on the Hit Parade and moving steadily up the charts.

Miller sat at the piano after exchanging glances with Nye. "Everybody ready?" he asked, looking over the band, as the musicians settled in after placing the sheet music on their stands. When he was satisfied that everything was in order, he gave a gentle four-count, Nye nodded at his players, and the band sprang to life. After Riddle's exhilarating musical intro, Sinatra jumped in with his crisp, energetic vocal: "I've got the world on a string, sittin' on a rainbow…" From the first few bars, we all knew that his voice was back and with a more virile sound. He did not finish the lyrics to the song, as the band played on; instead, he joked around with Artie Frye, the tenor sax man he knew from many other gigs.

"Okay, okay, guys," Miller said, cutting the arrangement short of the finish. "Let's take it from the coda."

When the band finished, Sinatra said, "Listen up, guys. The guy who wrote this marvelous song, Harold Arlen, and Nelson Riddle, the new cat who arranged it, are both supposed to be in the audience tonight, so let's play it like they wrote it." He turned to wink at

Ava, who had been sitting at a front-row table and looking on with her customary, alluring expression.

After *String*, Sinatra wanted a run-through on another Arlen tune, the deeply affecting *One for My Baby*. "Please, watch the tempo on this one, and pay close attention to the dynamics. Got it, guys?

The band followed instructions, and the sentimental lyric was gently voiced by Frank. Then the pace changed again, as Sinatra snapped his fingers to Cole Porter's *I Get a Kick Out of You*, the band grooving to his tempo. He grabbed the mike in his left hand, took it off the stand, turned, and winked at the band, as he sang:

I GET NO KICK FROM CHAMPAGNE
MERE ALCOHOL
DOESN'T THRILL ME AT ALL
SO TELL ME WHY
SHOULD IT BE TRUE…

Wow, I thought, if the rehearsal is this good, what is going to happen tonight when he gets hold of the audience.

"See you tonight, gentlemen—stay sober," he said, when he finished up and made his way back to the dressing room Ava by his side. He stopped for a quick interview with a local newspaper columnist from the Record.

I remained in the showroom to watch the tradesmen put the final touches on the set. Ten minutes later, one of them shouted from the stage, "Where's Frank?" It was an electrician, who had a question about a particular lighting setup.

"He's downstairs taking a haircut and a shave with Rocky," replied Willie B. Williams, in his rich, radio-caliber voice. "Should we get him?"

"No, I don't want to bother him now. Maybe you could ask him to catch up with me when he is done downstairs, okay?"

All day, the phones in the office rang off the hook, people wanting reservations for the Sinatra show. The girls in the office were going nuts, trying to sort out how to add more tables to the already packed house for the two shows. Sinatra solved the dilemma, when he offered to do a third show. Bill gladly accepted the offer.

Celebrities were set to attend in significant numbers—Yogi Berra and Mickey Mantle had locked in their reservations, and I think the whole New York Yankee baseball team wanted to see the show. By 6 p.m., the parking lot was full, and valets were beginning to park cars on Hudson Terrace, facing north. Soon, the cars were being parked so far afield, that a jitney was needed to bring attendants back in a timely manner. In addition to ballplayers, the crowd included show biz types, newspaper people, mob guys, and anybody else who was lucky enough to get a reservation.

The scene on the showroom floor was like a political convention. Waiter captains defused arguments about seating. Waiters and busboys moved at breakneck speed, trying to accommodate dinner orders that the downstairs kitchen, in turn, hurried to prepare; large orders of the most expensive items on the menu were in demand. Although there were about thirty people working steadily in the kitchen, it just wasn't the same without Bill's brother, Joe.

The lights finally dimmed, and the bandstand began to rotate, as Pupi Campo and his Latin Band played the final chorus of the most popular song of that year, the Mexican mambo instrumental Quién Será. Norman Gimbel had written the English lyrics to this song, which he called Sway, and it was recorded by many beloved Riviera performers, including Dean Martin and Sinatra.

As the bandstand slowly revolved, bringing the show orchestra upstage, Nye kicked off a hot version of *Mambo Jambo*, as the Donn Arden Chorus, consisting of sixteen gorgeous showgirls, made a dazzling entrance. The audience was mesmerized, as the ladies, with immaculate choreography, mamboed their way onto the stage. With the stunning entrance complete, the chorus moved into its patented production number, Bless all those Beautiful Girls. And all the beautiful girls, indeed, struck their most provocative poses, as they stood motionless on the revolving stage and circled the showroom. The atmosphere set the mood for Bill Miller's extravagant show. It had an almost magical way of getting the audience caught up in the moment, allowing them to forget their real-life woes.

When the showgirls exited the stage, out came Bud and Cece Robinson with their precision, ballroom-dance routine that captivated the audience with their graceful style. Singer-impressionist George DeWitt followed, and then droll Joey Bishop. Who opened with the line, "On my way across the George Washington Bridge, I saw this lady go right through the red light."

Bishop paused, and the audience waited expectantly.

"The cop stopped her and asked, 'Lady, didn't you see the light?'

"The woman replied, 'You've seen one, you've seen 'em all.'"

He continued, "I once called my mother during a hurricane. She got on the phone and said, 'Joey, I can't talk to you now, the lines are down.'"

And joke after joke, like that, rapid-fire, while waiters' captain Jack Osterdahl directed his charges with hand signals similar to those given on an aircraft carrier to communicate with pilots; and waiters whisked huge aluminum trays laden with food, held high overhead, flying saucers in search of tables on which to land; and photography girls snapped away with their Pacemaker, Speed Graphic cameras, taking pictures for anyone who wanted to capture their moment, their magical evening at the Riviera.

Before long, the huge dinner orders from the big-spending audience overwhelmed capacity. Dishwashers bogged down, and busboys and waiters crashed into one another on the steep stairs leading down to the kitchen. Bill, observing all of the goings-on, immediately took command of the situation and, running to the large window just inside the kitchen door, said to captain Bruno, "Open this window and tell the busboys to throw their dirty dishes off the cliff."

"What?" asked Jack Bruno, in astonishment.

"You heard me. Open that damn window before someone is killed falling down these metal stairs."

Better that dishes take the plunge, than people.

This was a night unlike any other at the Riviera: Sinatra returning as victor. When the lights dimmed and the spot came on for the main event, he drifted onto the stage in a most cool manner, accompanied by ravenous applause, to Riddle's rousing setup for I've Got the World on a String. Harold Arlen and Nelson Riddle were in the audience, just as promised, and they looked both proud and satisfied, as Frank took his tune to the bank.

This night was the wakeup call to the world that Frank Sinatra was back. This Jersey boy was riding high, wide, and handsome, hitting home runs with *They Can't Take That Away From Me, One for My Baby, You Go to My Head, I Get a Kick Out of You*, and on and on. He roared through, or caressed, 20 songs, leaving the audience drained from applauding, and Bill with the special feeling that he had mounted a show that history would recognize as one for the record books. What very few people in the audience realized that night was that Bill Miller had secretly invited some of his faithful employees, and their wives and kids to the show, giving them a chance to witness history before the Riviera became a parkway toll booth.

Sinatra, still as lean as he was at the start of his career, showed impressive stamina. By the time he finished his third, it was past 3 a.m. Some of those on hand for the second show stayed on for the third. I kept wondering if we were going to run out of plates, glasses, and silverware… and adrenaline. Luckily, we didn't. When the last of the crowd exited, the club all but collapsed.

"Everybody, go home!" shouted Bill. "We'll clean this place up tomorrow."

He seemed to be the only one who didn't look even the slightest bit tired, as he made his rounds to see if everything was in one piece. I waited for him to return to the showroom. Nancy couldn't keep her eyes open, and curled up in one of the banquettes.

"Hey Gio, what the hell are you still doing here?"

"I'm waiting for the fourth show to begin," I said, without cracking a smile.

Bill gave me a bear hug and, when he released me, he noticed Nancy asleep in a fetal position.

"Take her home, for godsake. In the morning, we'll climb down the cliff and try to find all that stuff that went out the window tonight—don't worry, Gio, our insurance is paid up…Seriously, we still should have enough dinnerware for two shows and, if we need more, we can always use the old stuff Ben gave us when he owned the place."

"How can we use those, Bill? They have Ben Marden's name on them."

"You're wrong, Gio, they have Ben Marden's initials on them."

The light bulb went on in my head. "I see, said the blind man, as he picked up his hammer and saw. Bill Miller, the man who has all bases covered."

"Tomorrow is another day," Bill said. "It always is."

I could hear the irony in his voice.

When I passed the Fort Lee Diner on the way home, Nancy tucked in the car, I saw owner Gus Grossman standing on the sidewalk out front. There were so many cars parked in the street in front of the diner that there was nowhere to park. I wanted to get the morning paper "hot off the presses," as we used to say, so I double-parked and bought a copy of the *Daily News*. Tomorrow is another day, I thought, just like the boss had said. Then, the thought occurred to me.

Tomorrow was already here.

Chapter 26

"Gio, what is this cardboard box full of scribbled notes doing in your closet?"

"Oh those—I have been saving them for when I write that novel I have always talked about. Anyway, what are you doing rooting around in my closet?"

"I just have the urge to clean all the crap out of our home. I don't know what is the matter with me lately, but I'm feeling very depressed and I'm hoping that staying active solves the problem. And besides, have you noticed how much weight I have been gaining in the last few months?"

"Come on, you're not gaining weight, you are just imagining that," I said, hoping to halt Nancy's complaining. "It's Saturday. Do you feeling like catching a movie tonight?"

"Not really; somehow I just don't feel like going out much anymore. I don't know what is coming over me, but lately I have no ambition to do anything, and I am getting a bit worried."

"Look, let's give Doc Shapiro a ring at the Riviera. Maybe he can have a look at you. What do you say?"

Two hours later, we were facing the good doctor in his little exam room at the Riv.

"I just feel kind of lousy," Nancy explained. "I don't have any energy, I wake up in the morning feeling a little nauseous, and I'm gaining weight for no apparent reason."

"Let me ask you something, Nancy, how old are you now?"

"I'm forty-nine and, usually, I am very active, but right now I feel like I'm ninety."

Shapiro brushed something off his chin. "Have you been missing your monthly period?"

Nancy looked at me as if to question the doctor's sanity.

"I can never have children, Doctor Shapiro." She paused, almost embarrassed. She turned to me with a look I knew only too well, the look of a child in trouble.

"Go ahead, honey, tell him."

Nancy took a breath and squared up before the doctor. "When I was young, I made a mistake and got myself pregnant. I was so afraid to have the baby, because I was not married at the time. Also I was a dancer, and I was trying out for a new show, so I decided to have an abortion. The quack nearly killed me. Immediately afterward, a real doctor told me that the abortion had done so much damage, I would never be able to become pregnant again."

Shapiro tugged on an earlobe. "I am sorry to hear that story, Nancy. Do you have regular menstrual cycles?"

"No, not really…sometimes I get one, then months go by and nothing happens. I never worried about it because I knew I couldn't become pregnant."

Shapiro nodded in an understanding way. "I can't do very much here, but I would like to have you come to my regular office and let me take a good look at you. Why don't you give my receptionist, Ann, a call and set up an appointment, and maybe we can get to the bottom of this."

When Nancy excused herself to go to the ladies' room, Shapiro took me aside. "I have a sneaking suspicion that she might be pregnant."

I was dumbfounded. "But it's…impossible."

"Hell, no. I have seen this before, and I think I am seeing it again."

A swirl of emotions seized me. "Nancy's forty-nine, doc. This seems like a dream…How can we find out for sure?"

"You have heard of the 'rabbit test,' haven't you?"

"Is that when they inject the woman's urine into a rabbit and, if it dies, she is pregnant?"

"Yes, that is what we commonly use to test for pregnancy."

"Then we have a problem, doc, and it ain't finding out if she is pregnant."

"What are you referring to, Gio?"

"I am just telling you that Nancy has this thing about killing animals. She won't go for it—not in a million years."

"Well if that's the case, we can use the 'bufo' test.'"

"What's that?"

"We use a frog instead of a rabbit, and if the frog produces eggs within twenty-four hours after being injected with the urine, the test is positive."

"Does 'positive' mean she is pregnant?"

"Absolutely: That is correct, she will be pregnant indeed," said the Doc.

"What about the frog? How do we explain killing the frog?"

"No, Gio, in the bufo test, the frog doesn't die. We use them over and over."

"Well, let's bring on the frogs."

Five days later, after Nancy was bufoed, and the results were positive, she was officially diagnosed as pregnant. When she came back from Doctor Shapiro's office, she was radiant with excitement.

"Gio, you're not going to believe it, but I am pregnant! I'm nearly fifty and I'm pregnant!... You're not upset are you?"

"Upset? I'm ecstatic!" I grabbed her and held her tightly, as tears welled up for both of us.

"I guess it's better late than never," she said, her voice cracking.

"Don't worry about a thing, Nan; this is the greatest news I could ever get. Pretty soon we'll have another Arigo to take care of."

"But they said I could never have children." Tears streamed down her face.

"Only God makes the final decisions, hey remember what that preacher told us when we got married about trusting in the Lord with all our hearts and not relying on our own understanding?" I said. "Let me ask you something, sweetheart, when is the baby due?"

"You're not going to believe this, Gio, but the doctor says I'm almost five months pregnant. *I told you* I was getting fat!" Happiness shone from her tear-stained face.

"Oh hell, Nancy, fat or skinny, you always look beautiful to me."

I was undecided about telling Bill and Abe and all the guys at the Riviera. But when I was talking with Mary and Molly over coffee in the office, I couldn't resist. Molly confided that both she and Mary had suspected something, just by the way Nancy had looked when I brought her to the club for the Sinatra show a couple of weeks earlier.

"What do you say we throw a nice, big, baby shower for her?" offered Mary.

"I love that idea," said Molly.

Word quickly spread throughout the club that a baby was on the way for Nancy and Gio and, in the kitchen, when the girls took coffee breaks, the topic of conversation always seemed to drift towards suggested names—for boy or girl—for our baby. Being that the showgirls were all in their late teens and early twenties, and none of them (as far as I knew) had ever had a child, all of the goings-on were of great interest to them. Nancy's pregnancy was educational to them; they all seemed fascinated by the fact that a new life was being brought into the world. Sure, most of them had younger brothers and sisters, but that had happened when they were kids. It seemed a special time for everyone, and not without irony— as the Riviera was bowing out, a new member of its family was about to take its first bows.

In late August, I informed Nancy that Molly was picking out new curtains for the office, and wanted her opinion.

"Why would Molly ask for my opinion?" Nancy asked.

"Because she values it—why else? She said she did not want anyone to know that she was going to change the office around," I was almost stammering to make up a story that sounded credible.

A week later, the first Sunday in September, Nancy was up early. Her belly was becoming huge, and she was extremely uncomfortable. About 1 p.m., she came out of our bedroom, wearing a dowdy-looking dress that made her look kind of frumpy.

"You're not going to the Riviera looking like that, are you?" I asked. It was the afternoon scheduled for appraising new curtains.

"And why not? There won't be anyone there but Molly and me. Anyway, since when are you so concerned about how I look, anymore?" There was a glint of sadness, maybe anger, in her eyes.

"What do you mean? I always love to see you looking sharp, like you always do when we go out."

She went back into the bedroom and, in about a half-hour, came out looking like a million bucks, wearing a beautiful maternity outfit that Mary Miller had sent her. "I was saving this outfit in case we had a chance to go out, Gio," she said, making an awkward attempt at a pirouette in the living room.

"Perfect, Nancy. You make the clothes; the clothes don't make you."

"Ah, stop the bullshit, Gio. I know I look like a cow right now, but give me a few months and I will be turning heads again."

"You're turning heads now. And I am not bullshitting you, Nancy. I love you, no matter how you look."

On the way to the club, we listened to the New York Giants' football game on the car radio. They were playing the Washington Redskins and, when we turned on the radio, it was already the second quarter. We listened to broadcaster Marty Glickman deliver the play-by-play in his distinctive, New York accent. By the time we left Route 4 and turned onto Hudson Terrace, we both had high hopes that the Giants, trailing by just a few points point at this juncture, would win this one. They'd better—I had twenty bills riding on them.

"What's Dusty Reale's car doing here?" Nancy asked, noticing the dancer's '49 Ford convertible parked among many others. "And what are all these cars doing here? I thought no one was going to be here today."

I shrugged. "I have no idea."

"Well, there must be some kind of a meeting going on."

"Guess so. No problem, though; you and Molly will meet in private."

As we climbed the five steps at the main entrance, I said "Look, I want to go down to the kitchen and see if I can grab a sandwich—my stomach is growling. You go and wait for me in the lounge, and I will rustle up some snacks for the two of you."

I had just turned the corner after leaving Nancy to walk into the lounge by herself, when I heard the twenty girls waiting for her shout, "SURPRISE!" Mission accomplished—I had put one over on her. The first and last time for that; Nancy was a sharp cookie. Guess the pregnancy had thrown her off-kilter.

By the time her shower ended, and we packed up all her gifts, it was almost seven o'clock. As we headed back to Hackensack, Nancy could not stop talking about the beautiful gifts that Mary and Molly had given her, and how much she loved the baby blanket from dancer Pat Cotton—it was decorated with both pink and blue bears, to play it safe. Judy Tyler's gift was two white outfits that would work for either a boy or girl, and the other girls had all bought tiny nightgowns, bootees, caps, and mittens. Nancy loved everything, and she was so happy and overwrought that, by the time we pulled into our driveway in Hackensack, she was sound asleep. Before I turned off the motor, I flicked on the radio to check the score of the Giants' game.

The Redskins won, 10-7. Shit, there went my twenty bucks. Betting is out, once the kid comes, I thought ruefully.

I nudged the expectant mother. "Nancy, Nancy, come on sweetheart, we're home." She opened those gorgeous, sleepy eyes and gave me the biggest smile, as she stretched her arms and grabbed the lapels on her unbuttoned coat to pull it around her.

"You go in the house; I will bring all this stuff in later," I said.

"Oh no, Gio, I want all this brought into the house now, right now."

"Come on, I'm tired; I'll bring it in later."

"No Gio, stop giving me a hard time. I want it brought in right now."

Experience has always taught me that I can never win an argument with Nancy. "Here's the house key," I said in a surrendering tone of voice. "Let yourself in and leave the door open, so I can bring everything in."

"Thanks Gio." She was smiling again. I guess soon-to-be mothers should have their way. "I'll make you some tea. And I brought you a nice piece of apple pie from the party."

"Love you, babe!" I shouted, as she opened the door to the house.

She turned and looked at me, as I carried an armful of gifts. "I love you, too, Gio."

For the next week or so, I would jump every time Nancy said she had a pain. I wished the kid would hurry up and get here, so I could concentrate on trying to find myself a job. Finally, after twenty-four hours of labor, our beautiful son, Gerard, was born in Englewood Hospital at 2:30 a.m. on September 17, 1953. I could not wait to tell the gang down at the Riviera all about it, when I went to work that night.

As I entered the stage door and shouted joyfully, "We had a baby," Al quickly asked me whether it was a boy or girl."

"Nine pounds, five ounces," I said.

"Gotta be a boy. We have a pool going on down here as to what sex the baby would be and how much it would weigh. Let me see... nine-five..." He leafed through his list of guesses. "Okay, the winner is Junior Jackson in the chorus line. Damn, I was close—I only missed by two-and-a-half pounds."

We each laughed, as if we'd had a few drinks. "Have a cigar Al," I said, as I proudly plucked the first one from the box of "Bearings" that I had brought.

By the end of the day, it seemed like everyone was smoking a cigar. When I went backstage before showtime, I saw one of Donn Arden's dancers, Janis, a Georgia beauty, all dressed up in her chorus-line outfit and ready to go onstage. She had smoked one of my cigars down to the stump, and wasn't finished with it yet. How odd it looked to see a goddess smoking a stogie.

"Put that goddamn thing out," shouted Mary Smith, the wardrobe mistress, as the girls lined up and readied for their onstage cue.

"Here, Gio darlin', would y'all be a nice guy and please put this chomped-up stump out for me?" requested Janis, handing me her soggy, well-chewed, cigar, as she hurried to find her place in the line.

"That's some lady, huh, Al? I guess those Georgia peaches are used to rolling their own down there."

Al's mind was on weightier matters. "Did you catch the Daily News today, Gio?"

"No, not yet; what's going on, anything good?"

"More bullshit from the Supreme Court. I don't think those judges have anything better to do than waste their time writing earth-shattering papers on their personal hobbies."

"What do you mean?"

"Get this: They ruled that baseball is a sport—not a business. Can you beat that? Now the Supreme Court realizes what any five-year-old kid from Fort Lee understands. Maybe they should put Buck Connell at the Fort Lee AC on the court, whaddayou think?"

"I don't think he'd look so good in those long, black robes, Al."

Al pretended like he was pondering that, then said, "Maybe not." Two seconds passed, and we broke out laughing.

"How are Nancy and the baby doing, Gio?"

"Fantastic. They are coming home tomorrow."

"Are you getting the place ready for them?"

"Yeah, I am doing the housework, and I've got most of my crap cleaned up," I explained. "I can't wait to get them home. You got any kids, Al?"

"Yes, I have one son. His name is Tommy, and he is thirteen. You must have seen him last Tuesday, when I brought him down here to see Victor Borge."

"Was that your son, the tall kid? I think I did see him. Was that your wife with him?"

"Yes, that was my wife, Mildred. The boss said I could bring them down here to see a show once in a while. Lou Gallo took care of everything for us. He even got them a table right next to the dance floor. Lou is an all-right guy, you know that? I tried to take care of him, but he said my money was no good here."

"The boss always tells me that anybody who works here is welcome to bring their immediate family down here, anytime, to enjoy a show." A sadness crept in; we could feel it. "You got any plans for when this place closes next month?" I asked.

"Not really. El Quain asked me to take over the Rustic Cabin parking lot concession for him, so I am going to do that. But I think I will need a lot more to cover my bills. The boss asked Chief Greco if he could find me some work as a special favor. They are talking about starting a parking authority in Fort Lee, and they need some-body to work it."

"What's a parking authority?" I asked.

"Charging people money to park. They're gonna put up these meters on a pole in the street, and people have to put dimes in them or get a ticket."

"Nothin's for free anymore, huh, Al?"

November was a memorable month that year. I saw Guys and Dolls right before it closed on Broadway. Our next-door neighbor volunteered to babysit, while Nancy took in the final performance. Late in the month, we had a newspaper strike in New York that lasted for eleven days. Bill was going nuts because he had just laid out a pile of money to book Eddie Fisher for the Riviera's final New Year's Eve show; because of the photo engravers strike, the boss couldn't advertise in the New York newspapers.

Some people thought that strikes were the work of communists, and the whole country was going crazy trying to identify every last one of them living in the U.S.A. General Electric announced that all communist employees would be fired. Eisenhower criticized Senator Joseph McCarthy for declaring that there were commu-nists in the Republican Party. McCarthy had his big guns trained on more targets than just the GOP. For him, it was open season on anything that moved.

Meanwhile, at the Riviera, no one was paying much atten-tion to anything except for the quest to find new jobs in the midst of an uncertain future. One chaotic afternoon, while we were all hanging out backstage, Juan, one of the Cuban waiters, told me that his younger brother, an idealistic follower of Cuban revolu-tionary leader Fidel Castro, had recently been killed in an unsuc-cessful sneak attack on the Moncada army barracks in eastern Cuba. The attack was connected with a revolt against President Fulgencio Batista.

I asked Juan, "Do you think this Castro has any chance of oust-ing Batista?"

He shook his head vehemently. "Not in a million years," he said.

It was then that I began thinking about the deal that Ben Marden was getting himself into with the radio and TV stations in Cuba. I brushed off those thoughts, because I believed that Marden and his cronies really knew what they were doing.

As the final holiday season at the Riviera rolled around, sadness prevailed within the ranks. We greeted each other like family members saying goodbye for the last time. No longer was there any hope that the Riviera would get a stay of execution. Half-hearted attempts at trying to create publicity to save the club were regarded by the press as not newsworthy. After all, how could anyone, or anything, stop the wheels of progress?

But we reminded ourselves that the show must go on, and Eddie Fisher was the chosen cleanup hitter to clear the bases at the Riviera...forever. Fisher was scheduled to perform on New Year's Eve, for the final hours of the final show. He was, simply put, a hot singer. His chart-busting hit records had earned him a berth as host of NBC's *Coke Time Variety Show.* His hits included *Anytime, Oh, My Papa* (which rose to number-one on the Cash Box charts), *I Need You Now,* (another #1), and *Wish You Were Here.* He planned to sample a new song, *You Gotta Have Heart,* for the show. As the curtain was about to come down for the last time, *You Gotta Have Heart,* from the Broadway musical Damn Yankees seemed to be the battle cry at the Riviera.

On New Year's Eve, the place was packed early. All the old faithful were there to say goodbye to the place, and to take with them a lifetime of memories they wished to preserve. The well-stocked freezers in the kitchen were emptied. Handshakes, hugs, and kisses were the order of the day for employees and entertainers alike. They were all taking the big ship on its last ride before it was scuttled.

Bill Miller's partners, Al Kevelson and Al Bierman, walked around like lost souls in those final hours. Everyone offered them condolences, as if they were at a funeral. As was his custom, Bill tried to lift spirits, but even he could not chase the gloom.

Along with Eddie Fisher fans, that final audience was filled with family members of the Riviera family. When the show started, it was obvious that some in the chorus line felt the emotion of the night, as mascara ran from their tear-stained eyes. Only when Fisher emerged, and when Nye and his orchestra kicked in with the first number, did the showroom regain its energy and resemble its old self. Fisher sang in his clear tenor:

ANYTIME YOU FEEL DOWNHEARTED
ANYTIME YOU'RE FEELING BLUE...

Our sentiments, exactly.

After the traditional countdown to the New Year, and the burst of cheering when the precise second arrived, no one was in a hurry to end the celebration. As usual, Bill had provided the hats, noise-makers, streamers, and confetti, as well as a never-ending supply of champagne to wash away the tears. When the merriment finally subsided, he stood by the main entrance and shook the hands of as many patrons as possible, as they filed out through the brass doors for the very last time.

In the aftermath, confetti was everywhere and silence was pervasive, except for a few lonely party horns sounding the death knell of the great nightclub scheduled to meet its executioner in the days that followed. Staffers, including myself, who handled cleanup chores, took a little extra time to look the place over, and breathe in the distinctive, exciting, and historic atmosphere for the very last time. After Al Austin checked the entire building, he returned to the showroom, where Bill and a few of his closest friends were drinking a toast.

"All's tight, boss."

"Hey Al, come on over here and have a drink with us," Bill said. Then he motioned for those of us still there to join in the final chorus. One for My Baby (and One More for the Road). We all stood together and sang—not quite Sinatra, but just as heartfelt.

There was nothing more to be said. The party was over.

Epilogue

On a Monday morning, four months after the Riviera closed, I was skimming through the Help Wanted ads in the *Bergen Evening Record*, when the phone rang. The baby was crying, and Nancy was frantic about how we were going to make ends meet. I had received a nice severance bonus from the boss, so I was okay for now, but between rent and diapers, we were beginning to feel the pinch.

"Hello, Gio, is that you?"

"Yeah, Bill?"

"Long time no see, huh?"

"Well, so good to hear from you. How are things?"

"Pretty good. The reason I am calling you is that I recently heard from an old friend of mine, Milton Prell, out here in Las Vegas, and he asked me if I was interested in running the entertainment operation at his new hotel, the Sahara. But right now I feel like a duck out of water because all my connections in the entertainment world are back in New York, and they're no good out here. Since he became the head of the Sands, Jack Entratter, who started out as a doorman at the Copa, has signed up just about everybody who's anybody out here. So I need to get very creative and come up with some good ideas on how to level the playing field. Understand?"

"Not really, but go ahead, tell me more." I was excited to hear the boss's voice again.

"It's like this: I was thinking that, instead of trying to come up with acts to compete with the Sands, how about I try to create something where there will be no competition, but we will still bring the crowds in?"

"How do you *do that*, boss?"

"By creating a lounge act that will be a tremendous draw."

"A lounge act? You mean like a piano player and a singer?"

"I mean like *Louie Prima*."

He let that hang there, and I thought about it for a few seconds. "In a lounge?"

"Why not? We'll have him go on at midnight and play until the sun comes up. I'm telling you, Gio, he'll pack the place every night. There's nothing like that in the desert."

Leave it to Bill.

"Right now he's at the Rustic Cabin. I stopped by the other day to say hello to El Quain, Al Austin, and the boys."

"All, right, so here's what you do: "Go up to there and have a talk with Louie. Tell him that I would like to speak to him about coming out to Vegas."

"Can I ask you something, Bill?"

"Sure, go ahead,"

"Please explain to me how you are going to fit Louie Prima into the Sahara Lounge with his ten-piece band?"

"It's the Casbah Lounge at the Sahara Hotel, and I want Louie to downsize his band to five or six pieces, and to include that girl singer he uses…Keely Smith's her name. I can bring in a sax player who has the best sound anyone has ever heard—Sam Butera—and team him up with Louie. When all the clubs on the Strip close for the night, the Casbah will cook with Louie Prima and his combo. Whaddaya think, Gio?"

I thought it was just the thing I was waiting for.

"I'm beginning to find my sea-legs again," Bill continued. "Maybe you and Nancy and the baby could come out here and start a new life in Nevada."

"Do you own the Sahara, Bill?"

"I have a ten percent stake in the place. The main owner is Milton Prell. He's quite a guy—honest as the day is long. He's from Missouri originally and came to California to open a 'bingo palace.' The place got such a good reputation for being honest that it became a giant success. He moved to Las Vegas and opened a place called the Club Bingo right across the street from the El Rancho Vegas. Remodeled it. Now he calls it, The Sahara, the Jewel of the Desert. Pretty fancy, huh?"

"Sounds impressive; what's it like?"

"Two hundred and forty rooms and a three-hundred-seat bingo parlor. The whole place has a very Moroccan theme—It has these giant camels out front. You're gonna like it. I'm putting you on the payroll as of now."

Did I mention that Bill was a persuasive guy? Now, all I had to do was convince Nancy. Was Las Vegas the place to raise a child?

First stop was the Rustic Cabin. I called Al Austin, who filled me in on Prima's schedule.

Bill had explained that he had found bookings for Prima and his band, when they first came to New York, so now it was payback time. I wondered why Bill sent me on this mission, rather than handle it himself. I would shortly understand.

I reached the Rustic Cabin around 5 p.m. on a Friday night. The help was just arriving, and Al and his boys were hanging out in the parking lot, waiting for the action to begin. Fifteen minutes later, Prima arrived in his orange and white Oldsmobile Fiesta convertible and parked right in front of the main entrance. I gave him time to open his trunk and take out his tux bag, before I walked over and introduced myself.

"Hi Louie, my name is Gio Arigo, and I work for Bill Miller. Can I speak to you for a moment?"

"Bill Miller? You mean Bill from the Riviera?" Prima's musical, accented, slightly hoarse voice was distinctive

"That's him. He's in Las Vegas now, and asked me to stop by and speak with you about an opportunity that you might be interested in. May I?"

He eyed me. "Come on in with me. We can talk in my dressing room."

A half-dozen messages were taped to the mirror in his dressing room.

"Sit down, I will be with you in a moment," he said, as he hung up his suit bag and quickly read the messages. When he finished, he turned to me and said, "What's on your mind, cuz?"

"Well, it's this way, Louie. Bill was just offered a share of the Sahara Hotel if he would run their entertainment operation. He asked me to come up here and speak with you about the possibility of you going out there, with your band. You know, for a long-term arrangement for you guys at the Sahara."

He seemed to stare at me for several seconds, as if still assessing my trustworthiness. "I don't know. Vegas is great, but I am pulling down some nice scarola right here. What color green is he talking about?"

"We didn't discuss that, but he did say that if you agree to come out there, you will make more money than you ever dreamed of. He said you could bet the ranch on that. What do you think?"

"I'm all ears, cuz, but I am not sure what to think. I really want to know what the deal is. What am I supposed to do to make all this dough you are talking about? I don't have to go out there and shoot some gavones, do I?" He made a motion as if he was holding a tommy gun and went, "Pow, pow, pow, pow."

"No, of course not, but there is one thing that he does want you to consider," I suggested, treading lightly.

"What's that?" he asked aggressively.

"You have to cut the size of your band and take on a few other musicians from New Orleans. The main guy I am talking about is Sammy Butera."

"I heard o' that cat, my brother Leon knows him well. How's the showroom?"

"I haven't seen it, Louie, but from what I hear, the whole place is first-rate. Boss wants you to play in the Casbah Lounge, which is supposed to be—"

"—*Me*, play the lounge! You could have heard Louie all the way to Fort Lee. "Are you for real? It took me all my life to become a headliner, and now you guys want me to play the *lounge*?"

"Not me, Louie, I have nothing to do with it. I'm just relaying Bill's message."

"Why the hell doesn't he call me himself, then?"

"Look, you can be sure of one thing. Bill would never do anything that would hurt you. Whatever he is asking you to do, he feels is in your best interest."

"You mean in his best interest. How can he expect me to give up the band I have now and start all over again playing in a *lounge*?"

"You'd be playing when all the other shows are over, up and down the Strip. They'd all be coming to see *you*. Bill expects this to be big, Louie. And, you know, he has a pretty good track record."

Louie's expression changed. A glimmer came into his eye. "I'll get back to you tomorrow; I've got to think about this. What's your phone number?"

I handed him one of my old cards, with a new number hand-written on it. "Don't use the Riviera number." I smiled wistfully. Call me at home in Hackensack. See, it's written down."

"I will call you tomorrow afternoon." He rushed off to the bandstand.

"Perfect Louie, perfect" He was already out of the dressing room.

The next day, he called as promised. The conversation went like this:

"Gio, I am finishing up at the Rustic Cabin next Saturday night. I talked it over with my consigliere, Keely, and she thinks we should take a shot at this. Me, I feel menza menza. Either way is okay with me. So we give it a shot. What do you say?"

"I say Bill is going to be very happy to hear the news. Do you have any idea when you can leave for Vegas?"

"Maybe in a week, after we finish here in Jersey. I plan on driving out there. I got to take the Fiesta with me. Some sonofabitch is always trying to steal it here. They only made a few of these cars, you know."

"I know everyone is talking about your car."

"I have to pay big tips to Al's kid, who parks the cars here, so he can hide it back down in the swamp when I'm onstage. The kid says there is a guy who comes here every Saturday looking for my car. Can you imagine that? He says the guy tells him he wants to repossess the car because I am not making the payments. So I missed a few, but those guys must think I'm *stunad*. Everyone knows I am good for it.

"You know, Gio, when I first came to New York, Bill Miller was the guy who got me a lot of bookings, so I feel kind of obligated to try to help him at his new gig in Vegas. Anyway, I hate the snow here in New York…Are you goin' out there too?"

"I think so, soon as I'm done cleaning up stuff for Bill here in Jersey."

Driving home, I had that feeling inside you get when that things are popping in your life. Nancy had agreed, in principle, to the move west. Now it looked like it was going to happen.

Bill was thrilled by the news. "Nobody beats Louie onstage for excitement," he said, transmitting his own excitement over the telephone wires. He asked me if I had been keeping an eye on the Riviera.

"Only the steel shell is left," I said. "Sad, Bill."

"You got to move forward, Gio—that's what life's all about. You should see what they are doing out here in Las Vegas. They're building places so fast, it would make your head spin. Seems like ever since they built the Hoover Dam and began setting off those atomic bombs in the desert, this place is wide open. I can't even count all the new joints out here. You'll see when you come. You'll be working exclusively for me, Gio. And I'll make it worth your while. You deserve it. You've really come through for me."

Exclusive for Bill Miller was more than good enough for me.

A week later, we packed up the car, bundled up baby Gerard, and took off. By evening, when we stopped for gas in Pennsylvania near the Ohio border, the attendant filling up our tank noticed the baby in the backseat, with piles of clothing carefully placed on both sides of his little sleeping box.

"Where are you folks headed?"

"All the way to Las Vegas," I said.

"Wow, that's some trip. Did you hear that Sammy Davis was almost killed in a car accident today?"

"Oh, my God, what happened?" Nancy said.

"He was on his way to California on Route 66. Terrible accident, that's all I know."

Driving into the night, I thought about Sammy and how nice he was when I met him at the Riviera with his father and uncle. I quietly said a prayer that he would pull through.

By the time we reached Las Vegas, after several overnights at roadside motels, we were a bit worse for the wear. Nancy's back ached from holding Gerard most of the way, and my eyes were playing tricks on me from the sun glare I had absorbed during the long ride. Bill was putting us up at the Sahara, so our first order of business was to set up the baby nursery, and allow Gerard and his mother to get some rest. I then went straight to Bill's office, where, with perfect timing, he was going over Prima's contract with him. Bill and I embraced, and Prima shook my hand. He seemed exuberant.

"Gio has a baby, Louie." Bill explained.

"A bambino! Minga! How did that happen?" Louie kidded, in his graveled voice. "*Come si chiama?*"

"His name is Gerard," I said. "I named him after my cousin, Gerardo, who grew up with me in Philly."

"You speak Italian, Gio?" Bill asked.

"Just a little," I said. "Look, I didn't mean to barge in on you guys."

"No, I want you to stay and listen to this. It's okay. You don't mind Louie, do you?"

"Of course not."

Bill offered Prima $3,500 per week, and said he would match that for Keely Smith, and for the band.

"Bread like that is nothing to sneeze at," Prima said, his expressive features animated.

On November 24, 1954, Louie, Keely, Sam Butera, and the band debuted at the Sahara's Casbah Lounge, performing five shows a night from midnight to 6 a.m. Bill had invented the concept of a lounge with big-name acts.

Meanwhile, my little family settled in a Las Vegas suburb known as Rolling Hills. Nancy found a new, three-bedroom/two-bath house for $15,750, just two miles from the Sahara. No down payment was required for veterans.

Bill and I were hell-bent to beat the drums for his new lounge act. He called me into the office during my first week, and told me he had a strategy in mind.

"Gio, tonight around ten, hit as many clubs as you can and pitch the show. Take a few of the girls from the line with you, and spread some dough around in the bars and restaurants. Invite bartenders and waiters over here to see our show. Explain that we're open until six in the morning, and tell them to come over here for a nightcap after they close. Tell them that, if they identify themselves as working on the Strip, we'll buy the first round.

"Also, get the word out at the late-night, breakfast joints. If we get those working people to come to the Casbah, then they will spread the word for us and, before long, we'll be packing this place seven nights a week. Let those other joints have the big talent shows; we are going to kick the gong around, doing it our way." People didn't realize that, in addition to being a dynamic performer, Louie Prima was an accomplished composer, who had written *Sunday Kind of Love* and *Sing Sing Sing*. He and Sam put together the kind of show that seemed to place the audience under a spell. The words to one of his greatest hits told the tale: "That old black magic has me in its spell." The Harold Arlen/ Johnny Mercer standard *Old Black Magic* became the signature tune for Billy Daniels, another classy lounge singer who defined the breed, but it was the cover version by Louie Prima and Keely Smith—with its wild pace and breathless vocal—that captivated the world.

For me, working with Bill at the Sahara was like being in the living room with your family. We spent three years there together, breaking attendance records in the lounge, while Bill established himself as one of the pioneers on the Vegas Strip. Just when I thought we were comfortable, he shocked me: "Gio, pack up our stuff. I just took shares in the Dunes."

Once again, I was bouncing off walls, but Bill calmed me by saying, "Relax, Gio, this is going to be a cakewalk. They know us out here now."

"Listen, boss, how long do you think you can keep this up— buying hotels like they were M&Ms, and running around like you're twenty-five years old?"

"You want me to get a room in the nursing home?"

"You're fifty years old now."

"So? What is that supposed to mean?"

"Maybe should start to think about cashing in some of your chips, and taking it a little easier."

"How can I quit something I love so much? I can go anywhere out here, and everybody knows who I am."

That was a heady feeling that Bill Miller never wanted to lose. He wasn't planning to stop with the Dunes—not by a long shot. He set his sights on Cuba and the new, 650-room Monte Carlo de La Habana hotel, whose owners wanted him to run the operation, and offered him a stake as well.

"I told them I'd jump if I can get some blue chip players on board with me," Bill told me. "You know, like Tony Martin, Sinatra, Donald O'Connor. I would put them on the Board of Directors, and they'd entertain there exclusively."

Bill said that the "nut" on the Monte Carlo was north of twenty million dollars.

"Can you imagine that? Look, we all know who is running everything down there, but let's face it, those guys are trying to go legit now."

"That's a comfort, Bill," I said, with more than a little sarcasm.

"Look, Gio, they got this guy Castro and his rebels running around in the woods down there, but my money's on Lansky and Luciano to maintain business as usual."

I took a minute to think about that one. "Bill, I can't believe this. Do you plan to move your wife and the whole family down there with you?"

"I have to see about that. Right now, I have no plans for that far ahead."

"Am I going with you?"

"Is the Pope Catholic?"

"Maybe in a pine box."

"Huh?"

"Nancy will shoot me."

Bill laughed. "Hell, in Cuba, the rebels are liable to shoot me."

"Looks like I'm under fire, no matter what," I said.

"Seriously, Gio, I've been assured by my political contacts down there that Batista does not find Castro to be a serious threat...I see you've been reading the papers."

"What about Lansky? Is *he* worried?"

"Not about getting shot, but, you bet your ass he's worried. He's got a big stake in everything down there. But, you know Meyer; he always comes out smelling like a rose.

"You know, Gio, I've got a lot of skin in the game down there with this project. I had to put up all my marbles to show good faith and get this thing off the ground. So the answer to your question is sure I'm worried about Castro, but I have too much invested to turn back. If the crap hits the fan, I will lose everything."

Neither of us said anything for about ten seconds, then, "What do you say, Gio, are you with me on this?"

"You know I'm with you, boss. I'll just have to take my lumps that's all."

"That's what I wanted to hear— here's hoping that nineteen-fifty-nine will be a great year for us Gio." He sounded buoyant, and it was catching. "Now listen, don't tell Nancy yet. I'm going down there to celebrate New Year's Eve and get the lay of the land."

That was Bill Miller, the most enthusiastic man I ever knew. But he was also a realist.

As he and his partners celebrated New Year's Eve and the construction of their new hotel in Havana, Castro and his troops raided the city, turning the island upside down. In an instant, Bill's stock in Cuba crashed, and there was more at stake for him than the profitability of a hotel. He grabbed the first plane out of there. When it landed in the Dominican Republic, Bill Miller realized that he had left Cuba with nothing more than the shirt on his back.

* * *

When Bill Miller returned to Las Vegas, he was visibly shaken from his Cuban experience. But with his customary fortitude and the resolve of a lion, he picked himself up, shook off the dust, and started all over again. His next venture was to buy into the Frontier Hotel, where, once again, he made a great success of himself. He followed this by setting up headquarters in the Riverside Hotel in Reno, then branching out to the Netherlands Antilles and the Bonaire. After this, it was back to Vegas and an executive position at the International, then on to the Flamingo. Bill really made the rounds, but he was successful at every stop.

And you guessed it—he dragged me along for the whole ride. Finally, he took what he called a "respite," and retired to Palm Springs, where he would go swimming every day, while waiting for the phone to ring with an offer of one more chance to open another hotel or nightclub.

The well-traveled Arigo family went back to New Jersey for good and lived happily ever after (and, as of 1973, we're still at it). I found myself a job selling real estate.

And I did write that book I had promised...You have just finished reading it.

THE END

Author Biography

Tom Austin is the son of Al Austin whom you have read about in this book. After studying show drumming with the Riviera drummer Erwin Russo, as a teenager Tom teamed up with Bob Gaudio of the Four Seasons and Jersey Boys fame and started their own band called the Royal Teens. The Royal Teens charted several major hits, the most famous being "Short Shorts" and "Believe Me" written by Austin and Gaudio.

On Tuesdays Tom's dad, a security officer at the Riviera, would take the youthful Tom to watch shows featuring Sinatra, Tony Martin, Vic Damone and all the other great stars of that era.

Tom went on to become an accomplished drummer and fine artist. His paintings hang in the permanent collection of the United States Coast Guard in Washington, DC. In addition, for the past 45 years he has owned and operated his own Real Estate and Appraisal Company. In 2011 he received the Status of Realtor Emeritus. In 2015 he was inducted into the New Jersey Doo Wop Hall of Fame. His memorabilia is on display in the Rock and Roll Hall of Fame in Cleveland.

Tom's first non-fiction book, *Bill Miller's Riviera, America's Showplace* is currently available at retail book outlets.